SURGING PASSION

Jim looked softly down into her upturned face. He jerked Sadie tightly against him so that he could feel the wonderfully soft swell of her breasts against his chest and the way she vibrated when near him. Her eyes darkened and looked bottomless. Suddenly he took possession of her mouth, felt her yield and then clutch at his back with trembling hands. Her lips parted. He told her with his deep demanding kiss that he wanted her.

She moaned softly, and he filled with intensity for her. He couldn't stop himself, but slid his hand to her side. And when she didn't shrink away, he grazed the side of her breast with his hand, wanting so very much to tear away the fabric that kept him from her. He wanted to feast his eyes on her. He wanted to know that she belonged to him, that there had never been another to win her trust, and never would be again.

Then somehow his hand was on her breast, filled with the womanly softness of it, feeling the hardened nipple pressing through layers of clothes and years of reserve to say she was responding to him, that she wanted him, too!

"Sadie!" he whispered, arching against her. "Sadie! Sadie!"

SWEET WHISPERS

SWEET WHISPERS

Samantha Harte

To Janet,
To the quietest
person I ever met! I promise
to write Ice Princess for you
Someday!

SH

PaperJacks LTD.

TORONTO   NEW YORK

AN ORIGINAL

PaperJacks

SWEET WHISPERS

PaperJacks LTD.

330 Steelcase Rd. E., Markham, Ont. L3R 2M1
210 Fifth Ave., New York, N.Y. 10010

PaperJacks edition published November 1986

This is a work of fiction in its entirety. Any resemblance to actual people,
places or events is purely coincidental.

This original PaperJacks edition is printed from brand-new plates made from
newly set, clear, easy-to-read type. No part of this book may be reproduced or
transmitted in any form or by any means, electronic or mechanical, including
photography, recording, or any information storage or retrieval system,
without permission in writing from the publisher.

To Mom, Dad and new families

Chapter One

Inside the suffocating Kansas Pacific coach, flushed, weary passengers nodded with the rhythmic lurching. At the head of the coach, several wind-burnt cattlemen slouched in their seats, staring at hands of tattered playing cards. Several seats back, a group of women wearing calico dresses and straw hats mounded with homemade cornhusk flowers shushed their restless youngsters and whispered together, eyeing the poker players. Two families of bright-eyed Swedish immigrant farmers strained to see everything beyond the sooty coach windows. What they saw was bewilderingly vast, nearly featureless and flat.

The locomotive's steam whistle shrieked. Its plaintive wail echoed across the wind-swept prairie where Kiowa Indians had roamed only a few decades before. Now, even the encroaching cattlemen were being driven farther west, replaced by homesteaders, small dusty towns and the twin silver ribbons of the railroad.

The train hurtled westward, leaving a swirling trail of black smoke in the parched August air. In the rear of the coach sat a young woman alone. Her widely set, green eyes were trained on the swiftly passing prairie outside her half-open window. Her narrow-brimmed hat with discreet gray grosgrain ribbons hanging down the back was pinned low on the front of her head.

She wore a muted gray woolen serge traveling suit, out of date and ill-fitting. Even to a casual observer, though, she was delicately proportioned, well endowed and astonishingly pretty.

Her lustrous black hair had been pulled back from her face and knotted at the nape of her neck. She had a pert chin, a wide, intelligent brow and lovely, rounded cheekbones. Her skin was as smooth and perfect as fresh cream.

About her was an aura of watchfulness, of careful caution. When one of the cattlemen chanced to catch her eyes, which appeared even larger and more alert behind her tiny, round-lensed, nickel-rimmed spectacles, he met with an instant look of reserve.

Sadie stared out of the window, her head nodding as the coach jolted. Her back ached. Her stomach was knotted with nervous anticipation. In the distance she saw a blue lake shimmering in the fierce Kansas sunshine. Fanning herself with a copy of Ellsworth's Primer covered in brown leather worn so thin the cardboard backing showed in places, she yearned for the cool-looking water ahead. She had been one of the few girls in her Indiana home town brave enough to swim.

Now as she reminded herself that she must conduct herself as a young woman beyond reproach, she shuddered to think of all that had already gone wrong in her life.

The train surged across the summer-scorched plain where the yellow buffalo grass grew waist high. In the distance the lake shimmered like silver, winking away to the horizon, until suddenly its glinting surface vanished, revealing a low sandy-colored bluff, a scattering of faded, sixty-foot cottonwoods and, finally, a town.

Sadie blinked, startled when the lake completely vanished, vanished just as quickly as her mother and all that had meant so much in the faraway, never-to-return time of her girlhood.

A conductor wearing a boxy blue uniform came forward from the smoker into Sadie's coach. "Warren Bluffs, Kansas!" Reeking of burnt Havana Queen tobacco, he came abreast of Sadie.

A smile flickered on Sadie's flushed face. Hesitantly, she met his inquisitive gaze before looking away again, her breath held.

"This here's your stop, miss," he said, his dark eyes quick on her face.

She nodded, sticking the primer inside her shapeless rose and brown carpetbag. The train screeched into the dusty town, which from a distance had appeared to be little more than a collection of sun-drenched shake-roofed shacks. Upon closer inspection, Sadie saw that Warren Bluffs had a look of care about it in spite of the eddies of amber dust that stirred between the one-room depot and some square, false-fronted stores beyond.

Sensing every eye on her back, Sadie rose and went out to the windy rear platform of the train. Excitedly, she clutched the ornate iron railing. When the train hissed to a stop, the conductor handed her down. She was the only passenger debarking.

"My baggage?" she asked, panting as the baking sunshine seared her cheeks. Squinting, she saw no one but an old man wearing ragged bib overalls sprawled on a bench in a wedge of shade that slanted down under the depot's eaves. He snored into the battered gray felt hat squashed over his face.

Her two camel-backed trunks dropped from the door of the baggage car. She cringed and smiled up at the conductor. Then remembering she mustn't create too vivid an impression, she turned away. The train jolted forward, gathering momentum until it was hurtling away into the blinding yellowish haze of afternoon sun.

Leaving her trunks and carpetbag, Sadie lifted her skirts

and stepped down from the platform, rounding the depot. A young clerk sat inside over a silent telegraph key. Ahead was a wide, empty, wheel-scarred street lined with sagging warehouses, an untidy lumber yard, some weedy vacant lots and an old log land office.

Beyond the tops of pale spreading cottonwoods, the sky hung cloudless, bleached nearly white in the heat. To the south were the residential streets, the few scattered lots slightly more grassy, but without the beautiful lake. It had been a mirage.

Faintly came the labored strains of a brass band playing "Tramp! Tramp! Tramp!" Intrigued, Sadie set out toward the sound. No one could be expected to meet her; she had purposely arrived a day early to avoid fanfare.

Reaching Cowtrail Street, Sadie saw the single-story sandstone city hall and courthouse slumbering in the center of a dusty circular street two blocks down. Several children raced around and then darted into the oaks and cottonwoods at the far side of the circle. In the other direction were two large general stores, a restaurant, a newspaper office and a barbershop. Beyond them stood a reeking livery barn, more widely scattered store fronts and, finally, several saloons rendered silent by the early afternoon hour.

Paintless farm wagons had been parked at random along the wide main street. Beyond the courthouse, a hand-lettered red, white and blue banner that said WARREN COUNTY FAIR drooped between two young black walnut trees. The band honked and brayed from a small whitewashed park pavilion nestled in the curve of the Smoky Hill River nearby. Milling in front of the pavilion was a crowd as faded and dusty as the Kansas tableland.

Thinking of home and her own long-ago school days, Sadie's heart stung with homesickness. She entered the grassy park, which was littered with abandoned quilts and willow market baskets overflowing with half-eaten pies, homebaked breads, jars of preserves and hastily abandoned luncheon napkins.

Babies slept in the shade, and children of all ages darted by, paying her no heed. From miles away farmers and their families had come to relax and visit before the grueling days of harvesting the new Turkey Red wheat.

At the far edge of the park, oldsters in shirtsleeves and suspenders pitched horseshoes. Far from their chink-clank sat a group of matrons in the shade of century-old burr oaks. Children, their shouts soft as memories, were running races along the distant grassy riverbank, where wild sunflowers rioted in profusion. Sadie unpinned her hat and removed it, enjoying the cooling air on her dampened scalp. She lifted her face and sighed.

A man caught sight of her looking so fair and alluring compared to the spreading, less defined ladies of the town. The sunlight caught her hair, making it glint blue as a crow's wing. Her face, undarkened by sun, seemed like a vision.

Her gray skirt tugged in the breeze. The ripple of a simple muslin petticoat winked beneath her hem. If by choosing such unbecoming clothes she had hoped to avoid attention, she had failed. The sheer simplicity of her attire, and the way she held herself and stood shielding her sparkling eyes from the sun, announced she was not of Warren Bluffs. She was different, a lovely, provocative, irresistible stranger in a place where strangers came no more.

Crossing the trampled grass, Sadie watched the band members — an assortment of bewhiskered old gentlemen, and flushed adolescent girls and boys — as they paused between songs. The old gentlemen in red suspenders and Sunday bowler hats mopped their brows. The youngsters looked longingly at the tables in the shade covered with faded red checkered clothes and pitchers of lemonade and tea with ice.

Four boys in narrow-brimmed straw hats, ragged knickers and faded plaid shirts dashed by yelling and cursing. With a start of surprise, Sadie watched the smaller three boys tussle in the grass in front of several farmers who were talking to some shopkeepers. The eldest boy, possibly fourteen, slipped in behind the men. His face was narrow, sun-browned, his eyes furtive and alarmingly clever, as if he had been schooled to be a ruffian since birth.

In astonishment, Sadie saw the older boy neatly dip his hand into the vest pocket of one distracted farmer, taking what appeared to be a large gold watch! With startling assurance, he relieved another man of a few coins and still another of a greenback dollar while jostling around the men pretending to be hiding from his playmates.

While Sadie gaped, more tendrils loosened about her flushed face. She was unaware of a pair of pale, piercingly blue eyes trained on her slim back.

Keeping the young thieves in the corner of his vision, the tall, lean man moved from his vantage point among the old lilac trees to have a better look at her. By the heavy droop of her twisted-up black hair, he suspected when unfurled it must hang below her tiny, cinched waist.

If ever she'd been in Warren Bluffs before, he thought, he would have remembered! Concerned that she might call out to the boys they were both watching, he angled in front of her.

She was wearing little spectacles and slid them to the end of her nose to glare over the rims.

As the pickpockets streaked away with their loot, Sadie noticed a man loping toward her, a tall, muscular, authorita-tive-looking man with sun-streaked brown hair and a tanned face.

Several other people were now eyeing her! She composed her face, remembering suddenly that she wanted to attract no attention. She should turn right around and get back on the next train! The people here were too sharp. They might easily catch her in a harmless but absolutely necessary lie.

Then her heart missed a beat. He wore a glinting tin star on his leather vest! His snowy chambray shirtsleeves were rolled back, exposing sun-bronzed muscled forearms and making him look fresh and casual, but Sadie felt that his approach was ominous.

He wore his wavy sun-streaked hair combed straight back

from his tanned, long-jawed face. His pale blue eyes were keen, observant. A tinge of a smile lifted one corner of his wide, sensuous mouth. He was coming directly toward her!

She lifted her face, letting the hot, dry prairie wind tug more of her hair free of the heavy knotted braid at the nape of her neck. She was surprised to see he wore no pistols. She thought all men of the law wore them, affording themselves that extra bit of self-esteem such creatures needed to feel like men.

With an effort, she kept her expression innocent of the alarm raging in her breast. He was attractive and moved with ease in spite of his remarkable stature. She sensed something warm about him, saw intelligence and sensitivity in those scrutinizing eyes.

He wore no hat but reached toward his forehead as if tipping one. "Afternoon, miss. I don't believe I know you." He glanced toward the place where the thieving boys had disappeared.

Her cheeks flamed. "I thought you were the sheriff."

"Not yet," he said, white teeth flashing in a self-assured grin. He winked.

Flustered, she turned to see the rampaging pickpockets darting into the crowd again. She stiffened. "You might turn your attention to those young hooligans, Deputy. I saw the elder boy pick three pockets just now. His young friends provided an excellent diversion."

His pale blue eyes narrowed. "Most folks aren't so observant."

Sadie scowled up at him. Surely this handsome wind-ruffled man couldn't be as corrupt as all the other men of authority she'd been forced to endure in the past several years. He had such a fine, wide brow. The way his eyes crinkled at the corners made him look kindly and strong. She admired his straight masculine nose, and his mouth was so wide and expressive. Must all attractive men be thieves and swindlers?

"You might consider arresting them. Four boys against a man of your size . . . it shouldn't be difficult." She brushed hair from her face.

He placed a wide, tanned hand on her sleeve. The wind ballooned his shirt. "Hold on, miss."

His touch on her arm was as warm and as penetrating as a concentrated beam of the sun's rays. Though her heart was already responding in completely impossible ways, Sadie drew away.

She looked bewildered, he thought. Her eyes were so clear, so open, so remarkably, shiningly green in that beautiful heart-shaped face. For a maddening instant he wanted to assure her that he was doing his job, perhaps not for those robbed farmers but ultimately for the town, but he had to keep silent.

Sadie saw nothing but the glint of the sinking sun on the deputy's tin star. Her head reeled as she heard herself speaking from a great distance. "It's your sworn duty to arrest . . ."

"Not so loud, miss!" His voice was low and calm. He moved in front of her, blocking her view of the boys as they retreated to the riverbank. "They won't be back for a while."

Sadie felt smothered in the heat. Her heart began to hammer as she squinted into the sun. "Boys begin with thieving. Then it's bank robbery and . . . and . . ."

The deputy was struck by the vivid flush on her delicately rounded cheeks. She began to gasp. Her beautifully full bosom rose and fell. Then suddenly her snapping green eyes became vacant. Her eyelids fluttered. Her head lolled back as if the weight of her thick hair had suddenly become too heavy to bear.

He grasped her shoulders. "Come over here in the shade. I'll catch those boys, but not today. Let me get you something to drink. You're not used to our heat." He pulled a kerchief from his breast pocket and flapped it in front of her blazing face.

The women across the way noticed their tall, handsome deputy assisting a pretty stranger to a bench in the shade. The old gentlemen on the pavilion craned their necks to catch sight of her rosy face. The farmers and their wives turned, frowning at the young woman whose slim shape made them dimly dissatisfied with their own roughly-hewn bodies.

While calling in their children, the women began drifting across the park. One matron hurried ahead, her brown gingham skirts swishing softly, her cloud of fawn-colored hair shining in the sunlight. The deputy had some fair thing drooping in his arms! And about time!

Sadie's voice came out in a breathy whisper. "Please, those boys . . ."

"I'll see justice is done, miss, but in my own way, in my own good time," he whispered close to her cheek. "Arresting Sheriff Wheeler's son today would have me out of a job. That would leave Warren Bluffs at the mercy of a —" The curious were pressing too close by then for him to continue. "Go back where you came from, miss, and leave the law to me."

"I can't, Deputy. Warren Bluffs is my new home."

His piercing eyes swept over her, taking in the choking, high-necked suit jacket and the dusty traveling skirt that accentuated her frail, slim figure. "Our new schoolmarm is supposed to be twenty-five and of iron constitution! You're just a girl . . . and if you don't mind my saying so, too darn pretty for this town!"

She noticed his tone had warmed in spite of his words. She managed a weak smile. "Nevertheless, I am Sadie . . . Evans." Trembling and uneasy, she rose from the bench. Her arms tingled as a strange chill washed over her. Then she sank into darkness.

The young woman slipped so naturally into the curve of the deputy's arm that for an instant he thought she was feigning a faint. Grinning uncertainly as his neighbors crowded nearer, he eased her back on to the bench. Her delicate bones felt tender against his big hands. Her cool silky hair unknotted and spilled across his arm. He looked down into her face and knew he did not want her to go away.

"What ails her?" someone asked.

A woman in gingham arrived at his side then, and he turned to Olive Crowley in relief.

Sadie moaned and fought the strong, gentle hands supporting her. With a gasp, she returned to consciousness and found herself reclining backward in the deputy's solicitous arms. Someone was slapping her wrists. Someone else thrust a vial containing spirits of ammonia beneath her nose. She caught a whiff of the biting odor and her eyes sprang wide.

"It's probably just the heat," the deputy was saying.

"Set her down here, Jimmy. Get her a glass of ginger beer. Let me loosen this tight collar, dear. You'll die of heat stroke in this heavy jacket." The woman's voice was as gentle as her hands.

Sadie felt so disoriented she made only the feeblest protest.

"You can't be Sadie Evans!" the woman went on, chuckling as she fanned Sadie. "We're expecting a . . . a *birch rod* of a spinster!"

With a cooling breeze on her damp throat, Sadie gratefully accepted a dripping hanky from someone and patted her face with it. "Oh, my, I have made a dramatic entrance, haven't I? Not at all the way I would have liked." She tried to laugh. Her green gaze swept timidly across the anxious faces peering down all around her.

"Not at all, dear!" the woman said, taking in everything about Sadie in a single, appraising glance. This Sadie Evans was well groomed, her voice mellow and warm, with a touch of a midwestern accent. Though her hands were slim and pale, she looked strong enough to wield a birch rod, and that's what the school children needed! "Just call me Olive. My husband, dear man, has a bank here in town. You're early, you know. Mayor Runyon said you were arriving tomorrow. Oh! Here's our Jimmy with your drink. Did you walk all the way from the depot in this heat, Sadie? No wonder you felt faint!"

Sadie sipped at the tart ginger beer as the onlookers assessed her, apparently finding her something less than what they'd hoped for.

"I was so eager to get started here . . . ." She struggled to rise and properly greet the ladies. She was making a perfect mess of everything, and all in less than her first hour in town!

"Stay right where you are, dear," Olive said, frowning sweetly. She turned when the crowd parted, admitting a small, regal matron dressed in heavy foulard silk. "Look who's here already! Miss Sadie Evans, may I present the president of the Warren Bluffs Ladies' Society, Mrs. Ethel Cadwallader. We ladies haven't quite won the right to vote on the school board yet, but Ethel is fighting her husband and the entire male population of Warren County on our behalf!"

"My pleasure," Sadie murmured, bowing to the birdlike woman with leaden gray hair and a tremendous scowl of open disapproval.

"We were led to believe you were a qualified teacher, Miss Evans," Mrs. Cadwallader said, raking Sadie's figure with a hard, knowing brown eye. "Exactly where did you obtain your teaching certificate?"

"I'm prepared to present my credentials," Sadie said confidently. "They're in my carpetbag at the depot."

Something elusive in the young woman's eyes sparked Ethel's irritation. This Sadie Evans didn't appear to be timid. On the contrary, she met her betters' eyes squarely, almost defiantly. Ethel would soon put a stop to that! And to think she claimed to be three years older than MargieBelle! She looked three years younger, and that wouldn't do!

"We requested a male teacher of unquestionably severe nature," Mrs. Cadwallader went on with her brows lifted haughtily. "I, of course, was not at all pleased when another woman teacher was chosen . . . it was against my better judgement. If we had wanted another female teacher, my daughter, MargieBelle, would have taken the job. Gladly."

Olive cast the woman a look of impatience. "Let's not discuss such things when Miss Evans isn't herself."

Ethel Cadwallader purpled and edged back, her expression stormy. "What makes you think she isn't always swooning into the first available pair of arms?"

Olive rolled laughing eyes and waved Ethel off as if she should be ignored.

Finishing the ginger beer, Sadie brightened, determined to overcome her momentary weakness. "I'm fine now, really, but I am a bit weary. Might I see where I'm to stay and send for my trunks? How soon can I look over the schoolhouse? I want to begin classes promptly next Monday morning at nine."

Mrs. Cadwallader moved in front of Olive. "Eagerness is all well and good, Miss Evans, but we did not hire someone intent on rushing headlong into —"

Olive interrupted, her broad red face split with a smile masking a controlling nature. "Why, Sadie dear, of course you must be worn out! You came all the way from Ohio? How many days on the train? Was the trip exciting? I've never been on an 'Iron Horse' myself. Scared to death of the things. Cinders flying about, and buffalo herds crossing the tracks. Mayor Runyon hired you in spite of a few minor protests, but you came highly recommended. We're all eager to get to know you."

Sadie smiled as if she was not writhing with uneasiness. "I've been . . . furthering my studies in the East. My education has often been interrupted . . . by work. I financed everything myself. I'm an orphan."

"We'll be like family soon enough," Olive said, chuckling. "Into your business at every turning, soliciting your assistance day and night with all our projects. Warren Bluffs is a busy place, in spite of its sleepy appearance. Jimmy! Why are you hanging about? Bees to the honey," Olive said, winking at Sadie. "What does a town like this need with a sheriff and a deputy, too, any more? Our wild cowtown days are over. The railroad pushed all the things to cause a town shame to Hays City! And good riddance." She linked elbows with Sadie as if they were old friends.

The deputy Olive had been referring to as Jimmy came forward and smiled down at Sadie with a terrible twinkle in his eyes. He had ceased to worry about her. She seemed quite capable of handling herself among these aging hens. He wondered if she was spoken for, and figured she must be. "Sheriff Wheeler needs me looking after things while he naps," he said, hugging Olive's shoulders. He hoped Sadie would not mention what she had seen moments before.

Olive laughed. "Isn't that the truth! Sadie, have you

officially met our handsome young deputy, James Warren? If the name sounds familiar, that's because Jimmy is the grandson of our town founder."

"You make me sound like I'm still wearing short pants, Olive," Jim said. "Call me Jim, Miss Evans. I've been a Warren Bluffs boy for almost thirty-one years now."

"I've known Jimmy nearly as long," Olive added, releasing Sadie's elbow. "I'd go with you to the boarding house, but I'm in charge of the barbeque supper tonight. I hope you like roast buffalo. Jimmy, why don't you take Miss Evans over?"

Sadie watched the townswomen discussing her from behind their work-roughened hands and hated to leave the welcome protection of her talkative new friend.

"I'd be pleased to, but I suspect Mrs. Cadwallader intends to direct you." Jim nodded to Sadie and Olive as he moved away, turning his attention to the riverbank.

"Indeed, I would think you'd like to get settled and rest, since you obviously aren't used to any sort of exertion," Mrs. Cadwallader said, still miffed that Olive had usurped her authority. She eyed Sadie's ill-cut traveling suit with a sniff of disdain. "I'll ask my husband to have the buggy brought 'round."

"I don't mind walking," Sadie said, wondering how she might win the approval of this small, iron-hard woman. Without it her job in Warren Bluffs was surely doomed.

"Ladies in this town prefer to ride," Mrs. Cadwallader said, regarding Sadie with a look of superiority. "I hope you're made of sterner stuff than you look. Fortunately *I* have no school-age children to entrust to your care. Only the grandchildren of a rather worthless son-in-law."

Inwardly seething but outwardly smiling, Sadie followed the woman out of the park.

Chapter Two

"You'll find Widow McClure difficult to live with," Ethel Cadwallader was saying, concluding an exhaustive description of the Warren Bluffs residents. She pulled up in front of 5 South Prairie Street and stopped. "She won't tolerate the slightest bit of frivolity. Only the best boarders stay in her house, you know. It's quite an expense for the school board to put you up here for the next five months . . . or until you take your leave of us. This house was built by Trudy's late husband — he was trafficking in cattle when he was killed. Some may tell you he died in a saloon brawl in Abilene, but don't you listen. Trudy McClure would die a dozen times over if she ever heard such talk!"

Sadie climbed down from Ethel's one-horse top-buggy. The clapboard boarding house was finer than she had expected, an imposing Victorian, two stories high and with a broad front porch.

The side yards had been planted with box elders, and a matched pair of vicious looking prairie thorn trees covered with two-inch spines stood in front. To the left was a fragrant — and impressive — rose garden.

From the house Sadie heard a tremulous voice singing an old love ballad. "I Love You Truly."

"That's Alvinia singing in the front parlor," Mrs. Cadwallader said to Sadie's inquiring look. "She's a spinster, like you, so you mustn't antagonize her by permitting gentlemen callers. I'd come inside, but I'm late helping at the serving line. If I leave MargieBelle to her own devices, she's liable to do nothing but make sheep's eyes at young Deputy Warren. We're pleased, of course, that he's taken such an interest in her, but she mustn't be too eager. It wouldn't look seemly. Good afternoon, Miss Evans. That boy I sent to fetch your trunks should be at the depot by now. They'll be along any time."

Sadie's head whirled with her quick dismissal. Mrs. Cadwallader turned the buggy in a tight circle and headed back for the park. Then, as an after thought, she leaned out to add, "Oh, by the way! We'll expect you to speak to the school board. Wednesday evening. That should give you plenty of time to prepare a speech."

The buggy rattled away, leaving Sadie grateful to be free of the hard-eyed woman, but uncomfortable about facing her landlady without an introduction.

A speech, she thought, groaning. Of all the jobs, why did she have to be best suited to teaching? Renewing her resolve, Sadie mounted the wooden steps, which were flanked by lavender petunias growing out of tin cans, and tapped at a door fitted with beveled ovals of thick glass. After a long silence, the door opened a crack. Sadie stared down into the pale innocent face of an older woman who smelled strongly of wood-violet dusting talc.

"I'm Miss Sadie Evans, the new schoolteacher," Sadie said, smiling amiably. "I understand there is a room waiting for me here."

The soft-looking, slightly plump woman looked puzzled. "Now, I don't know. Is this Monday already? You're not due until Monday, young woman!"

Sadie explained, and finally the woman let her in. "You

have a lovely voice," Sadie said, glancing into the parlor, where the keyboard cover for the eight-hundred-pound upright parlor piano lay open. In addition to the piano, the room held a parlor suite consisting of a tête-à-tête, reception chair and rocker all covered in maroon silk brocade.

"I'm a singing instructor, you see," the woman said, tremulously introducing herself as Miss Alvinia Dewey. She rambled on about her pupils while Sadie peeked out from behind the lace curtains to see if her trunks were coming.

Miss Dewey was probably no more than fifty, but she behaved as if she were ninety. She sang for Sadie, accompanying herself on the piano. "Wilt Thou Be True?" "Open Thy Lattice, Love" and "Come Where My Love Lies Dreaming." Sadie began to wonder if she was going to go as quietly to seed in this place as this sweet woman had.

Then Sadie heard excited talking and panting outside. Olive Crowley and another woman were bustling along the dusty lane.

Olive's friend had salt-and-pepper hair tightly knotted on top of her head, and she walked like a cowhand. They burst into the entry. "Land sakes! When Ethel said she brought you here and abandoned you I couldn't believe it. I'm Trudy McClure, your landlady. Have you looked at your room? Well, of course not! Alvinia, aren't you going to come on over for some fried chicken and pie? We know you can't tolerate that tough old buffalo steak the menfolks love so!" She thrust her hand out and shook Sadie's with strength and confidence. "How do you do! Welcome to Warren Bluffs!"

"You know how I get in the heat," Alvinia murmured in her childish tone. She closed her music and looked wistfully toward the door. "It's such a long way to the park, and I'm not as spry as I used to be."

Sadie smiled her hello to Olive and Widow McClure. "Miss Alvinia looks as if she'd like to be persuaded to go."

Olive nodded approvingly as she fanned herself. "I'll just run back to the kitchen for a sip of your famous lemonade, Trudy. Trudy's the best cook in town, Sadie. You're going to love living here. Don't pay any attention to whatever Ethel Cadwallader said to you."

"About what?" Sadie said, breathlessly swept into the kitchen with Olive while Widow McClure bustled upstairs to thunder about, throwing open windows.

"About anything! She left you here alone just to make you feel unwelcome, but you're as welcome as you can be! Now where's that dipper?"

The kitchen was spacious, spotless and sweet with the aromas of recently baked breads and pies.

"We came back to make you join us at the barbeque. No argument out of you. I know Jimmy wants to get better acquainted with a pretty young thing like you. You mustn't feel shy."

Sadie almost laughed, bowled over by the woman's breathless energy. "I didn't know I was invited. I'd love to come."

"Why, that Ethel! She didn't tell you to come over when you were rested? The very idea! She's a cat, and you can tell her I said so. MargieBelle's not much better, but she's still after a husband, so she daren't show her true colors too plainly. She's driven off every eligible man in town and is starting over at the head of the list!"

From the upper recesses of the house, Trudy McClure stopped thundering. "Everything's aired now, dear. Come up and have a look!"

Olive patted Sadie's shoulder. "You'll have the room next to Alvinia. I'm told the old darling snores," she whispered. "But it's a nice room. Good cross-ventilation. Are those your trunks?" She craned her neck to look out the front door. "I wonder why Cornell's driving the freight wagon. You don't mind having black children in your classroom, do you, Miss Evans? We've had so many families from the South settle up this way in the last few years." She waved out the door. "Cornell! Where's Mr. Biggins? Drunk again?" She turned back to Sadie. "Herman Biggins works at the depot when he's not sleeping. You may have seen him when you got off the train. Nice old man. Not bright enough to work at anything except odd jobs." She pointed to her head. "He's forgetful, but he gets the biggest thrill driving that freight wagon! Of course, he shouldn't drink — You've heard of our prohibition legislation, haven't you? We're liable to be a dry state come this time next year. We aren't long from our cowtown days. I remember what cattle and liquor did for Warren Bluffs' reputation. Sheriff Wheeler saved us from a passel of outlaws and rowdies, I can tell you!"

Sadie listened with fascination. "Please, you must call me Sadie. And I welcome all students to my classroom."

Olive nodded. "That's what I expected to hear. Mind, though, that Cadwallader clan'll have a number of their pesky little outlaws in attendance as well. Put them together with the Wheelers and you'll have yourself a circus for the first few days. But don't let any of them scare you. A bunch of high-and-mighty no-accounts, most of them. Have to be careful of Ethel, though. She has a lot of friends, or rather her money does. I'd like to see you get half a chance here. We need a good teacher."

"Who was the teacher before me?" Sadie called as the woman started down the steps toward the lanky black youth who was hefting Sadie's battered trunks from the freight wagon's bed.

Olive chuckled. "You haven't heard, then! I thought surely Ethel would've spelled that out clear enough. Sheriff Wheeler's daughter had the job last year. She got herself fired, yessir! And she deserved it. Mighty loose with her language, and mean as a range bull! She couldn't keep those heathen children in class for more than an hour. Preacher Whithers has been tutoring his children himself, and not liking it, I can tell you. His boys go on to college in Lawrence. Now Ethel, she was set on MargieBelle being the new schoolmistress. But MargieBelle was never a star pupil. She's taken piano from our Mr. Bennett for ten years, and she still can't play a note!" Olive charged on out to tell the boy how to handle a lady's trunks.

After many directions and cautions, the boy carried Sadie's

trunks to her second-floor room in the rear. Olive and Trudy rested in the cool kitchen while Sadie changed into a light-weight linen shirtwaist and tan poplin skirt.

The room was wonderfully simple, not so very different from her own room when she was a girl. The white enameled iron bedstead trimmed with brass knobs and the nightstand and four-drawer chiffonier with a beveled plate-glass mirror on top looked as if they'd come straight from a mail-order catalogue. She hung her traveling jacket on a hook behind the door and unlocked her largest trunk, which now stood beside an open window hung with blue dimity curtains. Through the window she could smell the roses in the side yard.

She almost wished she could forego the barbeque to rest, but resolutely repinned her hair and polished her spectacles. She couldn't hide.

Leaving her room unlocked, Sadie joined Olive and Widow McClure in the entry. They had coaxed Alvinia to go along and, chatting like old friends, the four women returned to the park.

Unfortunately, Jim Warren wasn't at the barbeque. Even so, Sadie spent an enjoyable evening meeting her fellow boarders and listening to their talk far into the cool evening beside the river.

At six-thirty the following Wednesday evening, Trudy and Olive walked Sadie to the meeting hall on the second floor of Cadwallader's store on Cowtrail Street where many of the Warren Bluffs residents had gathered to hear the new school-marm's speech.

Though the evening was oppressively warm, Sadie had chosen her gray serge because it was her most unattractive outfit. Her hair was smoothed back in a severe bun, and with the tiny spectacles perched on her nose, she hoped she looked old, serious and stern.

"You're on time. How nice," Ethel Cadwallader said the moment she spied Sadie. Her elaborate maroon China crepe gown rustled softly as she turned to indicate her husband. "I want you to meet my husband, George. He owns this store, as you've probably guessed."

Sadie smiled with reserve up at a large bearded gentleman in an aging brown worsted suit. From the way Mrs. Cadwallader conducted herself, Sadie had imagined they were one of the first families of the town, until Trudy informed her that quite the opposite was true. George Cadwallader had been a buffalo hunter in the early days, before a serious fall had forced him to take up trading. His store was the result of an advantageous marriage to Ethel, then a spinster of twenty-eight.

"This is my lovely daughter, MargieBelle," Ethel went on, introducing Sadie to her diminutive daughter.

Twenty-two-year-old MargieBelle Cadwallader wore a frilly white organdy dress better suited to a child of twelve. The childish sashed style accentuated the maturing curve of her face. Her hair was a fine shade of light brown, done up with big bows in an equally adolescent style with masses of dangling ringlets.

"It is such a pleasure to meet you, Miss Evans. What do you think of our town so far?" MargieBelle asked in an overly sweet voice.

"It's just like home," Sadie said, enduring MargieBelle's calculating scrutiny of her clothes, hair, hands and shoes. The young woman began to look uneasy.

"It wasn't always that way, was it, Ma? Not long ago Warren Bluffs was just as wild as Abilene! Oh, I see *my* Mr. Warren has found a moment to come by. He did promise to try! He's terribly busy keeping this little town in line, you know. He would make a good sheriff, some day, but my ma and I agree he'll do wonderfully well in papa's store. It's obvious my sister's husband doesn't have what it takes to be the manager of such a complicated family business. Oh, and Ma" — MargieBelle fluttered to the side and spoke so loudly that Sadie heard every word — "let's invite Jimmy to supper next Sunday. He's sure to propose . . . again. I'll bake my blue-ribbon cherry pie, and I suppose I could almost be persuaded to accept this time, if he tries to kiss me as often as he always does!"

Sadie was left standing alone again, and glad of it.

The hall was a huge open room of rip-sawn yellow knotty pine with an inelegant podium at the far end. Rows of round-backed oak chairs quickly filled with dusty residents in slouch hats and sunbonnets, followed by their broods of squirming children.

With a tight smile, Sadie made her way toward the front. Every eye was trained on her, and her stomach knotted. She wanted very much for them all to like her, but she knew she must also impress them with her strength and ability.

She noticed MargieBelle hanging on Jim Warren's arm and felt an unexpected twinge of irritation. She was surprised to see that he looked as if he wished to be anywhere but with the carnivorous little flirt.

With a private smile, Sadie made her way toward the podium. Though she doubted the truth of MargieBelle's boasts, she had no room in her life for a man, especially not a disturbingly attractive man who couldn't bring himself to arrest pickpockets.

Still, Sadie's courage was buoyed by the warmth of Jim's eyes when their gazes crossed. Trembling, fighting the nervous flutter in her stomach, Sadie straightened her back, reminding herself that she had faced far worse than this.

She reminded herself, too, that Ethel Cadwallader had probably dreamed up this speech more as a torment than a test of her abilities. Sadie was determined to prove herself more than equal to the job.

The room echoed with low chatter, but as the young woman in gray reached the podium, a gradual hush fell over everyone. Parents and their numerous children, arranged in descending order of size like so many stair steps, settled into rows of chairs. Palmetto fans began moving like the frail white wings of moths, stirring the hot, musky air.

A tall wiry man in a stained tan stetson stood by the open

rear door, glancing at everyone entering from the stairs leading up from the street. He greeted most, his eyes quick, slick, always moving back hungrily toward the slim young woman now standing before the assemblage, her head high, her little spectacles reflecting circles of lamplight. Her dark hair was combed so tightly back from her face it glinted like boot black. He worried his overlapping front teeth with a soggy-tipped toothpick.

A group of boys let out a whoop and dashed out the side door. Seconds later firecrackers danced beneath the vacant rear seats. People upset their chairs as they scattered. The younger children screamed. The confined space filled with acrid smoke and deafening noise.

Never flinching, Miss Sadie Evans remained rigidly still behind the podium. When at last the noise and commotion subsided, she gave everyone a radiant smile. Nodding to the three school-board members who were settling themselves with indignant huffs in the first row, she cast her calm gaze across the room.

"Now that we've re-enacted the Battle of Bunker Hill, let's get on with the business at hand. I am Sadie Evans, your new teacher. This evening I'd like to outline how I will organize the Warren Bluffs school. I'll give you a general idea of the studies I will pursue with your children . . ."

Her voice rang clearly and confidently across the upturned faces, many admiring, many not. Ethel Cadwallader, in the second row, shook her head at intervals.

Jim Warren watched the slim, pale young woman take command with her sweet voice and wondered where she had learned such courage.

All too soon her speech was done; she hadn't bored them for a moment. After answering several surprisingly good questions, she yielded the floor to the school-board president, Mayor Runyon, who should have introduced Sadie, but hadn't.

Jim supposed that oversight was Ethel's doing. He watched

Sadie moving off to the side, directly into the path of three eligible men, Ethel's own unmarried son, George, Jr., Olive's unmarried son, Ben, and a widower, Dr. Hamlin.

"Excuse me a moment, Miss MargieBelle," Jim said quickly, prying her sharp white fingers from the crook of his elbow. "I should be getting back to my duties now. Nice to see you again." He rose before she could squawk her usual protest and strode out the back, curious about the feeling of irritation he'd experienced when Sadie Evans looked up into the smiling faces of those three men.

George, Jr., and Ben had a lot to offer a woman. Dr. Hamlin was a well-established man with education. What did it matter, anyway? Jim thought. He had no time for courting. As he glanced back, however, he did think Sadie looked as if she'd appreciate rescuing.

By the time he reached her, Sadie had managed to nod polite but unencouraging smiles to the three attractive men and was turning her attention to some of the other people who were crowding around. She was pleasantly aware of the handsome deputy lurking not far away. Then she overheard one of the farmers she'd seen robbed detain the deputy. He asked about his chances of getting back his gold watch. Pausing, Sadie listened. Moments later she interrupted the hushed discussion. "Forgive me, Deputy, but I couldn't help overhearing. You've arrested the persons responsible for those . . . incidents at the park?" Her voice held a slight edge of sarcasm.

"Were you robbed, too, miss?" the farmer asked, scowling down at Sadie in surprise.

"Not exactly," Sadie murmured nervously.

"Deputy tells me Biggins did it, but I don't recollect bein' anywhere near that ol' coot all afternoon. I'm telling you, Jim, I don't think it's possible."

Jim drew a deep breath. "I'm doing all I can to clear this up, Seth, but at the moment Herman Biggins is in custody. The stolen items were found in his shack. I wouldn't worry. I've got your pocket watch locked up in my desk. I can give it back as soon as the judge comes through to hear the case. Evening, Miss Evans," he said, tipping his imaginary hat and moving away, obviously annoyed at the turn the conversation had taken.

"Pardon me, Deputy," Sadie said, detaining him. "I don't understand. This Mr. Biggins. Is he the man who works at the depot?"

"He does odd jobs around town. His predicament is nothing for you to be concerned about. Enjoyed your speech. Sorry about the firecrackers."

"Those young hooligans again, I see," she said, looking coolly up at Jim Warren. She found it difficult, however, to remain annoyed with him for long.

"Troublesome age those boys are at."

"All four of them . . . and this handyman in jail." She looked up at Jim and for a moment wanted to bring down his charade. Then reason prevailed, mingled with another emotion too alarming to acknowledge: attraction. She clamped her mouth shut. Surely, Jim Warren had a reason for handling the situation "in his own way." She wanted to think so, at any rate.

Besides, she reminded herself, she dared not become involved. She'd handle those boys — if they dared show their faces in her classroom — in *her* own way.

A new group of curious youngsters asking about the lessons she'd outlined surrounded her. As Jim drifted out of sight, she became engrossed in the pleasant task of acquainting herself with her new pupils.

By the time the hall was almost empty, Sadie was desperate for a little air. She went down the stairs to the outside where the long cool shadows cast by the newly risen moon filled the wide dusty street with pale light.

"I wonder if I could walk you home," Jim Warren said softly from the shadows. He fell into step beside Sadie as she moved away from the store.

Startled to find him waiting for her, Sadie spoke rather loudly in case anyone was listening to them. "It's kind of you to offer, Deputy Warren, but I'm not sure everyone's done with me yet."

"You sound as if you're a lone bone among a pack of hungry dogs," he said, chuckling. His appreciative eyes went over her face.

She tried to soften her expression. "I hope I'm not giving that impression."

"No, but I know how it feels being the object of Ethel Cadwallader's attention. I hear you're from Ohio. Where, exactly?"

Sadie had been warming to the deputy, but at once she was on guard again. Her stomach knotted worse than it had when she confronted the unreadable faces of Warren Bluffs. "A little town called Higginsville just outside of Marietta," she said automatically.

He nodded. "Small-town girl, then."

"I guess you'd say so." She prayed he'd ask no more questions. "My mother ran a boarding house."

"I was going to ask how you like Widow McClure and the rest of her boarders." His blue eyes were twinkling.

"I had no idea I'd be thrown in with the cultured element of Warren Bluffs! Imagine, the librarian, the music professor and the singing instructor all in one house! In the past two evenings I've heard every story they have to tell. Twice." She chuckled, knowing her nervousness showed. "I like them."

Shortening his long stride to match hers, he guided her along the dirt walk toward Prairie Street. "Been teaching long?"

Not trusting her voice, she shook her head. She found herself eager to remain in his company, but not if he was going to grill her with questions. "About this Mr. Biggins," she said to change the subject.

"If you don't mind, Miss Sadie . . . say, I hope you don't mind me using your first name?"

She shook her head, pleased and trying to hide it.

"And you'll call me Jim?" he asked, grinning wonderfully.

She flashed him a smile. "Not Jimmy?"

"Not if you know what's good for you."

Startled, she laughed. "Go on about Mr. Biggins."

"Let's not pursue serious subjects. You have a way of making a man feel as if he must leap to his feet and right all injustices. At the moment I'm powerless to free Herman. I know he's innocent, but there's no proof. The boys planted their loot in his shack that afternoon. Somebody happened by and found it all before I could . . . . I know it's a set-up, but — There I go, again, discussing serious business when I want to be charming you!"

Sadie didn't respond. She could scarcely fault Jim Warren for not doing his duty when hers was quite clear. She must speak up in this handyman's defense. At the moment she couldn't bring herself to do it.

"I've spoiled our walk," Jim said, watching her troubled expression and slowing his pace as the boarding house came into view. "I'd like to think you and I are on good terms."

Smiling up at him, Sadie brightened. "Really, Dep — Jim, haven't you enough young ladies hanging on your every word?"

"If you mean Miss Cadwallader . . . ." He began to grin.

"It was a very nice walk, Jim. Thank you for seeing me safely home. Isn't that the Cadwallader buggy coming up behind us?" She paused and glanced back. Uneasily she took a step backward and started away alone.

"I wouldn't like to think Ethel Cadwallader has you cowed, Sadie," Jim said, his face serious as he watched her abrupt retreat from his side. "You're free to talk to anyone in this town that you like."

Sadie raised her brows. "No one cows me, Deputy Warren. Certainly not Mrs. Cadwallader. I do value my new job, however, and would like the chance to do it for a day or so before someone like you gets me fired."

"Me!" he said, half laughing as the Cadwallader buggy drew alongside. He was forced to nod at pouting MargieBelle and her scowling mother. "Evening, ladies. Catching a ride, I see, Ben?" he said to Ben Crowley at the reins. Ben's eyes were fastened on Sadie with the greatest interest.

Obviously annoyed that Jim was not behaving according to

one of her inner plans, Ethel ignored him. "Miss Evans, you got away before I could speak to you." She began digging in her beaded reticule.

Jim rocked on his heels, his grin self-satisfied. "She did a bang-up job, didn't she, folks?"

Ben nudged MargieBelle.

MargieBelle shook her curls. "Ma, aren't you going to introduce them? Without an introduction, she wouldn't give dear Ben the time of day. Was that the way things were done in Ohio, Miss Evans?" MargieBelle asked sweetly. Her eyes were jealously narrowed, taking in the way Jim's attention remained on Sadie.

Mrs. Cadwallader withdrew a long key and handed it down to Sadie. "I'll be over at the schoolhouse tomorrow morning if you care to join me there. You can air the place and see what needs to be done. You'll have a modest account at my husband's store if you need furniture, books or slates. Everything must be listed and reported to the board, of course. Forgive me, Ben; Miss Evans, our friend Ben here said you scarcely acknowledged him at the hall this evening. While your reticence is understandable, I felt I should introduce you. Ben works in his father's bank. He's quite a catch."

Sadie was tempted to ask why, if that was the case, Margie-Belle wasn't attached to him. Thinking better of it, she merely smiled.

Ben Crowley climbed down from the buggy and bowed to her. "Very pleased to meet you, Miss Evans!"

He wore a formal black woolen frock coat with matching trousers. Sadie could see his resemblance to Olive in his friendly eyes and florid face. He appeared to be about Jim's age, though he was shorter and more pallid, probably because of his indoor occupation. She knew at once they'd be good friends, but nothing more.

"I didn't mean to be rude at the hall, Mr. Crowley, if indeed I was," Sadie said, unnerved at the way Ethel could twist anything she did to her disadvantage. "I hope you'll all understand that my only interest at the moment is my new job.

If that interest changes," she said, trying to give Ben Crowley a pleasant but impersonal smile, "you'll be the first to know. And now, if you'll all excuse me . . .?" Inside she was trembling. She wanted to run from the women in the buggy and the two men whose eyes glowed so brightly when looking at her. "Good evening."

As she neared the boarding house, she paused long enough to look back. The buggy was rattling away, MargieBelle's high-pitched chatter sounding loud and indignant. Jim and Ben had disappeared. She hoped Jim had been as discouraged as she intended him to be, but at the same time she couldn't help feeling a sharp stab of regret.

Jim Warren's grinning face filled her mind's eye. Would a time come when she might dare encourage his attentions? Probably by then he'd be long married to MargieBelle.

Lifting her chin, she let herself into the boarding house. She held the schoolhouse key tightly in her hand. This job was the only thing that mattered! She hurried up to her room before the others could return from the meeting and detain her. If she didn't have a job — this job — she had nothing left! When her life was secure, she might think about love.

Shivering, she shut herself into the tiny room that had quickly taken on the feel of a refuge. As soon as she had stripped off her suit, she crawled into bed in her corset and petticoat, huddling there, thinking that *soon* she might be able to fall asleep without straining to hear whispers about her. If only she had someone like Jim Warren to make it all easier . . . .

She shook her head and covered it with the pillow. The job came first! Only the job.

Chapter Three

The next morning Sadie had just crossed Cowtrail Street on her way to find the schoolhouse when she met Jim Warren coming from the other direction on a buckboard wagon.

"Morning!" he called, stopping alongside her in the dusty street. "I thought Mrs. Cadwallader was taking you to the schoolhouse for a look around."

Reining in her simmering temper, Sadie forced a smile. "I thought so, too. I've been waiting at the boarding house for more than an hour. I decided not to wait any longer."

"Knowing her, she's waiting at the school, drumming her fingers, eager to accuse you of being late." Jim grinned and winked.

Sadie suspected that was probably true. "Nice to see you, Dep — Jim." She shrugged, gave him a little smile, and started on her way once again.

"Can I give you a ride?"

In the early morning heat, her head was throbbing already, but she shook her head. "Thanks just the same."

She paused at the depot to watch a train shriek to a halt. Several people got on. She almost wished she was going with them. But where could she go? she asked herself for the hundredth time. Every town west of the Mississippi would have a Mrs. Cadwallader, or worse.

Jim stopped the buckboard just ahead of her. He had turned around and was heading in the opposite direction now. Leaping down, he swept his hand through his sun-streaked hair and grinned. He wore a faded blue plaid shirt beneath his vest. His foot was braced against the little iron step on the side of the buckboard, and his work-worn denims strained across his muscular thighs, accentuating the length of his legs. He was by far the finest figure of a man Sadie had ever seen. She longed for him to go away from her at once!

Sighing, she cocked her head and adjusted her spectacles. "Just as surely as I accept a ride from you, Mrs. Cadwallader will happen by and misinterpret it."

"Not this time. She'll see exactly what I mean for her to see, that I find the new schoolmistress intellectually stimulating. I'm trying to better my meager education." He winked again.

Sadie pulled a hanky from the pocket of her smothering brown wool skirt and patted at the beads of sweat that were collecting on her forehead and throat. Remembering that Ethel said the ladies of this particular town preferred to ride, Sadie approached the buckboard with gratitude. She allowed Jim to hand her up.

Sitting as far from Jim as she could without falling off the spring seat, she swallowed over her dry throat. What could they talk about? Jim had her tongue-tied!

"Tell me about this meager education of yours, Deputy Warren," she said at length, a teasing note in her voice.

"I learned my three R's at the knee of our librarian, the famous Mr. Charles. He taught the entire time I was in school." Jim clucked to the horse, moving the buckboard north along Prairie Street.

"Which was for how many years?" Sadie asked, pretending to be very prim.

"About eight years, total," Jim said. "I started late. When I was sixteen I ran away to join up and do my part to preserve the Union."

"I had no idea!" Sadie said. "And your parents?"

"My mother died when I was three. Childbed fever. My father was in Lawrence when Quantrill went through." His face reflected a moment of pain. Then he went on. "I was raised by my grandmother. She died three years ago. A finer woman there never was. And strong." He grinned and began nodding. "She would have approved of the way you handled yourself last night at the meeting hall. I couldn't help but laugh when I thought how Justine Wheeler would've flown into a rage over those firecrackers. You have a cool head, Miss Sadie Evans."

"I was terrified," she said, looking down while her cheeks colored. "What became of you after the war? You haven't been the deputy for ten years to a . . . a man like this sheriff I've heard so much about."

He steered the buckboard onto a narrow lane overgrown with weeds. "Looks as though no one's been up to the old schoolhouse in a while." He flashed her a playful grin, and her blood tingled. "I, Miss Sadie Evans, was an Indian fighter."

She cocked her head. "You expect me to believe that?"

"Yes, because I was. We've had Indian raids in Kansas until quite recently. Mostly in western Kansas, luckily. The militia needed volunteers, so I volunteered. When grandma became ill, I came home. After she died, I decided my abilities were needed here."

Reluctant to pursue that subject, Sadie turned to one that had plagued her in the small hours. "In all that time you never married?"

He gave her a look that revealed he was pleased she was asking. Then his expression turned serious. "I never felt I could ask a woman to share my life. For years I was away living a reckless nomadic life. Now I'm not likely to be shot without warning, since most of our saloons will be closed if the prohibition legislation passes the voters. For the most part, the townspeople are quiet. Without drunken brawls to break up, there's little for me to do. We have an occasional difference of opinion between the ranchers and farmers. There's a bit of thieving . . ." When he saw that she wasn't going to go on about the pickpocketing incident, he sighed. "Unless we're overrun by outlaws, I don't see an exciting future ahead. Recently I have thought about taking a wife."

Sadie bit her tongue to keep from mentioning MargieBelle Cadwallader. Instead, she turned her attention to the schoolhouse, which sat in the middle of a featureless field by the riverbank. Hundreds of sentry prairie dogs stood alert on the mounds surrounding the building. "Oh, look!" she said, laughing and pointing. The small blond gopher-like creatures barked the alarm and disappeared into burrows.

The schoolhouse was of graying board-and-batten pine, with a shake roof that probably leaked. A leaning rusty iron fence ran along the road. Behind the building was a small sway-backed three-sided hay barn where horses could be tethered during school hours. Firewood and dried buffalo chips, unpopular but indispensable for fuel, could be stored in the rear. Beyond that was a long, wooden stockade-style fence leading to the twin outhouse. The six-foot-high fence bisected the privy, serving to keep the boys' and girls' sides separate.

"Being here again makes me feel about ten years old," Jim said, squinting as he looked around.

"And if you were ten, what would you think up as torment for the new teacher?" Sadie asked as he helped her down into the knee-high grass.

"A frog in her desk would be an absolute necessity," he said, forcing the low iron gate open. He scuffed his way up an overgrown path to the battered door, his eye trained on the ground.

"What about snakes?" Sadie asked, shuddering as she gathered in her swirling hem.

"I wasn't a bad boy, Miss Evans. Just loveably mischievous."

She tried to smother a laugh. "I see!"

"A bucket of water over the door might cool your enthusiasm for this job," he said, taking the key from her and working it in the rusted iron padlock. He glanced up as he edged his way in. No bucket was poised on a rafter, ready to fall onto his head. "No one's been here since Justine was fired. That was last November. Want me to send someone to help clean up? This is a lot of work for one woman to do."

Sadie pushed in behind Jim, blushing as she bumped against him. She surveyed the wreckage inside. Every crude pine desk had been overturned. The black boards — stained planks mounted on the wall — had been deeply gouged with obscene words. The teacher's podium had been smashed. Heaps of dirt and leaves had collected in the corners.

Sadie experienced a thrill of anticipation. "This is just the sort of work I enjoy, Deputy Warren!" She went to inspect a broken pane in one of the four tall, narrow windows.

Jim righted several desks, arranging them one after another so that the rear of one heavy seat became the desk top of the seat behind it. Then he lounged against one, regarding Sadie. "You're a remarkable woman, Miss Evans."

Growing intensely uncomfortable, Sadie moved quickly away. "No different from anyone else." She felt his eyes on her. She hadn't been so aware of herself as a woman for a long time. A tingle began bubbling in her blood. Glancing up, she saw his eyes soften. A gentle, pensive smile curved his lips. "You might help right the rest of these desks, Deputy. Then I'm sure you have your own work to do." Sadie was alarmed to find her voice growing strained and husky. She was trembling.

He set to work immediately. He was done before she had even had time to inspect the cloakroom. The walls of that narrow windowless closet had been gouged by a vengeful hand, too.

"They can't even spell some of these words," she said, meaning to sound amused. Instead, the tightness in her voice betrayed her uneasiness.

When Jim came up behind her, she was trying to straighten the bent nails that had been intended as coat hooks. She whirled, her heart pounding, and looked up into Jim's face, feeling herself go weak. He was too much of a man for her! She was suddenly unbearably aware of the breadth of his shoulders. Her eyes drank in the exhilarating muscular swell of his chest, the narrow tautness of his waist, and those sturdy legs. As he edged in after her, she backed away.

He looked as if his own reaction to her presence in the dim narrow space was far more disturbing than he liked. He felt as if his every schoolboy fantasy was coming true.

She stood a head shorter than he, her full bosom rising and falling rapidly. She wasn't afraid that he'd hurt her. On the contrary, she felt what he was feeling, that she was a woman, that he was a man.

His ardor swelled. He wanted very much to kiss her. He wanted to sweep her into his arms and crush her to his chest. He wanted to hold her and pet her and possess her, but instead he forced himself to scan the bent nails, estimating how many new ones she'd need. He couldn't seem to concentrate.

"I'll look around for any vermin that might trouble you, Miss Evans. Then I *will* have to be going." His voice was low, thick.

She straightened, the tension draining from her face. A grateful softening came into her beautiful green eyes. He wondered who had taught her to fear a man who wanted her.

Impatiently, he turned, grazing his shoulder sharply on the doorframe. He had to put as much distance between himself and the woman of his dreams as possible without actually running from her.

He made a quick check of the outhouses, finding them alive with spiders, but otherwise safe. The hay barn was busy with field mice, but that probably wouldn't bother her too much, unless one showed up in her desk or in her lunch pail.

Wishing he were one of the lucky youths soon to be facing her in that classroom, he started back toward the buckboard. He caught sight of Sadie collapsed in one of the dusty little seats, one hand covering her eyes.

She was strong, but she needed him, he thought. With a

twinge of surprise, he realized he desperately needed her, too. He had been waiting for that brave little beauty all his life!

Sadie found a broom in the cloakroom next to a box of musty books stored on the floor. Glad to be alone, glad for work to occupy her mind, she swept the cloakroom, and then the main room — which was fifteen feet by twenty — until she was overheated and covered with grit.

The defaced blackboards bothered her. She decided they must come down, but she lacked the strength to pry out the nails. The list of supplies and tools she needed became so long she couldn't keep everything in her head.

Dusting her hands at last, she went outside. Looking up the wheel ruts that passed for a road, she wasn't surprised that Mrs. Cadwallader hadn't yet come. The woman probably hoped the work facing Sadie in the schoolroom would force her to quit.

Sadie inspected the hay barn and outhouses, finding the mice and spiders. She shuddered, but soon enough everything would be clean again. She sank down on the doorstep to rest.

She was definitely not up to this summer heat. She could see the green of the park not far away. To the south were the lush back yards of Warren Bluffs' finer homes. To the east ran Prairie Street. The jailhouse was also on Prairie Street, she thought, just across the tracks.

The jail, the sheriff, the handyman in the cell . . . . She chewed a knuckle. She couldn't bear the fact that she'd said nothing about seeing the handyman at the depot.

She rose, looking at her filthy hands. Then she went through the schoolhouse, removed the board from brackets bolting the side door closed and stepped down to the watering trough. She worked at the pump until fresh, cool water splashed into the dusty hollow-log trough. After washing and cooling her face, she set out.

The Warren Bluffs jail was among the few field-stone buildings in town, a solid unfriendly block with a door and a single window in front. The moment Sadie stepped inside, the cool press of musty air repelled her. On one side wall was a locked oaken rack of carefully oiled rifles. To the rear were three small cells and a door to a back room. The handyman snoozed on a cot in one of the cells, looking just as he had the afternoon Sadie saw him at the depot.

Before her stood a battered double-pedestal oak desk piled high with yellowed papers and heavy mugs of vintage coffee. Behind it sprawled a tall, wiry man in greasy denims and a dirty brown plaid shirt, his ankle-broken, poorly resoled knee-high parade boots up and crossed on a stack of "wanted" circulars. His stained hat was drawn down over his face. His ungainly thin hands were laced over his shallow chest. "Back already?" he muttered beneath the hat.

"Excuse me, Sheriff." Sadie fixed her eyes on the ornate tin star pinned on his vest. "I wonder if I might have a word with you."

His chair righted with a loud thump. The prisoner woke and snorted. Looking groggy, the sheriff gaped at her, his eyes gradually sharpening and narrowing. His face was like weathered leather, deeply tanned and heavily lined around his eyes. His untrimmed, bristly, sun-bleached mustache concealed a grim, turned-down mouth.

"Howdy, Miss Evans. What brings you here?" He reached for a toothpick and sucked it, eyes narrowed. He approved of the pallor around her eyes and mouth as she began to speak, and he decided he liked her shape even better close up.

"I'm concerned about the vandalism done to the schoolhouse, Sheriff Wheeler," she said, sounding more confident than she felt. "I need someone to take down the blackboards. They can't be repaired, but someone could pry them off the walls for me and reblack them on the back side. I understand the handyman who might do these chores for me is here in jail."

Otis Wheeler rose, shifting his bony shoulders around inside his overlarge shirt. He let his eyes roam freely over Sadie's sternly upturned face. He felt like laughing at her. She was mighty tiny for an uppity woman.

He looked pointedly at the now dusty front of her white shirtwaist and the full dark skirt that disguised the swell of her hips. He rubbed his nose with the back of his hand. "Didn't know about no vandalism. You'll have to report that to the school board, I expect. Herman can't help you with them blackboards. But there's plenty of men in town who'd be glad to take them down for you. What did you say was wrong with them?"

"They've been gouged with obscenities. Misspelled ones. Sheriff, Mr. Biggins can't possibly be responsible for stealing the items found in his shack after the fair. I arrived that afternoon. I saw him sleeping at the depot. Moments later I saw . . . children running through the park. Picking pockets." Her face turned hot and crimson.

The sheriff's eyes bored into hers. "I beg your pardon, miss, but that ain't for you to be concerned about."

"But I am concerned! That man is innocent!"

Mr. Biggins leaped to his feet. "Didn't I tell you that, Sheriff? I was plumb asleep at that there depot most all that afternoon. Even ol' Seth said he didn't think I had the brains to get his watch out of his own pocket 'lessen he'd feel me doin' it!" Herman clutched the iron bars of his cell. His seamed face shone with renewed hope.

Sadie found the sight of him so pathetic that tears sprang to her eyes. "I know you want justice served in your town, Sheriff Wheeler," Sadie went on, her voice small.

"Call me Otis," he said, coming around the desk. A look of amazement and alarm twisted his weathered face. "Who you been talking to about the thieving that day?"

"No one, really. I saw the boys . . . ."

"Which boys is that?"

"I surely couldn't say. They were all strangers. I haven't been able to sleep since I heard this innocent man was behind bars for something he didn't do!"

"Let's talk outside," Otis Wheeler said, taking her arm and steering her out the door. As soon as the door had shut, his manner darkened. "You keep your nose out of my business, and I won't tell you how to teach the youngun's in this town!"

Sadie swallowed with difficulty. She felt weak with fear. The last person in town she needed as an enemy was the sheriff. Yet perversely she pressed on. "I must insist you take down my testimony on behalf of Mr. Biggins. I know you want to do the right thing. It was only natural to think the poor man was guilty when —"

"I don't need no little schoolmarm making up excuses for me," he said, glaring down into her face. "I don't need no trouble from you, either."

"That's the last thing I want, Sheriff. It's my obligation as a teacher, however, to set a good example for my students. If a child came to me with this problem, I would surely advise him to bring the information before the good and honest sheriff who is so . . . looked up to by his . . . friends." She tried a slight smile.

The man sputtered. Abruptly, he glanced up with a peevish frown. "You've been talking to my deputy. I heard you been seen hanging around with him. Let me tell you this, Miss Evans. Folks don't take to schoolmarms who can't keep their eyes off the eligible men in town. Or the rest of the men either." His dark eyes glittered. He began to smile, revealing overlapping front teeth. "You still want to swear out a testimony?"

Jim Warren strode up behind Sadie. She had never before felt more relieved as she turned and looked up into Jim's puzzled, faintly worried, but very welcome face.

"What's going on, Otis? Have you decided to arrest her, too?"

The sheriff released Sadie's arm with a sniff. "Says she seen Herman at the depot last Sunday. That don't account for the stolen items turning up in his shack, though."

"Maybe those boys became frightened and hid what they took in the first place handy." She turned to Jim quickly. "I couldn't keep myself from telling the sheriff about some children I saw running in the park the other afternoon."

"What children?" Jim asked, his eyes turning dark with concern. He glanced at Otis to see if the man suspected Sadie had any idea who the boys really were. Otis seemed to want to believe she didn't.

"I haven't any notion who the children were, since I've never met any of them."

"Maybe they were from out of town," Otis mumbled. He kept his face turned away as he thought. Then he smiled and looked down at Sadie like a cornered, dangerous dog. He opened the jailhouse door and re-entered the jail. "I expect we can let Herman go for now. Herman, you got to testify when the judge comes through."

"Sure, Sheriff! Where would I go, anyways? I don't know no place but this here town! Thanks, miss!" Herman rushed to Sadie the moment his cell door was opened. She was just coming back inside. He seized both her hands and shook them in passionate gratitude. "Thank 'ee! Thank 'ee!" He was out the door, scuttling away before another word could be said.

"That was generous of you, Otis," Jim said, coming in and taking an extra chair from the wall. He looked amazed. "Care to sit down, Miss Evans, so we can take your statement?"

"Oh, of course," Sadie said, sitting gingerly across from Otis.

In short order, she gave her testimony, omitting the portion where Jim told her the leader of the pickpockets was Otis Wheeler's son. She didn't know that for a fact. She was still being honest by not mentioning it.

As quickly as possible, Sadie made her goodbyes and escaped from the oppressive atmosphere of the jailhouse. Before returning to the school for a long afternoon of work, she hurried to Cadwallader's store and told the clerk what she needed, asking for everything to be delivered as soon as possible. Then she rushed to the boarding house for a nibble of lunch and several minutes of trembling self-reproach in her room.

She couldn't have lived with herself if she hadn't said something, she kept reminding herself as her fit of trembling became worse. She was glad she'd helped free the poor old man, but now she'd made another enemy. And she was afraid! This was a nice little town. She liked the schoolhouse. And she liked Jim Warren. She didn't want to have to leave!

After a few moments, she steeled herself. Taking an old pair of gloves, and a kerchief for her hair, she set out in the blistering afternoon heat for the schoolhouse.

Ethel Cadwallader waited within the protection of her top-buggy. Her face was flushed, her prim blue suit dusty. Sadie saw the woman parked in front of the schoolhouse the moment she turned onto School Road from Prairie Street. She had a good long time to contemplate the upcoming encounter as she trudged along in the heat.

Reaching the buggy, Sadie called, "Good afternoon." She turned in through the gate while tugging at her gloves.

"Miss Evans!" Ethel snapped, struggling down from the buggy. "I find all this very disturbing. Not only have you gone off from a job scarcely begun, but you left the schoolhouse door unlocked. I must warn you, the school board will have no patience with a careless schoolmistress!"

Sadie whirled, counted to five — she had too much to say to count to ten — and flashed Mrs. Cadwallader a brief but confident smile of dismissal. "Leaving the door unlocked was an oversight. I do hope you'll forgive me. Considering the condition of the building, however, it hardly seemed worth-while to worry about vandals. They've come and gone long before this afternoon. Pardon me for being short with you, but I am frightfully hot! I assure you, this school will be in perfect order by Monday morning." She seized the broom and began sweeping furiously. The air filled with clouds of dust. "Oh, do move out of the way before some of this dirt gets on you! I've already made my first order for a new desk, a box of chalk and some windowglass for the broken pane over there. It's such a shame this fine building was left in this condition for so many months." Sadie hoped her reproach didn't go unnoticed.

Left speechless by Sadie's bustling activity and torrent of words, Mrs. Cadwallader stood in the doorway, holding a hanky over her nose and mouth.

With the air sufficiently filled with dust to keep the woman at bay, Sadie ducked into the cloakroom to tie the kerchief over her hair. She hoped to find Mrs. Cadwallader gone by the time she came out, but her antagonist wasn't one to give up so easily. Sadie began dragging desks into rows.

"It would be best if you arranged the desks facing this direction," the woman said.

Sadie knew Ethel would contradict any arrangement she chose and so went on dragging desks as if she had been working too hard to hear the woman speak. When Mrs. Cadwallader said nothing more for several minutes, Sadie paused for a breath. The woman's eyes were riveted on the defaced blackboards.

"Disgraceful!" Mrs. Cadwallader gasped, averting her eyes.

"It most certainly is," Sadie said, putting her hands on her hips and nodding her head. "I'm having them taken down and turned over. You're welcome to help me blacken them as soon as they're back up. I mix egg whites with the carbon left after burning potatoes to a char. The mixture works better than paint. I would love to have a few pots of flowers in the windows, too. And I'll need to redo those penmanship letters." She indicated the alphabet painted along the top of the blackboard. "Are you handy with a brush, Mrs. Cadwallader?"

"You know perfectly well a woman my age could not climb a ladder!"

"Margie Belle, then?"

"Certainly not! You seem to be amusing yourself at my expense, young woman. Let me warn you. The slightest misstep will have you on the train heading out of town before you even know what has happened."

"I don't intend to make any wrong moves, Mrs. Cadwallader," Sadie said, her voice low. She felt suddenly reckless. Her anger was so close to the surface she knew she must drive the woman away before it erupted.

"You've already made a good many wrong moves. Your conduct is under the closest scrutiny. You've been the talk of the town since you fainted on Sunday afternoon. The true test, however, is yet to come. Can you teach? Can you conduct yourself like a lady? Can you refrain from making eyes at eligible men? My friends and I have no intention of letting a woman of questionable morals teach our children. I am referring specifically to walking after dark with Deputy Warren. Unchaperoned. And riding alone with him in a wagon only this morning. Really, Miss Evans! That man is taken. I made that quite clear from the first. In any case, one would think you could restrain yourself just a little. If you came here only to find a husband —"

Sadie's mouth popped open. She was about to unleash some of the words gouged into the boards behind her, but at once realized Ethel was purposely provoking her. An argument would justify firing Sadie on the spot. If Ethel's power didn't extend as far as immediate dismissal, at least she could recommend that Sadie be fired.

Realizing Ethel probably didn't have the authority to fire her, Sadie closed her mouth. She unclenched her fists and forced a businesslike smile. "You can rest assured I have no interest in a husband — or even a gentleman friend — at this time. If I did, I certainly wouldn't stoop to stealing one already taken — if he was in fact taken. I wouldn't need to."

At once Sadie realized she'd said too much. Ethel Cadwallader's face reddened. Her eyes bulged with rage. "I know about young women like you!" she snorted and stormed out, leaving Sadie cursing herself.

Chapter Four

Widow Trudy McClure's boarding house had a large, well-appointed dining room with ample space to seat Trudy at the head of the mahogany table and her four boarders at the sides. An extra place, reserved for a possible guest, was always set at the foot of the table.

Sadie found her fellow boarders somewhat dull, but was grateful that they were too absorbed in their own pursuits to pry too deeply into her background. Their table talk revolved around sufficiently dry cultural subjects that Sadie felt quite safe in their company.

Mr. Corwin Charles, the librarian, had been the school teacher in Warren Bluffs' earliest days. He had the dreamy look of a poet, wore stiff collars and addressed Trudy, Sadie and Alvinia in the most formal manner possible.

Now that he had retired, he kept to his books and only ventured out for work and evening walks. He was a private man who looked as if he had not quite realized his life's dream in Kansas.

Mr. Lawrence Bennett was the oldest boarder. He gave music lessons in the front parlor. Sadie had already been treated to the mind-numbing monotony of his pupils' scales and finger exercises. He wore a neatly clipped graying beard and had an old-world manner that quite suited his friend Mr. Charles but revealed his dislike for most people, ignorant young children in particular.

Alvinia Dewey basked in the attentions of these two gentlemen, who treated her with exquisite deference. Her voice pupils sometimes combined efforts with Mr. Bennett's piano students. The results were truly deafening.

Sadie felt worn out from her long day cleaning the schoolhouse. Emotionally drained from her encounters with the sheriff and Ethel Cadwallader, she had rushed home to wash up for supper. Now she sat wearily listening to Mr. Charles and Mr. Bennett discussing President Hayes' insistence that he would serve only one term.

Hoping to excuse herself and slip upstairs, Sadie expressed her desire to have a likeness of the president for her classroom and then rose as a knock came at the front door. "Would you like me to see who it is?" Sadie asked, since Trudy hadn't finished her meal.

"No, dear! You look worn through. Go on up to bed. We understand."

Sadie was halfway up the stairs when she heard Jim Warren's voice at the door. For an instant she tingled with pleasure. Then she hardened her heart. She could risk no entanglements!

"Sadie, Jim's here to see you," Trudy called as Sadie reached the top of the stairs.

Sadie's hand went immediately to her dust-laced hair.

"You look fine, dear," Trudy whispered, smiling in a remarkably understanding way. "It's perfectly all right with us if you'd like to visit with Jimmy on the porch for a few moments."

Seeing no way to refuse without making an undue fuss, Sadie forced herself to smile and returned to the entryway. Mr. Bennett's dark opinion of this meeting was written clearly on his face as he pressed past into the drawing room. Alvinia looked aghast!

Mr. Charles kept Jim cornered for ten minutes before Trudy managed to distract him.

Sadie then joined Jim on the porch. The suffocating heat of the day had dissipated, and the night air was refreshingly cool and sweet. In spite of her impatience, Sadie couldn't help but respond to Jim's smile as he led her to the swing at the far end of the porch where thick wisteria vines climbed toward the roof.

"I know you're tired, Sadie," he said softly, "but I had to say something about this afternoon."

Sadie sank onto the swing. She took off her spectacles and polished them. "I'm a bit worried that I won't have the schoolhouse clean by Monday. Mrs. Cadwallader is probably parking her buggy on School Road, preventing anyone who might like to help me from coming to the school." She smiled. "I shouldn't have said that, but she was rather unpleasant to me today."

"Mrs. Cadwallader is an unpleasant woman," Jim said, leaning back against the railing, his hands in his pockets.

Even in the shadows his face noticeably softened as he gazed down at her. Sadie thought how attractive he looked with his hair combed back and those penetrating pale blue eyes. He saw far more than most people realized. She felt awkward under his scrutiny.

"That was a good thing you did for Herman," Jim said.

"I believe in honesty," Sadie said softly, wishing they could drop the subject.

"And I wanted to thank you" — his voice dropped to a whisper — "for not mentioning all you knew about the pickpockets. I'm after bigger fish."

She looked at him sharply. "I don't wish to make Sheriff Wheeler my enemy. With Mrs. Cadwallader convinced I'm not right for my job, I already have quite enough to handle. If her daughter is so suited to teaching, why wasn't she hired?"

Jim grinned. "MargieBelle Cadwallader's only interest is her latest package of ribbons and lace from Kansas City. Her deepest thought concerns the correct size of her bustle. I'd venture to guess she doesn't want to be a teacher. Ethel wants it for her, in the event MargieBelle doesn't snare the right husband. Any husband, in fact."

Sadie cast Jim a sidelong glance as if to say she knew who the intended victim was for Ethel's and MargieBelle's snare.

Jim went on as if he hadn't noticed her piercing look. He knew Ethel had made it clear that she had him in her sights. He wondered if it was presumptuous to mention that MargieBelle didn't interest him.

He thought Sadie looked weary. She sat primly on the swing, her hands folded just so in her lap, her shirtwaist bearing faint smudges of dust. He admired her pluck and courage.

Why was such an attractive young woman settling for a position in this fading little town? She had such a lovely face. Her features were delicate, her skin fair. He had seen her smile a few times, but she seemed strangely subdued for one so young. It struck him suddenly that she might be in financial straits. That would explain her dated clothes. To think that such a lovely, intelligent woman had been left penniless . . . .

"You're staring at me with the most unsettling look on your face," she said, peering up at him with sparkling eyes. Then Sadie realized she was flirting and looked away.

"I think you know I find you interesting," Jim said softly.

Sadie stiffened. Suddenly she rose. She faced him as she had faced Ethel Cadwallader that afternoon. "I meant what I said the other evening. My job is my only concern."

"I know that's what you said. At the time I felt it was mainly for Mrs. Cadwallader's benefit."

"No. Yours too, Jim." She glanced up at him. She went warm all over. She hoped he couldn't see the responsive color rising to her cheeks.

To keep her from escaping inside, he put his hand on her arm. "Can we be friends, at least?"

"Oh, certainly." She gave him a brief smile, noting the depth and darkness of his eyes as she looked at him. She began weakening, and found herself swaying toward his strength. She wanted nothing more than to let him put his arms around

her. As quickly as that thought surfaced, she dashed it away
and balled her fists. No man was going to put his arms around
her ever again! "But only friends," she added very softly.

"I guess it was impossible to hope you weren't spoken for.
Who's the lucky man?"

Of all the lies she was being forced to tell, this would be the
easiest, she thought. She tried to speak, but couldn't bring
herself to tell Jim there was someone waiting for her back in
the East. She shook her head. "I'm so tired . . . . Please forgive
me if I go in now. There's no man for me, lucky or otherwise.
I think you know that as the school teacher I am expected to
avoid —"

"I'm quite a respectable man in this town, Sadie! I wouldn't
think of jeopardizing your position." He was looking at her
with such questioning eyes.

Sadie wished only that he would leave her alone. "I value
your friendship, Jim. Let's leave it at that."

He hadn't removed his fingertips from her arm. "There's
great sadness in your past."

She glanced up, hoping alarm didn't reflect too brightly in
her eyes. "But there were happy times, too. That's what I want
from Warren Bluffs. A new home and happy times again."

He grinned suddenly. "I'm a patient man. I'll see to it that
Ethel has no reason to question your social life. But you have
to promise me something." He grinned.

"And what, pray, is that?" She peered up at him with a
playful smile.

"That you don't give unfair advantage to the other men in
town who are also struck by your beauty and intelligence."

Sadie chuckled as she slipped past Jim. "Good night,
Deputy."

Once safely in her room, Sadie peeled off her dusty clothes and
washed her hair in the enameled washbasin. While combing
out its heavy, silky length, she stood at the window looking out
over the prairie. How good it was to be where she could see so
far, to be where the air was fresh and the night so still.

She turned to look at her little room. Already the comforts of home softened the austere furnishings. Her second trunk had been stored in the cellar. Her meager wardrobe of shirt-waists and dated, gathered skirts now hung on hooks behind the door. The other trunk stood open beside the window. In it were her books. *Gems of World Literature, Every Woman's Cooking, Williamson's Medical Companion,* The Woodline editions of Browning, Emerson and Longfellow, *The Farmer's Encyclopedia, A History of Our Great Nation,* the 1872 edition of *The American Almanac* and *Webster's Pronouncing and Defining Dictionary.*

She had placed a tintype likeness of her mother in a heavy oval frame on the dresser. Save for that, she had no other personal mementoes in the room. The quilt on her bed, done in a double-wedding-ring design, was colorful. It had attracted Trudy's admiration at once, but to Sadie it served as a painful reminder, one necessary at times like this when her impressionable heart was telling her to think of Jim. Handsome, smiling Jim Warren!

She had yet to see Jim take care of the young pickpockets "in his own way." Until he did so, he would remain suspect, in spite of her assurances of friendship. Never again would she take a man at face value! Certainly, she would not waste her time believing gentle words and seemingly honest intentions.

In bed, however, Sadie had no control over her fantasies. She imagined Jim coming to her in some shadowed place to envelop her in his strong arms and dazzle her with his kisses.

She was, after all, a healthy young woman. While her heart might be locked against further assaults and her mind as sharpened as any carving knife, her body and her emotions raged on. Because she dared not let a man into her life, she was doubly aware of the effect of Jim Warren's smile. She thought how it might feel for him to touch her . . . and more. Her imagination spiraled out of control, in her longing for all that she must deny herself.

By Saturday afternoon the schoolhouse looked very nearly presentable. Sadie had enjoyed a respite from Ethel's disapproving eye. She had scrubbed the floors, hammered in new coathooks and painted a fresh alphabet above the newly turned and blackened boards at the head of the room. Herman had come by and done the chores like an eager child.

She dared not schedule any work for the following day, a Sunday. Relieved that her work was nearly done, she now hoped to outline her lessons and begin thinking ahead to the students who were soon to sit at those heavy pine desks.

As the shadow grew long across the scarred floor planks, Sadie heard the rattle of buggy wheels outside. She glanced up from her place in the first desk. Ethel Cadwallader stepped down from her top-buggy into the tall grasses. By the woman's expression she was obviously thinking the schoolmarm should have had the grass trimmed, but Sadie knew that the children would soon trample it.

"I'm surprised to find you here, Miss Evans," the woman said, entering without invitation. "My, this room looks almost civilized. I thought I'd come see if indeed you'll be holding classes Monday. I wouldn't want my grandchildren coming over if you're only going to send them away."

"I'm glad my work meets with your approval," Sadie said, rising.

"I wouldn't go so far as to say that, but you do appear to be making an effort. I suppose you've noticed the fence to the privies is in need of repair? It's important that you have no unpleasant incidents . . . . I'm sure you know what I mean."

Perversely, Sadie kept an innocent face. "What *do* you mean? I doubt it's likely to fall on anyone."

Mrs. Cadwallader puffed like an indignant sparrow, but her eyes were as fierce as any eagle's. "I'm referring to peeking."

Sadie tried not to show her amusement. "I would think that children brought up on farms and ranches would have had their share of sex education. If you feel there's a problem with the children of this town in that regard . . ."

The woman purpled at Sadie's insinuation that the Warren Bluffs children had prurient minds. "Indeed not! That's what we're trying to prevent!"

They were prevented from pursuing this amusing subject

by the arrival of a wagon. It circled the schoolhouse and drew up in the rear.

"What is *he* doing here?" Mrs. Cadwallader demanded.

Sadie turned to see Jim climbing down from a delivery wagon. In the bed of it stood her new desk. "Perhaps Mr. Biggins is unable to drive again today."

"As for that, young woman, you would do well to mind your business here in the schoolhouse and refrain from visiting the likes of Sheriff Wheeler."

Sadie might have asked why, if Jim hadn't loped in.

"Delivery for —" His cheerfulness dwindled as he caught sight of Mrs. Cadwallader and her tremendous frown. "Good afternoon, ma'am. So nice to see someone finally helping Miss Evans with all her preparations."

Sadie silently cheered his veiled reminder that no one had offered to lighten her work load. "What brings you here?" she asked.

"In this civilized town there's very little to keep a deputy busy. Since Herman had other business I decided to help with your desk. Herman would never be able to get it in here for you, in any case. Where do you want it, Teacher?"

Sadie showed him the space she'd left at the head of the room. While he was outside wrestling the cumbersome desk to the ground, Mrs. Cadwallader took the opportunity to draw Sadie aside.

"What is he really doing here, Miss Evans?" she asked. Her expression showed clearly that she assumed something untoward was going on between Sadie and the deputy.

Sadie wasn't about to skirt the issue. "If you think I'm encouraging him, you're very wrong. I certainly didn't invite him here."

"A woman has more ways of extending an invitation than with words!" Mrs. Cadwallader snapped. Her eyes raked Sadie from head to toe. "I thought I informed you —"

"I have no control over where Jim Warren takes himself!" Sadie interrupted. "Perhaps you should speak to him on the matter."

Of course, Mrs. Cadwallader couldn't do that, Sadie knew.

He was a reluctant quarry. It wouldn't do to tell him too plainly that he was being stalked.

A few minutes later, Sadie smiled to herself as Mrs. Cadwallader pointedly invited Jim to dinner for the following day, saying that MargieBelle had been taken by a fit of baking and had filled their house with enough pies for an army.

"Kind of you to think of me," Jim said, red-faced as he maneuvered the heavy desk through the side door and shoved it into place before the newly blackened wallboards. "It's wonderful that you're welcoming Miss Evans with a Sunday dinner party. As you know, my grandparents' house has been closed for two years. Otherwise I'd welcome her myself."

He straightened and wiped his brow. The heat in the schoolhouse was oppressive. In spite of Sadie's sweeping, he had stirred up some dust, which now swirled lazily in the shafts of sunshine slanting through the windows.

Mrs. Cadwallader looked stricken and silently furious with Jim. He appeared genuinely puzzled by her reaction to his words.

Inadvertently he had pointed up the general assumption that someone was going to welcome Sadie socially, and that that someone was surely going to be Mrs. Cadwallader.

Sadie realized Mrs. Cadwallader's awkward position. Quickly she interceded. "I'm afraid I've already made plans for tomorrow," she said in an easy lie.

"How clumsy of me," Jim said, reading Sadie's eyes. He saw that no one had invited her.

Looking at Mrs. Cadwallader, he tipped his imaginary hat, but his expression was clearly reserved. It was as close to a reproach as he was going to give the scowling, huffing woman. "You'll relay my regrets to MargieBelle, won't you, Mrs. Cadwallader? I have to be on duty tomorrow. The sheriff has something going on at home. He didn't say what."

Mrs. Cadwallader was speechless, both because he had declined her invitation and because Sadie had saved her from embarrassment. The look in her eye was confused. Sadie knew the woman did not want to be in her debt!

"Thank you for coming to help," Sadie said, not meaning to

rub in her advantage, but aware that was how it would surely sound to Mrs. Cadwallader. "I'm about finished here for the day. Goodbye."

Sadie excused herself and went out to see what other items had come from the store. She heard Jim escorting Mrs. Cadwallader out to her buggy. The woman's voice was solicitous. Jim's voice was reserved, almost clipped.

Sadie was just carrying in the box of small items she'd ordered, as she heard the buggy roll away.

Jim came back inside. "This is beginning to look more like a school all the time. Where am I to sit, teacher?"

Smiling to herself, Sadie turned and regarded him with a critical eye. "Judging by the expression on your face, I had better put you right where I can keep my eye on you." She indicated the front desk facing hers.

"That's exactly where I want to be," Jim said, squeezing into it. "You're a very nice person, do you know that?"

"Kind of you to say so." Self-consciously she stacked the chalk in her drawer. Then she arranged the books she'd brought from the boarding house in an orderly row along the back edge.

"You shouldn't have let her off so easy. Not that I meant to embarrass her like that. I assumed if she was inviting me to dinner in front of you that you had also been invited."

Sadie smiled a little more. "You assume a lot."

"Well, she should have invited you."

"Her purpose was to show me that you are" — Sadie felt her cheeks begin to redden — "'taken' is a word she has used."

He leaned back. "You're beautiful when you blush."

"I'll accept that as the observation of a friend," Sadie murmured, knowing it was fairly impossible for the two of them to avoid flirting with one another.

"And you're determined," he added.

She nodded. "I suppose if I tell you I mean to go home now, you'll ask to drive me."

"You suppose a lot, too, teacher. I'm just trying to be a good citizen. *Has* anyone invited you to dinner yet?"

"Olive Crowley has asked me for next Sunday. She assumed I'd be tired tomorrow and preoccupied with thoughts of my first day."

"She's a perceptive woman, one of my favorites. She reminds me of my grandma." He leaned forward then. "If Ethel gets too much for you, will you tell me?"

Sadie looked around and then laughed to herself. "I forgot to order myself a chair!"

Jim chuckled, apparently aware that she occasionally avoided answering a difficult question just as he did. "I'm glad to see you're not entirely perfect," he said.

"Far from perfect, Deputy," she said softly, meeting his eyes. For a moment she was captivated by his gaze. She wanted more than anything for him to rise from that desk and come at her with the intention of kissing her.

Quickly veiling her eyes, she went for her sunbonnet and took up the empty box she would refill with books and carry to school early Monday morning.

"I would like to drive you. You do look tired."

"Thank you. I accept, and not just to prove my independence from petty tyrants like Ethel. I'm exhausted! How can I get in touch with Mr. Biggins about more repair work? Mrs. Cadwallader is concerned that the privy fence will afford some child the chance to peek at another."

"Really?" Jim asked, laughing as he took her arm. He led her outside into the waning heat. He locked the door for her and took her around through the high grasses to the wagon. "I'm surprised she remembers the sort of thoughts schoolchildren have."

"Why, Deputy! Schoolchildren are only interested in avoiding their lessons and making life miserable for their teacher."

"Not this schoolboy. If you want to know where the peephole is in the privy fence, you've only to ask me!" He handed her up to the wagon seat. This one was unsprung and as hard as Mrs. Cadwallader's eyes.

"You're shocking me," Sadie said, stifling a smirk. "If my

students are anything like you must've been, I shall have to teach more than reading, ciphering and history."

"I think you're going to be very surprised by the students," Jim said. "And they'll be very surprised by you."

He guided the wagon around onto the road, which was beginning to look more used, and headed back toward Prairie Street. When they reached the store, Sadie quickly climbed down and thanked Jim rather loudly for delivering her desk. She was sure they were being watched from all sides.

He just smiled at her, as if reading her thoughts, and bade her good day.

She hurried into the store to order the chair and then started for her boarding house feeling lonesome for Jim's company, but glad that she had escaped Jim. It was getting harder and harder to keep him out of her thoughts!

Chapter Five

At six o'clock on Monday morning Sadie was dressed in her gray serge and on her way out the boarding house door just as Trudy was rising.

"Won't you wait for breakfast?" Trudy called as Sadie started down the lane.

"Too nervous," Sadie said, smiling and waving.

Besides, Sadie thought, the walk at this early hour was quieter and cooler. And she *was* nervous. She had no idea how many students she would have. She vaguely recalled Ethel Cadwallader mentioning grandchildren. Then there was the matter of the pickpockets.

Her uneasiness was not evident as she walked briskly north along Prairie Street, across Cowtrail Street, past the depot and across the Kansas Pacific tracks until she reached School Road.

The school was still a quarter of a mile away on her right. Mercifully, she was the first to arrive this bright September morning. She was thinking how truly miraculous it was that she had this job and this chance for a new life. She unlocked the door and stood for a moment, savoring the silence. Then she opened the barred side door for cross-ventilation and hung her hat in the cloakroom. Her hands were shaking.

In less than an hour, Mayor Runyon's grandchildren stepped down from a fine, black top-buggy and formally greeted Sadie at the iron gate. Betty Runyon was tall for fourteen, her dark hair knotted, her white shirtwaist and skirt impeccable. She was an attractive, serious-looking girl with a reticent smile.

Her sixteen-year-old brother, Walter, was obviously the Warren Bluffs dandy. Handsome, and handsomely dressed, he wore the expression of a sorely taxed blade only gracing the schoolhouse with his presence under duress from his father, the lawyer.

Close on their heels came Christa Roberts, a bubbly, darling fifteen-year-old bedecked in a calico dress more suited to a Sunday sociable. Her father owned the town's other store — rival to Cadwallader's. Christa was friends with Betty, and made no effort to conceal her infatuation for Walter who, at Sadie's bidding, finally sauntered inside.

Moments later a fringed Michigan surrey arrived with the preacher's four children, who ranged in age from nine to sixteen.

"Please go in. Write your names and ages on the blackboard. We'll have a test later to determine your grades."

The Whithers children looked incensed. They were all at their proper grade levels or beyond they declared, but finally filed inside to comply with Sadie's request. They were formally dressed, a sober and not particularly handsome group. The girls wore starched white linen. The boys wore well-made worsted trousers with suspenders. Sadie dared to feel encouraged.

All at once the remainder of those interested in attending the first day arrived. Before Sadie could take a breath, she saw the three young pickpockets and their older leader streak around from the rear. Two sullen girls of about twelve and a brother and sister in tatters crowded in together. The tattered girl, scarcely seven, was teased by one of the pickpockets. The first quarrel erupted to the accompaniment of the little girl's wails!

Sadie herded everyone inside. Several shy children had entered by the side door and taken seats in the rear. Sadie recognized Cornell Johnson, the lad who had delivered her trunks, and his frightened-looking younger sister. A homely adolescent girl in a poorly stitched calico dress and bonnet huddled in the farthest corner.

The Runyon and Whithers children took all the forward seats, leaving the middle of the room for the rabble who had arrived all at once. Five empty seats remained.

"Good morning," Sadie said brightly to the boys in their hats and the girls in their tight braids and hair bows. She introduced herself, hoping to set everyone at ease. She asked those who had not written their names on the blackboard to come forward.

The ragged brother and sister whimpered, so Sadie wrote their names: Dooley and Bonnie Terrison. Their father was a wheat farmer.

The delivery boy and his sister wrote their names beautifully. Cornell was fourteen, his sister, Annabelle, twelve. Their father was a smithy who had onced worked on an Alabama plantation.

The cringing homely girl in the rear burst into tears when asked to write her name.

"Her father runs a saloon," Christa Roberts volunteered, her tone reflecting a disapproval she had probably learned at home. "She and her mother dress hair."

Some of the children giggled.

Sadie smiled encouragingly at the homely girl. "Just tell me your name and age. I'll mark it down for you."

"Winnie Akins," the girl whispered. "I'm thirteen."

"And can't read a word!" someone whispered.

Sadie let her calm gaze move across the room. "I'll tolerate no teasing. We're here to learn. Anyone with the courage to do so, will."

The leader of the pickpockets swaggered to the blackboard.

He scrawled a barely legible "Marty Wheeler" at the bottom of the list. "I'm fifteen," he announced, raking Sadie with a look that sent shivers of disgust through her blood.

She was shocked that a boy so young would have such worldly eyes. Clearly, he knew a great deal about being a man. He knew exactly how to stare at Sadie's womanly attributes.

His younger sister, Susanna, and her best friend, Dawn Shockley, were the two sullen girls. Neither could write legibly.

With some discomfort, Sadie realized the room was filled with Shockley children. The eldest, sloe-eyed Dawn, would be the object of all the peeking at the privy fence. She recognized Dawn's brothers, Mike, Freddy and Danny, as the pickpockets. An additional brother, Herbie, seemed friendly and out of place in the sharp-faced family.

These were the Cadwallader grandchildren! Sadie's heart stood still to think what Mrs. Cadwallader would say if ever she learned her grandsons were thieves!

Twin boys of thirteen wrote their names well enough, and Olive's little grandson wrote best of all. Another boy of eight informed her he could read the pictures in the catalogue in his privy, much to the merriment of the Shockley clan.

The students totaled twenty-three, with a predominance of boys. Sadie stood before them quaking in her shoes, but hiding it well. Half the students were adolescents; and half, she knew, were bound to torment her. She began an oral examination to determine the extent of their knowledge and, by the end of the morning session, she knew how she would rearrange everyone. She dismissed for lunch.

The Runyons drove home in their top-buggy. The Whithers' driver returned with their surrey. The rest of the town children scattered, leaving Sadie staring in bewilderment at the ranch children, who would remain through the lunch hour. The respite she had hoped for each day was not to be.

She ordered them into the shade to complain over the contents of their lunch pails. She had thought to walk back to the boarding house for lunch, but couldn't leave the children unattended, particularly when the group was made up of the five sharp-faced Shockleys and the two ragged Terrisons. She'd have to bring her lunch, but for that first day would have to go as hungry as the Terrisons, who had brought nothing.

Sadie passed the hour writing her students' names in a ledger and watching from the corner of her eye as the Shockleys whispered about her.

The afternoon session went surprisingly well. Sadie met the returning students at the door and assigned seats. Soon she stood before them, pleased by the arrangement that would afford her the greatest control over the most troublesome children, who were already fidgeting in their seats.

"I have divided you into four groups," she began. "On my right is the first grade. This next row is the second grade. This row," she said, looking down at scowling Marty Wheeler, "is what we will call the middle grade, for those in third through ninth. On my left will be the upper grade for those at the secondary level. Now, who can name the president of our country?"

The preacher's eldest stood and correctly recited all nineteen presidents, their terms of office and their vice-presidents. Backwards.

Overwhelmed, Sadie smiled. "Who can tell me where the name of the State of Kansas came from?"

She was glad no one answered. "It comes from the Kansa Indian word for wind. It may possibly mean 'smoky wind,' for the smoke blown from the great prairie fires."

The class erupted with tales of sweeping fires they had seen, and the afternoon began in earnest.

The first week passed with amazing swiftness, leaving Sadie exhausted each day. The Shockleys did their best to annoy her with stares, giggles, fits of blessed but sullen silence and suggestive whispers.

There was a rash of petty thefts. All evidence pointed to the hapless, catalogue-reading eight-year-old Newcomb boy who,

Sadie knew, was innocent. Marty Wheeler continued to look at her as if he meant to ravish her. Indeed, Sadie was careful walking to and from school. For the most part, she felt everything was going as well as could be expected.

She obtained the names of school-age children not in attendance and mapped a strategy to visit their outlying ranches and farms.

Jim had not stopped by to charm her, and she was acutely aware of his absence. Sadly, she wondered if she'd discouraged his attentions too well. Wasn't there some way she might retain his friendship *and* her fragile reputation?

On Friday the obligatory frog appeared in her desk drawer. She proceeded with a lesson on reptiles. When a painstakingly printed note appeared in her hat after school that day, she whirled, thinking someone lay in wait for her. Only Marty Wheeler had the depraved knowledge necessary to insinuate such dark threats.

> Watch yerself, teacher, I can git my hands on you. You will wish you was dead and gone away. I am waiting to ketch you alone. Git out of town!

Sadie had to wonder why she was such a threat to her tormentor. She supposed that she wasn't a personal threat precisely, more just an object of interest.

These children were independent and stubborn, just as their parents were. They resented her authority. They chafed at the confines of a schoolroom. It was only natural for the one with the poorest upbringing and morals to try to have a bit of fun with her.

On Sunday afternoon she presented herself at 2 Park Circle across from City Park at the home of banker Leroy Crowley for dinner.

"We're so glad you could come!" Olive said, pulling Sadie into their lovely little Victorian home, where she was introduced to Olive's adult children.

Both John and Forrest were married. Little Jerome Crowley was there, along with his infant cousins. Ben, whom Sadie recalled from the night of the town meeting, was waiting there to sit solicitously across from her in the parlor and grill her with questions.

Sadie feared she had been invited more to expose her to Ben's attentions, than for dinner. At last she escaped to the kitchen to help Olive and her daughters-in-law lay a veritable feast in the shaded grassy backyard.

"If Ben asks too many questions, just tell him to pipe down," Olive laughed as Sadie fanned herself in the fierce afternoon heat. "He's eager to please you. He thinks he's looking for someone to court, but I don't think he's ready yet."

"I haven't the time for beaus," Sadie hastened to put in.

Olive laughed as if to say she knew better. "Ben was engaged to Cassie Whithers, the preacher's eldest. A lovely girl. She met a fellow in Lawrence last spring and eloped. We were all astonished! She didn't even write Ben an explanation."

"I had no idea there were more Whithers children," Sadie said, hoping indeed that Ben didn't have any intentions toward her.

Olive chuckled. "Preacher Whithers has taken God's injunction to be fruitful and multiply quite literally!"

Sadie smothered a chuckle.

"They already have one son away at college, so education is important to them, as you can imagine. I was hoping they might stop by later on. Preacher seems quite pleased with your teaching so far."

"I'm glad to hear that."

"Is that Jimmy's voice I hear in the parlor? Go on in and say hello to him. The two of you make a darling couple!"

Sadie's face reddened. She made feeble protests, but let Olive shove her inside nevertheless. She found herself happily smiling up at Jim as he caught sight of her in the dining room.

"I hear you have the young hooligans of Warren Bluffs tamed already!" he called, drawing her into the parlor to talk of the frog, stink bugs and crickets that had appeared in her desk that week. She said nothing of the note or the privy-fence peephole.

Half way through dinner Jim was called away, leaving everyone at the picnic tables to wonder what mischief was being made on a hot Sunday afternoon. At dusk Ben insisted on walking Sadie back to her boarding house. She could hardly decline, in view of her suspicion that someone might be lying in wait for her. She could only hope that Jim would not interpret the walk as "unfair advantage."

Ben was wonderfully kind to her. Eventually he strayed to talk of his lost love. Sadie could see he was clearly still in love with the young woman who had jilted him. She thanked him for his escort and hurried up to her room for the rest she needed to face her second week in the school.

As she walked to school the following morning, Sadie saw Marty Wheeler loitering between some buildings. Susanna Wheeler was already at school, lingering by the door with a handful of wildflowers in her fist. As soon as Sadie was inside the iron fence, Susanna thrust the sunflowers into Sadie's face.

"These are for you," the girl said, attempting to smile. Her expression seemed set in a perpetual scowl, like her brother's and father's. Sadie was at once on guard for a hidden bee or spider. "These are very nice," Sadie said, taking the bouquet and going inside. "Why don't you bring a little water for them?" she said, hoping to show the girl she was willing to be pleasant.

Appearing nervous, Susanna went through the side door. She worked the pump until she had filled the large tin cup Sadie kept for thirsty children. Sadie arranged the flowers in the cup and put them on the corner of her desk. With satisfaction, she plumped them with both hands and then waited for her students to straggle in. It was a very encouraging gesture!

She had just taken attendance and settled everyone into a lesson when her hands began itching and she noticed tiny blisters rising along the sides of her index fingers and thumbs.

Glancing at the flowers on her desk, she went quickly to them and hunted for leaves like those she remembered growing on vines in the woods behind her mother's boarding house. Seeing nothing suspicious, she supposed the itching could be coming from something else. Then as her cheek began stinging where she had rubbed it moments before, she knew with a certainty she had somehow touched the irritating oils of poison ivy.

Almost at once she heard snickers. Turning, she found all eyes on her. The well-behaved students looked puzzled, the troublemakers expectant.

Saying nothing, Sadie took the cup of flowers outside and dumped them in the rubbish heap. She scoured her hands and washed the cup again and again. With her hands dripping and stinging and her cheek inflamed, she marched into the classroom and fixed her eye on Susanna Wheeler.

"I would conduct a lesson on the identification and perils of poison ivy, but I tend to think that your bouquet was rubbed against the leaves so I would have nothing to show the class. Susanna, if you're itching anywhere you must wash immediately before you risk getting the poisonous oil in your eyes or mouth."

Susanna's snapping eyes rounded with alarm. She flashed her smirking brother a look of hatred and raced outside to scrub her reddening hands.

Sadie's eyes smarted with tears as she resisted scratching her hands. The blistering spread all across her palms. She went outside to question Susanna who, though poisoned herself, refused to say where she had got the flowers or whose idea it had been for her to bring them.

"Very well," Sadie sighed. By now she was in agony. "Go inside and complete your lesson. I'll see to you and your brother after lunch."

"I was just trying to be nice!" Susanna wailed at the door for all to hear.

Someone inside muttered, "You don't know how."

Sadie insisted the girl take her seat. She endured the remainder of the morning session with the grit of a martyr.

She wouldn't give the person responsible for her torment the satisfaction of knowing she was in pain.

At lunch she asked the ranch children to take their lunch in the city park. It was a good half mile walk away. The walk to and from would keep them occupied for an hour. Betty Whithers offered to take Sadie to the doctor's office, but Sadie declined, only to wish she had gone in the surrey moments later when she again washed and knew there was little more she could do for her rash at the school.

Setting out at once, she made the doctor's office in good time and was ushered into his examination room without delay. Dr. Gary Hamlin was a kindly gentleman, in his early forties, with thinning hair and drooping mustaches. He looked her over with the same hungry familiarity that she had noticed on their first meeting at the town hall.

"How did you get poison ivy on your hands and face?" he asked as he bathed her hands in a soothing solution. "The only patch of it I know about is miles from town." As he daubed the solution on her cheek, she felt as if he was making love to her and wanted to draw away.

"I'm not sure."

"You're not going to like the looks of your face for the next few days. Do you want to close the school until you're better?"

"I wouldn't dream of it," Sadie said. She was eager to be on her way.

As she was leaving, the doctor detained her. "Would you allow me to call on you some evening?" he said, looking at her with intensity.

Sadie managed a small, painful smile. "You're very flattering to a woman who must look quite awful right now," she said. "Perhaps when I'm back to normal."

"I'd advise you to change your clothes." His neck began to redden. "You may have the poisonous oil somewhere on them."

"Oh, that's a good idea." She started at once toward the boarding house.

Trudy was aghast at the sight of her. "You must stay here and rest!"

"I wouldn't give the little . . . vixen the satisfaction," Sadie muttered, marching into her room and carefully disrobing. "I'll wash these myself later. No sense in the laundress risking this rash."

"Am I to understand that some school child deliberately gave you poison ivy?" Trudy was shocked.

Sadie became alarmed. "You mustn't tell anyone! It wouldn't do for the children to think I tattle out of school."

"Of course not!" But Trudy looked as if she meant to spread the news the moment Sadie was out of sight.

Sadie started back for school thinking that she must throw away the drinking cup before some poor child got poisoned oils on his lips from it. She marched with such determination she was quite dizzy by the time she reached the school. Fortunately her recent work had strengthened her constitution. She didn't faint.

Although it was nearly one o'clock, none of the children had returned. Sadie had avoided her mirror and so didn't know how she looked. She took her lunch to the side yard and sat on a bench in the shade to eat and plan the correct punishment for the poisoning. Clearly, without proof, she couldn't punish Susanna, particularly when she was sure Marty was the devil who had thought up the prank.

While she sat, she heard a giggle nearby. She rose quietly to scan the area around the school. The prairie dogs perched on their dirt mounds stared back at her.

The river was not far off. Along the banks grew some cottonwoods and scrubby bushes. She heard the giggle again and tiptoed nearer. The gurgle of the water slipping by masked her footsteps.

Sadie stared into a dense cover of bushes to see Dawn Shockley in the ardent embrace of Marty Wheeler. It was evident he was already well acquainted with the girl's ripening body!

Sadie was so startled she scarcely knew what to do. Frightened suddenly by the enormity of what she was seeing, she turned quickly and fled back to the school. The sight of that stilll immature girl in an intimate embrace, her budding breasts brazenly exposed, left Sadie breathless and confused.

She surged through the side door and collided with Jim Warren. His arms went around her so naturally she hardly noticed them.

"Oh, please —" She pushed at his arms and managed to make him back away.

"Hello, teacher!" he said, peering into her face. His smile dropped away. "Whatever has happened to you, Sadie!"

"I can't think about that now! I just saw —" She looked up into Jim's face with alarm and went red to the soles of her feet. "Marty Wheeler and that Shockley girl are —" Tears stung her eyes again, and she whirled to escape to the privacy of the cloakroom.

All was silent. She was alone and she wept, not so much because two children were making love on a river bank, but because she was afraid she herself was doomed never to make love!

"Sadie, it'll be all right," Jim said, coming up behind her and turning her.

She went into his arms, pressing her good cheek against his vest. She felt the edge of his tin star dig into her hair. His hand cupped her head and smoothed the flyaway tendrils. For a blessed moment she thought of nothing but the warmth of him against her, the solid protection of his strong arms around her, the wonderful dusty, sunny aroma of his clothes and the sound of his breathing.

Then he was lifting her face, studying her inflamed cheek. "Poison ivy," he said.'

"I've just returned from the doctor." She explained Susanna Wheeler's "gift" and then tried to turn away. "I must look horrid, but I have to finish the day. I can't let them think something as small as this will drive me away. They're only angry because their sister's not the teacher." Then she looked pleadingly at Jim. "That is why they're tormenting me, isn't it, Jim?"

"I like the way my name sounds when you say it," he whispered, still holding her within the circle of his arms. "Do you want me to speak to their pa?"

"You mustn't do that! I have no idea if Susanna was aware that the flowers she gave me had been rubbed against poison ivy . She has a rash, too. As for Marty . . . . I didn't intend anyone to see this, but perhaps I should show it to you."

. She had tucked the threatening note in a box of books that were stored in the cloakroom. She pulled it out and watched as Jim read. His mouth tightened.

He looked into her eyes. "He's too clever to get caught leaving these for you. Chances are he made Susanna print this. Will you tell me if he leaves another?"

Sadie hung her head and finally nodded. "I was so sure I could handle this myself."

"Have you eaten?"

She nodded. At last she straightened, lifted her face and sighed. "I am awfully glad you came by. You have a way of brightening my day."

His eyes glowed. He moved a little closer. "I knew you liked me."

She put her rash-swollen hand against his chest to hold him back. "Don't make me keep pushing you away. I've missed your visits."

"I've missed seeing you, too. I would've walked you home from Olive's house yesterday if I could. Instead, I had to let Ben look after you. He behaved himself, didn't he?"

She smiled. "You know that he did. His heart was recently broken, so I'm told. You have no rival in that man . . . except for friendship," she added coyly, looking up and smiling at him.

"And the good Dr. Hamlin? Has he asked permission to call yet?"

She tried to move around Jim and go into the classroom. "Let me by, or I'll stand you in the corner. Yes, as a matter

of fact, Dr. Hamlin did ask to call on me. I couldn't very well
say no, you realize. I want you to understand."

"Well, I don't." He put out his hand and blocked her exit.
He was smiling in spite of his harsher tone.

"Jim," she said, moving closer to him than she had intended.
She felt the intensity of the attraction between them flowing
back and forth like a warm tide. She got lost in the look of
yearning in his eyes. She thought he was going to kiss her. "Oh,
you mustn't! You'll get the poison ivy on your lips!"

He straightened. "I was only *thinking* of kissing you, Miss
Evans. I wouldn't have dared try yet."

"Do move out of my way!" she said, delightfully embarrassed. She was unable to understand how she could feel so
happy whenever he was around, especially when she looked
like a scalded chicken. "I heard the —"

She wasn't able to finish. There in the classroom sat Mary
and Sara Whithers. Nearby was Winnie Akins watching
round-eyed. The Davidson twins had just taken their seats.
They wouldn't look at Sadie. Tattered little Bonnie Terrison
stood huddled next to the cloakroom door, listening. She
burst into giggles.

"We heard you sparkin', teacher," Bonnie crowed, skipping
to her seat. She sang, "Teacher's got a beau-u-u-u!"

Jim edged from the cloakroom, his tanned face looking
darker and rosier than usual. He raked his fingers through his
hair and grinned. "Just trying to find out who wanted to hurt
teacher with the poison ivy."

"Jim, don't say anything! I'll handle this," Sadie whispered,
taking his sleeve and ushering him out the side door like an
errant student.

"If there's anything else like this done to you I want to
know!" Jim said, his tone suddenly serious.

"I'll run straight to your door," Sadie whispered, turning to
take up the remains of her lunch. "That is, if you'll tell me
where I can find you when you're not on duty."

"I'm always on duty. I sleep in the jail's back room."

"That's terrible!"

"Not when I care about this town and everyone in it. I have little use for my grandparents' house."

Sadie glanced up to see Marty Wheeler strutting up from the river bank. As the youth caught sight of the deputy, his stride faltered. He veered to the left, skirting the schoolhouse.

"I wonder if Dawn will have the courage to come to school after what she's done," Sadie muttered.

Jim looked solemnly at Sadie. He took her shoulders gently. "Life starts young on the frontier."

"I know, but at twelve? If Mrs. Cadwallader knew, she'd have a stroke."

"She probably does know. It probably galls her to know the kind of people she has in her family. That's why she's such an unpleasant woman."

"And she was concerned about peepholes! I suppose I have to keep this to myself."

Jim nodded. "Unless something comes from it."

"Mercy!" Sadie whispered. Then she realized what she was discussing — sex and pregnancy, and with Jim! — and her entire body reddened. She collected herself. "Would you be so good as to escort me home today?" she said very softly, hearing the heavy footsteps of Marty Wheeler entering the schoolroom behind her.

"I won't be late," Jim said, beginning to grin.

"I put tardies in the corner." She let a little smile play on her lips.

"I'd like to see you try." He turned and was gone, leaving her glowing. All too soon, however, the feeling of comfort gave way to a vague unease.

The students had taken their seats for the afternoon session.

"Did you call the deputy about the poison ivy on your flowers, teacher?" Herbie Shockley asked in all innocence. His siblings shushed him. He reddened and slumped into his seat.

Sadie stood behind her desk and surveyed her class. "Susanna was only trying to be thoughtful by bringing me flowers," she said, watching from the corner of her eye as Susanna stiffened in surprise. Marty just smirked.

Dawn Shockley darted in the side door, her face flushed, a leaf in her hair. She scuttled to her desk. Sadie resisted staring at the girl. Dawn knew one very important fact of life that Sadie did not — what it felt like to be a woman.

Beginning to tremble, Sadie sank to her chair. "I'd like to begin this afternoon's lesson with —"

"Miss Evans?" came a trembling voice.

Sadie looked up to see Dawn's hand raised. The girl held a quivering card in her hand. "Grandma asked me to deliver this to you . . . but I forgot . . ."

Sadie watched in horrified fascination as Dawn tiptoed to her desk and handed over a hastily scrawled invitation. Sadie could only wonder if Marty had waylaid the hapless girl, but as Dawn took her seat again, Sadie watched through her downturned lashes as Dawn gave Marty a sultry smile.

> The pleasure of your company is requested
> at Cadwalladers'
> 4 Park Street, Saturday, 7:00 P.M.
> *R.S.V.P.*

"Please thank your grandmother for me, Dawn, and tell her I'll send my acceptance by messenger tomorrow."

"I'll take it, teacher!" Herbie cried, waving an arm. "I'll take it to grandma!"

Chapter Six

September 13, 1879

Jim made his regular nightly circuit of Warren Bluffs' east side, where once the rattle of honky-tonk pianos had disturbed the staider residents' sleep half the night. The music was quieter now, and many of the old saloons were boarded up. A few had been taken over by struggling new businesses. Akins' Smoky Hill Saloon had its doors open across the way as the dust from a herd of longhorn steers driven in that afternoon was still settling.

Farther east were the cattle pens that had once teamed with beeves driven up from Texas. There, longhorn cattle had waited shipment to the packing houses in Kansas City. Since the railroad had gone through to a new terminus at Hays City, Jim had watched his home town sink into oblivion. As many residents now left the town as moved to it.

Sometimes he missed the old days. He'd been only a boy then, but life had been exciting in Warren Bluffs. He couldn't remember when Warren Bluffs had last seemed truly alive . . . until the afternoon Miss Sadie Evans arrived, that is.

Smiling, he emerged on Cowtrail Street across from Akins' saloon. Thirty-five years before, this had all been rolling prairie. His grandfather's soddy had stood fifteen miles to the south on what was now Warren Road. By the time Jim came along, the old man had built a real house, with lumber shipped in from eastern forests.

"Evening, Willie," Jim said, ambling into the saloon. "Everything quiet tonight?"

Willie Akins glanced around his nearly deserted establishment and grinned. "I could be closed and make more money. The cowhands moved on to the Turkey Red up the street about an hour ago. They was hunting the fairer sex."

"Still planning to move west if the legislation goes through?" Jim asked, leaning on the bar. He waved away a beer and winked. "Got to go to a party at Cadwalladers' in a while. Can't have the taint of liquor on my breath."

Willie sniffed a laugh. "That woman's determined to throw you and MargieBelle together. You got sense enough to see that, don't you, Jimmy?"

Jim grinned. "Schoolmarm's supposed to be there."

"Oh, I see! My girl tells me that schoolmarm is as pretty as a picture. And nice, too. She treats my girl with care. It ain't Winnie's fault she moved around so much she never got book learning. And now, here we'll probably be moving again."

"You could find other work in Warren Bluffs," Jim said.

"This is all I know. And this is what I like. Winnie'll find a good husband in the west, anyway."

"She's a good girl. Any more trouble with empty kegs and bottles turning up missing?" Jim let his gaze move slowly around the room. Henry Shockley and Lester Peck nodded their greeting from a corner table.

"No more of them missing, but them kids has been at the old saloon down the way again. I wouldn't like to think they're fixing to burn the place down. My place could burn, too. This whole town, in fact. I ain't got insurance for that. I'd like for Winnie to finish out the school year before we have to pack up. Can you get that place boarded up tighter?"

"I'll see to it. Have you been able to guess who the boys are?"

"Ain't no guessing to it, Deputy!" The bartender leaned closer, whispering. "It's them Shockley pups, and Marty. Somebody ought to tell Otis about that boy."

"Otis has been none too stable lately. If I could just investigate a bit longer . . ."

"Investigate all you care to, Jimmy, but I'm telling you, somebody's distilling wheat whiskey up in the bluffs somewhere. I seen Biggins with a bottle of stuff wickeder'n rat poison. Herman could turn up more than pickled some fine night. He could turn up stiff as a post. I think —"

Jim waved the man to silence and straightened. "I'm going over to the party now. Sheriff will take my rounds for a few hours. He's not much for parties."

"Not at Cadwalladers', anyhow," Willie said, snickering, seeing that Jim dared not discuss his most important problem.

"Maybe I'll get me a dance with the schoolmarm." Jim grinned.

"Folks say she's a bit stiff-necked."

"With Mrs. Cadwallader wanting MargieBelle in the schoolhouse and taking no pains to keep it a secret, I think the poor woman feels unwelcome."

"I'll tell Winnie to take her something nice come Monday morning. Is it true what I heard about the poison ivy?"

Jim sighed. "I've got my eye on that one, too. Evening, Willie. Boys." He tipped his imaginary hat to Willie's customers and stepped out into the cool evening.

He ran his fingers through his hair. Folks thought him strange that he didn't wear a hat, but he'd never gotten over the feel of a Cheyenne Indian's grip on his hair back when he was with the volunteers. The Indian had been shot before he could lift Jim's scalp, but ever since then the pressure of a hatband always brought the incident to mind. Jim wanted to forget the bitter feel of near death.

Seeing nothing amiss in town, Jim headed for the Cadwallader residence off Park Circle and was somewhat surprised to see their large side yard hung with glowing paper lanterns and teeming with everyone who was anyone in the town. Their house was not so large as one might think from the airs Ethel gave herself. It was a tall, fussy Victorian structure with a round cupola. They'd raised a son and two daughters there. Now, with half the town crowded into it, the place seemed cramped and stuffy.

He wedged himself into the entry hall, calling hello to all the faces that lit up at the sight of him. He was looking for one small, dark-haired woman with huge, fascinating green eyes. He didn't see Sadie anywhere.

He had managed to make his way to the parlor when MargieBelle seized his arm. She hung on him like a nagging child. Sometimes he thought she was playing a part, speaking lines her mother had coached her to say.

"Oh, Jimmy! I'm so delighted you were able to come tonight. Let's go tell Sheriff Wheeler he has to leave now. I want you to stay as long as you can, and I want you all to myself. Eew, you've been walking across town. I can smell the pens on you!"

"That herd of longhorns was a big one. I thought I should check on them. Your ma wouldn't want a stampede or a bunch of rowdy cowhands spoiling her party." Jim forced himself to smile down at MargieBelle's elaborate cascade of curls. Her ruffled gown was equally elaborate. She reminded him of something that ought to be put out of harm's way on a shelf somewhere.

Much to his amazement, however, her gown had an alluring neckline. This was the first time she'd ever displayed her bosom at what could only be considered a home affair.

She dragged him to where the tall, wiry sheriff stood watching everyone. Otis Wheeler let his slick eyes play along the neckline of MargieBelle's gown as she coyly reminded him that it was Jimmy's turn at the party. Otis smirked and gave Jim a knowing look that conveyed his assumption that the prim little bitch MargieBelle would soon be lifting her expensive skirts for Jim out on the lawn somewhere.

Envious, Otis ground his teeth. He bid a few of the guests

goodnight, though he made a point of ignoring his hostess, and left by the side yard as stealthily as he had arrived twenty minutes before.

The moment he disappeared down the dusty lane the atmosphere of the Cadwalladers' party lightened. More guests spilled into the side yard, where little candles in paper lanterns cast warm pockets of light across the lawn. Ethel's prized roses gave off a heady sweet scent. From the drawing room came the tremulous voice of Alvinia Dewey singing "Rosalie, the Prairie Flower" to Mr. Bennett's piano accompaniment.

Ethel Cadwallader made the circuit of her downstairs rooms and the side yard with the timing of a prison guard. She caught dashing young Walter Runyon in the pantry actually kissing little Christa Roberts on the lips.

"You two children should be ashamed!" she said, ordering them to the sides of their parents. Ethel made her opinion of such behavior quite clear. Within moments of the discovery, everyone was whispering.

Christa's father escorted her home.

Jim watched it all while on MargieBelle's tether. He was content to let her lead him around so long as she didn't expect him to talk to her. He was thinking of Sadie, wondering why she wasn't there. He wondered if he would ever be able to engage her in more than friendly banter. If he did, surely Mrs. Cadwallader would see them and spoil it. He'd have to convince Sadie a drive out of town would be a good idea, their only hope of avoiding curious eyes.

At last MargieBelle steered him out the side door and down into the yard where he could breathe. The punch table had been set up there. He dutifully poured two little cups. Margie-Belle sipped at hers, pursing her lips in a distracting manner. Then she led him through the rose garden to the rear where the Cadwalladers' yard met the Crowleys' yard. He could see Olive carrying pies from her back porch to Ethel's. He marveled that two such different women could live side by side all these years and remain on speaking terms.

MargieBelle drew him into a shadowy arbor. There, the

smell of roses was even stronger. She rubbed against his arm. Startled, Jim looked down to see her bosom pressed against him in a blatantly suggestive way. She was awkward and self-conscious in her seduction.

"More punch?" he asked, wanting to bolt.

"Oh, Jimmy," MargieBelle said, looking desperate, turning up her face just in case he felt moved to kiss her. "At last we're alone!"

He turned away so that she couldn't see his pained expression.

She moved against him even more brazenly. In spite of himself, he couldn't help thinking of MargieBelle's half-exposed breasts swelling up as she nudged his arm with them.

Then he smiled, for if Sadie had been standing beside him in this way, he would have had his arms around her and his eyes on that soft flesh. He would have been thinking about how to slip away to private places with her so that he could kiss her.

He had once courted MargieBelle until he realized what a bear-trap of a woman she was. And he had paid his share of calls on Cassie Whithers, who had shocked everyone with her elopement. There had been other girls of interest to him, too, not the least of whom were two saloon girls in western Kansas who had introduced him to the pleasures of manhood.

He was no saint, but something about the way MargieBelle moved against his arm reminded him of those saloon girls and their practiced devices. He frowned down at MargieBelle, wondering how many other men in town she'd rubbed against.

He began speculating again on the man in Sadie's past. She'd been hurt, he knew. She seemed sure of herself, and looked as strong as any Cadwallader, but the other day when he had put his arms around her he had felt her trembling. He had felt the way she melted against him, needing him.

Alarmingly, his ardor swelled as he thought of Sadie. He didn't want her to arrive at the party and find him in the shadows with MargieBelle. He didn't want Ethel finding him there either. Ethel was expert at twisting circumstances to suit her wishes. He happened to know he was the primary object of her current schemes. Ethel wanted his family name for MargieBelle and a controlling interest in the old Warren acreage.

"Oh, Jimmy," MargieBelle breathed, boldly pulling his hand to her breast. "I can't bear the way you toy with me."

She was soft, but he suspected she wore padding. It seemed such a foolish thing to do. He deftly pulled his hand away. "I think your pa has spiked the punch, MargieBelle. Let's go back to the light."

"Ma and pa like you, Jimmy," she cooed, seizing his face. She dragged his face down so she could kiss him.

He yielded only to prevent her from crying out. He was sure she would if he resisted her seduction. Keeping his lips relaxed and completely unresponsive, he stared at MargieBelle's fluttering eyelids. He pitied her suddenly. She would make some lucky man a good wife, but he wasn't feeling that lucky.

Her lips were soft. She even parted them a little. He felt mildly stirred, but his pity had a chilling effect. Finally he pried her hands from his neck. He moved swiftly away from her, saying nothing, thinking that he needed no shotgun in his back on his wedding day.

"Jimmy! Oh, Jimmy, please!" MargieBelle whispered, coming after him.

"I'm worried about the schoolmarm," he said to show her just where his attention lay. "Your mother did invite her, didn't she? Warren Bluffs mustn't be rude to the poor young woman. She needs this job."

In fascination, he watched MargieBelle's pleading, sexually soft expression ice over with disappointment. "I hate you, Jim Warren! You're the lowest form of bastard!" Her words were hissed, but he was certain any number of couples dancing on the lawn to Alvinia's rendition of "Black is the Color of My True Love's Hair" could hear her.

Jim whirled and gave her a sharply reproachful look as he whispered, "Don't spoil the party for your parents with a scene."

"Get out!" She stood with her little fists balled.

He decided she would not make any man a good wife. Then he heard Sadie's voice. His blood was immediately on fire. He turned, feeling his face already splitting into a grin. He watched as she appeared on the steps at the side door, talking earnestly with Olive, who had just delivered two pies to the refreshment table.

"Pie," Jim heard himself say like a hungry boy. He started toward the table.

Sadie looked as if she'd forgotten about the party. Her knotted black hair was drooping, with long tendrils trailing at her temples and the nape of her neck. Her cheeks were alarmingly flushed. Jim wondered if she'd had trouble on the way over.

As he drew near, he saw that her tan skirt was covered with water stains and dust. "Evening, Miss Sadie. Everything all right?"

She glanced up at him. She looked upset but not frightened. She also looked tired. Her rash was nearly gone. She was panting, and the rapid rise and fall of her unpadded bosom fired his longing to get her away somewhere private.

Olive patted Sadie's shoulder. "Don't worry about a thing, Sadie. We'll send Dr. Hamlin out there right away. They won't feel in the least beholden to anyone. So good of you to go to them! You didn't walk!"

Sadie looked vastly relieved. "Yes, I did. I had no idea the Terrison farm was so far! She smiled at Jim as she went on. "Bonnie Terrison whispered to me yesterday after school that they had a new baby at their house. She said her mother was feeling poorly. I was so pleased by the news I decided to go out there to see if I could help in some way. Bonnie's such a dear . . . and teased so much because of her ragged clothes. I suppose I thought to encourage Bonnie's parents to dress her a bit better. But those poor people! I found —" Sadie glanced around, realizing how many guests were eavesdropping. "Never mind that. There was so much that needed doing. I just did what I could. I had no idea the phrase 'just down the road a piece' meant seven miles! I left this morning thinking I'd be back in a few hours to rest and bathe before Ethel's party. Goodness, I must look like a harridan!"

"You always look lovely," Olive said, winking at Jim. "Doesn't she, Jimmy? Fetch her some punch. We'll sit her down somewhere."

"Too tired to dance?" Jim asked, as Olive moved away to solicit help from her friends on behalf of the new, sickly Terrison infant. Then Olive went to find the doctor, who was dancing.

"Let me catch my breath," Sadie said as Jim guided her toward a line of assorted household chairs along the high hedges. He got her a cup of punch before the doctor passed by. Jim stood aside as Sadie whispered to the doctor about what she had observed of the Terrison woman's condition. Jim gathered that Sadie had spent an exhausting day attempting to clean up for the poor farm family. And she had walked fourteen miles, too. As soon as Dr. Hamlin was rushing on his way, Jim took a seat beside Sadie and offered her the cup of punch. "Everything else all right with you?" Jim asked, wanting to whisk her away.

She looked at him with a weary smile tinged with sadness. "I'm fine, though worn to a tatter." She plucked at her dusty, stained skirt. "Everyone here is dressed so beautifully. I had intended to come looking . . . better than this, certainly. Now that I've stopped walking, I'm growing chilled. I forgot my shawl." She lowered her voice. "Those farmers live in a house made from blocks of prairie dirt and grass! And they're so desperately poor! The man hadn't called Dr. Hamlin because he couldn't pay. No one had been out to help them. It's likely no one even knew they needed help."

Jim gazed down at her rosy face and wanted so desperately to kiss her he almost couldn't contain himself. "A teacher does so much more than just teach," he murmured.

She seized his hand, drawing strength from him. "There was so little I could do!"

To the tune of "A frog he would a wooing go," the guests at

the Cadwalladers' party watched Jim Warren leaning most solicitously over the overheated, brilliant-eyed schoolmarm. When she caught his hand, a few ladies gasped at such bold behavior.

She hadn't even dressed for the occasion! In her dusty shirtwaist and stained tan skirt she looked as if she'd scrubbed floors all day. A few people were amazed to think she had so few social graces. She might have *tried* to dress better than that. A few others were more generous and supposed that as a working woman she didn't have party gowns.

MargieBelle watched from the shadowed arbor. She ground her teeth in anguished frustration. When she caught her mother glaring at her, she shrugged helplessly, indicating that she had failed again. Jim treated her like an annoying little dog. She wanted to tear the pink satin bows from her curls and run sobbing up to bed. Instead, she had to stand silently and watch a disheveled Sadie Evans charm Jim.

Ethel saw that everyone was watching Jim ignore her daughter. Her blood surged with hate for the impudent, disrespectful little schoolmarm whom she had invited to the party only to prove that the Cadwalladers were not deliberately trying to snub her.

Ethel moved down the steps into the yard. She stood unnoticed for several minutes beside the deputy and Sadie. At last Sadie saw her hostess and stood up, wincing as if the effort pained her. Ethel trembled with rigidly controlled hostility. "So good of you to come, though my invitation did say seven o'clock." Ethel managed to smile tolerantly. She obviously didn't expect better of Sadie's sort.

"The party is lovely, Mrs. Cadwallader. MargieBelle's dress is very becoming. I hope you'll forgive my appearance. I was already so very late I felt that if I stopped off at the boarding house to change I might fall asleep and not arrive at all. I couldn't allow that to happen."

Mrs. Cadwallader looked curious, and then frowned because Sadie didn't go on to say what she had been doing all day to make her late for such an important function. At last Ethel dismissed the ploy to engage her sympathies. "Jim, I wonder if you'd give me a moment of your time. I have something important to discuss with you."

Jim nodded. "Of course. Don't leave without telling me, Sadie. I want to know more about . . . your day."

Sadie smiled wearily. She watched the two move back into the house, away from the guests. She was wildly curious to know why Ethel was taking Jim aside.

The moment Sadie was left unattended, the males at the party descended on her. She accepted her host's offer to dance. The big ex-buffalo hunter led her into the gentle lantern light on the lawn, never noticing how stiffly Sadie moved to the sprightly music. Ben Crowley danced with Sadie next. Then the preacher turned her in dizzying circles.

At last Alvinia's voice gave out. Mr. Bennett consented, after much urging, to continue playing. As he began a difficult classical piece, the dancing couples dispersed.

Sadie took her chair again. She wondered if she dared empty her shoes. Finally she slipped into the shadows and unbuttoned them. Her feet were blistered and raw. She wanted nothing more than to go home to bed. She felt faintly disgusted to be dancing when Bonnie Terrison's mother lay alone out in that stuffy, dirty soddy with four frightened little children and a newborn waiting for her to rise from childbed and get on with her chores.

"There you are!" MargieBelle said, startling Sadie. She raked Sadie from her trailing hair to her dirty stockinged feet. She appeared to be at a loss for words.

Sadie tapped out the remainder of the gravel and pebbles from her shoes. "I'm truly sorry I'm late to your mother's wonderful party."

MargieBelle's control snapped. "Don't give me that simpering schoolmarm stuff, Miss Evans. I want you to know I'm on to what you're trying to do to me. I won't have it! Do you understand? I won't have it!"

"I can't imagine what you're talking about," Sadie said, sighing. She pulled her shoes back onto her burning feet, wishing her hands would stop trembling.

"Jim Warren is my beau! I think it's disgusting the way you're trying to seduce him!"

Sadie straightened. She looked down into MargieBelle's livid face and then at her plunging neckline. She couldn't keep from chuckling. "Seduce him? I don't think so, MargieBelle."

"I am *Miss* Cadwallader to you. Oh, my mother and I know your kind! You'll amuse yourself with Jim. Then you'll move on. You won't last here in Warren Bluffs. You don't belong here!"

"I believe you're wrong about that, MargieBelle. I'd love to stay and match insults with you, but I really am exhausted. If I'm such a nuisance, I'll just go home."

"You can't do that! You'll make us look bad."

Sadie kept her arms relaxed. "What do you want me to do?"

"I want you to stay away from Jim Warren! We're going to be married."

"I am doing my level best to avoid contact with any man in this town. I can't seem to convince Jim to keep away. He is, after all, a grown man and can go where he pleases."

"Then you admit you don't like him!"

"I didn't say that," Sadie said, chuckling softly. "Uh-oh, I see him coming, now. You don't want him to see us quarreling, do you? You want him to believe you're an even-tempered woman, I should think."

MargieBelle's eyes bulged with helpless fury. She quickly masked the look as she turned and smiled sweetly up into Jim's face.

"I'm going to have to leave," Jim said, his expression strangely tight. "See that someone escorts you back to the boarding house, please, Sadie." He glanced at MargieBelle. "Some unpleasant people in this town are trying to make Sadie believe we don't want her here."

"The very idea!" MargieBelle gasped in false horror.

Mr. Bennett was just beginning to play "Beautiful Dreamer."

"I know you'll understand if I dance just this once with

Sadie," Jim said, smiling down at MargieBelle. "Just to make her feel welcome."

MargieBelle gaped as Jim led Sadie into the grass.

"Wait, I haven't buttoned my shoes," Sadie said, beginning to laugh.

"Take them off," Jim whispered.

"I couldn't! I'd be the talk of the town."

"You already are. Take them off and dance with me. This is our only chance. If I don't get out of here soon I'll lose my temper."

Knowing everyone was watching, especially MargieBelle, Sadie slipped off her high-buttoned shoes and tossed them to the side. "The grass feels so soothing on my feet." She let Jim sweep her into an embrace, and he danced her expertly around the yard. "I hope you don't mind if I droop on your arm. I'm nearly done in," she said.

"I'd offer to walk you home, except that I know how that would look."

"Sometimes small towns are a bit tiresome," Sadie said.

"Your rash looks better."

She saw the caressing way his eyes went over her face. She wanted him to kiss her. "I've had it before. Each time the reaction is worse."

"You got into poison ivy as a child?"

"It grew near my mother's boarding house," she said, remembering those hot summer days when she was a happy child free to run and play.

"Your father's dead, I assume."

She nodded. "He died when I was very small. I scarcely remember him. Mother had to open the house to boarders when I was nine. We couldn't manage without their rent."

"And your mother?"

Sadie wasn't able to answer immediately. "She died about two years ago. The doctor said it was something to do with her . . . heart." She drooped more heavily. "I'm sorry. I miss her."

"Why do I get the feeling you weren't with her when she died?" Jim asked.

Sadie's blood tingled back to life. "Let's not talk of the

things that sadden me," she said, noticing that MargieBelle and Ethel were watching them. "What did Ethel say when you went inside with her?"

"We mustn't sadden the teacher, but we can anger the deputy," Jim said teasingly, but his eyes had taken on a flat color that alarmed Sadie.

"I'm not prying. Only trying to stay awake." She squeezed his hand. "You have a very intimidating frown, Deputy."

"I don't mind you asking, Sadie. I only mind having to answer that Ethel wants to support me in the November election for sheriff."

"Knowing her, she would expect something in return for her support."

"I think I'll go now before I say or do something I'll regret in the morning."

"You don't strike me as a man who has ever regretted a thing," Sadie said, trying to bring back his smile.

He did smile down at her, warming her, erasing her fatigue. "You have a way of brightening my day, too, teacher."

He excused himself then. He slipped away, nodding briefly to Ethel as if he had been called away and had to rush off.

Sadie staggered back to her seat and hurriedly replaced her shoes. She looked up to see MargieBelle seething before her.

"What did you say to make him rush off like that?" Margie-Belle demanded, her eyes anguished.

Ethel joined them and shushed her daughter. "Jim has a great deal to ponder, dear," she said to MargieBelle with a small knowing smile. "Sadie, you know of course, that Jim is hoping to overcome Otis Wheeler in the coming election for sheriff. I've pledged Jim my support."

"Oh, Ma!" MargieBelle gushed, squealing happily like a girl. "I just knew you would. I'll bet Jimmy's pleased."

"Oh, certainly," Ethel said smugly. "He's sure to win with our support."

Sadie rose. "And sure to be grateful, too, I'll bet," she said, but not maliciously. She saw through Ethel's efforts to make her think Jim could be controlled.

Momentarily at a loss for a retort, Ethel looked at Sadie with a certain wariness, as if she had misjudged Sadie's strength and must think of a new offensive strategy.

"I know I'm out of place at your lovely party in my walking clothes," Sadie said, edging toward the path leading to the street. "I wonder if you'd forgive me if I went home? I was out at the Terrison farm all day. I lost track of how much laundry I did. And the toddlers needed bathing. Mrs. Terrison was still confined to childbed, so I cooked for her. The family hadn't had a decent meal since she went into labor. If my guess is right, she was in labor for nearly two days . . . and then delivered herself, alone. I tried to bake enough biscuits to last them for several days. I've asked everyone who can spare a bit to donate it to help ease the doctor's fee. We don't want a struggling family to feel ashamed of needing our help, do we? I thought perhaps MargieBelle might have something tucked away in her hope chest to offer the infant. I haven't a thing." Sadie felt her throat catch. She forced a brave smile. "I was afraid this afternoon the newborn might not last the night."

Ethel was struck dumb. She stepped back as Sadie started away.

"Thank you for inviting me," Sadie said, escaping the yard and the pairs of eyes drilling into her in astonishment.

". . . laundry for that filthy family . . ." was all Sadie heard before she quickened her pace, nearly breaking into a run.

She couldn't erase her memory of Pete Terrison's expression as he watched her bathe his wife's bloodless face. He was a harsh embittered farmer by the twist of his mouth, but afraid for his woman. Sadie was worried, too.

At the corner, Sadie looked up at the courthouse and its pretentious little dome. A tall man standing in shadow on the steps started slowly toward her. At first she didn't recognize him. In her state of mind she thought of gathering up her skirts and making a dash for her street. Then the moonlight glinted on Jim's tin star.

"Carry your books, teacher?"

She burst into a nervous laugh. "You frightened me!"

"Forgive me."

Gratefully she took Jim's offered elbow and let him lead her into the blue shadows beneath the cottonwoods lining the circle. The stately houses of Warren Bluffs' best families looked on with stiff dignity.

"I know a short-cut to the boarding house," Jim whispered.

"Anything to get me out of these shoes as soon as possible."

He led her south on Park Street to a vacant lot between two small clapboard houses. The rear of the McClure boarding house loomed across the waist-high grasses.

"Won't there be snakes in the grass?" Sadie whispered, feeling suddenly too tired to be brave.

"The snakes in the grass are all back at Cadwalladers' having fun discussing us." He swept her up into his strong arms.

"Oh, Jim! Don't! What if someone sees us!"

"They'll envy us," he said, starting off through the grass.

Sadie laughed. "If I was in school and cornered like this I'd have to give a lecture on prairie grass. This is bluestem," she said, waving her arm to indicate the field. She laughed more loudly and caught a tight hold of Jim's warm neck. He was so wonderful!

"Say that again," he murmured.

"Blue —"

He stopped and brushed his lips against her pursed ones. "I like you, Sadie. Very much."

"Don't say that. Put me down." She struggled weakly, her blood rushing, and then surrendered when his lips pressed more urgently against hers.

"Bluestem what?" he whispered against her lips.

"Grass —" With her mouth slightly opened, Jim kissed her a third time. He hugged her body tightly in his arms, arching over her so that she felt completely in his control, and completely safe.

His lips were soft and pliant. They moved with careful urgency over her mouth. She fancied she could taste the punch he had drunk at the party. Then she felt her hairpins give way. Her hair unknotted and spilled down over his arm to swing heavily at his side. His grip behind her back tightened. He had her drawn so tightly against him, and was suddenly kissing her so deeply, she felt delirious and faint.

"Let me breathe!"

"I don't want you to breathe, or think, or anything! I want you to stop holding yourself back and kiss me!"

"I have to hold back!"

"I won't hurt you, Sadie. I care too much."

She was suddenly struggling, reminded of another time when she had been caught up by her desires. "Put me down. I'll go on alone in spite of the snakes in the grass!"

He didn't put her down, but he did loosen his hold. He crossed the grassy field to the rear of the boarding house. "I didn't mean to frighten you, Sadie."

"It's all right." As soon as they reached the edge of Trudy's truck garden, Jim set her down on her wobbly legs. She took off her shoes, remembering dancing on the cool grass. "You didn't frighten me. I was put in mind of something . . ."

"You've been hurt once," Jim whispered, his expression unreadable in the darkness. A slight breeze came up and the moon went under a cloud. "By a man."

She thought a long time before answering. "Yes. I was engaged once. And . . . betrayed."

"I'm sorry."

"I need your support and your friendship, Jim. Maybe I need even more, but I don't dare let myself think about that."

He moved quickly to her and gathered her into his embrace. He kissed her gently, holding her against his body in a way that told her he had wanted to kiss her for a good many days now.

She slipped her hand between their lips so he couldn't go on kissing her. "If I could just feel secure with my place in this town, with my future here . . . maybe I could think about . . . more."

"I want to take you riding," Jim whispered. "I want to show you my grandparents' house where I grew up. I want to show you everything that I love about this town."

"How do you feel about Ethel supporting you for sheriff?" Sadie whispered, keeping her face turned away.

"Not much, if I'll be expected to —"

"I know," Sadie said. "She expects you to marry Margie-Belle. How soon?"

Jim's breath went out in an exasperated sigh. "Soon. Before the election. I won't do that just to get votes! I don't have to."

"And if you refuse to marry MargieBelle?" Sadie asked.

"I really don't care what she says about me, Sadie! I'm the better man for the job. Otis Wheeler has outlived his usefulness as sheriff and should step aside. Because he won't, I have to beat him in the election."

"And you won't use anything that people might interpret as mud-slinging, like the fact that his son is a thief."

"I'll catch the kid at something worth catching him for. And there's more. I'll use it if I have to, but only at the right time . . . and only as a last resort." He moved away, smiling in the darkness. "I suppose I had better restrain myself. There's one way Ethel Cadwallader could hurt me. Through you."

Sadie started to move away, frightened by how happy and yet how afraid his words could make her.

He grabbed her arm. "Will you go riding with me?"

"Oh, maybe. Some day . . ." She smiled back at him. "And I'm not being coy."

"Not you, teacher. Sleep well, Sadie."

"And you, Jim."

"Not me, not when I've just been kissing you."

Chapter Seven

After the church bell stopped pealing the following morning, Warren Bluffs rocked with whispered news. Ethel Cadwallader's eldest, George Jr., who was all of thirty-three and had been living at the Grand Hotel on Cowtrail Street for more than a year, hadn't just been late to his mother's party.

He hadn't shown up at all. A telegraph dispatch had come in at the depot early saying he'd taken the seventeen-year-old daughter of wheat farmer Eb Meeker to Abilene and married her! Everyone was convinced the girl was in a precarious state — in other words, pregnant.

Ethel's eyes bored into anyone brave enough to meet her gaze as she and MargieBelle marched, heads high, from the church a few hours later. Everyone knew George, Jr., was a trial and no-account. None the less, his outright flouting of decent moral behavior and his disregard for family were a surprise. George, Sr. found a bottle somewhere — some claimed he bought it and not at any saloon, either. While Ethel, MargieBelle and their parlormaid cleaned up from the party the night before, George, Sr., got drunk and sat sprawled in the kitchen saying he hoped his boy had had his fun, because it was for sure the last he'd ever have, being married now.

Monday afternoon, while Sadie outlined the events of the American Revolution, assigned essays to the upper grade and a list of dates to the middle grade, dictated spelling words to the second grade and took the first grade aside to practice the alphabet, twenty-five-year-old Dorcas Terrison and her newborn son died quietly in their soddy seven miles north of town.

At that moment Bonnie was standing in her tattered smock and pinafore, twisting her shaggy braids and reciting her letters. Dooley Terrison had just correctly spelled "minute man." Pete Terrison, their father, stood in a dusty swirl of sunlight slanting into the desolation of his sagging soddy and asked Dr. Hamlin what he should do now with his motherless four children. Gary Hamlin shook his head, clapped the trembling farmer on his bony shoulder and went out to his rig.

School recessed Tuesday. Everyone went to Mrs. Terrison's funeral and Preacher Whithers read a fine bit over her pine box, drawing tears from all. That night Sadie couldn't sleep. She had washed that poor woman's face. She had rocked the failing infant. The memory of that long hot afternoon filled her with desolation. She felt peculiar and feared that somehow she was failing in her efforts to find happiness and security in Warren Bluffs. If she hadn't been sure that Jim Warren's kisses would surface in her dreams, she would have packed and left town. She wasn't sure why.

Perhaps she was coming to think of Warren Bluffs as home, she thought. She wanted nothing to go wrong here. To have someone die, someone she had tried to help, left her feeling helpless and vaguely uneasy. Were the good times coming to an end . . . so soon?

Wednesday morning Sadie arrived at school determined to shake off her feelings of gloom. She found the padlock hanging open. Immediately on guard, she crept inside and found her classroom a shambles. Her desk had taken the brunt of the punishment. It has been smashed to kindling. The misspelled obscenities were back on the blackboard, gouged so deeply she had to wonder again at the vandal's determination.

The scene was as chaotic as her emotions. Someone wanted her gone! She picked up her Webster's dictionary and sighed heavily. Its spine had been broken.

She assembled the students in the yard for morning session. Then during lunch she paid a call at the jail. She arrived trembling with rage.

"It looks as though it was done with an ax," she said, sinking into the chair across from Jim's desk. She described the condition of the school, her shaking voice betraying her feelings. "I thought you'd want to know."

"It must have been done yesterday during the funeral," Jim said, looking soberly at Sadie. "I don't recollect seeing Marty at the church or graveyard."

She shrugged. "Or any of the Wheelers." Then she straightened, lifting her head. Just being near Jim relieved her of much of her burden. "I've felt glum since Mrs. Terrison died, but I'll get over it. I'll have to."

"You look tired, Sadie. You need a break." Jim's expression brightened when he saw that she understood he was asking her to go riding again.

She managed to smile. The tension in her neck eased. "I haven't even been teaching a month. I don't need a break yet!"

"Warren Bluffs was aware the youngsters would be a tough bunch to teach. These incidents may have little to do with you personally."

"I've told myself that," Sadie said, rising to return to school, her courage buoyed. "But I had thought I was making progress."

"You are!" He rose too. "I'll bet most of your students were upset to see the schoolroom vandalized."

Thinking back, she recalled their anguished expressions and nodded. "I was so upset myself I scarcely noticed. Why, I've been behaving like a frightened schoolgirl! Whoever said this job would be easy?" She found herself leaning toward Jim, longing to go into his arms, and had to draw herself up. What a weak and foolish creature she was! She straightened and forced a confident smile. "Thank you for being here when I needed a . . . friend. Bonnie and her brother weren't at school this morning. I heard Mr. Terrison say at the graveyard that he would take his children back to the East to see if any relatives would take them in." Momentarily, her heart caught. "Oh, Jim . . . If only there were something I could do for them!"

"You've been a good influence on Bonnie," he said, taking her hand and rubbing her knuckles. "She'll never forget you. I'll come by later to have a look at the damage."

Tingling, she withdrew her hand from his grasp and, with a private smile of pleasure, slipped back into the sun. How good it was, she thought as she returned to the school with a lifted heart, to have Jim there when she needed cheering up.

By the following day three fathers had been by to stack the shattered desks on the woodpile. They nailed new planks to the walls and blacked them. The stench of charred potato hung in the air. The teacher's new desk was delivered and the town carpenter brought several new seats for the children. Classes resumed as before. At the end of the week, Pete Terrison rolled away in his loaded farm wagon, with Bonnie waving a tearful goodbye from the tailgate.

Sadie put on a brave face. "Remember to be good," she said, grasping at the child's hand as the wagon rolled along.

"Can I write to you, Miss Evans?" the little girl called, trying to smile.

"Of course . . . just as soon as you learn all your letters!"

"I have a loose tooth in front!" Bonnie called more loudly. The last of her words were lost to the muffled thunder of the wagon wheels going over the Kansas Pacific tracks. Sadie waved until her arm ached.

Saturday afternoon Sadie looked in both stores for a new skirt and shirtwaist but found nothing she liked. Christa Roberts, still confined in disgrace behind her father's yard goods counter since the Cadwalladers' party, told Sadie what a good seamstress Lettie Johnson was. "She could make whatever you want, Miss Evans —" Christa was interrupted by two ladies moving through the crowded store, whispering loudly.

". . . dancing barefooted in public! Did you *ever*?"

Christa looked up at Sadie. Her cheeks reddened with secret admiration. "Everybody's talking about you, Miss Evans!"

"Talk can sometimes be misleading, Christa —"

The other woman whispered on. "It's a disgrace, I tell you! Giving that poor child the rod for only misspelling a word. If I hear tell she's taken the rod to my boys for something puny like that, I'll speak to the school board about her! Why, Mrs. Wheeler says that woman is going out to the ranches sticking her nose into everybody's affairs — telling them to wash regular and move their privies away from the house for the sake of high-jean, or some such. Who does she think she is?"

Sadie's blood began rushing hotly. Whispers! Always whispers about her. "What are they talking about, do you know, Christa?" Sadie asked.

Christa looked alarmed. "You haven't whipped anybody at school! Last week folks was complaining that you hadn't raised a hand to anybody yet. I can't figure it."

"*Were*, Christa. *Were* complaining." Sadie stepped into the narrow aisle. She was trembling as she forced a smile. "Good afternoon, ladies! Oh, Mrs. Davidson, I didn't recognize you at first. Your boys are doing so well in their studies. Burt's way ahead in his reading." Sadie stopped herself, wishing she didn't sound so like MargieBelle.

Mrs. Davidson's mouth dropped open the moment she saw Sadie and realized her gossip had been overheard. Her round face flushed crimson to her hairline. "How do, t-teacher! T-this is Lindie Purcell," Mrs. Davidson finally introduced her friend. "Her children are too young to attend school yet."

Mrs. Purcell was a thin young woman with a wind-dried severe face. Her eyes coldly appraised every inch of Sadie's person. "My husband's the barber. He hears all about what goes on in this town."

"I'm sure," Sadie murmured.

"We're real good friends of the Cadwalladers. We didn't have the pleasure of meeting you at the party last week, but I saw you." She gave Sadie another scathing once-over. "You looked mighty romantic dancing with Jim Warren barefooted on the lawn in front of everybody."

Sadie kept her smile from souring. "Excuse me for asking, ladies, but I couldn't help but overhear you both discussing punishments that supposedly went on in my classroom over spelling words. Who told you these things?"

Both women stiffened. "We heard plenty about all that goes on in your classroom, Miss Evans."

"I can assure you ladies I've punished no one. My students are well behaved. Aside from the vandalism on Wednesday, I've had no serious trouble with them. I've no reason even to speak sharply to any of my students, much less give them the rod as I heard you mention. I wanted to be sure you knew that."

"Mike Shockley has told us every single thing that's been happening out on School Road," Mrs. Purcell said, although her eyes registered growing doubt at Sadie's confident expression.

Sadie gave a relieved chuckle. "I should have guessed. Mike Shockley! Mike is a bright boy, of course. He's several years behind in his studies, but we're working on that a day at a time. He has a fertile imagination, too. He spends too much time with one of the troubled striplings of this town, but there is little I can do about that. I'd like to think you ladies believe me when I say I've never given the rod to any student. Nor do I ever intend to. An hour on what I call a 'thinking stool' in a quiet corner is usually sufficient to restore a child's self-control. If you'll excuse me now, I really must rush off to attend to the remainder of my errands. Good day, ladies."

Trembling, Sadie moved quickly away. When she was out of sight she paused and heard them ask Christa if she had *ever*! Who *did* she think she was!

"Why, Miss Evans is a fine teacher!" Christa said, sounding

upset. "Those Shockley hooligans would try the patience of a saint!"

Sadie fled from the store.

Pranks. Vandalism. Outright lies. She had truly not expected the torment to go on this long! What could be wrong? Was it her fault? Was it time to move on? The mere thought of tearing up her fragile new roots filled her with anguish. She had to stay; she had to find a way to get people to lend her a little support.

That evening Sadie took a constitutional along the dusty residential streets, calling a helo to every person rocking on a porch. Naturally, she was asked to stop and chat.

After only a few evenings, Sadie knew which of her students were spreading imaginative stories of bizarre assignments and punishments. Sadie set all her curious new friends straight on the matter, but while she felt assured of their approval, the atmosphere in her classroom grew even worse. For her every step forward, the Shockleys dragged her two steps back. Rather than risk losing her temper with them, she finally felt that her only recourse was to buy that small "thinking stool" at the end of the following week. After keeping the three most imaginative Shockley brothers on it for an hour each, a semblance of order was restored.

During the last weekend in September, Sadie found the livery man willing to lend her the use of his best buggy. She drove out to the Garley ranch. A black family newly arrived from Louisiana with four school-age children were living in a dugout soddy in the side of a hill and were attempting to graze a few cattle, most of them on the roof. The local wheat farmers wanted them to move farther west where grazing was more likely.

They were friendly and honored to be visited by someone as illustrious as the learned and prim schoolmarm. Sadie drank something called "rootberry tea" with them, a brownish concoction sweetened heavily with sorghum. Dirt sifted into her hair every time a steer wandered across the dug-out soddy's grassy roof.

Ivy Garley and her little brother, Jesse, began attending school when they could be spared from home. They were both in the first grade. Cornell's sister, Annabelle, took them under her wing. Soon their father was assisting at the blacksmith's shop in town and singing Sadie's praises for finding him friends and a job that paid cash money!

Sadie's next visit took her to a ragged squatter family living east of town. The only school-age child there was fifteen-year-old Junie, and she was six months pregnant. Junie's father kept Sadie at bay with a shotgun. "Don't need no more do-gooders out here! They done their damage right good."

Sadie turned her buggy around and went back to town, wondering if the man had been referring to damage done to his young daughter. That, too, she decided to keep to herself.

On her fellow boarders' advice, Sadie began planning a winter pageant for her students, a project designed to show off talent, draw community support and generally keep the youngsters' minds occupied with higher ideals rather than pranks.

Mr. Bennett agreed to contribute his best piano student. Alvinia suggested a small choir. Sadie decided to direct a tableau titled, "Christmas in Kansas."

Indian summer remained warm and golden, and plans for the pageant did indeed distract the children. A sense of routine settled comfortably over Sadie and the school. Jim went away for several days to assist with a large cash shipment for the Crowley bank. She felt unaccountably nervous the entire time. By the time he returned, the weather was again hinting at the coming cold.

Late one rainy afternoon Jim arrived in the livery buggy to drive Sadie back from the school to the boarding house. The sight of him in the schoolhouse doorway warmed Sadie's weary heart. The day had been a bit trying, with mud everywhere an impish child could think to put it.

"I'll wait out here until class is over," he said, grinning as he shook back his rain-damp hair. She looked so lovely standing before her class in her crisp white blouse with big soft sleeves and a high lacy collar, and her dark skirt smudged with small chalky handprints. She looked more like a mother than a teacher. Her cheeks were flushed and her eyes shining as she struggled to hold the attention of so many of varied ages and abilities now all eyeing her because her beau was hanging about.

Holding back a grin, he went out, shutting the door softly. He scanned the sodden field as he shook the water from his rain slicker. The sky was low and grey over the distant scattering of cottonwoods. He was glad to be back. Riding shotgun on a cash shipment was a risky business in these times. He had been surprised at how jumpy he'd felt.

He could hear the softly inquiring voice of Sadie inside the schoolhouse, and the piping answers of her younger students. Since she had come to Warren Bluffs, his life had seemed fuller. Filling his chest with cool, moist air, he felt foolishly like bursting into song. To have his town and Sadie there waiting when he returned seemed as close to perfection as he was ever likely to get. If he could just break Otis's twisted hold . . . He resented the power a man like Otis had, a power born of holding something over every voter's head in the county.

Jim heard another buggy coming up on the road. He led his rig around to the side door so Sadie wouldn't get soaked climbing aboard. The preacher's surrey stopped near the iron gate. Waiting in the covered rig, Jim heard the children pour out the door moments later as Sadie dismissed the afternoon session. Walter Runyon brought the family buggy from the protection of the hay barn, waved to Jim and drove his sister home. To stay in office, Otis even had something on the mayor, Jim knew. In the mayor's case it was a brief but damning affair with a dressmaker who had come through town and been discovered entertaining a number of male callers several nights running.

The Runyon surrey was just rolling away as Jim got down from his rig. He hadn't noticed the Cadwallader buggy arrive. Ethel's and MargieBelle's grating voices filled the schoolroom as they barged in.

"It's time someone put an end to this high-handed notion you have of giving a recital!" Ethel began, sounding as if she was backing Sadie into a corner.

Jim positioned himself just outside the door and stood, hands in pockets, listening. He was pretty sure Ethel had not seen him parked on the far side of the school.

"Religious doctrine is not to be taught in public school!" MargieBelle cut in, her speech sounding rehearsed. "I don't know where you get your high-flying ideas. I certainly wouldn't expect these ignorant children to perform for the entire town, nor would I dream of . . . of . . ."

"Usurping," Ethel prompted.

"Yes, usurping the preacher's authority in church."

Jim could hear Sadie wiping the new blackboard. "What gives you ladies the idea I can't conduct a simple pageant?" Sadie said softly. "It's intended only for parents. You needn't attend. I think it's important to involve my student's parents in school activities, particularly when certain students insist on telling bald-faced lies about what goes on in this schoolhouse. Besides all that, I have Preacher Whithers' complete approval. He is writing the narration for the manger scene, and his wife will coach the children in church school. It's a joint effort," she said in a rush to finish before being challenged. "In addition, we will sing patriotic songs and Cory will be reciting the rather ambitious 'Paul Revere's Ride.'"

MargieBelle was momentarily overawed. "Well . . . to go to such lengths. . . . Why don't you just accept the fact that the students don't take to you? As far as we can see, they're trying to drive you away."

Mrs. Cadwallader made an effort to sound conciliatory. "MargieBelle's far better suited to teach these students. After all, she has grown up with them."

"I'm sure you'd make a fine teacher," Sadie said. "By the way, congratulations on the marriage of your son, Mrs. Cadwallader."

Jim smothered a laugh. Sadie didn't flinch from antagonizing the old dragon.

"I'll not stand here and listen to you insult me! We intend to discourage this recital," Ethel snapped.

"But the children are excited by the idea."

Jim heard MargieBelle strolling around the room, examining the slates left on the desks. She dropped each one hard enough to risk cracking it. Evidently she was reading the markings on some. "I'd have them much farther along than this," she muttered with a sniff and a sigh as if to say she supposed Sadie was doing her best.

"I'm sure you would," Sadie answered.

Sadie's agreeable attitude suddenly alarmed Jim. Perhaps she was growing weary of sparring with Ethel and Margie-Belle. Fearing she might be thinking of leaving town, he decided to intervene on her behalf.

"Afternoon, ladies," he said, going to the side door and shaking back his dripping hair.

He relished Ethel's look of horror as her eyes swept over his drenched hair and slicker. She knew at once he'd heard her every word. She slashed a sidelong glance at Sadie as if to say she realized the trick that had just been played on her. "Jim, you'll catch your death," she muttered, her tone flat.

"What are you doing here!" MargieBelle squawked, looking as is she was trying desperately to remember exactly how nasty she'd just been to Sadie. She dropped a slate she'd been smirking at and forced a smile. "I-It's so nice to see you . . ." She faltered, perhaps considering an endearment. ". . . Jim," she said finally, reddening.

"I came by to give Sadie a ride home to keep her out of the rain. I've been stuck out back in the mud." That was as close to a lie as he was going to let himself get. "If I'd known you ladies were planning to fetch her . . ."

As Ethel blustered, he grinned in spite of himself. Ethel made a few agreeable noises, as if to say giving Sadie a ride had been her intention. Then she sucked in her cheeks, knowing he would always get the better of her.

"MargieBelle's just been telling me that she'd make a far better teacher than I," Sadie said, looking weary. She went into the cloakroom for her hat. She didn't meet his eyes.

"Oh, I'd make a fine teacher if given half a chance!" Margie-Belle chirped, tugging at her gloves and smoothing them with exaggerated care. "Sadie's doing the best she knows how, but nothing would be more perfect that a Warren Bluffs girl teaching in this classroom." She sidled up to Jim and gazed sweetly up at him. "Don't you agree, Jimmy?"

Jim watched as Sadie came out of the cloakroom pinning on her hat. She adjusted her spectacles. Her green eyes seemed enormous and childlike. Then she gave MargieBelle a warm, startling smile.

"I have to agree you should at least be given a chance to show your teaching skills," Sadie said to MargieBelle as she gathered her books together and tidied her desk.

MargieBelle's expression clouded. "Do you mean . . . you're quitting your job?" Her face was drained of color.

"Of course not," Sadie said. "But you and so many others are convinced I'm not right for it. I'd hate to think any one of you was correct. After all, my main concern is the education of my students. I wonder if you'd care to come to school — say, tomorrow — and teach? What is your field of interest? English? Mathematics? Mine has always been history."

"I couldn't do that!" MargieBelle cried.

Her mother nudged her sharply.

"I mean, I'd feel odd . . . side by side with you. It would hardly be a clear test of . . . teaching ability if you were here. The students don't . . . take to you. They'd be like they always are." MargieBelle looked to her mother anxiously for assistance, but Ethel only smiled smugly.

Sadie went on. "I agree that it would be hard on the students to have two teachers. Would you like to teach alone for an entire day?"

"She'd be glad to show her superior ability," Ethel said before MargieBelle could answer.

MargieBelle managed a hasty smile and blinked her eyes at Jim. "That's very generous of you, Sadie. Do let me know when you'd like me to take over."

Jim wondered how long Sadie had been planning to call Ethel's and MargieBelle's bluff.

"I have little planned for tomorrow," Sadie said. "Would you care to meet me here at seven? I could show you what we've been doing. You could take the rest of the day."

MargieBelle squirmed. Her mother nodded with satisfaction. Then she jabbed MargieBelle's side again.

"Oh! Of course. Tomorrow, then." MargieBelle looked ill.

Ethel strutted to the door. She thrust her umbrella into the rain, opening it with a satisfied snap. "You're a wise person, Miss Evans. Come along, MargieBelle. You have your curriculum to prepare. I think you should begin the day with . . . ."

MargieBelle flashed Sadie a thinly veiled grimace, skirted Jim and his amused look and dashed after her mother. "Ma, I'll just teach whatever she —"

"You'll teach what I say you'll teach, young woman! Get in that buggy and don't say a word. Just listen to me. I'll tell you everything you need to know to prove to every last man, woman and child in this town that you are the one for this job!"

The pattering rain drowned out MargieBelle's agonized plea to reconsider and Ethel's last hissed words. MargieBelle scrambled into the buggy and it jolted wetly away.

Heart hammering, Sadie sagged against the edge of her desk. "I hope I haven't just given away my job." She rubbed her aching neck.

Jim grabbed her and turned her for a kiss. "Brilliant!"

"Don't tease me about this." Her eyes were dark with worry.

He kissed her smartly. "You know she'll make a mess of everything. She'll be so nervous . . . ."

"That will hardly make for a fair comparison of skills."

"Is she going to remain calm if Mike Shockley brings firecrackers?"

"Or stink bugs." Sadie looked up into his eyes, warming to him. She laughed softly. "Maybe it will prove to her and her mother that I can teach . . . a little."

"And while she's trying valiantly to fill your shoes, Miss Evans, you and I will go driving. I'll have a picnic lunch packed for us. We'll go far away."

"It sounds lovely, but it's raining." Sadie let him draw her into the circle of his arms. "And you're wet. Were you eaves-dropping?"

"Of course. They weren't very nice to you."

"I don't expect them to be," she whispered.

She felt so slim and frail he began to worry that she hadn't been eating properly. She was too serious, too troubled by things he couldn't help or change or even guess at.

"Tomorrow it will not dare rain," he said, lifting her chin and kissing her. Her lips were so sweet, so tremulously desirable he almost wondered if he was going to be able to behave himself. He wanted nothing more than to make her his in every way possible. "Tomorrow we'll leave the world behind. I'll make you smile all the day long."

"I'll worry about my students."

"I won't let you. This plan of yours will work," he said.

"It wasn't a plan at all, just a weary concession."

"Then I admire your quick thinking. Nothing would be better for MargieBelle Cadwallader than a taste of reality. If Ethel wasn't constantly at her back, goading her, MargieBelle would be a reasonably nice person."

"And you'd like her."

Jim looked softly down into her upturned face. He jerked Sadie tightly against him so that he could feel the wonderfully soft swell of her breasts against his chest, and the way she vibrated when near him. Her eyes darkened and looked bottomless. Suddenly he took possession of her mouth, felt her yield and then clutch at his back with trembling hands. Her lips parted. He told her with his deep demanding kiss that he wanted her.

She moaned softly, and he filled with intensity for her. He couldn't stop himself, but slid his hand to her side. And when she didn't shrink away, he grazed the side of her breast with his hand, wanting so much to tear away the fabric that kept him from her. He wanted to feast his eyes on her. He wanted to know that she belonged to him, that there had never been another to win her trust, and never would be again.

Then somehow his hand was on her breast, filled with the

womanly softness of it, feeling the hardened nipple pressing through layers of clothes and years of reserve to say she was responding to him, that she wanted him, too!

"Sadie!" he whispered, arching against her. "Sadie! Sadie!"

She tore herself away and staggered a few steps back. Her face was crimson, her eyes unfocused and dazed. She pressed her shaking hand to her bosom and smiled uncertainly. "You make me forget . . . so much!"

He slid his hand to cup her cheek. "Tomorrow, if you want, I'll make you forget . . . everything."

Her eyes flared open. She looked at him as if half frightened, half desirous of that forgetting he promised. She fumbled with her crooked little hat, couldn't find her spectacles and discovered them dangling from his fingertips.

He returned them to her, wondering why she bothered with them when it was obvious she didn't need them. She put them on with both hands and then nervously tidied her hair.

He wanted to unfurl her hair, open her buttons and invade her reserve. Tomorrow, he whispered to himself, he would take her to the bluffs, and then to his grandparents' house where he had been a boy, a lad, a youth . . . and now, a man. With a sudden charge of warmth that began to center unbearably in his groin, he knew he loved Sadie. No harm must ever come to her, he thought, as he silently led her out to the buggy to see her safely home.

Chapter Eight

Carrying the apple pie all the way to the schoolhouse proved tiresome, but Sadie wanted to surprise Jim. The morning was brisk but clear, promising a beautiful day for a picnic.

MargieBelle and her mother were waiting in their top-buggy at the schoolhouse along with the Shockley boys when Sadie arrived. "I'm going to do this on my own," MargieBelle said, urging her mother to go as she climbed down. "Please, Ma?"

Ethel frowned down at her daughter and then, with a grim expression, snapped the lines and drove away.

Balancing the pie in one hand as she went to unlock the door, Sadie again found the padlock undone. "Wait, Margie-Belle. Let me have a look around inside, just to be safe," Sadie whispered, edging nervously inside.

"What could be wrong in here?" MargieBelle asked, pressing in behind Sadie in spite of Sadie's warning.

"I see nothing out of order," Sadie said, looking around and supposing that in her haste the afternoon before she might have forgotten to lock up. "Let me show you what I had planned for today," she said, shaking off her unease.

Quickly, she listed the lessons she had planned to teach. "We intended to rehearse the tableau after school, but I'll begin that next week."

MargieBelle wandered around the room looking silly in a fussy lace shirtwaist and a skirt with layers of pleats and ruching. As if she cared nothing about Sadie's instructions, MargieBelle unpinned her flowered hat and wandered from window to window like a bored child.

Sadie was about to open her desk drawer to get a piece of chalk when she heard strange scratching noises inside it. Those knavish Shockley boys. . . . She edged the drawer open a fraction of an inch and was met with several pairs of panic-stricken beady eyes! Pressing the drawer closed, she saw that MargieBelle was primping in front of her reflection in one of the windows.

Several children had just arrived, so Sadie went out to explain MargieBelle's presence. The Whithers children grimaced as they alighted from their surrey. "But it's only for this one day," Sadie assured them.

Winnie Akins looked sickened at the news that Sadie would be away for the day, but as Jim rolled up in an open buckboard wagon moments later, Winnie's eyes began to shine. She slipped into the school with a pleased secret smile.

MargieBelle had seated herself at the teacher's desk and was smiling smugly as she leafed through the almanac, when she caught sight of Jim in the doorway.

Before MargieBelle could gather her wits and speak, Sadie lifted the napkin-covered pie from her desk and presented it to Jim.

"Is this for me?" Jim sniffed appreciatively as he took it, gingerly lifting a corner of the napkin. "My favorite! Didn't I tell you it would be a beautiful day? Morning, Miss MargieBelle."

MargieBelle's eyes were sharpened and narrowed. "You're going out together? You planned to all along?"

"Good of you to afford us the opportunity to get away," Jim

said, bowing at MargieBelle, his grin wide and his eyes filled with mischief. "Sadie needs a break." He glanced around at the sharp-eyed Shockleys who shrank in their seats when Jim's gaze fell on them.

MargieBelle fixed Sadie with a hate-filled glare. "It's hardly proper!" In agony, MargieBelle watched Jim taste a bit of piecrust. Flouncing to her feet, she went to the door and saw curious children peeking into the wicker hamper tucked behind the buckboard's seat. Herbie Shockley was licking white icing from his fingers. At the sight of his Aunt Margie-Belle's shocked expression, he reddened and ran. MargieBelle spun on her heel. "You're going to be out all day?" She looked horrified and ill. "On a picnic?"

"Don't worry about Sadie," Jim said, taking Sadie's arm and leading her through the doorway. "I'll see she doesn't freckle."

Sadie turned, momentarily reluctant to leave MargieBelle in charge of everything she had worked so hard to set to order, but MargieBelle's glare kept Sadie from changing her mind.

"You'll find the chalk in my desk," Sadie said, turning away to link elbows with Jim. Finding those mice would show MargieBelle what she went through with exhausting regularity.

"Your chariot awaits, m'lady," Jim said loudly enough for MargieBelle, still trembling with fury in the doorway, to hear.

Sadie let him hand her up. He came around and put the pie in a sheltered spot next to the hamper, then climbed up next to Sadie. He helped adjust her shawl so that she'd be warm in the early morning chill, making quite a show of keeping his arm around her shoulders, until MargieBelle heaved a disgusted sigh and went inside the schoolhouse, slamming the door.

"I feel guilty about leaving her," Sadie whispered.

Jim hugged her shoulders. "A day with those wily creatures will do her good."

"The boys have filled my desk drawer with mice," Sadie whispered.

Jim burst into laughter. He grabbed up the lines. "Git up! Maybe it's not fair to leave MargieBelle to that, but at least she won't suffer a rash from it for a week."

"The children will be horrid to her." Sadie twisted around to look back anxiously. She already heard shouting.

Jim turned onto Prairie Street and drove to Cowtrail Street where everyone watched as they passed. "The whole town knows you've given the day to MargieBelle."

"And what is everyone saying?" Sadie said, straightening, resigned.

"They're saying the deputy's sweet on the schoolteacher. He ought not to be so bold as to drive her right through town, but they're saying she seems awfully nice for someone from Ohio. And MargieBelle Cadwallader would be a sight easier to stomach if she'd get off her high horse."

"What are they really saying?" Sadie asked, finding herself always smiling when with Jim.

Jim tipped his head back and grinned. "They're saying they wish to hell they were sitting on this buckboard with you instead of me!"

"I can see I'll get no serious answers from you this day." Sadie hugged his arm. His friendship was a wonderful tonic.

"That's right."

Shortly after they left town, heading south toward the bluffs along the river, Jim reached behind the seat and brought out a fine black silk parasol.

"Where did you get this?" Sadie asked, grateful to shield her face from the burning sun.

"Olive sent it over last night about half an hour after she heard you were going driving with me today. Excellent grapevine in this town!"

"I like Olive," Sadie said. "She's a good woman."

"And Warren Bluffs likes you, in spite of what a few small-minded people have tried to make you think."

"I understand all of that, really," Sadie said. "It's not pleasant to deal with women like Ethel and MargieBelle, but

I've dealt with worse. I didn't come here expecting to fit in immediately. Years ago a new family moved to my home town. I was grown before we felt they had become one of us."

They drove for a while in silence. The road angled to follow the wide curve of the river where the bluffs rose higher, bleached, rugged and pale in the morning sunlight.

Sadie quickly relaxed against the seat. "I did need this," she said, breathing deeply. "This is a beautiful land, so vast, so much room to breathe."

The air was faintly tart, made sweet and moist by the rain the day before. The prairie had been parched to a uniform tan. Sadie smelled autumn in the wind and felt nostalgic.

"I'll show you my grandparents' house first," Jim said, turning onto a narrow, overgrown twin track that meandered toward the river.

"Tell me how your grandfather came to settle here."

"He intended to graze cattle brought up from Texas, something like they do in Missouri and Illinois. That's why he bought so many acres. His connections knew the railroad would cross the plains near here. Someone with enough land to receive the beeves stood to make a fortune."

"Did he?"

Jim grinned. They had reached a twisting road cutting along a low bluff. Emerging from a jumble of boulders, they looked up at a rise where an abandoned soddy sagged in the glaring morning sun. "Granddad chose this spot because he could see so far. He once saw a Kiowa hunting party ride by — six or seven braves — but he was more troubled by speculators and outlaws then he ever was by Indians. Those were rowdy days. Nothing like now."

"Is it safe to have a look?" Sadie asked.

"Not any more." He flicked the lines across the horse's rump and headed along the river where the water spread shallow and clear among the rocks. It reflected the sky's blue and the overhanging branches of the cottonwoods in a perfect mirror image.

Sadie became conscious of a restful silence. A caressing breeze brushed across her face. She let the shawl fall from her shoulders and twirled the parasol.

Jim smiled and leaned close. "The sun shining through the parasol makes lace shadows on your face." Then he kissed her lightly. "I've been waiting all morning to kiss you."

"Folks will count the hours until our return," she murmured, secretly thrilled by his kiss.

"We can go back after lunch if you want."

She chuckled and shook her head. "I wouldn't miss a moment of this lovely day!"

He looked relieved as he stopped before a bleached, lonely looking clapboard house half a mile from the soddy. Pensively, he stared up at it. "I was a boy when Granddad built this house. I know every foot of his land. As a youth I spent days on horseback wandering all through these bluffs. We had cowhands then, and kept quite a herd." He indicated the sagging outbuildings and the long-abandoned corrals. "Then Granddad grew weaker. My father took work in town at the law offices. I lost my father and grandfather in the same year — my father to a renegade's bullet, my grandfather to a broken heart."

"It's sad to see the house empty," Sadie said. "I can see the care that went into building it."

"Each summer I straighten up a bit, but until a family lives here again it won't look as I remember it," Jim said.

"Why not rent it to someone?"

Jim glanced at her and chuckled. "If I did that I'd have to admit I'm never coming back here to live. Want to look around?"

She nodded and let him help her down. He looked as if he wanted to kiss her again, but restrained himself and led her to the house.

Inside, the furniture was covered with sheets. A heavy layer of grit now lay over everything in the once-proud parlor. The kitchen and pantry were lined with narrow shelves where Jim's grandmother had stored jars of put-up preserves.

Sadie's throat caught at the sight. "It reminds me so much of home," she whispered, turning into Jim's ready embrace. She clung to him.

He lifted her face and kissed her, allowing himself a leisurely taste impossible anywhere in town. Then without a word, he led her up the creaking stairs to view the four bedrooms.

"The furniture's lovely," she said, peeking under some of the drapes, acutely aware of the beds . . . and of Jim so close behind her.

"Everything was shipped all the way from St. Louis in freight wagons. My grandmother wanted all the comforts of civilization. She expected to live out her life in this wilderness, and she did."

"My grandparents came over the Cumberland Gap. Moving west must be in our blood."

"I knew you were of good stock," he said, grinning, his hand lingering at the small of her back.

Sadie smiled ruefully.

"What made you decide to become a teacher?" Jim asked as they went down.

Sadie stiffened. "It seemed the only thing I could do."

"In view of your broken engagement," Jim added for her.

She nodded.

"You said you were betrayed. That's a strong word for a broken engagement, isn't it? Did he marry your best friend?" He was grinning a little, but his eyes were serious.

Sadie tried to hide her growing discomfort. "I'd rather not talk about him. After all, today I'm only supposed to be happy, if I remember your promise."

"I promised that . . . and more," Jim said, attempting to draw her close again.

She looked up into his eyes, silently letting her expression tell him that mention of her engagement had put her off. Feeling vaguely uneasy, she went out onto the porch and gazed across the vast wind-swept prairie. The horizon was an unbroken hazy line far in the distance. "Where will we have our picnic?"

"You're not hungry already?" he asked, coming up behind her after locking up.

"Just curious."

"Feel like doing a little exploring first?"

"I'd love it!"

"I'll bet you were a tomboy." He went to the buckboard and brought the hamper into the shade, with difficulty fitting her pie inside.

Sadie felt the mood lighten. "I was just an ordinary girl with a penchant for romantic adventure," she said, swishing her skirts like a schoolgirl.

"If it's adventure you're looking for, I'll take you to the wickedest wilds of my grandfather's ranch!"

"It's your ranch now, isn't it?"

"Yes, but I don't think of it that way. Come on! This way. Do you want the parasol?"

"On an adventure? Hardly. I don't mind a few freckles, if you don't."

"But you're so pale. You'll burn." He took her hand and led her down the weedy track. His hand was warm and strong and sure around hers.

"Hadn't you better see to your poor horse?" she said, laughing as she saw he'd completely forgotten it.

"You've turned my brain to pudding," he said, grinning.

"Then I'd better keep my wits about me or we'll never find our way back to our lunch. I went to a lot of trouble to bake that pie."

"I suppose it's your mother's old recipe," he said, taking her hand again after he'd released the horse from the traces and tethered him in the shade near some good grass.

"No, Trudy's recipe."

They started down the road and were soon to the river. "It looks nice enough to wade in," Sadie said, crouching to take up a handful of water to drink. She patted her warm cheeks with her wet palms.

"I've never known a woman to enjoy the small everyday pleasures as you do, Sadie," Jim said, watching her with a more serious look than she liked.

"Perhaps it's because I never had very much. I had to make do with everyday pleasures. I learned, more or less by accident, that they're the only ones worth having."

As she stood, he swung her into his arms. He wasn't wearing his tin star now. She was free to lay her head on his chest and listen to his heart hammering.

He dipped his head and kissed her thoroughly, kissed her so hard her head bent back until he held her arched tightly against him. Again his hand stole to her breast. Her body charged with lightning as he touched her. Everything in her screamed to say no, that he must not touch her that way, but she remained locked against him, tasting his lips and saying not a word to stop him.

She returned his kiss with an intensity she hadn't intended. Finally she dragged her lips away. Panting, she was alarmed by the waves of desire coursing through her, making her want to throw away all cares and have with him all that she so yearned to have with one very special man.

He could make her feel so reckless! "Show me these wickedly wild places you told me about," she said, moving away along the bank.

His face was flushed. His eyes reflected the same overpowering intensity she was feeling. They should not stay together alone, he thought. But when he indicated the way to go, she followed without hesitation.

They came to a small creek emptying into the river on the far side where it trickled down from the bluff.

"Want to cross?" he asked, huskily.

"My shoes *are* a bit too hot," she said, glad to stop and let him unbutton them.

After he slipped them off and held the laces together so that he could carry them for her over his shoulder, she peeled down her stockings. His eyes were on her, watching hotly. Her bared legs felt cool as she lifted her skirts and stepped gingerly into the cool water. She sank into the silt and had to lift her hem high almost to her knees. "Oh! It's deeper than it looks!"

Grinning as if he had known that all along, Jim yanked off his boots and finally decided taking them along was useless.

He tossed his boots and her shoes into the shade. "Now you can't run from me," he said, following her into the water without bothering to turn up the cuffs of his denims.

She felt young and playful again. "What makes you think I would run from you? Have you thought that you can't run from me, either?"

He stopped and splashed her with such a huge sweep of water that the side of her shirtwaist got drenched. She let out a squeal of laughing indignation and immediately turned to splash him. In moments they were both soaked.

Laughing, and shaking his dripping hair from his face, he came to her and removed the little spectacles from her nose. He dried them carefully and then folded them, placing them in his shirt pocket. He peeled off his vest and flung it back to the bank. "Now, Miss Evans, I want you to let down your hair."

They stood together in the middle of the river, looking into each other's eyes. The water rushed urgently around their legs. Sadie could do nothing but hold up her skirts and let him pluck the pins from her hair.

The sun-warmed length of it tumbled down her back, while the breeze blew a few strands across her face. He gathered it and held it back for her.

"I wanted to see if your hair was as long as I imagined," he whispered as if someone might overhear them.

"Why, Deputy! One would think you lay awake nights thinking about unpinning my hair," Sadie said equally softly.

He smiled as he kissed her. Then he stood back, tucking her hairpins in his pocket along with her spectacles. Her soaked shirtwaist clung wetly to her corset cover. He could see the thin blue ribbons threaded through the lace around her neckline. His hands itched to untie the bows.

The front her wet skirt sagged, hugging her thighs. Knowing he could not go on much longer looking at her in that way, he crossed quickly to the far side of the broad, shallow fording place and waited for her to join him there. He watched her step gingerly through the mud, her raised hem exposing her pale rounded knees and the tantalizing wink of lace trim on her pantalets.

He was wild for her. He couldn't stop himself from pulling her into his arms as she reached the bank. She fell easily against him, her eyes languid, her lips full and parted. His mouth moved all over her face. He was aware of nothing but the taste of her soft, trembling lips, the warmth of her mouth, the smooth silkiness of her cheeks, the pulsing tenderness of her throat.

He clutched at her long hair, tangling his fingers in it, bringing her head back so that he could kiss the hollow of her throat. Then he plucked two of her shirtwaist buttons open. He fought to kiss the soft white swell of her bosom.

"Oh, Jim!" she gasped, holding his face and moving him away so that he was forced to look at her. Her cheeks were flaming, her eyes soft and unfocused, drugged by his touch. Her lips trembled with a kind of dazed joy. "Wait! Let me think a little longer. Please. . . ." She smiled hesitantly.

He wanted her so badly he was no longer in control. He grabbed her again and smothered her face with his kisses. She laughed softly, delighting in his desire, but again she held him away when he moved to kiss her bosom.

With one trembling hand she held the shirtwaist closed at her throat. She moved to a boulder and sat, lifting her hem to expose her muddied feet. Her expression sobered somewhat as she looked at them.

He moved quickly to bring handfuls of water to her feet and calves. As he rinsed her feet, the touch of her silky legs fired him even more. Quickly he moved against her, half crouched before her and kissed her, his hands stealing deftly up the sides of her thighs to the sanctity of her hips. He was almost beyond reason now. He thought only of how to move her gently to the grass beside the boulder and possess her there.

She received his kisses like one starved and finally tore her mouth away, panting as she laid her cheek against his. He could feel the heat of her skin. He burned to have her.

"Sadie, it doesn't matter what's in your past. I'll never hurt you. I want only to give you all of myself."

She drew back, a gentle sadness in her eyes that alarmed him. "But it does matter," she whispered, lifting her face so that the sun shone fully on her. There was a faint sheen of tears in her eyes.

"No matter what happened . . ." he started to say, thinking — fearing — she had been thoughtlessly used and abandoned by some lout.

A slight smile flickered at the corners of her mouth. "Let's just walk a little farther. Please." She pushed his hands out from beneath her skirt but brought them quickly to her lips and kissed his fingertips. "You're such a wonderful man. I wouldn't like to think that I might hurt you."

A charge of alarm went through him. It hadn't occurred to him that she might be married. "Have you a husband somewhere that you're running from — or who deserted you?"

Her face reflected instant surprise. She laughed, moving quickly to kiss him, her lips soft and comforting. "No, I'm not married. Please, please, just a little time . . . ."

She got lithely to her feet and pulled him up beside her. She started on ahead, pulling him after her, but her legs felt weak with desire. She was so nervous she couldn't begin to think.

Wild thoughts skittered through her head. She remembered another man who had made her want to throw aside caution. Luckily — or perhaps unluckily — she had not given in.

Now she was thinking of giving in again. But she could only imagine that Jim might think less of her if she did. She wondered if some day he might think less of her in any case. Could she live with herself if she did not have this man's love for however long he was willing to give it?

Looking as if he had regained some of his composure, Jim again took the lead and preceded her along the twisting creek into the shadows of the bluffs, where even the soft breeze couldn't reach. The sun shone high above them, but they were cast in cool shadows. The only sound was the gurgle of the water tumbling over rounded stones. When they had climbed quite a distance, Sadie was thirsty again. Jim stopped and cupped his hands and she drank from them.

They had come to a small level ledge under the brow of the bluffs. They were deep within the bluffs now, in the privacy of the shade and the coolness of the late-morning shadows.

He tugged her hair from her moist cheeks, his eyes so intent she felt hypnotized by them. As he moved to kiss her, she held him off only long enough to open his shirt buttons. She tugged his shirttail from his denims and felt her body ignite with what she knew was a yielding fiery desire to be possessed.

They said nothing in those brief moments as he stripped away his shirt and stood over her. She found a sheltered spot and sank down where she unbuttoned her dress with care and opened her shirtwaist. He crouched then and pulled the ribbons of her corset cover so quickly she sucked in her breath.

His eyes were riveted on her breasts as he freed them from the thin cotton cloth. Then his tanned hands closed over them. He was on his knees, easing her back, slipping to her side to lean over her and kiss her face lightly.

He kissed her breasts, and then it was as if he was no longer thinking but only wanting her. He was there over her, his weight solid and comforting, his breath fast and urgent against her lips, his hands softly pressing her skirt up and away from her legs. He trailed his hand along her thigh to her hip where his touch had stung her so fiercely only a while before.

This time she felt no hesitation. She needed him. In spite of the fact that nothing might ever come of this love, she wanted this moment for her own. She wanted to belong to him, to feel his hands taking possession of her, to feel his lips on hers, and his eyes drinking in the swells and valleys she had kept private for all these years.

Then he was there for her, deep and mind-numbing! She knew nothing but the feel of him in her, the fierce possession, the mystery revealed within her. They moved as one, two flames burning together.

She felt herself returning from some faraway land of brilliance and darkness where she had known nothing but the joy only Jim could make her feel. He had taken her away from the world and made her forget everything, just as he had promised he would.

She felt weak and dazed. She lay very still as he moved from her body and covered her. Then he cradled her close to his chest and they lay together in the shade for a long time without speaking.

After a time he rose and went to the creek to wet his hands. He'd done up his denims, but his chest was still bare. For those silent moments between them, Sadie pretended he belonged to her. Indeed, she knew that for this day he did belong to her. She needed only to reach for him again to have the ecstacy he had given her before.

He bathed his face and then brought a sip of water in his palms for her. Her breasts were still bare, the nipples bright and erectly pink. He slipped his hands behind her back and partially lifted her against him, kissing her cheek, then her throat, and finally her breasts.

He looked into her eyes for the answer to his question and saw that she was willing again. Looking as if he disbelieved his amazing luck, he moved over her again and this time their lovemaking was slow, delicately nurtured, until the flames leaped even higher. They moved together, their wide eyes locked, his hands covering the softly rocking delicacy of her breasts, and her fingers clutching his forearms. She grasped at him urgently and then, as if he knew nothing but her body and the pleasure of if, he arched into her in one final burst of glory.

The sun was past its mid-point and moving to the west by the time they righted their clothes and started back for the river. Just as they were coming out of the shadows, Jim stopped Sadie and turned to her for one last look into her eyes.

Her cheeks were flushed, her expression soft and un-guarded. She caressed his face with her eyes, and then she smiled a smile of radiance that filled his heart with triumph.

"You love me, don't you?" he said, walking beside her to the river's edge.

"Let's not talk of love yet," she whispered.

"You're wonderful." Unbelievably, he wanted her again! There in the middle of the river, with the water rushing around her breasts . . . . "You're beautiful. I love you, Sadie."

She quickly put her finger to his lips. "Sh-h-h! I'm hungry. Let's eat."

"Why don't you want to admit you love me?" he asked.

She gathered up her skirts, unmindful of how much of her legs she showed this time, and ran slowly through the water to the other side. She grabbed up her shoes and stockings and ran back toward the house.

He watched her move so quickly from him, knowing she was not afraid. She looked so slim, so fragile. She went to the horse and patted him, and then as Jim crossed the river, she took the hamper from the shade and spread the cloth Olive had also sent for their picnic. Jim thought of Sadie lying naked on it, but then he squinted up at her and a shadow passed over his mind.

She was still keeping at least one part of herself from him. He did not have possession of her yet, and until he had all of her, even that secret part, they could not talk of love.

Chapter Nine

Though it was not yet three o'clock, Sadie and Jim found the schoolhouse deserted. Uneasily, Sadie scrambled down from the buckboard. "MargieBelle must have dismissed early. I wonder why."

Trembling as she crept into the hushed schoolhouse, Sadie braced herself. Something awful must have happened, and she would be blamed. The desk rows were uneven. A few slates had fallen to the floor. She picked one up and found it cracked.

Her desk top was bare. The center drawer hung open like a lolling tongue; broken pieces of chalk lay scattered everywhere behind her overturned chair. Sadie could almost picture the mice scattering. Strangely, she didn't find the thought amusing now.

As she stooped to pick up her books that had fallen to the floor, she glanced through the half-open side door and saw a corner of MargieBelle's ruffled hem. "MargieBelle?" she called, leaving the books.

Jim was just coming in behind her. "Is it safe to enter?" he asked softly, a note of amusement in his voice.

Sadie didn't turn to answer, but rushed to the side door.

With balled fists, MargieBelle sat on the bench just outside the door, as rigid as a statue. Her tangled hair had fallen to her shoulders, and it stuck to her sunburnt cheeks where perspiration trickled from her scalp. She must have been sitting there for hours. Her shirtwaist sleeve was torn, her skirt dirty along one hip.

"What happened?" Sadie cried, stepping outside. Her heart stood in her throat. "Are you all right?"

As if she had been waiting for hours for this moment, MargieBelle lifted malevolent eyes and fixed Sadie with a look of undying hatred. Her lips pulled back from her teeth. "You planned that little trick with the mice."

"I most certainly did not!" Nevertheless, a wave of guilt washed over Sadie. "For weeks I've put up with pranks far worse."

MargieBelle looked as if she wanted to rise with dignity and march away as the wounded party, but fury seized her. She leaped to her feet. Blinking, as if she couldn't decide what to do, she suddenly seized two handfuls of Sadie's hair and yanked her head back and forth. "You bitch! You dirty no-good bitch! I could kill you for that! You made me look worse than a fool!"

"MargieBelle, are you craz— Don't! You're tearing out my hair!"

MargieBelle wrestled Sadie backwards toward the watering trough. Her teeth were bared and her eyes blazing. Sadie felt shards of pain radiating in her scalp. She was so shocked by the attack she didn't have time to think. Instinctively, she curled her fingers into claws and blindly defended herself, going for MargieBelle's eyes. It was all she knew. Dig! Dig fast and deep! Kick when the chance came. Bite!

Waves of pain leapt along her scalp as MargieBelle jerked even harder. Then MargieBelle squealed as Sadie's rigid fingertips grazed hurtfully along her temple.

Jim vaulted through the side doorway. "Sadie! Don't!" His face wore a look of amazement. He pulled up short, gawking at the two tussling females, his expression changing from astonishment to anger and disapproval.

Sadie stumbled backwards against the edge of the watering trough. MargieBelle still held her by the hair. Rough wood gouged the back of Sadie's knees. Flailing, she regained a bit of control, and then realized she was still trying to get her fingers into MargieBelle's eyes. A stunning quiver of horror went through her as she drew back. Then she seized Margie-Belle's curls. "Let go or I'll rip out *your* hair!"

Propelled backwards, Sadie splashed into the trough. Then with a blinding pain across her back, she hit the opposite side of the trough, upsetting it. With MargieBelle atop her, she landed heavily in the dirt.

Instantly, Sadie had the advantage. She rolled, straddling MargieBelle and grabbed her wrists. "Let go of my hair!" She jerked MargieBelle's curls with one hand. "Let go!" Finally she felt her own hair released, but then MargieBelle's nails dug into her forearms.

"Get off me, you bitch! Are you trying to kill me?"

Looking down at MargieBelle and resisting a powerful urge to slap her, Sadie fought her twisted wet skirts, and finally stood, trembling. "You're no lady, MargieBelle Cadwallader!"

MargieBelle scuttled from beneath her, her eyes wide. "Neither are you!"

Seized with a violent fit of shaking, Sadie jumped when Jim came from behind and touched her soothingly. Filled with shame, she edged away. How could she have fought like that? She wanted to run and hide. It would have been better to take whatever MargieBelle wanted to do to her than let Jim see her behave in such a savage way.

Jim turned from staring at Sadie and looked down at MargieBelle. "You attacked Sadie."

"Don't look at me that way!" MargieBelle snapped. "She had it coming!"

Sadie smoothed her disheveled hair with weak and trembling hands. She did not deserve to be treated like that, she thought, trying desperately to hold back the tears that burned her eyelids.

"What started this?" Jim held out his hand to MargieBelle. Giving the outstretched hand a look of loathing, MargieBelle got to her feet unassisted. "Sadie filled her desk drawer with mice. Then she went traipsing off with *you!*" Her narrowed eyes raked Jim as if she meant to spit on him. She dusted her skirt and straightened her shirtwaist. "I was just trying to . . . to . . . . I don't want your damn job, Miss Sadie Evans! I only want to be left alone! I don't need you to make a fool of me in front of my mother. I'm miserable enough as it is. Ma will be here any time now. Don't think I'll forget this. You're finished, Sadie Evans! I'll see to it you're fired. Today! You can start packing."

"Don't make such rash threats," Jim said softly, raking his hair back in a gesture of impatience.

"They're not threats, you — you cheap excuse for a man! To think I wanted to marry you. Well! You can forget any hope of that. . . Or of becoming sheriff. Ma will withdraw her support. The two of you can rot, for all I care."

"Sadie didn't put those mice in her drawer," Jim said evenly. "The children did."

MargieBelle's eyes bulged. "You were in on it, too? My lord, I almost died of fright! They came spilling out and were clinging to my skirt . . . . I almost died, I tell you! And those damned brats *laughed*!" She burst into a fit of hysterical sobbing. "I'll be a laughingstock."

Jim tried to comfort her, but MargieBelle flung his hands away. "Don't touch me!"

Sobbing and hiccuping like a child, she marched from the schoolyard just as her mother's buggy turned in from Prairie Street. Halfway up the road, MargieBelle's step faltered as she looked up and saw her mother coming toward her. Then she shook back her tangled curls and went on, fists rigidly at her side.

Sadie watched MargieBelle meet the buggy and climb

aboard. She could faintly hear MargieBelle's wailing tale and she saw her gesture wildly toward the schoolhouse and Sadie. At intervals, Ethel looked in Sadie's direction, and she could feel the heat of her hate.

At last, Sadie went inside, took the broom from the cloak room and began sweeping furiously. Jim watched her from the side door. What they had shared only hours before seemed now like a dream.

"Where did you learn to fight like that?" Jim asked softly.

Her grip tightened on the broom handle as she paused. "Where did she?"

His chuckle seemed forced. "I suppose we were wrong to leave her to the mice and the mercy of the schoolchildren."

"Yes, we were." Sadie threw back her head to keep her tears in check. "She all but forced me to let her take over, and I had to go and let something like this happen. She'll get a great deal of sympathy, and I'll lose my job. Worst of all, the children will be without a teacher again. MargieBelle can't teach them."

"That was proven beyond a doubt."

Sadie's heart twisted to remember the joy of the previous hours, now spoiled. "Will anyone remember the prank was intended for me? Would anyone care if I had been frightened out of my wits by a drawer full of mice?"

Jim stretched and sighed. Then he started toward the door. "You wouldn't have been frightened out of your wits, Sadie."

She sighed, too. "I suppose you're right. Jim, I only wanted a laugh out of this. I didn't want to hurt MargieBelle. I feel so . . . responsible." She could hardly stand the sense of shame she felt for having left knowing how frightened MargieBelle would be by the mice.

"If it's any comfort, I doubt you'll be fired, Sadie. You're too interested in the welfare of the Warren Bluffs children." Jim's voice was warm and comforting. She tried to keep from melting at the sound of it.

She tried to smile. "Thanks, Jim." Suddenly she felt a spark of renewed hope. She still had him on her side. "Thanks very much for . . . a beautiful day."

"I'll drive you home," he said, still looking worried and faintly puzzled.

She shook her head. "I need some time alone. To think."

They called it a meeting to report her first month's progress to the school board, but Sadie knew she was being called to account for the incident about the mice in the drawer.

Knowing she would be thought petty, she nevertheless said nothing of what MargieBelle and her mother had done to provoke her into leaving MargieBelle to the mice. She made no excuses. "I heard the mice in the drawer and left, knowing Miss Cadwallader would find them." The school board members, Mayor Runyon, Leroy Crowley and George Cadwallader, Sr., were left to draw their own conclusions.

When the meeting was over, Sadie left without speaking to anyone. Nothing more was said about a dismissal. She went home to rest, clutching her first month's pay of twenty-three dollars and remembering that women teachers commanded three times that in the northwest.

Trudy was full of talk for days afterwards. "MargieBelle said you pulled her hair! She said you tried to scratch out her eyes, but I said, 'Why would Sadie do such a thing?' And she admitted she tried to slap you. Is a word of what she says true, Sadie? Did the two of you really fight like two cats in an alley?"

"I only want to forget the entire incident," Sadie said, half wishing she'd never gone on the picnic with Jim.

For the remainder of the week, Sadie made her usual evening constitutional work in her favor. She refused to satisfy curiosity about the incident with MargieBelle, asking only for help with her pageant.

By the following week she had involved every child in some aspect of it. She received permission from George Cadwallader, Sr., to stage the production in early December at the meeting hall over his store. Rehearsals began that Wednesday after school.

Sadie saw Jim regularly, but not alone. The weather cooled suddenly. The days became blustery, the nights frosty. They would not be riding into the bluffs again, she thought, alone and aching for him in her room.

At night Sadie burned to be with Jim. Occasionally, they shared a few stolen moments at the schoolhouse, or while walking in the evening. Their eyes would meet. The need to be together would flare again, but MargieBelle's attack had deeply disturbed Sadie.

While the majority of the townspeople still appeared to have faith in Sadie, the opposition to her was also surprisingly strong. She dared make no more mistakes. She wanted desperately to succeed in Warren Bluffs. Without her teaching job, her only hope for employment lay in the hazardous, mind-numbing factories of the East. As much as she desired Jim, she was willing to forego her immediate passion in the hopes she would eventually be accepted by her new friends.

Jim sensed Sadie's reticence. Short of inviting her to his grandparent's house, he had no way of being alone with her. He steeled himself to be patient and went about his daily tasks with dogged determination.

Ethel did, indeed, withdraw her support from Jim's campaign for sheriff, and added loudly in all related conversations that MargieBelle no longer wished to receive him as a caller. Ethel's new hostility forced Jim to spend more time keeping in touch with the county's voters. When he wasn't on duty, he went to neighboring towns to campaign for honest law enforcement. Yet for miles, men remained loyal to the great lawman, Otis Wheeler, whom they remembered from the cowtown days of central Kansas.

Nevertheless, just as many people remembered, with admiration that Jim's father and grandfather were both more fathers of the state than any Wheeler. Besides, Jim openly supported the legislation for prohibiting the sale and distribution of strong spirits in Kansas, while many knew that Otis Wheeler opposed it.

The time away from Warren Bluffs helped keep Jim's

thoughts off Sadie, except at night when they both lay on opposite sides of town remembering those moments alone in the bluffs.

Jim wanted to settle their relationship, but, like Sadie, he found himself pulling away from the intensity of his feelings. He was waiting. For what, he didn't know. Perhaps it was that he had known Sadie so short a time. Perhaps it was that he was waiting for that locked door inside of her to open to him. Perhaps it was only that he didn't understand the feeling of being in love. He dared not trust his judgement in the face of such mindless desire.

"You must be either a wise man or a shepherd, Marty," Sadie said with growing exasperation. She drew on the last of her strength for that late Thursday afternoon. She looked up at the smirking youth. "As I've said a dozen times this week, you can't play the role of Joseph. I find it difficult to understand why you have to keep pestering me about this."

He snickered, enjoying her efforts to control herself. "Just trying to help you out, teacher," he said, grinning in that knowing way of his. "Pa says we got to keep a real close eye on you."

Outside the nearly deserted schoolhouse, the cool blue shadows lengthened. A moaning wind swept across the prairie, reminding Sadie that All Hallow's Eve was a week from tomorrow — the sort of day perfect for the likes of of Marty Wheeler and his pranks.

Winnie Akins sat in the back row stitching on her blue costume. Her family had been thrilled when Sadie chose Winnie to play Mary in the tableau; they had bought blue linen for her costume, a flowing sack-like gown to be tied at the waist with a thick soft cord.

Feeling Sadie's eyes on her, Winnie looked up and smiled sweetly. "I should be going soon, Miss Evans," she said, glancing uneasily at Marty lounging against the corner of Sadie's desk. Winnie wouldn't risk walking home at dusk as long as Marty was about, Sadie knew.

"Run along then," Sadie said.

She frowned at Marty. Each day for the past week, he had remained after school for no other reason than to complain about the part she felt him capable of playing in the tableau. As a shepherd or a wise man he needed only to stand in the background. To ask him to do more would surely tax his abilities and risk provoking trouble. Marty was aware of his part's simple nature and enjoyed acting the fool during rehearsals.

As Winnie slipped out into the wind and hurried away, Sadie got up to tidy things before sending Marty on his way. She didn't want him following Winnie either.

As she moved about the room, Marty leafed through her ledger.

"You might bring in some kindling for the morning," Sadie said, uneasy at being alone with him.

"I'll come by early and warm you up, teacher," he murmured, watching her face reddened.

"What did you say, young man?" Sadie felt like a fool to be blushing.

Snickering, he took her chair and followed her every movement with devilish eyes. "I said —"

"Never mind!" Sadie scowled at the new, jet-black pot-bellied stove standing in the middle of the room. The school board had had it delivered the previous Saturday, certain proof that they expected her to last in her position through the winter. She dreaded lighting it for the first time. What mischief would the Shockley boys get into with a hot stove at their disposal?

Marty cleared his throat as if swallowing a chuckle. "Ever been with a man, teacher?"

Sadie's heart leaped with embarrassment. Marty's low, husky voice sent shivers up her spine. "Don't be vulgar. Go home. I'm about to leave myself, now."

Marty grinned as he leaned his chin on his crossed forearms. He stared at her from between Ellsworth's Primer and the crack-spined Webster. "You're mighty pretty, Miss Evans. I think I love you." One index finger stole up his nostril. He dug thoughtfully and then resumed his intense gaze. "Yep, I love you all right. Clean through."

Sadie went for her cape and hat. Her heart had begun to pound with anxiety. "I'll speak to your father if you say another word. Go home!"

In the cloakroom, as she was pinning on her hat, she heard Marty steal up behind her. She whirled. "Go home immediately!"

"I know you got a hankering for me, too, Miss Evans. We could have us a little fun 'fore I go." Marty's upper lip was beaded with sweat.

Forcing herself to remain calm, Sadie tied her cape around her neck. Keeping her flinty eyes locked with Marty's darkly smiling ones, she was relieved when his gaze finally flickered away. "Get out of here," she whispered in disgust.

"No use telling my pa what I'm saying. He don't mind. Besides, every man in town knows what you want. You got that look." Though he was speaking boldly, his face grew red and he began shifting from foot to foot. She was not flying into the hysterics he expected.

Considering the wisdom of slapping his impudent face, Sadie couldn't restrain a shudder of fury. She was half afraid what Marty was saying might be true. Someone might indeed know about the day she and Jim had made love in the bluffs. She might very well have the look of a woman in love.

"You need a man, teacher. I can see plain that you do. I won't tell nobody." He moved imperceptibly closer. "But I could make you feel fine."

She caught his cheek in a palm-stinging, resounding slap and watched his head jerk to the side. "Get *out* of here!"

Blinking, Marty gawked at her. Red marks flared on his cheek. His eyes hardened as he fingered them. "I'll remember that."

She met his look with equal hardness. "I hope you do. I know the sort of boy you are, Marty Wheeler. Say another word and I'll not only speak to your father, I'll visit Dawn

Shockley's father as well. How that poor girl avoids pregnancy, I don't know. You needn't stay after school any longer. In fact, you had better clear out of here as soon as I dismiss each day, or I will take your presence as a direct challenge. You're excused from participating in the pageant."

"Didn't want to be in your damned stupid sissy pageant anyhow," he said, moving away, the look in his eyes ugly now.

Her threats obviously didn't bother him. She wondered if she would be forced to defend herself as she had with Margie-Belle. Her threat to visit Dawn's parents was an empty one. The last thing she wanted was for Dawn, as bothersome and sullen as she was, to be forced into a shotgun marriage with a creature like Marty.

"Go home," she hissed, ready to push him out the door.

"You're going to be sorry you ain't been friendlier to me," he whispered back, disappearing into the gathering darkness.

On Monday after lunch the mayor's granddaughter discovered the cameo brooch that was usually pinned to her woolen cape was missing. It turned up in Jerome Crowley's pocket. Sadie knew Olive's grandson hadn't taken it and refused to be lured into punishing the boy.

After school, Cornell's sister, Annabelle, couldn't find her knitted hat. The Shockley boys swore little Douglas Newcomb had taken their pennies. Mary and Sara Whithers found their capes on the floor in the cloakroom. Sadie sent everyone on their way after a stormy rehearsal. "I won't tolerate more pranks! To stop them, I'll call in your parents if necessary," she called.

When the mayor's grandson lost a small gold pocket watch the next day, Sadie knew trouble was brewing for the weekend's spooky holiday. A stolen penknife turned up in the lunch pail belonging to the preacher's youngest child. His sisters found dead mice in their hats. Their shrieks and screams delighted most of the boys and even some of the girls.

Terrified of being blamed, the faint-hearted Newcomb boy avoided school for the remainder of the week.

Worried that her threat to call in the parents hadn't prevented this new rash of pranks, each day Sadie faced a class growing more tense and suspicious. Sadie was quite certain that Marty and his cronies were behind all the pranks, but she had no proof.

On Thursday afternoon Marty leaped to his feet. "Who took my whittling knife?" he demanded with the indignation of a judge. "I got that whittling knife from my famous big brother. I want it back, and I want it back right now!"

The children sat mute in their seats, frowning at him as he carried on. Sadie wondered then if she was correct to assume that Marty was masterminding the pranks to punish Sadie for rejecting his ridiculous advances.

Susanna Wheeler's hair bows disappeared that afternoon and turned up in the mud the following morning, All Hallow's Eve. Susanna threw a tantrum so violent Sadie began to wonder if the girl might have been capable of gouging the vengeful words in the blackboards during the last act of vandalism.

Upon returning from lunch, Dawn Shockley found the word "hussy" written on her desk, in mud. The girl burst into humiliated tears. "Who did this?" Her eyes filled with wild fear. When no one spoke, she rushed out. Sadie fully expected a visit from Dawn's parents that afternoon, but no one came.

Rehearsals had been pandemonium all week as the children accused one another of the pranks. The mayor's grandson, Walter, and the delivery boy, Cornell, got into a fist fight after rehearsal, when Walter accused Cornell of taking his watch.

Sadie intervened, forcing the hot-tempered youths apart, receiving an accidental glancing blow to her shoulder that alarmed both boys enough to make them forget their accusations in their attempts to apologize to her.

"Shake hands and forget this incident. We'll learn who the guilty person or persons are next week. For now, go home." Sadie was proud when the boys parted in a gentlemanly manner.

Marty had stopped coming to rehearsals. All week long,

however, he had gotten detailed reports of everything that was said after school from Mike Shockley, who arrived breathless at the Wheeler shed each afternoon. Marty saw to it that no one in the school was spared as a victim of a prank. He lay awake for hours each night in his bedroom in the lean-to addition behind his father's ramshackle house, planning just how next to annoy his "ice duchess." Miss Sadie Evans would be damn sorry she had called him a boy, he thought, smiling into the darkness.

On All Hallow's Eve, Marty was left to his own devices when his cronies had to attend a party at their grandmother's house. After nearly getting his rump speckled with birdshot when he skulked through someone's backyard in search of mischief, Marty went home to quietly get himself puking drunk in the shed on his pa's hidden whiskey. He was violently sick all weekend. Jim Warren called it the quietest Halloween weekend in memory.

But come the following week, the respite Sadie had looked forward to did not occur. Bleary-eyed Marty nearly busted a gut when snooty Christa Roberts discovered Walter Runyon's pocket watch in her reticule. "I didn't take it! How could it have gotten in my bag?" she cried in horrified anguish. "I would never do such a thing!"

Marty needed only one last grand prank to destroy the ice duchess's authority, he thought, watching her from his butt-numbing seat in the third row. Without a teacher, he'd be free of his mother nagging him to go to school, and his pa would be glad to have the sharp-eyed, clever lady away from where she might catch on to their schemes. As his pa always said, an honest woman was the most dangerous kind.

While Marty waited to put his final plan to destroy Sadie Evans into effect, he sulked and grumbled continuously. Beginning that Monday he made it known to one and all that something grossly unfair was afoot at the Warren Bluffs school.

"There's a bald-faced thief at that school, Pa. Miss High-and-Mighty Evans don't do nothing to stop him. It's plain as day who's doing it, too." Marty scowled across the dinner table night after night. The cramped, cluttered room looked murky in the flickering lamplight. "Miss Evans don't punish her pets, Pa. All she does is pick on me and my friends."

Susanna listened with shining eyes, suspecting that her brother had a delicious plan to make that stuck-up Miss Evans look so bad she'd be laughed or driven out of town! Imagine anyone saying to a Wheeler that God's talents were being wasted on gossiping and tale telling.

Justine wiped her mouth with the back of her hand. "I can't wait till they fire her, Pa. I'll get the job back, what you bet?"

Otis just leaned forward, fixing Marty with a piddle-freezing stare. "I don't give a damn if you have the job or not, Justine," he said without looking at his homely, dull-witted daughter. "You, boy, you just listen up good. I want all I can get on her. I got a feeling about her."

His wife scowled, her long jaw set as she dished more stew onto his plate. "What feeling is that, Otis?"

"Shut up, woman. It's a feeling, that's all. She ain't going to cause us no trouble, 'cause we're going to get to her first."

Dawn Shockley met Marty on the way to school, as she did each morning. "Did you find out who wrote that word on my desk yet?"

He tried to kiss her and feel her swelling breasts, but she put him off.

"I ain't doing nothing more till I know who thinks I'm a hussy! You find out and fix him, or I'm not letting you touch me ever again! You hear me, Marty-smarty Wheeler?"

"Ain't I got enough to worry about without you hounding me, too? I'm getting blamed for everything, you know," he said, angry that she wouldn't cooperate.

"Well, if it's not you that's doing all this stuff at school, who is it?" she demanded, looking as if she had assumed he was doing it all.

"I don't like to say, but I know, o' course," he said, according to his ingenious plan. "It's her pet. If one of us got caught taking all that stuff she'd keep us on her goddamned dunce stool for an hour. Let it turn out to be one of her la-dee-da favorites, and she looks the other way."

"You ought to do something about it, Marty," Dawn said, eyeing him from beneath the hood of her short cape. "After all, you're the man of the school. Ain't ya?"

He grinned and stole a kiss. "I'll do something all right. You'll see."

On Thursday of the week following Halloween, Marty overheard the preacher's youngest boy complaining just before lunch that Jerome Crowley had no right to be the pageant's narrator.

And Winnie Akins had just completed her pageant costume.

Standing just outside the schoolhouse door, listening, Marty held his breath to keep from laughing.

"Why cause this uproar now, Cory?" Miss Evans was asking Cory. "All along you've wanted to recite 'Paul Revere's Ride.'"

Cory scuffed his feet. "Somebody said being narrator is the best job and Jerome got it because he's your pet."

Marty snickered. Somebody said . . . . All he had to do was breathe different and the whole damn school took it as gospel!

"What an idea! Yours is by far the more difficult piece," Miss Evans said. "It's much too late to find a replacement for you, or for you to learn the narrator's lines. I should think you'd be proud to recite for your father. I wouldn't like to think you've fallen prey to someone interested only is disrupting our pageant."

Confused, Cory grumbled that he'd recite after all and spent the remainder of the day stewing.

While Miss Evans broke up a staged fight in the schoolyard during lunch, Marty crept into the school by the side door and got to work. He was just scuttling up the road a few minutes later when he heard Winnie Akins begin to screech. He knew she had just peeked in the paper-wrapped parcel containing her fancy-dancy costume, which she kept in the cloakroom.

"Miss Evans! Miss Evans! Oh-h-h . . . . It's ruined! Someone's ruined it!"

Sadie was just leading smirking Mike and Danny into the schoolroom by their prominent little ears when she saw Winnie in the cloakroom doorway, holding up her costume. Someone had hacked two circles and a triangle from the front and a square from the back.

Sadie released the Shockleys' ears. They were already snickering and pointing as they dashed outside. "Winnie! How awful! Quickly, put it away," Sadie said in embarrassment. "Don't carry on so, honey. We can find you something different to wear."

Winnie flung the gown to the floor and ran. "I hate this school!"

The following day, just after Sadie dismissed for lunch, Marty remained in his seat and tripped Jerome Crowley as the slight, increasingly nervous boy passed on his way out. "Steady there, weasel," Marty snickered, catching Olive Crowley's grandson and giving him a friendly pat. "Don't want to fall on your pretty-boy face, do you now?" Surreptitiously he slipped something into the boy's hip pocket.

An hour later Marty loitered near the iron gate watching for Jerome to return from lunch at his grandmother's. "Hey, weasel, come here." Marty held a closed jackknife with a white bone handle in his scrawny fist. He had carefully worked blue threads into the joint between the first blade and handle. "I found this next to Cory's desk. Put it back in his pail, will you? That's a good little weasel."

Jerome took the closed jackknife and frowned. "I don't hafta do nothing you say."

"Better not keep it or Cory'll think you took it."

The Runyon buggy turned in toward the hay barn from the road behind them. Jerome looked up, his huge blue eyes filled with alarm.

"Don't let them see you with it," Marty whispered. "They'll say you took it, along with everything else. Put it back now."

"You do it!" Jerome said, unable to understand why he suddenly might be accused of stealing again.

"Naw, go ahead. I'll keep everybody out while you put it

back. You can trust me, weasel. But don't tell nobody I helped you, or we'll both get the dunce's stool."

Marty grinned as he watched the little boy tiptoe into school.

Sadie was watching Walter tether the buggy horse in the hay barn, when she heard the surrey coming up the road. The Shockley boys were chasing prairie dogs behind the school, and Douglas Newcomb and Herbie Shockley were shooting marbles on the far side of the water trough, where the dirt was level and smooth.

The sun felt warm on her face. She was glad Douglas Newcomb had returned to school, because for a time she'd suspected him of some of the pranks.

Her thoughts turned to the two new children, absent today. This had been the first day in two weeks that nothing had happened. The rash of pranks coincided with their entry into school. She wondered if the Garleys possessed enough devilment between them to cause such remarkable trouble.

After she'd finished eating, she went to the trough to dip water into a new speckled tin cup. As she drank, she saw movement inside the school. At the nearest window she watched in astonishment as Olive's grandson, Jerome, stood beside his own desk, staring intently at Cory Withers' desk. Something about his furtive manner kept her silently watching, horrified to think that at last she had concrete evidence of which student was a guilty participant in the pranks. What was the child up to? She'd tan his hide!

Jerome approached Cory's desk and looked behind and under the seat. Finally he looked in the cubbyhole beneath the top.

With a lightning-quick motion, he thrust something into the cubbyhole and fled outside, looking guilty and filled with terror.

Trembling with indignation, Sadie slipped inside the moment he left. Surely Olive's grandson couldn't be stealing! Yet Cory had called Jerome "teacher's pet" often enough that Jerome might want to take a small boy's revenge on him.

At the other door she watched Jerome standing by the gate

looking nervous and disoriented. The Shockleys sidled up to him, poking fun, as usual, and pushing the boy. Then one of the Shockleys plucked something from Jerome's hip pocket and held up two raggedly cut circles of blue cloth.

Grabbing the stunned little boy, the crowing Shockleys went through all his pockets, finding a matching triangle. Jerome looked stricken.

Hooting with laughter, two of the Shockleys watched the third hold the circles of cloth to his chest while wiggling in a circle like a hoochy-coochy dancer. Then the boys saw Sadie watching, dropped the scraps and dashed away.

Feeling dizzy, Sadie sagged against the doorframe. Was it Jerome who had mangled Winnie's costume? But why? Gathering her strength, feeling anger bubbling just beneath her rigid control, Sadie marched outside.

"Stop right there, young man!" she shouted as Jerome bolted. She reached the gate and plucked the blue scaps from the grass. "You and I have something to discuss! Come inside at once."

Everyone had returned for the afternoon session and stood silently in the road watching Jerome struggle with his conscience. Finally he plodded into the school like a condemned little man.

Sadie fought to keep her voice even. "Johnny, Walter, Cornell, keep order out here while I speak privately to Jerome."

She stepped into the school and closed the door. For a moment she couldn't bring herself to speak. The school smelled of damp wool and chalk dust. The room had cooled and now echoed with her thumping heartbeats. "What were these pieces of cloth doing in your pocket?"

Jerome quaked with terror as he turned to face her. He started shaking his head, worrying his hat with small chubby hands. "I don't know, Miss Evans! I never seen them before!"

"You have no idea how these things came to be in your pockets?"

"No, ma'am!" He shook his head solemnly.

She supposed someone might have put the pieces in his

pocket. A skilled pickpocket could slip something into a pocket as easily as out of one.

She went to Jerome and crouched before the trembling boy. "You swear you know nothing about how Winnie's costume got cut up?"

"Yes'm! Cross my heart and hope to die eating a snake's gizzard." A tear rolled down his rosy left cheek.

"I don't believe snakes have gizzards," she said abstractedly. Then she remembered seeing him take something from Cory's desk. She straightened, noticed all the round-eyed faces pressed against the windows, and went to the Whithers boy's place.

"I didn't take it, Miss Evans! Honest, I didn't! I didn't! I wouldn't!"

Had Jerome put something back into the desk's cubbyhole, she wondered? She reached into the recess and felt the cool length of a small jackknife. She held it out for Jerome to see. "Did you put this in there?"

His eyes grew so round she wondered if he was going to burst. "But I didn't take it!"

"Who told you to put it in there? Why would you?"

Her questions overwhelmed him with terror. Another tear rolled to his chin.

She pried one of the knife's blades from the handle and saw the threads caught in the joint. The evidence was becoming so very convincing. "Are you trying to make it look as if Cory cut up Winnie's blue costume?" she asked softly, touched by Jerome's quivering lower lip.

Then she saw the corner of a bit of fabric tucked beneath Cory's slate. She pulled out a ragged square of blue linen.

Jerome drew in his breath and looked ready to faint.

Before Sadie could ask him again if he was guilty, Winnie burst into the room. With fresh tears coursing down her plump cheeks, she looked at Sadie. "They're saying you won't punish him! They say you'll let this go on because you like him best! That ain't fair! You got to punish him! He ruined my Mother Mary gown! He needs a good whippin'."

"Hush, Winnie," Sadie whispered, tormented to see

Jerome's face whiten with terror. "I don't whip students." She wanted to comfort both children, but she felt rooted and rigid. They were her dearest students!

From the doorway the students who had spent the most time on the thinking stool whispered, "Teacher's pet," with a particular vehemence.

Sadie whirled. "Come inside and take your seats!" She was as close to losing her temper as she had ever been in her life. When everyone was seated and silent, Sadie held out the blue scraps found in Jerome's pocket, and the knife he'd hidden in Cory's desk.

"If Jerome is guilty of defacing Winnie's pageant costume, then he must sit on the thinking stool for an hour —"

"That ain't long enough!" Mike Shockley shouted, leaping to his feet. "He oughta be on it for days. He oughta be expelled!"

More huge tears welled in Jerome's eyes. He kept shaking his head while looking at Marty as if betrayed.

"He done worse than us," Danny Shockley snapped.

"One hour," Sadie pronounced with finality. "Unless . . . Jerome has something to say in his own defense." She looked hopefully down at the trembling boy.

"I didn't do it, Miss Evans! I didn't do nothing." He looked about ready to say more, but when his eyes met Marty's dark ones, he stiffened and closed his mouth.

"He made my Mother Mary gown nasty!" Winnie wailed, leaping to her feet. "I'm sick of the way everybody in this school tries to make me feel low. I'm as good as the rest! I'm not nasty — not like some!" She cast Dawn a look of hate.

Sadie flung the evidence to the floor. "Hush, Winnie!" She braced herself on the edge of the desk. "Hush, everyone! Sit down." For several dizzy seconds she covered her eyes, trying to think, trying to understand the nagging feeling in the back of her mind. Something about this whole incident was bothering her. Finally she decided she had to go with her hunch.

"Jerome, take your seat — no, at your desk." Sadie drew a

ragged breath and straightened. Her blood was rushing suddenly. If she was wrong she'd be in serious trouble. Her authority would be destroyed. "Class, I don't believe Jerome cut Winnie's costume."

Eyes rounded, Jerome slipped to his desk like a ghost.

Sadie's gaze settled on one narrow face that reflected no surprise. Her voice came out like ice. "Marty Wheeler, please stand."

Marty looked around with a "Who me?" expression. He grinned as if to say he figured the teacher had lost her mind. Skinny, homely, his hair ragged, his eyes glinting, he stood up slowly. He scratched under his arm until Sadie's frigid stare made him stop.

"Did you cut Winnie's costume?"

"Couldn't have, teacher. Some nit stoled my whittling knife. Or did you forget about that 'cause it ain't nothing to you? You're always trying to pin stuff on me, and I'm plain weary of it! So's my pa."

"Empty your pockets, Marty." Sadie's voice remained calm.

Smirking, he pulled his trouser pockets out. They were dark, ragged with holes and empty.

Sadie went up to him. For a revolting moment their eyes remained locked. Then she dipped her hand into his shirt pocket. She pinched at the lint at the bottom and pulled out tufts of white cottony fuzz, bits of shreaded tobacco, cornbread crumbs . . . and frayed, inch-long blue threads.

"In view of the way Winnie's costume was cut, I'd say you are the sort to think up such a stunt. You may sit in the corner the remainder of the day, Marty Wheeler."

Someone snickered loudly.

Marty bristled. "For me it's all day, is it?" His neck reddened. "You can't make me!"

"The many pranks you've pulled during the past two weeks warrant more than a mere three hours on the stool. You may be allowed to stretch every fifteen minutes. Sit!" Though trembling with rage, she never blinked. When Marty didn't move, she seized his grimy ear and guided him to the corner.

Marty looked as if he wanted to throttle her, but he'd do nothing so long as anyone was watching. He slumped onto the stool in a huff.

For the remainder of the day Sadie felt Marty's hatred radiating from the corner. She set the children to working sums and then sat contemplating how to protect herself from Marty when the day was done.

"Class dismissed, except for Marty. I want you to stay after for a few minutes," Sadie said with icy calm at three of the clock.

In moments the room was empty. The excited voices of the liberated children died away, except for Johnny and Walter, her eldest students, who were waiting outside with the surrey and buggy until she sent Marty home. Gratified by their gesture of protection, she turned on the slit-eyed pickpocket slouched on the thinking stool.

"I expect you've spent the afternoon thinking how to get even with me for humiliating you in front of this class," she began, startling Marty as she closed her ledger with a snap. "I'll give you one last warning. If you have the courage to return to school on Monday, I'll take that as your pledge that nothing more will disrupt my classroom. You'll steal nothing. You'll leave no threatening notes. You'll say nothing to me or any student of a vulgar nature. In short, you'll conduct yourself as a gentleman."

"What'll you do if I don't?" He spoke with contempt.

"I'll tell your father you were picking pockets in the park on Warren County Fair Day."

He sniffed a laugh. "You didn't see nothing of the kind."

"Danny, Mike and Freddy Shockley helped you take a gold pocket watch, some coins and a greenback dollar. You hid those things in Mr. Biggins' shack later that day. Mrs. Cadwallader would surely think you'd corrupted her grandsons if she learned the details. She'd see the Wheeler family run out of town. That could anger your father, since I recently heard she is considering supporting him in the election." Fickle woman, Sadie added to herself.

He laughed. "My pa won't give a tinker's damn about that two-bit stuff. Or the Cadwalladers."

"Then I'll advise the town council that their sheriff is protecting a thief and arresting innocent people in his place. It will be a simple matter of contacting the governor to have your father removed from his office." She moved close enough to see a flicker of uncertainty in the boy's furtive eyes. "I am done with your pranks, Marty Wheeler."

With a grunt of disgust, he shoved past her, bruising her shoulder as he stormed out. He flung the iron gate so wide that the fence sagged back. In a fit of rage, he stomped one side of the fence into the grass.

"I don't give an ice-cold damn in hell if you do tell my pa! He's going to fix you. He's going to fix you good!"

Chapter Ten

November 10, 1879

Marty was not in school the following Monday morning. Giving no indication that she was concerned, Sadie conducted her classes in the first true peace the little schoolhouse had known in weeks. She hoped that Marty had quit school and she would see him no more.

Rehearsal went well. Jerome remembered his introduction. Cory knew his recitation by heart. The rest of the students enjoyed themselves, and Winnie was hard at work stitching a new costume from yard goods Sadie had bought herself.

When the last student left that day, Sadie straightened the rows, wiped down the blackboard and then went for her hat and cape. Engrossed in her thoughts, she looked up to see Sheriff Otis Wheeler lounging against the door frame. He looked so like Marty — right down to his negligent, insolent manner and expression — that immediately Sadie was on her guard.

Without greeting the man, she barred the side door and

tied on her cape. "I suppose you've come about the incident with Marty last Friday."

Otis slipped off his tan stetson and smoothed back his corn-colored hair. Then he stroked his long, bristly blond mustache. "The boy tells me you humiliated him in front of everybody."

"I'm sure that's how he saw it," she said. "I'm about to leave. We could discuss Marty's unacceptable behavior on the way." Oddly, she found herself trembling, afraid to approach the door as long as Otis was there to block her way.

"You got something against me?" Otis asked, his voice low and menacing.

"Not at all, sheriff. Did Marty explain why he was punished in front of the class?" Her voice betrayed a slight tremor.

Otis smiled slightly and rubbed his nose with the back of his hand. "Said something about dirty pockets."

Sadie chuckled. "Please sit down. I'll explain." She took her seat behind her desk where she could hide her trembling fists. She felt safer there.

"I'll stay where I am, if it's all the same to you."

Trying to remain calm, Sadie listed the many incidents that had led up to the ruining of Winnie Akins' pageant costume.

"Just how was it cut up, did you say?" Otis asked, never taking his eyes from Sadie's bosom.

For a moment she endured the unpleasant rush of blood to her face and neck. Finally she stood and sketched the damage done to the gown on the blackboard. She drew two hasty circles where the wearer's breasts would be, and a triangle farther down. "There was also a square cut in the back." Quickly she erased the suggestive picture.

Otis snickered softly. "You think my boy done that?"

She explained how Marty had contrived to make Jerome the guilty party with the knife, and then explained why finding threads from the ragged blue linen scraps in Marty's pocket proved he'd had the scraps on his person.

"And that's enough to put my boy on that damn little stool of yours for three hours?"

"He's been nothing but trouble to me, and it was high time he learned to stop disrupting this class! And . . . he has made vulgar remarks to me." She leveled angry eyes on Otis.

He just went on smirking, his own eyes low-lidded and insolent. He strolled behind her, trailing his finger along the shadows of her sketch on the blackboard, looking around with that infuriating half smile. The hair on the nape of her neck began to prickle.

"What kind of remarks?" he asked softly.

"I wouldn't care to repeat them," she said, hating the nervous break in her voice.

"You got to admit you're a damn pretty woman. Marty's just a growing boy. Got his mind on . . . plenty of things, including pretty women. I wouldn't like to think you'd encouraged him and then —"

"I've done no such thing! If that's what you came here to suggest, you can just leave!" She stood and moved toward the door.

Otis was quick to block her way. "Ain't no use getting uppity about all this. It ain't nothing but a little harmless funning. You got to expect a little of that in the schoolhouse. My girl Justine took her share, I can tell you."

"Let me pass, please." She was terrified.

"Now, just hold on. There ain't no call to get your back up with me. I'd like for us to be friends." He moved a little closer.

She didn't want to back away and reveal that she was afraid. She smelled alcohol on his breath and was surprised. A brief glance at his eyes showed them to be slick and half-focused.

"It's mighty nice having a pretty female new in town." His voice came oily and soft. "I can't say as I blame my boy for saying things out of turn. 'Course, he's only a boy. He don't know the right way to approach a pretty, cultured woman like yourself. I think you and me could be real good friends. That deputy of mine ain't a bad sort, but he don't know the half about women as I do. I know things about women that most of this town ain't never heard of. I could tell you about some of it."

"Let me pass."

He placed his long, battered thin hand on her arm. "One thing I know how to do is make a woman feel like a real woman. I got ways of pleasing a woman maybe even your kind ain't heard of yet. Don't go getting stiff-necked on me. Just hear me out. I know your kind. I seen it plain that first day you came to me. I says to myself, Otis, there's a woman looking for the best man in town. And here she's figured out a real smart way to come calling on me. I seen how you looked at me that day, Sadie. You was plumb shocked to find a real man in this out-of-the-way dust hole. I'd say you and me could be real close friends." He slid his hand to her shoulder. Then he moved swiftly to take hold of her chin. "Close friends."

Sadie jerked free and took several steps away from him. She was shaking with revulsion far stronger than anything she'd felt with Marty. She had believed she could bluff Marty into leaving, but she wasn't sure of Otis at all. By the time he left she might not be good for much ever again.

Swiftly he had his hands on her shoulders and backed her to the wall next to the cloakroom door. As his face lowered and his mouth opened, she twisted away. She lost her balance and stumbled into the cloakroom.

"Now, is that any way to be?" Otis whispered, lunging into the cloakroom after her. He seized both her wrists and wrestled her into a corner. "I been real nice to you. I ain't said I think you're a damn fool for humiliating my boy in front of the town, but that's what you are!" He punctuated his words with flickering, unfriendly smiles. "Thinking about screaming, are you, teacher? Or are you thinking about how good it'll feel when I lay you on the floor —"

"Let go of me!" She was shocked to think he would speak to her in such a coarse manner.

"Going to claw out my eyes?" He chuckled. "Didn't think I knew about that, did you? I know everything in this town. Real ladies don't go for the eyes. They ain't bred to it. You ain't no real lady, Missy Evans. I even wonder if you're a real school teacher."

He blocked her effort to knee him and pressed her into the corner more roughly. Then he slathered his mouth over hers as she twisted to avoid his kisses. She felt his cool wet lips and tongue moving on her cheek and wanted to scream.

Finally she managed to slap him hard, striking the side of his nose with the heel of her hand. As he clutched at his face, she kicked his shin and was out of the cloakroom.

"Say a word about this," he shouted in a muffled nasal twang after her, "and I'll tell everybody what you offered me here in this schoolroom!"

She whirled in the doorway. "Nobody'll believe you!"

"It'll be your word against mine . . . and my boy's. He'll say he's had you every day after school. He may already be saying it. He's bright." Otis sauntered from the cloakroom, wiping his bleeding nose on his sleeve. "You surely are one stupid little fool, Miss Sadie Evans. I ain't a man to have against you."

"Nobody," she panted as she floundered out, reckless with fear, "will believe you! I have friends in this town now. And you're nothing but a drunkard!"

"You can still make me forget all this," Otis said, grinning and leaning in the doorway. "I like my women to fight me. You and me could have some real good times."

Sadie picked up her skirts and ran until she could run no more.

If she'd broken his nose he'd have to shoot her, Otis thought. He stayed in the schoolhouse until the bleeding stopped, then walked out, leaving the door hanging open. He considered the idea of getting Marty to burn the place down. 'Course, to do that, they'd have to make it look like somebody else done it. She'd left him in such a state he couldn't think just who that someone might be.

Otis found himself back at the jail before he realized it. Jim was sitting in his chair reading the local newspaper sheet. "Out of my way," Otis snarled, shoving Jim out of the chair.

"Been in a fight, Otis?" Jim asked, holding his temper as Otis slammed in, flinging the door shut.

Jim stood, a wry smile softening the hard glint in his eyes. "Get out. I got thinking to do."

Jim left at once.

The man was too damned agreeable, Otis thought suspiciously, wishing he'd been able to provoke him instead. He wanted to sink his fist into that pretty-boy face.

Otis stared at the headline detailing theft of empty whiskey bottles from the Akins Smokey Hill Saloon. Another announced the coming of the new telephone line from Abilene. He crumpled the paper into a ball and threw it. Damn her, he thought. He wished she'd been more receptive. Her lips were as soft as rose petals.

Taking out letter paper, Otis hunched over the desk and began the painful process of printing words he wasn't sure how to spell.

It was nearly dusk and time for Jim to begin his rounds. Instead of moving off down the street, though, he loitered just outside the jail, his hands jammed in his back pockets. He wondered where Otis had been.

Easing to the window, Jim looked in. Otis was writing something, clutching a thick pencil and licking the lead every few letters like a schoolboy. Sighing, Jim wondered why he suddenly felt so uneasy. He settled onto the chair outside the door and drummed his fingertips on his knee.

Less than an hour later Otis came out, his lips compressed into what was a strangely self-satisfied smile. "You still hanging around? Lazy son of a bitch."

"There's blood all over your sleeve," Jim said evenly, content for the moment to bait the man.

Otis turned, squinted into the darkness and then spat not an inch from Jim's boot. "Ain't you got nothing to do, Warren?"

"It's quiet tonight. I'll make rounds in a while. There's dried blood on your cheek, too."

Otis's chin jutted out. "Keep your goddamned eyes to yourself, or I'll put them outa your head!" He shook a rumpled envelope at Jim. "Ain't nothing says I can't take your badge any time I see fit."

Jim was able to make out only a portion of the crude lettering on the front of the envelope. He watched Otis limp down the street — was Otis falling-down drunk? — and cross the tracks to the dry goods emporium where the postmistress kept her rows of cubbies and her postage scale. Jim had seen Otis write only one other letter, when a wanted outlaw with a price on his head made the mistake of staying long enough in town to be identified.

A few moments later Otis emerged from the emporium and started for home. Jim stood and stretched, thinking of going over to the restaurant as he usually did about this time. On the way he stopped at the emporium.

"I was about to go home, Deputy," the postmistress said, as she locked the door to her enclosed corner. "Have you a letter for me, too?"

He shook his head. "Sheriff wondered if he spelled that address right."

She giggled. "I already corrected it for him," she said. "It wouldn't look right for it to go all the way back to Ohio with 'Ohia' on it."

"Thanks," Jim said. "He said for me to pick up the reply when it comes in. Would you let me know when it does?"

"On the trail of a desperate outlaw, Deputy?" she asked with an excited giggle.

"No," Jim said, grinning easily. "Just a little business the two of us cooked up together."

"I'll bring it to you as soon as it comes in. My packets arrive with the first train at five."

He tipped his imaginary hat and went out. "Obliged, ma'am."

While Jim ate, he pondered the blood on Otis Wheeler's cheek. For some uneasy reason he wanted to talk to Sadie and decided to intercept her as she made her evening circuit of the residential streets.

By about the time Trudy would have been done serving dinner at the boarding house, Jim was waiting at the corner of Prairie and Cowtrail Streets where he often met Sadie and walked with her. When she hadn't come by after half an hour, he strolled up to the boarding house.

"Why, Jimmy!" Trudy said, drawing him in the door the moment she saw him. "I've got pie left over. Come in and have a bite while I clean up." She nearly dragged him back to the kitchen.

"I find it impossible to believe that you have pie left," he said, nodding his hello to the boarders sitting in the drawing room.

She closed the kitchen door and clutched at his sleeve. "Sadie hasn't come home from the schoolhouse yet!" she whispered. "Sometimes she goes out to the ranches to see about more students, but that's usually Saturday afternoons. It's not like her to forget to tell me she's going to be late. And she has never missed supper before. I'm worried!"

He smiled to reassure Trudy. "She's probably doing something in connection with her pageant and lost track of time."

"You heard about that little scene at the schoolhouse Friday?" Seeing that he hadn't — since he'd been traveling around the county most of the weekend — Trudy gave him a detailed acounting of Marty Wheeler's punishment on the thinking stool. "I've been worried about her all day! Think what that wicked boy might try to do!"

"I'll go out to the schoolhouse and see her safely home," Jim said, giving the woman a hasty goodbye. He was unable to mask his feeling of alarm as he strode out. It was no wonder Otis had been in a temper!

Stopping by the livery barn to borrow a horse and lantern, Jim pounded out to the schoolhouse. It was deserted, and the door had been left standing open. He tied the horse, noted the bent fence and broken gate, and then lighted the lantern. He felt faintly sick at what he might find inside. If anything had happened to her. . . . He'd kill Otis. He's do it with his bare hands!

Inside he found few clues to what might have happened to Sadie. While the rows of desks were straight, her own desk was askew, and her books were about to fall over.

He found her little hat, hatpin and several hairpins scattered on the cloakroom floor. He trailed large droplets of dried blood back into the main room and saw a long handprint on the doorframe. It was too high to be Marty's, but narrow enough to belong to Otis.

That's when he noticed Sadie's spectacles lying under one of the desks. One lens was cracked. He picked them up, his chest suddenly heaving with the effort to breathe. Finally he folded them and tucked them into his shirt pocket. His jaw ached he was clenching it so hard.

He found nothing outside though he walked with care. "Sadie?" he called softly, walking all the way to the river and searching both banks for five hundred yards. "Sadie, are you out here?"

Standing perfectly still, he listened, thinking he might hear her calling to him. When he heard nothing, he finally returned to the school.

Sadie walked until she was ready to collapse. In the darkness the twin wheel tracks leading north were hard to follow. She stumbled again and again in the potholes. She didn't care where she was going, only that she was going away from Warren Bluffs on the first road available.

By dark she was exhausted and thirsty. She remembered taking the road weeks before when visiting the squatter family.

Her fear and anger finally cooled. She walked on, feeling somewhat foolish now, wondering if she should turn around and go back. She had already missed supper. There would be questions. . . .

Dared she face that classroom again? Her students needed a teacher, but she needed safety and security. She didn't need Otis Wheeler or his son threatening to ravish her every time she stood up to them.

Another convulsive shudder went over her as she remembered Otis's hands on her. She felt so alone and helpless in spite of her bravado. He could easily have overcome her. She wondered why he hadn't. Perhaps he was just as cowardly as his boy. She might only have to fight him off a few more times to be free of him. But oh, she so wanted just to do her job and be left alone!

She began to wonder if she was too tired to make it back to town. Then she noticed the squatter's sod shack tucked against the hillside, and decided to ask for water there. As soon as she approached, a hound began baying.

"Who's out there!" came a shout.

"Hello!" Sadie called. "It's the schoolteacher. I've been walking a long time, and I'm thirsty. Could you spare a little water?"

The door to the shack fell open, and feeble yellow light filled the doorway. Sadie couldn't imagine living there, in such squalid poverty. A man's silhouette darkened the doorway as he stepped out. He had his shotgun again. "Water, is it?"

"If you please. I hate to trouble you so late, but I am so weary. I had no business taking such a long walk." She hoped she was putting the nervous, suspicious man at ease. He was probably used to people coming by and hounding him to get off their land — and used to filling them with birdshot, too.

He moved the long menacing barrel of his shotgun in the direction of the creek down the hill. "Drink yer fill, lady."

She went down there and sank to her knees to drink. The cool water tasted so sweet and reminded her so of Jim that for a moment she feared she was going to cry. Then she heard the squatter's cautious footsteps coming up behind her.

"Got any notion of birthin', schoolteacher?"

"Do you mean do I know how a baby is born? Yes." She struggled wearily to her feet, dusting herself off. "If you'd like me to tell your daughter a little of what I know about the process, I'll be happy to."

"Don't have to tell her nothing. Just git in there. Help her pull it out. It's coming early."

Sadie felt faint. "Junie's in labor?"

"Quit your jawing and git!" He waved the shotgun at her. "I ain't no use to her." He scratched beneath his long graying beard. He was wearing nothing but a faded dirty union suit.

Sadie trudged to the shack and stooped to go inside.

Junie lay on a pile of prairie grass covered with a quilt. She was stark naked, her belly swollen and shiny in the feeble light of a single buffalo tallow candle. Sadie moved the candle away from where it might tip and ignite the dry grass of the bed.

"How are you feeling, Junie?" Sadie whispered, squatting beside the girl and taking her hand. Suddenly she was chilled all over with nervous sweat. Junie clutched at her hurtfully, but smiled. Sadie's heart raced so fast she was certain she would faint in the fetid, smoky heat of the soddy.

"What can I do for you, Junie? Do you want a doctor? I know of a woman who does midwifing, if you'd rather."

Junie answered with a gathering wail, crushing Sadie's hand, arching her back, thrusting up her engorged breasts and spreading her legs until a smoothly distended birth-canal opening, already filled with the infant's head, showed. Her wail trailed off into a moment of breathless, quivering silence. Then, expelling her breath with a loud ah! Junie relaxed for a few seconds.

Sadie twisted around to look up into the bland face of the man watching from the doorway. The look chilled her. There was no time for a doctor or midwife, but she scarcely felt up to this new and terrifying challenge. "I want clean water and something to wrap around the baby. I'll need a knife . . ."

With her head reeling, Sadie turned back to watch the young girl arch again to meet the contraction. More of the baby's pale head bulged out.

Sadie could really do little but watch as the girl's efforts peaked again. She was stretched tautly white. The man brought a cooking pot with steaming water — Sadie was amazed to realize so much time had passed. For her it had stood still. She rinsed her hands. Massaging the area around the baby's head, Sadie made soothing sounds to relax the girl.

"Don't hurry. Give yourself time to stretch. This is all perfectly . . . natural. . . ." Sweat trickled down her back. She definitely felt faint!

Miraculously the girl's skin did stretch even more over what Sadie thought was a perfectly enormous infant head. And then the girl arched suddenly again. With a gush, the infant's head pushed into Sadie's trembling hands. Slippery, wet, coated with a thick white something, the infant seemed to turn of its own accord and thrust one shoulder after another into the world.

Sadie stared down at the tiny, perfectly formed little body in her hands. The eyes were tightly closed, the male genitals proudly pink and startlingly large. The infant twitched. Sadie lifted him quickly, wiped his face with the front of her shirtwaist and then slapped his tiny creased rump.

He reddened. His mouth opened. She slapped him again, feeling a sensation of panic rise in her chest.

Junie's eyes rounded. She reared up and seized her son and shook him. "Cry!"

With a sharp gasp, he inhaled and then let out a tiny high-pitched shriek that sent shudders of joy through Sadie. She blinked and realized her face was awash with tears. Laughing, she wiped them away. "He's going to be all right!"

After a few moments she tore some of the gathering threads from her petticoat's ruffled border and tied off the cord in two places with them, slicing through it in between with the squatter's hunting knife.

After a while she washed Junie's sweaty, grimy young body and covered her. The baby suckled a moment and fell asleep. Sadie sagged back against the crumbling soddy wall and laughed raggedly. "I am definitely not paid well enough!"

The squatter came and went as Sadie dozed against the wall. The night grew colder. Finally the man slipped inside and closed the door. He sat and leaned back against it, cradling the shotgun in his lap. He offered Sadie a square bottle of un-labeled spirits. "Thankee, ma'am. Yer a good 'un."

She sniffed at the bottle. Not wanting to offend him, she

sipped a little. Tears immediately sprang to her eyes and she gagged when she tried to swallow.

He grinned.

"Where did you get this?" she croaked, coughing.

"Found it."

"Where's your wife? Wasn't she here last time I came out?" Sadie dusted herself and then adjusted a ragged scrap of quilt over the sleeping new mother.

"She died." His eyes turned to his daughter and grandson. "They would've been fine."

Sadie nodded wearily. "Yes, she would've done all right without my help, but I'm proud just the same that I was here to share this beautiful moment with you both." She looked at the child, who seemed so tiny and fragile now. She could see he was far stronger looking than the limp Terrison infant had been. "I'll bring something for the baby to wear tomorrow," she said, beginning to close her eyes.

He was already shaking his head. "Don't want nothing from you."

"Of course, but I would want to repay you . . . if you can spare something to eat now. I missed supper."

His eyes softened. He handed her a joint of roasted rabbit from a nearby cooking pot, and then, after she'd eaten, she slept.

Chapter Eleven

Sadie woke at dawn. The squatter's daughter was sitting up on the quilt-covered buffalo-grass mattress, nursing her newborn son. Sadie couldn't help but stare at the girl's milk-engorged breasts and feel a thrill to see the way the baby eagerly sucked at the dark nipple.

They drank thin coffee together and talked of doings at the schoolhouse. Then Sadie knew she had to start walking if she hoped to reach town and change into clean clothes before the beginning of school.

As she followed the dusty twin track away from the soddy, a biting wind pulled at her tangled, unfurled hair. The vast land spread all around her. The sky reached forever, high, pale and cold. But though she shivered in her cape, she felt strangely refreshed. The birth had renewed her faith that somehow soon all would be right with her world.

In the distance she saw a horse and rider cantering. She hoped for a ride to town, as her feet were beginning to ache. Suddenly the rider heeled his mount and pounded toward her.

Jim was leaping to the ground and sweeping her into his

arms before his horse had stopped. "Sadie! I've been looking for you all night!"

Then his lips were on hers. His mouth was warm and urgent, his hands hard and crushing on her back as he held her against him.

She sought his mouth with equal urgency, overjoyed that he was the first person she should see on this strangely beautiful cold morning.

Abruptly he held her at arm's length. He took in everything about her appearance from her unknotted dusty hair to the strange bloody stains on her shirtwaist. He plucked some dried grass from her tangled curls, his eyes tight with anguish. "Where have you been?" His voice was husky, betraying the terrors he'd felt all night while searching for her. "I've been along every road from town twice."

She took his trembling hands and held them to her cool cheeks. "I was helping deliver a baby!"

His face worked with disbelief. He frowned, and his mouth opened. Then he smiled just a bit. "I know what I saw at the schoolhouse, Sadie! Tell me what happened there!"

She shook her head. "It's not important. I-I decided to come out this way to see how Junie Scott was doing . . . and she was in labor. I really didn't do a thing for her but hold her hand, but — oh, Jim! It was so beautiful! A new baby, so pink and perfect!"

She threw her arms around his neck and held him, wanting to erase the look on his face that told her he suspected some of what she'd been through the afternoon before. She wanted to make him forget that there was anything to worry about. Then she took his face in her hands and looked up at him. "I've needed you . . . I wish we could be alone again."

He stared incredulously at her. Then he was kissing her, holding her and hugging her to his chest as his hands moved possessively over her back. "I thought I might find you hurt or . . . dead!"

She didn't want to make light of his fears, but she did smile a little. "You've been a deputy too long. I'm sorry you were worried. Forgive me. I . . . I had no idea I'd be gone all night."

"You're not telling me everything."

"I'm all right. Really! That's all that matters. I promise I won't go off again without telling you."

He fumbled in his shirt pocket and pulled out her spectacles. His silence was enough to tell her he suspected she got on quite well when not wearing them.

She looked at the star-shaped crack in the right lens and for an instant the feel of Otis Wheeler's scrawny body against hers made her understand fully what Jim had feared he'd find. "Oh," she said, taking the spectacles. "I suppose I'll have to have new ones made. I do hate them so. Always have."

He stared at her, looking as if he wanted to shake the truth from her, and then he stepped back. She hoped he wasn't angry.

"Can we hurry? I don't want to be late for class," she said.

His mouth tightened. His eyes grew dark. He circled the horse, patting him, and then mounted. He reached down and Sadie took his hand. She mounted behind him and then held his waist tightly.

"It was so beautiful," she murmured. "It makes me wish. . . . It made me think of you, of that day in the bluffs. I haven't been able to get that day out of my mind." She laid her head against his back and heard his heart pounding.

He took a deep breath. "If you were . . . hurt in some way . . . would you tell me?"

She understood what he was asking, but if she said a word about what Otis had said and done, Jim might make a terrible mess of a situation that might blow over. "If I was ever hurt in a way that affected . . . us, I would," she whispered. She could feel the muscles in his back tighten.

"I'm saying to myself that there's a reason why you won't confide in me. For some reason you don't trust me," he said thickly.

She hugged him. "You know that's not true." But even as

she said it she realized that she didn't trust him completely. She couldn't. She didn't trust a single person on earth — not completely.

"From now on, I'm not letting you out of my sight," he said between his teeth. He wheeled the horse and they trotted toward town. "I don't give a damn what's said in town. I care about what happens to you. I'm going to be a burr and stick to your side."

She chuckled and hugged him more tightly. "I won't mind that a bit."

When they reached town the streets were already busy with end-of-the-week commerce. People turned and stared as they rode in. Sadie was clinging to the deputy's back and looking as if she'd been dragged about the countryside.

She hated the way everyone stared at her. She ducked her face, wishing herself invisible, wishing they didn't have to ride straight through town under the gaze of all eyes. And she wished she was not straddling the horse, with her arms around Jim and thinking about the sensations coursing through her body.

If ever she had wanted Jim, this was the moment! She could scarcely keep from squirming more tightly against his body and letting him know with a special soft moan in her throat that she was remembering what they had known together.

"I'll drop you off at the boarding house. Are you sure you want to teach today?"

"Of course. I'm only a little tired. Oh, and I promised to take something out to the Scotts for the baby. I doubt the poor thing has any clothes, and it was cold in that soddy. Jim, did you know that the Scott woman had died? He didn't say how long ago, but it can't have been very long. I was out that way less than a month ago."

"Unless he makes trouble, I leave his sort alone. He's poor. He doesn't need the law on his back, too. But when you're ready to go out, I'll drive you. No more walking, Sadie. I don't intend to live through another night like last night."

"I'm very sorry, really."

"Why do I keep thinking it's not your fault that you were out that way on foot?" he said sharply as they reached the boarding house.

She didn't answer.

He held her hand as she slid from the horse. Already Trudy was rushing down the front steps and into the street, exclaiming over Sadie's disheveled appearance.

Sadie shut out the woman's questions and stared up into Jim's troubled eyes, trying to tell him in silence what she wanted him to believe.

His expression softened. "I'm going to take this horse back to the livery barn. I'll be back in about an hour to walk you to the schoolhouse. They won't mind you starting a bit late."

"Make it half an hour," she said, smiling.

She turned to Trudy and explained about the Scott baby without exactly saying how she happened to "find out" about Junie's labor.

While Sadie washed her hair and changed her clothes, Trudy excitedly sent out the word that Miss Sadie was back, safe and sound, and that clothing was needed for a newborn. Sadie knew there was nothing better to distract the gossips than the tale of a birth unattended by doctor or midwife. All the ladies would be concerned about an unmarried school-teacher assisting with it. They would never stop to remember that she had been missing.

With her hair still damp, Sadie twisted it into a severe knot and pinned it. She had lost so many hairpins lately she'd have to get more, she thought, finally looking squarely at herself in the mirror over the dresser.

For a moment as she stared into her own eyes, the whole of the previous day flashed across her mind in all its emotional turmoil. She was aching for Jim, and the intensity of her need alarmed her. She was staying in a town where she was not only not wanted but in physical danger as well, and all because she loved Jim Warren.

There, she thought, looking away. I've admitted it to myself. To love him was to be in the greatest danger of all. She should leave town at once and choose another out-of-the-way place to live out her life in privacy and peace.

She felt terribly alone suddenly, for in spite of the few friends she had gained in her two months in Warren Bluffs, there was not a one she could talk to, really *talk* to.

Perhaps the whispering would have died down if, less than an hour after Jim Warren brought Sadie back to town on the back of a horse, he hadn't been seen escorting her to the schoolhouse, too.

He had a strange belligerent expression on his face. Folks couldn't remember when they'd seen him look more dangerous. He was one to ask questions, to watch and think . . . and wait. For months, folks in town knew, he'd been watching and thinking and waiting for Otis Wheeler to give the opening he needed to step into office as sheriff.

Folks were skeptical that Jimmy Warren could do it. After all, Otis hailed from the old days. He'd gunned down outlaws in the streets of Warren Bluffs when they were lined with nothing but saloons and chippy cribs. He'd fought drunken cowboys with his fists. Though those days were gone from Warren Bluffs, folks had to wonder how Jimmy, a lad they could remember wearing short pants and riding riot with his little friends, could ever top that.

As for the little schoolteacher Jimmy was so obviously sweet on, she had to have been up to far more than birthing the night before. Not a person in town could remember Jim asking more questions than he had that night — in every store, at every house.

Jim waited outside Roberts' store while Sadie hurried inside to buy some hairpins. He held no rifle, but he looked on guard nevertheless.

"Heard you got yourself lost last night," a clerk said as Sadie selected her purchases and placed them on the counter.

She smiled amiably and explained about the baby. She spent several precious minutes picking out a warm blanket as a gift for Junie's baby. Then she asked for it to be wrapped, and realized that she was purposely making the clerk squirm for asking her such forward questions.

"Heard all kinds of speculation on what became of you," the weak-chinned man said, apparently not the least uncomfortable about telling Sadie the gossip to her face.

"I'm sure you did," she said, suddenly wary.

He smiled up at her. "Some folks wondered if you'd gone off with some man."

Sadie's eyes widened involuntarily. She fixed the man with an indignant frown. "Does Mr. Roberts realize what a rude clerk he has employed in his store?" She had half a mind to walk out.

The little man smirked and smiled like a whining alley dog. "I heard you get on with men pretty well for a —"

She slapped him.

Startled to think she had done such a thing without intending to, Sadie stepped back from the counter. Instantly, Jim was at her side. The thunderstruck little clerk looked up at Jim's steaming expression and finally began to squirm in earnest. "M-morning, Deputy!"

"Tell me what he said, Sadie," Jim said softly.

The store was as silent as a Sunday afternoon. Moments later Christa's father arrived from the office in the rear. He was flushed with alarm. He cast the writhing clerk a scathing look.

Sadie whirled and pinned Mr. Roberts, whom she knew to be an exceedingly proper man, with her glare. At first she said nothing, wanting to know first what the proprietor thought of her before deciding if she was going to repeat what the worm of a clerk had said.

"Whatever is wrong, Miss Evans?" Mr. Roberts asked, his

tone dripping with solicitude, his eyes darting about his hushed store.

"As I'm sure you've heard," Sadie said very softly and very gently, "I was called away last evening to help deliver the baby of an indigent family outside town. Your employee seemed to think it perfectly acceptable to repeat some gossip he'd heard concerning my absence. He said —" She counted to ten, wondering suddenly with a rush of confusion and alarm, if she was overreacting. Perhaps the little worm had only been trying to ask to call on her.

Jim took her elbow. "Whatever Boyce said, it must have been an insult. I heard the slap outside."

"Why, Jim, I can't imagine what would make him — you're fired, Boyce! Get—"

Sadie turned anguished eyes on Mr. Roberts. "Wait a moment, please." She put a trembling hand over her aching eyes. "Now that I think of it, I'm sure this man didn't mean what he said in the way that I took it. I tend to forget some of the people in Warren Bluffs are simple and lack a graceful way of expressing their interest in me. Please, don't fire him on my account. Let's forget the incident."

The clerk looked frightened and amazed.

"Sadie, are you sure?" Jim whispered, looking incredulous.

"I don't need any more trouble," she said so softly that he sensed rather than heard what she said.

"It's a misunderstanding, Wilbur," Jim said. "She's tired after being up all night with that newborn. Why don't you just deliver those things she wants to her boarding house later. Put them on my bill. Sadie, it's getting late. Are you sure you wouldn't like to rest today?"

She hung her head and let him lead her outside. "Let's just go," she said desperately.

They were across the tracks about to turn onto the School Road before Jim spoke again. "What did the weasel say?"

Sadie's nerves had calmed as they walked. The clerk had said what he meant; she had taken it the correct way . . . and reacted like a guilty woman, she thought, furious with herself. She was losing control.

"Sadie?"

"He said something about how well I get on with men." The heat of embarrassment began staining her cheeks again. "I was warned yesterday that Marty might be gossiping about me because I put him on the thinking stool for so long." She caught Jim's black look from the corner of her eye. "Don't ask me about it again, Jim! I have to go to school today. I have to see if Marty's in school. If he is, that means I've begun to exert some amount of authority over him and he won't give me any more trouble."

"And if he's not?"

"Then I have a few more battles to fight."

As they neared the school she felt a strong sense of reluctance to face the children. She wanted to run away with Jim and hide within the circle of his protecting arms.

"I don't understand you, Sadie," Jim whispered huskily.

"What don't you understand?"

"I know you've been treated badly here. I don't know all the reasons why. Maybe it's because you're so beautiful. . . ." He looked as if he wanted to take her into his arms.

She smiled a little. She loved to hear him say he thought her beautiful. "That has nothing whatever to do with how I'm treated, and you know it."

"I've asked myself if another schoolmarm would have had as much trouble here as you have. I suppose anyone would have. Mr. Charles retired because the youngsters were so unruly. I guess I'm wondering why you continue to put up with us. Why, of all the teachers we've hired, are you the one determined enought to stick out all the pranks and gossip. . . ?"

She dared not look up for fear the reason would be plainly written on her face.

"There are other towns in need of teachers," he said softly. "I lie awake nights fearing you'll decide one of them might be easier."

She shook her head. "I understand small towns, and I understand people. I must prove myself here." She sighed. Her reasons sounded hollow even to her own ears.

"But why here? Why not prove yourself somewhere else?"

They had reached the school. The Runyon buggy was in its customary place in the hay barn. Someone had righted the iron fence and fixed the broken gate hinge with a little wire. There was a small bouquet of the last of the season's wild sunflowers lying before the gate.

Jim stooped and picked them up. "These must be for you."

"Watch out for poison ivy," she whispered, but she took the bouquet without hesitation. As she stared into the wilting blooms, a small smile lifted her lips. The children had left them for her. They were waiting quietly inside. "Do you shave yourself while looking in the mirror?" she asked softly, suddenly glowing with happiness.

He looked faintly amused and puzzled. "I stop by the barber every morning."

"Well, tomorrow morning, when Lloyd Purcell is shaving you, look in his mirror and ask yourself why Miss Sadie Evans has faith in Warren Bluffs."

Chapter Twelve

Clutching the bouquet of wilted sunflowers, Sadie went into the school. All her students were present except Marty. His seat was conspicuously vacant.

"Excuse me for being late," she said, studying her students while she unpinned her hat.

The Shockleys' eyes burned with excitement. Winnie looked worried, and the others seemed restless, too. Detecting an unpleasant odor coming from the cloakroom, Sadie discovered a carefully wrapped box in the corner where she usually hung her cape.

She snatched up the reeking, soggy package and took it quickly outside. She almost made it to the riverbank before the box fell apart in her hands, dropping horse dung at her feet. Luckily none got on her clothes.

Stooping at the riverbank, she washed and then returned to the school. The hushed whispers ceased at once. "Can anyone tell me about the package?" she asked, her voice heavy with weariness.

"Marty came by." Cornell offered.

"Did not!" Susanna snapped in defense of her brother.

"Did too!" Jerome shouted.

Sadie stood for a long moment looking earnestly at each young face. She could truthfully say she liked and cared about each of the children. Stiffening her back then, she turned toward the blackboard. She couldn't seem to remember what she had intended to teach that day. Her mind was an exhausted blank. If only she could retreat and regroup, just for a short while.

"It's such a beautiful day, I think we might all benefit from a surprise holiday." Turning, she watched the looks of puzzlement and surprise crossing the upturned faces. Many began smiling. "Class dismissed for the day," she said, giving her students a smile. "Enjoy yourselves."

For a stunned moment the students were silent. Then the younger ones were on their feet, rushing and jostling into and out of the narrow cloakroom. In moments they were through the door and scattering in all directions.

The older students looked as if they thought Sadie had some ulterior motive for dismissing, but Sadie let none of her weary thoughts show in her expression.

When at last she was alone, she sank into her chair, checked to make sure her drawer was empty of mice and gave the room a quick inspection to see if anything else needed attention. All was well. All was perfectly well, and for a few precious moments she could think.

Letting her chin rest on her arms, she sighed deeply. She had all but told Jim she loved him. She had all but said she was staying in Warren Bluffs because of him, yet everything in her was urging her to escape before it was too late! But escape where?

She was tired. She should have gone to bed for the day. She knew she shouldn't remain alone at the schoolhouse, but felt reasonably certain Marty or his father would not arrive to accost her for a few more minutes. By then she'd be hurrying back to the fragrant warmth and security of Trudy's house.

For the time being, she stared dreamily at the far wall. Strangely the barnyard odor still clinging to the air in the schoolroom made her think of home and the year she had been eight. They had had a cow then. The odor and the tart November air coming in the half-open schoolhouse took her back to the time when all had been so perfect, so simple.

A picture of her mother's little boarding house under the protection of the huge old elms came to Sadie's mind, a picture of weather-beaten board-and-batten walls, slightly crooked old windows, a generous yard and the hedges of old lilacs that bloomed white in the spring.

Sadie clearly pictured her mother standing on the back steps of the service porch, a tall, lean woman, strong and always smiling, but with a touch of sadness in her eyes. She had a huge heart and a gentle nature. Sadie remembered her mother's black hair, heavily laced with gray, and her gown with the big bell skirt made of faded lavender calico. In Sadie's memory she was shaking her head and laughing, waving her arm now for Sadie to come inside. "You can teach the chickens and the goat to read after lunch, Sadie!"

She wore a threadbare pinafore, and her long spindly black braids danced on her shoulders as she ran into her mother's waiting arms.

The boarding house had a veranda where her mother's boarders rocked on warm evenings. Back among the elms where the woods lurked, waiting to reclaim what civilization had stolen, was a shed where Sadie played pirate with the neighbor boys, where she received her first kiss at eight, and where she first spun her dreams of becoming a wife, mother, and teacher.

Her home town had been small and secluded until the railroad built a spur two miles away. She remembered the neighbors complaining that the railroad brought too many strangers, though everyone had to agree that those strangers and their money brought prosperity. Sadie and her mother, Elinor, had fewer worries, thanks to that spur. The upstairs rooms were always filled. Elinor had welcomed all kinds — mostly men — so long as they were clean and quiet and complimented her cooking.

As the town grew, the respectable, clean, quiet strangers came and went, seldom staying long enough to be more than a name in her mother's ledger or a half-remembered face across the dinner table.

Sadie's mother did well enough to send Sadie to the high school forty miles east. Those years away were wonderful but lonely for Sadie, boarding as a mother's helper to a family of fourteen. Though her days had been busy and full, she had missed her mother. She returned home at seventeen determined to remain with her mother always. Though she still hoped to marry, she expected to find a husband willing to stay on and help at the boarding house.

Sadie discovered, however, that her years away had changed her, making her too educated to attract the countrified affections of the boys she once played with.

One by one her friends, most of whom could scarcely read, married and began families. Sadie reached her eighteenth birthday never having entertained a single serious beau. "Some day the right man will come along," her mother assured her, and that was when both women realized that Sadie's future husband would probably be found among the strangers who shared their table.

By the time Sadie was twenty and no likely man had come to sweep her off her feet, she and her mother began to consider whether Sadie should take a permanent teaching job, either in town or in one of the towns nearby. Before anything could come of the talk, however, Sadie's mother fell ill. For several weeks Sadie cared for her while taking over all her chores. In spite of everything, she had been happy, ignorantly, wonderfully content.

Sadie sat at her desk in the schoolhouse for a long while. She had expected to grow old in that boarding house with her mother. Certainly many gentlemen boarders had expressed an interest in Sadie, but none had received her mother's imperceptible but absolutely necessary nod of approval.

When Sadie turned twenty-one, she and her mother began piecing the double-wedding-ring quilt top, as if trying to summon Sadie's future husband with each hope-filled stitch.

In March of that year, about when the pieced top was ready to be joined to the backing, a young man arrived, battered valise in hand, wearing the ill-fitting but unmistakable suit of a traveling salesman. He was stocky and strong, with curly hair and coffee-brown eyes. He was the handsomest man Sadie had ever laid eyes on.

He had a beautifully sculpted mouth, and he smiled in a lazy provocative way that made Sadie want more than anything to be noticed by him.

Though polite in the extreme, he at first paid no attention to Sadie. At twenty-eight his only interest seemed to be in making his weekly rounds to sell lightning rods to all the locals and farmers. He went out every day, sometimes staying away far into the night. He was the most diligent man ever to cross her mother's threshold. He was clean and quiet, and he minded his manners at the table. He got on well with the other boarders and displayed no vices. His low, vibrant voice filled the simple boarding house with warmth and excitement.

Sadie began taking extra pains to dress in fetching styles. Her mother began laying a feast at each meal. And with every inquiry into the background and daily habits of this handsome young stranger, Sadie's mother began nodding her approval ever more vigorously. By June she was openly smiling and asking him to join her in the drawing room on warm evenings.

He called himself Rayford Storm. "I have a bounden duty to save hard-working farmers and the good citizens of every town in this great country from the terrors of a cloudburst and God's wrath by electrical fire!" he said more than once, grinning as if he knew he was being theatrical.

Sadie chuckled, remembering those first evenings in the drawing room as he pitched his wares. Within a week the boarding house roof bristled with iron spikes from every corner.

What a charmer Ray had been! What an absolute delight to a lonely, sheltered young woman. Sadie had thought she would never love another man as she loved him, and now here she was in this fading town in Kansas where her love for Rayford Storm had driven her.

Of course, it hadn't been love, she thought, rising finally to check the schoolhouse windows and make sure she was completely alone. She stood in the front doorway of the schoolhouse, and then the side doorway, remembering how breathless she had been to sit across from Ray at her mother's table and watch him eat.

She remembered the first time she sat alone with Ray on the veranda, feeling nearly faint with hope and excitement. She had been so overcome by her feelings she had never noticed the sparkle in his eyes when he looked at her. She shouldn't have trusted her desires then, she thought, and she shouldn't trust them now when Jim Warren made her feel the same way!

She had to sit down suddenly. She dared not stay in Warren Bluffs another day! Jim Warren had her breathless with desire! He had her longing for him, dreaming about him, spinning impossible futures that included him. He had no idea how deeply she needed and wanted him. He had no conception of how much she would be hurt if a time came when he no longer wanted her.

Trembling suddenly, Sadie took paper from her desk drawer and then unstoppered her bottle of ink. She smoothed the tip of her quill, knowing she shouldn't put a single word to paper. But because she so desperately needed help she was willing to risk contacting the only person alive who knew her well enough to say whether she should stay on in Warren Bluffs.

Sealing the letter half an hour later, Sadie let out a ragged sigh. Adelaide would know what she should do. Then she wondered if she dared even send the letter! In all the time she had been in Warren Bluffs she had sent no letters and received none. In a town so small, surely someone would notice if and when a reply came. And from where.

Looking up from his desk, Jim saw schoolchildren racing past the jail. He stood and stretched, wondering why Sadie had dismissed early. Grim possibilities suddenly flooded his mind. Grabbing his coat, he started out the door. He felt uneasy for Sadie, knowing she was in trouble and fuming because she refused to confide in him.

When he reached the schoolhouse, he saw through the window that Sadie was sitting at her desk with her hands over her face. He tapped at the door before going in.

"Oh, Jim," she said, straightening and flushing prettily. She stood up quickly and brushed her skirt. "I've been sitting here thinking I must go home before Marty gets the idea I might be alone."

He came to her desk, watching every flicker of her expression, and perched on the corner of it. "I was worried about you. Why did you dismiss early?" He reached for her hand and caught it. She seemed reluctant to be touched at first, but quickly relaxed, allowing him to draw her closer.

"It seemed the most sensible thing to do. I was too tired after all. I should have listened to you." She smiled so softly he wanted to gather her into his arms.

Jim noticed the neatly addressed envelope lying on her desk. Miss Adelaide McAllister, Lincoln, Indiana. "Friend of yours?" he asked, indicating the letter with as much nonchalance as he could manage.

She swallowed. Her smile looked a bit forced. "A-a friend from my schooldays. I've . . . asked her advice on how to handle . . . Marty and the other troublemakers. She and I studied together to be teachers."

He nodded, smiling to show he believed her. "I'll walk you to the post office," he said, standing. Then he sniffed the air. "Smells like a livery barn in here."

She nodded with a rueful smile. "The morning wasn't without incident."

Jim's mouth tightened. "One of these days I'm going to

catch that boy at one of his pranks. I'm going to either turn him over my knee and give him a good caning, or —"

"I'd say he's too old to benefit from that."

"Or I'll beat a little respect into him with my fists." Jim flexed his hands.

"Isn't it a beautiful day?" Sadie said, slipping the letter into her pocket and leading the way out of the school. "Leave the door open to air the place. I'll come back later."

Jim shook his head as he joined Sadie in the sunshine. "I'll lock up for you later. You take the day off. Get some sleep."

She smiled up at him, her eyes strangely troubled, even a little frightened and sad. "Thank you for taking such good care of me."

Quickly, while she seemed approachable, he kissed her. "That's how you make me feel, Sadie. Protective." He wanted to draw her into his arms, but felt strangely that an invisible wall had sprung up between them where only a few hours before he had felt her clinging to his back on the horse, giving him lascivious ideas.

She was so changeable, so mysterious. He wanted to hold her and shake her and make her cling to him again, but she was like a frightened but determined wild creature, cornered by Otis's misbegotten boy and fighting on to the last. The last of what? he wondered.

They walked back toward town in silence. "You seem very thoughtful all of a sudden," Jim said. "Thinking of the newborn?"

"Oh . . . yes, in a way. I suppose it put me in mind of home." She chuckled, though she didn't meet his inquiring gaze. "Pay no attention to me, Jim. I get foolish when I've had too little sleep."

"Still got faith in Warren Bluffs?" he asked, annoyed by his insecurity.

She smiled up at him. "I have faith in you, Deputy."

"I want to see you tonight." His words were heavy with meaning. He needed to be reassured that she had not changed.

She glanced quickly away. "I want that, too, but —"

"We could go to dinner. We could sit and rock on Trudy's porch." He took her hand. That would have to do, he thought, wanting so much more.

While he waited for her reply, they walked all the way to Prairie Street. At last she spoke, her voice soft and faintly playful. "I think I'd like to have dinner with you, Deputy."

He wanted to hold her now and keep her to himself. She had such a strange wistfulness about her. It was as if she was counting the hours until something irreversible took her from him forever. He stopped, his thoughts filling him with alarm. He watched her hand tremble as she tucked her letter into the mail slot. Otis had written a letter. And now Sadie has written a letter, too.

Jim's hands drew into fists. When she glanced up at him, her eyes were faintly moist, her cheeks flushed. He could feel their moments together slipping away.

At six P.M. Jim arrived in front of the boarding house in a hired buggy. He was wearing his best suit, a dark worsted frock coat and matching trousers that he usually reserved for appearances before the circuit judges. He'd had his shoes shined, his hair trimmed, his nails buffed and his cheeks shaved to a shiny, nearly raw red. He'd endured the teasing of half the men and women in town who caught him looking like a young man going a-courting.

He *was* going courting, he thought with a flushed grin. He'd bought a nosegay of hand-made silk violets at the ladies' dress shop to present to Sadie. He wanted the entire town to know his purpose. He had taken Sadie to the bluffs with no more hope than to kiss her. He had struck pure gold with her, and yet he had thought he could not approach serious subjects with her so long as she kept secrets from him.

Now all that seemed like the excuses of a gun-shy bachelor. He loved Sadie. This night he intended to make that completely clear to everyone, especially her!

Sadie stepped out from Trudy's entry hall wearing a snug but simple gown embellished by none of the usual ruffles and doo-dads. She had coiled her hair into a mass of ringlets on top of her head, and completed the style with dangling sausage curls alongside her neck. There would be no unfurling her hair tonight, he thought with disappointment.

None the less, he trembled with desire for her and thought her the most beautiful woman in the world.

"Evening, Deputy," she said sweetly as her eyes swept admiringly over him.

"You look lovely," he said, offering the silk flowers.

"Oh." Her eyes lifted to his. "They'll always last, won't they?" she whispered, allowing him to pin them to her shoulder.

His hands trembled when he touched her.

The boarders watched from the parlor windows as he led her out and handed her up onto the buggy seat. Then they were driving away and grinning like two adolescents into the privacy of the darkness.

Sadie was still feeling a sense of bittersweet longing as they drove into town and stopped at the rustic little place that called itself a restaurant. She could think of little to say, for it seemed so wicked to lie to Jim when all she longed to do was throw open her heart and lay her life openly and honestly before him.

He had taken nearly as long to prepare for their evening together as she had. Feeling wildly confused and secretly afraid that every moment spent in this town was bringing her closer to disaster, Sadie thought how much she would have liked to be wearing a lovely silk gown of yellow with flounces of lace and a luscious petticoat beneath. Instead, she had to be content with this plain cast-off, knowing somehow that Jim saw beyond it to the woman he believed her to be.

For this night, she thought, and perhaps for the last time, she would go on being that woman.

They ate a simple but hearty meal in the surprisingly crowded restaurant. They talked of nothing important and spent more time smiling and blushing at one another than eating. Most of the patrons, they later realized, had come to watch them!

Miraculously, Sadie's melancholy mood lifted. In spite of the curious people watching her, she forgot her fears and her memories. As before, Jim's penetrating blue eyes and beguiling smile made her forget. She saw only his endearing face, his gaze fixed on her alone, telling her with a private twinkle that he desired her. She felt his love flowing around her like a warm wind. She savored each moment with him, memorizing this special night for safekeeping in the winter soon to come.

When again they boarded the buggy, she sat close to him, holding tightly to his arm, daring anyone to say she was wrong to want Jim's love and protection. "It was a wonderful dinner," she whispered. "Thank you."

Jim snapped the lines against the horse's rump and started back toward the boarding house. A cold wind ruffled his hair. The sky was black and low with storm clouds. Instead of turning at her street, however, he kept going, driving on around the courthouse circle to the road leading out of town toward his grandparents' house and the bluffs.

"Where are you going?" she said, tugging at his arm as the horse picked up its pace. A prickling of alarm started in her stomach.

"I'm taking you back to the place where we were able to leave the world behind," Jim said, his face shadowed.

"But we can't! You said we'd sit on the porch —!" She pulled away. "Jim, please!"

Jim turned to her and kissed her cheek lightly. "I want more than sparking from you, teacher."

She laughed softly, forcing the alarm from her voice. Didn't he know how helpless she was with him? Hadn't he already made her reckless, willing to allow something to happen between them that should never have been? "Please take me back before we completely scandalize everyone."

"Does it matter what anyone thinks of you? Aren't you trying to think of some way to tell me you're going away soon? Isn't that what your letter was for, to find another job?"

She went cold. She hugged his arm again, burying her face against his shoulder. "No, it wasn't about that at all! I told you. Jim, I can fight everyone in this town, but I can't fight you. I can hold out a little longer, if you can. Maybe Marty's left school for good. I can go on if he isn't there to torment me."

He gave a strange smile. "Can you?"

"Of course, if you don't compromise me." She put a hand to his cheek. "I do want to stay and be your . . . friend."

He went on smiling. "Reach into my breast pocket, Sadie."

"Why?"

"I have something for you."

She drew away, suddenly, afraid. "Stop the buggy, Jim. I'll walk back to town." She twisted away and started to climb down.

"Sadie!" he said, grabbing her arm. He tugged on the lines and the buggy rolled to a halt.

She was slipping to the dusty road before he could speak. In amazement, he watched her gather up her skirts and start back toward town. Then he leaped to the road and started after her.

"I can make it if —" She was panting, perhaps even weeping.

"Sadie, stop!" Jim said, striding to reach her. He swung her around and felt her struggle half-heartedly in his arms.

Then he kissed her, holding her gently as she continued to struggle. He tasted the salt of her tears on her lips and cheeks. Why was she crying now after all the other things that should have made her cry and didn't?

"I won't betray you!" he whispered against her lips. "I know you think I will —"

"I don't think that at all. Please, Jim! Let me go back to town. All we need is a bit more time. And yes, I was thinking of going away, but I can't. I do love you. Oh, God, I do love you!" She took his face in her trembling hands and kissed him.

Her passion was so startling, so arousing, Jim almost thought to make love to her there in the road scarcely half a mile from town. His arms encircled her in a possessive frenzy, and his mouth met the demands of her own. "Sadie, my love," he murmured against her lips. "I love you, too!"

He sensed she was throwing aside her fears and doubts. She was giving herself to him completely. He didn't understand why and, strangely, now he was even more afraid for her. He held her as if he would never let her go! "Marry me, Sadie!" he whispered hoarsely, burying his face in her neck. "Marry me!" He started to reach into his breast pocket.

"Oh, don't!" she cried, clinging to him, kissing him again and again, holding back his hand. "Don't ask. Let's just get into the buggy and go to the house. I want to be with you. I want this one night with you to remember for always."

He held her away, staring down into her tear-streaked face. "Tell me what you're hiding!" He began to shake her gently. "Tell me. Trust me!"

She let him shake her. She wanted to tell him, but the words were frozen inside of her. She began to cry openly, and finally he released her. He stood glaring down at her, trembling with fury.

"Why don't you trust me?"

She didn't respond.

He must never know, she thought with cold realization. She wanted to drop down in the dusty road and sob. She could not tell him. She would never willingly destroy what they had.

Her tears dried. She watched his face reflect the turmoil of his thoughts. Then he seized her shoulders. She felt the bite of his fingertips in her flesh.

"I don't care what's in your past!" he said with finality. "I love you."

He turned and dragged her back to the buggy. He pushed her up onto the seat and ran around to climb up beside her. He whipped the horse, and the buggy bumped wildly away from the town. Sadie held tightly to the seat, faintly terrified by Jim's anger. But he was taking her to the house, and they would have what they needed from each other one more time.

He didn't even unhitch the horse when he reined in at the yard of his grandparents' house. He pulled Sadie down after him and took her to the door, his determination rousing the flames of her need for him. He'd brought the key, she noted, as he unlocked the door. He'd intended to bring her here all along.

They lighted no lamps. They mounted the stairs to the bedroom where the four-poster stood covered with a sheet. He pulled the spread away carefully, exposing the bare mattress beneath. He sank to the edge of it and held out his arms. "Come to me, Sadie."

She went slowly into the circle of his arms. Carefully he untied her cape from around her neck as she unpinned her hat. Then she watched him unbutton her bodice and unhook her skirt. When she was standing before him in her corset and pantalets, she helped him to remove his coat, and his boots.

All was silence between them; words were their enemies, thoughts their downfall. She looked only at his eyes, at his hands pulling at her corset-cover ribbons and the laces of her stays. When she stepped out of her lacy drawers, she was naked in the darkened barren bedroom.

In the distance was the haunting howl of a prairie wolf. Wind whistled through a crack somewhere in the old deserted house. A few raindrops pelted the windowpane.

She heard none of it. She saw only Jim's eyes drinking in the fullness of her breasts, the delicate curve of her waist and the alluring swell of her hips. She belonged to him.

He pulled her close, holding her waist as he kissed her belly. Then he trailed his hands down over the curve of her bottom and along the backs of her thighs.

She couldn't move away from him.

When he looked up, she crouched, smothering his face with her breasts before unbuttoning his shirt. She spread the fabric back over his broad, warm shoulders and smoothed her palms over his satiny muscles.

This was the man she loved. This was all that mattered.

Suddenly he grabbed her and pulled her against him as he fell back onto the mattress. He held her tightly to him, relishing the feel of her soft warm breasts against his chest. She squirmed and laughed a little as he held her on top of him and then, cradling her bottom in his hands, he rolled her over and lay against her, mindful of the warm delicacy of her body quivering to his touch. He kissed her face slowly, tantalizingly, tasting every creamy inch.

He moved his hands around her hips to her belly, and then down to part her legs so that he could be as close to her as possible. She moaned against his neck, her breath quick and hot. "I love you," she whispered, her throat tight. "I love only you."

Then he kissed her deeply, feeling her body responding to the movements of his hands in the cradle of her thighs.

"Oh, Jim! Oh! . . . Jim . . ." she whispered.

She plucked at his waistband, but he would not let her find satisfaction so quickly. He moved his mouth to her breasts, and then to other recesses. She clutched at his hair and gasped with delight.

She was so sweet. So very sweet.

When he could no longer wait, he stood, looking down at her. She was so lovely, so delicate, so eager. He dropped his trousers to the floor and lowered himself over her writhing body. He felt her hands grasp at his back, tasted her mouth, felt her gasping breaths make her breasts push up against him.

He took possession of her, wanting to blot everything from her mind but his desire for her. He held her pinned to his body for what seemed like an eternity, a forever heaven of warmth and sweet satisfaction. He blotted everything from his own mind, sought the ultimate with her, and found in the brilliance of it that it was he who was possessed.

Chapter Thirteen

The sudden storm acted as Jim and Sadie's ally. When at last the wind and driving rain slackened enough for them to return to town, it was very late. Those who might have wondered what time Jim had returned Sadie to the boarding house had long gone to bed. And Sadie had good reason for her straggling, tangled hair — the storm had drenched them, "forcing them to take refuge at Jim's place."

Sadie lay awake in her own narrow bed at the boarding house for the rest of the night remembering what she and Jim had had there in his grandparents' house. It had been a taste of the happiness awaiting them, if only the future could be tamed.

She put all thoughts of leaving Warren Bluffs from her mind. In the morning she believed she'd been foolish to think anyone might discover what lay in her past.

Though there was talk as the days crept by, it became common knowledge that Jim and Sadie were courting. If the Cadwalladers had any opinion on the matter, they kept it to themselves. By Monday morning, Sadie arrived at the schoolhouse feeling amazingly optimistic. She loved Jim Warren! It seemed absurd to think that anything might go wrong when she had that magnificent passion to keep her smiling!

Even the children behaved well. Rehearsals resumed. Sadie refused to let herself worry about the vacant seat in the third row, relishing each day Marty remained away. She arrived and departed with her students, leaving no opportunity for trouble, and dined with Jim each evening.

She regretted sending the letter to her friend, for the trouble with Marty had passed, she was sure. She heard no gossip and encountered none of the Cadwalladers. Even the Shockley children seemed able to behave when Marty wasn't around to incite them to mischief.

For the first time Sadie dared to feel encouraged — and liked. Nevertheless, she had to stop by the post office early each morning to see if a reply had come to her letter. She hoped none would. By the end of the week she was convinced Adelaide had wisely decided not to answer.

On Thursday she passed the emporium relieved to forget her moment of weakness when she penned the letter. The postmistress came out just behind Sadie, flagging down Jim, who had been crossing the street to call a good morning to Sadie.

"Deputy! That letter you were expecting has just come. I just took it out of the mailbag. Morning, Miss Sadie. Now let me check — Oh, there's one for you, too! Isn't that nice!" She held both letters out.

Frost the night before had killed the last of the weeds and grasses drooping alongside the emporium. "Thank you," Sadie said with forced cheer as she took the letter. "I do believe winter is on its way."

"If it's not the heat, it's the cold. Well, would you look at this, Deputy!" the postmistress exclaimed, interrupting herself. "There's another letter for Sheriff Wheeler! He has been busy, hasn't he?"

Jim pocketed both letters. "I'll take them over to the jail," he said.

Sadie glanced as casually as she could at her letter, noting the unfamiliar return address. "That's strange," she said to herself as a charge of alarm went through her. "I-I hope she's all right."

She glanced up at Jim to see if he was going to walk her to the schoolhouse. "Everything all right with you?" she asked.

"Fine," he said, with a distracted smile. He nodded his thanks to the postmistress and started away. "I've got something to tend to, Sadie," he said. "I'll talk to you later."

A chill went through her as she watched him lope away. Something was different. Something had changed. Huddling beneath her cape, she rushed on toward the school. Halfway there she stopped and opened her letter.

Dear Miss Evans,

Knowing your need for discretion I am answering on my personal paper. Adelaide met with an accident shortly after a man calling himself Starling visited her. I regret to inform you that she has died. I've taken the liberty of thinking your problem through. It would be unrealistic to hope your new friends will be able to overlook your past circumstances. Involvement with men seems to be your downfall. I advise you to leave your position with all haste.

The letter was signed by a woman Sadie didn't know. For a moment she couldn't go on. Adelaide gone? It wasn't possible!

Aching with grief for her lost friend, Sadie tucked the letter deep in her bodice and glanced around to see if anyone had noticed her stopping. She forced herself to remain calm and to lay aside her grief. Everything would be all right. All she had to do was be patient!

The morning passed quickly in the schoolhouse as Sadie conducted a spelling bee. She was pleased to see the progress of her students, particularly in the first two grades. Cory Whithers triumphed over everyone, spelling "hippopotamus" with assurance, and soon it was time to dismiss for lunch. The day had warmed enough for Sadie to eat in the sun on the bench where she could see the ambling traffic on Prairie Street.

* * *

Sheriff Wheeler:
Your request for information puzzles me. I don't know nothing of any young woman named Sadie Evans ever living here. We got no boarding house run by any woman called Evans, and none with a daughter fitting the description you gave. You got the wrong town, friend.

Morley Rose, Sheriff,
Higginsville, Ohio

Jim stared at the letter, his teeth and jaw aching, a headache settling dully behind his eyes. All right, he thought. Sadie isn't from this town in Ohio.

That meant very little, he told himself, refolding the letter and tucking it back into the envelope. He wanted to thrust the sheriff's letter into the potbelly stove across the jail's main room, but he hesitated, wondering if he was going to have to show it to Sadie. She must have a good reason for saying she came from this town when she didn't, he told himself. By the end of the afternoon, however, he was determined to know from where she hailed.

The muscles in his neck were taut cords, and he had a feeling of dread building in his belly. What might be in her past didn't matter, he thought, trying to fit her into any number of roles, from scandalous actress to uninhibited harlot.

He laughed to himself over them all. It didn't matter. It just didn't! He loved her. But it galled him that she wouldn't tell him herself, that she wouldn't trust him, that he had had to read another man's mail to find out.

He pulled the second letter from his coat pocket and studied it. He had a feeling that when he opened it he would know her secret. Did he want to? He loved her as she was. Nothing from her past would change the woman she was at this very moment. And this very moment she was the woman he loved and wanted for his wife.

He put the unopened letter on the desk and rose to pour himself more bad coffee from the tin coffee boiler. He hadn't realized that Otis had written two letters. This one might have nothing to do with Sadie.

Chuckling humorlessly, he went back to the desk and sank into the chair. How many more letters had Otis written? How many telegraph dispatches might he have sent? At any moment Otis might receive a reply to one and learn the truth. Jim decided he had to know everything about Sadie to protect her.

He held the envelope over the steaming cup of coffee and watched the glue along the sealed edge soften and curl away. As he pulled out the letter inside, a newspaper clipping dated more than two years before fell onto the desk top, face up. His blood ran cold as he read.

CONNERSTON DAILY REPORTER

North Rushing, Indiana. After only three hours deliberation, jurors found notorious train robber Rayford Stark, his female companion, Sadie Whiting, and four others guilty in the train hold-up at Wicke's Crossing September 29th. Stark and his gang received fifteen years each to be served at Lanceville Prison. Miss Whiting's ten-year sentence was commuted to two at the Lincoln Women's Workhouse. Miss Whiting fainted upon hearing the verdict. Her widowed mother was restrained and carried out. Miss Whiting claimed innocence from the outset. Stark testified that the twenty-one-year-old woman had assisted his robberies by hiding "loot" in her bedroom. She was arrested with a valise containing twenty-five thousand dollars taken at gunpoint from the Wells Fargo agent plus valuables forcibly taken from passengers. Justice has served to rid our state of a gang thought responsible for robberies and murders throughout the Ohio River Valley.

Jim read the clipping three times before he was able to tear his eyes away. This news story had nothing to do with Sadie! It couldn't. Then sighing, he rubbed his eyes and opened the second letter.

. . . can't say as I have heard of any young women fitting your description. But the name does bring to mind a case that interested me a couple years back. I've enclosed my clipping . . ."

The letter was signed by the federal marshal in Kansas City. Ol' Otis was looking far and wide for information about Sadie, Jim thought with a nervous chuckle. Though the marshal had no reason to link the two women except by first name, Jim was beginning to have a dismal feeling that the damning detail was the "widowed mother."

The clipping crumpled as he closed his fist around it. Robbery. Prison. The companion of this outlaw named Stark. . . . He rubbed his aching eyes.

Rising abruptly from his seat, Jim jammed the clipping into his pocket. He thrust the two letters into the stove and watched them disappear in little flares of flame. How strong was his love? he asked himself as he turned to Otis's stack of wanted circulars received from lawmen from as far as a thousand miles away. After a search of several minutes, he pulled out a yellowed, tattered sheet, from three years back.

— WANTED —
* * * $1000 reward * * *

Rayford Stark. Aliases: Stanson, Storm, Stutts and more; age 30, 5'10", black hair, brown eyes; scars: bullet — left shoulder, knife — lower abdomen and right forearm, lash marks — back, nick — right ear. Wanted for: armed robbery, larceny, break-ins, confidence games, rape, possibly murder. Armed and dangerous. Personable.

Jim's heart was pounding so fast he couldn't think. Suddenly he was laughing out loud, roaring with the absurdity of it all. His Sadie, the companion of this outlaw? Never! He'd show her the clipping and the circular. They'd have a good laugh over it. She'd tell him her secret then, simply because nothing in her past could be as damaging as this.

He folded the poster and stuck it inside his shirt. His mind rushed back to the day Sadie had arrived in town. Not another person in Warren Bluffs had noticed what Marty and his little weasels had been doing that day. A person wouldn't recognize the pickpocketing tactics unless . . . unless that person knew a lot about thieving.

She had been so insistent about his arresting the boys. Had it all been a ploy designed to make him think. . . ?

He thrust the disloyal thoughts from his mind. Feeling disoriented, he pushed out into the street. He shivered but didn't return for his coat. He just starting walking, plodding along, unable to stop himself from going to Sadie.

It didn't matter. It didn't matter! he repeated to himself. Whatever she had done before, it didn't matter. It was over. She had come here to begin a new life, and he loved her! Dear God, he loved her!

He threw back his head. The clipping had been about some other woman named Sadie who had a widowed mother. His Sadie had never embraced all he fought to obliterate!

Rehearsals for the pageant were going so well Sadie decided the students needed to meet with her only twice a week. Everyone had gone home but Winnie — who had completed a new costume and was proudly modeling it for Sadie — when Jim marched up School Road late that afternoon and swung in through the gate.

Then he was at the door, standing there looking so tall and wonderful with his sun-streaked hair whipped by the cutting wind outside. He wore no coat, only a soft blue chambray shirt stuck hastily in his denims. One side of his leather vest flapped in the wind, the tin star pinned on it winking in the slanting afternoon sun.

His face was red, accentuating his penetrating blue eyes. For a moment Sadie looked at him, seeing nothing but his eyes, thinking of nothing but the way the clear pale blue felt as it sliced through her like the bitter breeze swirling in the open doorway. She had never seen his eyes look so piercing. Or his mouth so hard.

"Oh, hello," she said, sounding feeble in the face of whatever great turmoil filled his mind. "Winnie, you can run along now. I'll walk back to town with Deputy Warren."

Winnie looked up at Jim with the glowing eyes of an adoring admirer. She changed out of her costume in the cloakroom and donned her jacket and bonnet. "Afternoon, Miss Evans," she said, giggling as she tied on her bonnet.

The moment the young girl was out the door, Jim took two more steps into the schoolroom. He closed the door softly, holding it as if to keep everyone and everything out. His eyes never left Sadie's face.

Sadie wanted to laugh and ask what demon had chased him to the schoolhouse, but the burning penetration of his eyes kept her silent. She rubbed her arms to warm them and then stopped, arrested by the strange humorless twist to Jim's face.

Jim searched her beautiful puzzled features for the reassurance he so desperately wanted. Her black hair was slightly mussed, hanging in tendrils at her temples and nape just as it had that first day. He wanted to seize her and shake out her pins and kiss her. He wanted to ravish her there in the sanctity of the schoolroom. He wanted to drive the doubts from his brain. He wanted her back for himself. But now . . .

No, he told himself. No! All he wanted was to ask her, to hear her say the clipping referred to some other woman named Sadie.

He couldn't remember what he'd done with the clipping. Then he had to tear his eyes from her. Her expression was so soft as she looked up at him, so trusting in spite of her silence. She believed he'd never hurt her, that he'd never betray her. Was he about to now, he wondered?

He swallowed, startled to feel a thickness in his throat. He wanted to say something to prove he didn't for a moment think she had once helped rob a train. He tried to imagine her holding a gun to a Wells Fargo agent or to a coach filled with trembling, terrified passengers.

His cheeks tightened into a semblance of a smile. The light was going out of her eyes. She was growing frightened. He had to speak. In that terrible moment he knew what she would be saying when he asked.

His shoulders lowered. The tightness left his back. He found the crumpled clipping in his shirt pocket and pulled it out. He smoothed it flat as if it was very precious, very fragile. All at once he felt old and tired. His heart became as heavy as a stone.

"I know who you really are, Sadie," he said softly, his husky voice filled with finality. "I know what you did."

Just as if he had thrust a knife into her breast, he watched the light in her face twist with pain. Her face went frighteningly white, as if she was dying before his eyes. She sagged, as if her legs had gone weak. Trembling visibly, she reached to grasp the desk for support and missed. She laughed sadly, her lips beginning to twitch with scarcely controlled tears.

The wash of icy hot terror that flooded her veins was worse than anything she had ever known. Her mind dimmed, and she fumbled again to grip the edge of her desk.

Everything began whirling. She could hear a droning voice

in the distance of her memory, a voice that had made her mother shriek with despair, a voice that had made Sadie's innocence and trust wink out forever. "Guilty! Guilty! Guilty!"

But she was not back in the town where she had grown up. She was here in a schoolroom with four rows of desks and Jim standing in the doorway. A red apple that Olive's grandson had brought that morning stood on the corner of her desk. Her books were stacked there, and the words on the blackened wall boards showed three months of progress of children who had known no teacher in nearly a year.

This was her new world. She'd chosen it, fought for it, and made it her own. She had believed that if she tried hard enough she could stay and make a new life for herself. She had wanted to believe it could be done.

But the other world had betrayed her innocence. Her own world had long betrayed her trust. She should not have been so foolish as to think she could start again. Her future was the factories of the East or the dance halls of the West, where she could disappear and no one would know or care about her past. That was the future Rayford Storm had left her to.

She lifted her eyes and saw the anguish written on Jim's face. Oh, dear Lord, how she loved him! How she hated to see the look in his eyes that revealed all she knew he must be thinking.

He thought he knew who she really was! He thought he knew what she had done. And he believed. She felt a blinding pain in her heart. He believed!

His love had been such a healing thing for her. She had given herself to him. She had given him everything. He had said he wouldn't hurt her, wouldn't betray her. . .

Now she could see that she had hurt him, just as she feared she would. She had betrayed him by all the lies she had been forced to tell from the very first moment they met.

She heard herself say, "Oh," again. Now that everything was crumbling between them, she knew their love had been a dream from the first. Now they were finally meeting as the strangers they really were. This was their beginning. That other time — those moments in each other's arms — had been between two imaginary people, now lost forever to reality.

Her sudden sense of relief was almost dazzling. Though she didn't want to leave Warren Bluffs, for this one quiet moment she was again the young woman she had been months before arriving in the dusty little town. How good it felt to remove the heavy mantle of lies she'd worn for so many weeks.

With Jim, the lies were now done. She looked up at him with all the love she held trembling in her heart and wondered if he was all she believed him to be. Or was he lies, too? She could see he was growing more and more troubled because she was not denying his words.

She loved him, she thought sadly, but she had feared all along that he wouldn't understand what lay in her past. She drew herself erect, steeling herself against the pain throbbing in her heart, and turned away to get her cape and hat. The schoolroom felt very cold. The fire had gone out.

"I was afraid I would hurt you," she whispered from the safety of the cloakroom.

He said nothing until she came out again. He had moved closer and was holding out a newspaper clipping.

She recognized that particular one even at a distance. "That was one of the kinder ones," she said softly. "And it didn't include a picture."

He caught himself and made a strange choking sound as if he expected her to read it and deny it.

She tried to smile. "Yes, Jim. I am Sadie Whiting. *That* Sadie Whiting. I spent the last two years in prison. I'm not twenty-five. I'm twenty-three. The woman who recommended me for this job was my prison matron. Adelaide McAllister."

He jerked a folded piece of paper from his shirt, opened it and held it out. The name leaped out at her. *Rayford Stark.* She had to look away. She didn't want to cry now. No amount of tears would wash away the stain of her past.

So, she thought, it wasn't the crime, the sentence or the prison term she'd served that made Jim's eyes look so cold and dark, but the man who had betrayed her. The man in her past.

She shivered as she brushed past Jim. If he could believe that she had ever given Ray what she had given him. . . .

How could Jim know that she hadn't, she asked herself as she emerged in the chilled, growing dusk. He had just learned that everything he knew about her was false. She was a stranger. Tears welled in her eyes in spite of her vow never to cry over her lost innocence again.

She lifted her skirts and began running. Jim didn't call after her.

Chapter Fourteen

At the last minute Sadie cut across the field to the park and slipped back to the boarding house from the rear. She couldn't think. Memories she had managed to repress for months were whirling in her mind, making her reckless.

She saw Ray's face swimming before her burning eyes almost as clearly as if she was seeing him there sitting across from her at her mother's dining table. Sadie saw it all so clearly. She was there again in her mother's boarding house that first time Rayford Storm had smiled at her, really noticed her as a person, as a young woman.

Her mother had just said something about the pie she was serving, when Ray had looked up, his eyes suddenly smoldering and mysterious. While Sadie's mother was turned away to cut another piece, Ray looked at Sadie, studying her, thinking his mysterious thoughts and finally letting his provocative gaze rest on Sadie's bodice. She had felt afire.

"Sadie baked this herself," her mother was saying.

"What else are you good at, Miss Whiting?" he asked, letting his beautifully shaped lips blossom into a blazing, irresistible smile.

Sadie understood now what he had meant. At the time she had thought him interested only in her virtues as a prospective wife. She couldn't have guessed that he was sizing her up for something far different.

That summer Ray became like a member of the family, helping with the heavy chores around the boarding house, even though he was tired after a long day on the road selling his lightning rods. He was charming, eager to help, lavish with his praise for Sadie and her mother's cooking, and for Sadie's obvious virtues as a young lady of spotless reputation.

He began staying in the drawing room after supper each night rather than going out. While discussing the weather, or something Sadie had just read, Ray's eyes strayed, but he was perfectly content to play the gentleman. Sadie dared to believe she had found that rarity, a man she could love forever.

Now she was still running from him. Halfway across the grassy lot behind the boarding house, Sadie realized she had been rushing along in a daze. If she had seen anyone, she hadn't been aware of it. It would seem very strange to Trudy if she arrived by the back way. She couldn't think, couldn't imagine what her next step should be. She went on, around the portico to the front steps. Alvinia was giving a lesson. Mr. Charles and Mr. Bennett were on the veranda, rocking, their knees covered with woolen lap robes, grimacing each time the voice pupil hit a sour note.

"Afternoon," Sadie said, barely meeting their eyes as she rushed inside.

Trudy was laying the table. "Goodness, it's getting cold out there! Tell those foolish men to come in before they catch their death. Supper's almost ready." Then Trudy paused as Sadie rushed past. "Sadie, are you all right? You look . . . peculiar."

Sadie drooped at the foot of the stairs. She forced herself to keep back the words that wanted to gush out and destroy her charade. She covered her eyes with a trembling hand. Whenever she was nervous, she felt faint. "I've felt ill all afternoon. I must be coming down with the grippe. I think I'll stay in my room tonight."

Trudy looked as if she wanted to lay her hand on Sadie's forehead.

"I don't want you to catch anything," Sadie said, holding out her hand to keep Trudy away. She rushed up the stairs.

"I'll send for the doctor!" Trudy called up.

"No, please! I'll be perfectly all right. I just need . . . rest."

"Can I bring you a tray later?" Trudy looked stubbornly determined to follow and minister to Sadie's needs.

Sadie shook her head and made a face as if to say she had no appetite. "Please, Trudy. I'll . . . oh, please!" She dashed to her room and pressed the door closed behind her.

The silence rang in her ears. She turned the key in the lock. Her head was spinning so fast she had to sit down. She did feel ill!

Think! she commanded herself. Jim wouldn't betray her. He'd say nothing. She could go on as before, at least long enough to secure another job. But what was the use of going on without him? How could she face another hostile, suspicious, self-righteous town?

Dear Lord, how had he learned about her? If he had suspected her and had written to someone . . . . Who would he write to? It didn't matter! She couldn't stay.

Dizzily, she rose and started pulling her clothes from the hooks behind the door and dropping them unfolded into the trunk by the window. How would she be able to leave without explaining — or lying — to Trudy? If she left, she must go with whatever she could carry!

Gasping for breath, she staggered to the window and threw it open. The prairie looked so vast, so lonely and desolate. She drew huge gulps of the cold air into her lungs, hoping her head would clear, but it only made her more dizzy. To begin again, more alone than ever, knowing she would not be able to make a single friend . . . .

She sank to the bed suddenly, grabbed up her pillow and smothered her face in it. Teaching again was out of the question. Such a job put her in touch with too many people.

There was really only one choice left. She'd been a fool to run from it. Only one profession accepted a woman with an alias.

In her memory loomed Stark's saturnine face and his sultry brown eyes. "I love you, Sadie," he had whispered late that summer. "Come walking with me this afternoon."

She had strolled into town to buy groceries with him, but always she kept him at arm's length, as she'd been taught to do. She accepted none of his offered gifts of jewelry. Even at the time she had thought it odd that he should possess so many mementoes belonging to his "dear, dead mother."

"Let's walk to the end of the lane and find a place to sit," he said at least a thousand times. "We're never alone."

"You know I can't do that, Ray," she said sweetly and primly as usual. "If you want to talk we can sit on the porch swing."

And they had, but that had led quickly to chaste kisses and, finally, groping, which he claimed he was unable to control. "I can't keep my mind off you!" he always said, thrilling her. He seemed to enjoy risking being seen kissing her.

If Ray got too bold, she always rose like a queen and went inside for the evening. She had behaved with Rayford Storm as a perfect young lady beyond reproach. She had known what she was doing, too. Willing to settle for nothing less, she was leading him relentlessly toward a proposal of marriage.

Rayford resisted, just as her mother had said he would. He went off for days, though he always returned saying he hadn't been able to stay away. Eventually, he had the run of the house. Her mother wondered aloud if it was proper to have an eligible boarder when her daughter was of marriageable age. "You might have to leave soon," she said once to Ray, hoping to force his hand.

"I couldn't." He looked stricken. "Haven't I behaved like a complete gentleman?"

"Certainly," her mother said. "But I do have to consider my daughter's prospects, and there has been some talk among my friends."

Only once had Sadie seen Ray near her bedroom door, and she had asked him what he was doing there. His room was at the head of the stairs on the second floor. She shared hers with her mother off the kitchen. She was afraid he had been thinking of compromising her.

"I thought I heard mice," he said, later causing an uproar as he insisted on searching every room. He found the mice, too, and began making regular checks, placing and emptying the traps and convincing everyone, boarders and townspeople alike, that he was gradually taking over the duties of the man of the house.

In September he made his manly needs clear to Sadie. "I can't go on living so near you and . . . suffering," he said, his eyes seductive, his hands stealing closer and closer to her breasts when they sat together on the porch swing.

"I'm very sorry you're suffering," she said demurely, not quite certain at the time what suffering he referred to. "But if you don't stop trying to . . . touch me, I'll have to go in!"

He had kissed her then, kindling her youthful fires. "What will make you give in?" he had whispered.

Her mother had schooled her well. She knew just what to say. "Our only hope of intimacy is . . . within the sanctity of . . ." She wasn't actually to say the word marriage, for that would be too forward of a well-bred, decent young lady. It was up to Ray to say he wanted to marry her.

She had struggled with him that night. And the next. And each night she despaired that he would ever propose. Finally one day he returned to the boarding house after a two-day absence. He was strangely cheerful, laughing with a twinkle and looking like the cat that had just stolen the very last of the cream. He wore a new suit and sported a large, valuable stickpin in his cravat. His hair was perfectly brushed and gleamed with macassar oil. In his hand he clutched a nosegay of fresh flowers.

On the porch he got down on bended knee. "Miss Sadie, will you consent to be my wife?"

"Oh, yes, Rayford!" she had whispered without hesitation, throwing her arms around his neck and kissing him full on the mouth.

"I know your mother can't afford the expense of a wedding," he whispered quickly, taking both her hands so that she couldn't rush inside to tell her mother the delightful news. "And besides, I know young girls as beautiful as you love romance. Let's slip away by moonlight and elope." He kissed her hungrily.

She drew away. "But my mother would be heartbroken to miss my wedding!"

"I have always longed to carry away my bride in secret . . . and enjoy her in privacy. You know how newlyweds are hounded in these small towns, their most intimate desires paraded before everyone. On our wedding night do you want to find a cowbell tied to the bedsprings? Do you want your mother and each and every boarder to know the exact moment we climb into bed together?"

Sadie had agreed to elope.

Now she looked down at the double-wedding-ring quilt on her narrow bed and laughed to think she had ever been convinced by that. A jangling cowbell even during the most intimate moments of her wedding night consummation would have been better than the fate she chose.

She jumped then at the sound of knocking at her door.

"Sadie, I'm terribly sorry to disturb you, but Jim's here to see you. I told him you're not feeling well, but he's being very insistent. I don't think he's himself. I've never seen him like this. Should I try to convince him to come back some other time?" Trudy tapped again. "Are you all right?"

Sadie tried to keep her voice even. "I'd rather not see him just now, if you don't mind." Her heart was suddenly racing. Wasn't Jim done with her? Had she misread his reaction?

Trudy rattled the doorknob until Sadie dragged to her feet and turned the key, opening the door. Trudy looked understandably agitated. Her eyes widened. "You haven't even taken off your hat and cape! I'm sending for Dr. Hamlin!"

"Don't trouble yourself, please," Sadie pleaded, trying to smile. She managed to look green. "Ask Jim to stop by in the morning. We'll talk then, on the way to school."

She had to keep going, she told herself. She had to keep pretending!

"You're not going to teach school if you're ill!" Trudy said. "You look as if you need —"

Jim stormed up the stairs. He had gotten his coat and his cheeks were red. His expression was strange, though perhaps not as dark as it had been at the schoolhouse.

"Jimmy, she's indisposed!" Trudy exclaimed, looking astonished and faintly scandalized. "You must go back down at once!"

Jim pressed Sadie's door wide. "You'll excuse us," he said to Trudy. "Sadie and I need to talk privately."

Trudy's broad face worked with a thousand bewildered thoughts. "Is something wrong? Have the two of you had a spat?" Then her expression cleared as understanding dawned. "Why didn't you say so, Sadie? Of course you both must talk. But Jim, you can't stay but a minute. Sadie doesn't look at all well. And you may not go in her room! If you need privacy, use the parlor."

Jim withered Trudy's knowing smile with an expression of blazing impatience. Looking hurt, Trudy thundered down the stairs.

Then he turned to Sadie. His voice was barely audible. "I shouldn't have let you leave without saying anything more to you. I'm sorry, and I'm sorry for embarrassing you this way, but I feel you owe me an explanation."

"I don't have to explain myself to anyone," she whispered, trying to close her door on him. Just to have him near brought her intense heartache. "Believe anything you like about me, Jim. It doesn't concern me. I'll leave on the first —"

"I want you to tell me your side of the story! I expect you to, because we were friends — and I hope we still are. The clipping does say that you claimed innocence . . . ." He forced the door inward again.

She whirled on him. "I did, and in spite of that everyone I knew reacted to the accusations just as you did. They believed them. No one believed I was innocent. Not even my own mother!"

He cautioned her to lower her voice. "*I* believe you, Sadie. I want to hear your side. You owe me that." He turned to the side. "It's just a little misunderstanding, Trudy," he called down the stairs. "She's not ill at all. Just sulking."

"I'm doing no such thing!" Sadie cried, coming back to the door. "Oh, Jim," she whispered. "What possible difference can explaining make to you or anyone in this town? Even if the truth doesn't get out now, it will soon enough. I was foolish to hide it, foolish to think I could teach. I have no choice but to go."

His eyes shot to the clothes hanging out of the trunk. Then he seized her arm and forced her down the stairs. "Come on! We're going out for a short walk, Trudy. Don't worry if we're gone long. We may get dinner somewhere after we've made up."

Sadie saw him wink at Trudy. He steered Sadie out onto the porch, thrusting her hat and cape into her hands. Trudy caught the wobbling hall tree he'd snatched them from. The temperature outside had dropped considerably since nightfall.

"This is ridiculous. You'll have the whole town talking about us!" Sadie hissed, throwing the cape around her shoulders. Her teeth were chattering.

"Which only proves how much you want to stay," Jim said shortly.

"What I want means very little in the face of what people will think of me once they hear I am a former convict," she whispered.

"Don't call yourself that."

"It's what I am! It can't be erased." She struggled against his grip on her arm. "I don't want to explain myself to you or anyone! You've already made up your mind about me. One newspaper clipping and everything you knew about me became void."

"You know that's not true," Jim said, guiding her firmly down the walk to the street. The livery buggy stood waiting. "Get in. I admit I'm shaken by what I learned today, and — all right, I did wonder for a moment if it was true. Can you blame me? If you're not guilty, you certainly have acted the part with this story you cooked up about your background."

She managed to jerk free. "Tell me the name of a single town that will hire a woman fresh from prison as their school-marm!"

"Will you get in the buggy, please?" he said softly.

With a whimper of frustration, she finally allowed him to hand her up.

"We're going to go somewhere private, and I want the whole story. Nothing left out, regardless of what you might think I will feel about hearing it. I want the whole truth and nothing but. You're not running away any more. Whatever happened to you, we'll fight it. If you were innocent, we'll appeal the judgement."

Her hiss burned her throat. "*If!* Always that horrible word, '*if!*' I *am* innocent, Jim, but that is no longer the point. The point is, I was in prison for two years! Nothing will ever change that! You can't convince me this town or any other will accept such a background in their schoolteacher even if my name *is* cleared. I lived among thieves and prostitutes. I shared their food, listened to their stories, learned their curses. I was *one of them!*"

"People will accept you as my wife," Jim said flatly, turning the buggy and urging the horse to a trot.

Her breath went out. "Are you just being stubborn about this, Jim? I can't marry you!"

He laughed a little. "You know I still love you. Would I be here if I didn't?"

"At this very moment you don't sound very much like you love me," she snapped, wishing she could get away from him. "You sound bitter, and you sound as naive as I once was." She didn't want to be forced to tell that stupid, humiliating story all over again.

He seized her, letting the lines fall and the horse find his own way out of town. "Maybe no one has ever loved you as much as I do, Sadie. Love isn't all flowers and kisses. Sometimes it's fury!" He scorched her lips with a bruising, demanding kiss that let her taste no small portion of his anguish.

"You're hurting me!"

"I want to . . . to shake you for not trusting me with your secret, for leaving me to find out by accident, in the way most likely to make me doubt you. You could have told me everything right from the first. No, you had to lie and make me think there was another man still in your heart, or . . . I don't know what I thought! It wouldn't have made any difference then, and it doesn't now!"

"I wish I could believe that," she whispered as he grabbed up the lines again.

The cold wind tugged at her hair. She was frightened of his anger and his so-called furious love. How could she convince him she was innocent? She hadn't been able to convince a judge and twelve good and honest people from her own home town!

How could it not make a difference? She was changed! She was forever ruined by the life she had led for two years behind those high gray stone walls, with those creatures and the lessons in reality they had taught her.

"You'd better believe it doesn't matter to me," Jim said with soft emphasis. "It's just possible we can still keep this quiet."

Her heart twisted with the hopelessness of it all. "And if we can't?"

Sadie thought at first that Jim was taking her to his grandparents' house, but he passed it, drove the buggy across the fording place in the river and continued up a barely visible twin track that eventually brought them to the top of the bluff.

From there she could see Warren Bluffs huddled in the curve of the river. Darkness had fallen. All across town yellow light spilled from windows, and the smell of wood smoke drifted on the cold night wind. Jim hadn't lit the lantern. The moon rose and the stars came out. The cold settled over them. Jim slipped his arm around her shivering shoulders.

She felt cold as she began her story. She told Jim she was really from North Rushing, Indiana. She told him of her years living with her mother and their various boarders. She told him of her years away at high school.

Then she told him of the day a man calling himself Rayford

Storm took the room at the head of the stairs, a man who supposedly sold lightning rods, who parted his hair down the middle and slicked it back with fragrant pomade. He had always paid his rent on time and acted the perfect gentleman.

"Get to the part I want to know about," Jim said impatiently in the darkness, his hand hard but reassuringly firm on her shoulder.

"I am trying to tell you the whole truth, as you insisted," Sadie said, her teeth chattering more from nerves than cold. "I want you to understand — if you can — how I came to be involved with that . . . man."

He sighed heavily.

"He proposed in September," Sadie said at the conclusion of her brief description of Ray's courting. "He said we would elope the following Saturday night. He gave me some money to hire a buggy and said for me to meet him a Wicke's Crossing where the train tracks crossed the road to Connerston."

"Sounds like a strange kind of elopement to me," Jim muttered. "Weren't you suspicious?"

"Are you going to listen or keep interrupting?"

"I'm going to listen."

"Of course, I was uneasy about the whole thing. I knew my mother would be heartbroken to miss my wedding. But I did think an elopement sounded exciting . . . and I was embarrassed whenever I thought of the cowbell."

"Cowbell?" Jim asked, his voice scoffing.

She had omitted any reference to Ray's desires for her. She explained haltingly about her determination to avoid having everyone know when they got into bed by the ringing of the cowbell tied to the bedsprings.

Jim gave a bitter laugh. "You were worried about a little thing like that?"

"Yes!" she cried. "I don't think you can imagine what an innocent I was! I had no more notion of what was done in the marriage act than a vague fantasy of kissing and touching. I knew nothing else. I swear!"

Jim said nothing.

She forced herself to continue. "Ray said he was going to go to Connerston to find a justice of the peace and rent us a room for the night. He made me think he was planning something wonderfully romantic."

"How?"

"He said the word suite, not room. I imagined a bridal suite at one of Connerston's finest hotels. He said he had to buy a wedding suit, and that he was going to pick up something very special for me to wear. Mother and I had always been so very careful with money. If I had not agreed to elope, I believed I would have to wear my Sunday dress and be glad for even that much. Ray made me imagine an elegant lace gown . . . ." Her voice fell to a whisper. "I was completely taken in by my girlish fancies."

"All right, he convinced you to rent a buggy and meet him . . ."

"Yes, there at the rail crossing. I did as he asked. I was frightened but excited. I slipped out after mother was asleep. I rented the buggy from a man I'd known all my life. Ray had said for me to tell him that mother had suddenly been taken ill and had to be rushed to Connerston for an operation."

"The man didn't offer to help, or fetch a local doctor?"

"Our local doctor was a drunk. And it was common knowledge that Ray and I were courting. The livery man knew my mother trusted Ray enough to let him take over many responsibilities around the boarding house. If I said Ray had sent me to get a buggy to take my mother to a competent doctor, I would be believed. Ray had a way about him . . . ."

She waited for Jim to offer some other question. He didn't.

"I arrived at the crossing only moments after the night train passed by. The smell of the engine's smoke was still in the air. It was cold that night, like it is now. I heard some rustling in the bushes, and Ray came out carrying a valise . . ."

Her memory carried her back to that dark, chilly night. She was huddled in the buggy, fretting about what lay ahead for her in the hotel bridal suite and worrying about her mother. Ray's oiled hair was mussed as he emerged from the bushes along the tracks. He had a strange glitter in his eyes that told her he was thinking of the night ahead, too. Or so she thought.

"Have you been here long?" he called out, running to the buggy and climbing aboard. "Let's go!"

"But Ray —"

He tore the lines from her hands and lashed the rented horse's back until they were hurtling along, bouncing and banging in the ruts of the road. The valise fell heavily to the buggy's floor panels. She grabbed it up and held it, thinking of the fine wedding suit and lace gown Ray had bought for them inside it.

"Did the train stop and let you off?" Sadie asked, wondering how he had come to be at the crossroads, miles from town.

"That's what I did all right. Stopped the train and got off. Are you excited, my darling Sadie? Will you be ready to give yourself to me tonight after we're married? All of yourself?"

She tried to hug his arm, but they rolled along so fast and bounced so hard she couldn't. "Yes, if you agree to be . . . gentle."

"Gentle? Oh, I'll be gentle," he laughed.

When they were several miles away, Ray reined in abruptly and grabbed her. His lips closed fully over hers. His tongue thrust deeply into her mouth, forcing her back until she was almost lying in his arms.

"Oh, please! You said you'd be gentle!" she cried, trying to push him away.

"Can't say no any more," Ray hissed, his hands closing over her bodice.

He was almost on top of her, ravishing her mouth, moving against her in a way that told her he had no intention of being gentle, no capability of it.

She had almost screamed in terror as her bodice began to open to his insistent, knowledgeable fingers. She felt his kisses burn a trail to her throat. She could still feel the way his day's growth of whiskers scraped her chin raw.

Then came a moment of confusion as a bright light flared somewhere to the side of the buggy. Another flared, and then another. She tore her face free and stared as several riders circled in close, all huge threatening shadows. They held torches high so that every detail was revealed — her half-opened bodice, Ray's hands on a determined route up beneath her skirts.

Ray fell away from her with a muttered curse, saw the men and at once lashed at the horse. Two mounted men ahead seized the horse's harness.

"Run, Sadie!" Ray shouted, diving from the side of the buggy, landing and rolling, trying to make a dash for the cover of the woods.

Half a dozen men were on him at once.

For a bewildered, completely innocent moment Sadie thought the men were defending her against Ray's ungentlemanly attack.

"It's all right," she said, clutching her bodice closed. "He was just a little overexcited. We're . . . eloping tonight."

The mounted men crowding around the buggy laughed. Sadie made no move to get down. She waited trustingly as one large man dismounted and came to the side. He wore an ornate tin star on his coat and held a long-barreled pistol pointed right at her breast!

"Kindly hand over that valise, little lady."

"It has our wedding clothes in it! If you've come to rob us . . ."

"Your stories ain't going to work on us, little lady. Wedding clothes? Well, I got to give you credit. It's a unique idea, but I ain't so stupid as you and your partner there seem to think." He seized the valise, threw it to the ground and jerked it open. Then he lifted several banded bundles of greenbacks into the glare of the torchlight. "Planning to wear this to bed tonight, was you? What a pretty sight! Sorry to spoil your plans, honey, but you and your lover-man there is hereby arrested for the robbery of the night train out of Connerston about an hour ago."

"There's been a mistake!" Sadie said in horror. "Tell them, Ray! Tell them we're on our way to be married! You must have picked up the wrong valise — Ray? Ray!" She wanted to grab the reins and lash the horse herself, but the sheriff was reaching for her.

Ray was chuckling from the darkness. "Don't she lie like a queen, boys? I guess you got me this time, but there ain't a jailhouse that can hold me. You know that. I got friends all over these woods!"

"Don't count on it, Stark," the sheriff said, jerking Sadie to the road, where he held her with one iron-hard arm clamped around her chest.

"I haven't done anything!" Sadie screamed, fighting to pry his hand from her breasts. "You can't arrest me!"

"Little lady, I got you red-handed! You met this varmint at the crossing where he jumped the train. If we'd waited here in the woods another minute or two he would've given us quite a lot to look at. Next time we'll time it better, eh, boys?" he laughed, giving Sadie a knowing wink. "I got to admit I never would have thought this sort of thing of you, Sadie. I hate to think what this'll do to your ma. Unless there's more we don't know about. Maybe she's in on it, too. Wouldn't be surprised."

"It's just me and Sadie on this one," Ray said as he was led away. "You can see that it's been one of my more enjoyable jobs. Forget the story about eloping, Sadie," Ray called back from a distance. "They got us on this one, but we'll make it work somewhere else. I tell you, boys, this little gal is one of the best I've ever worked with."

Sadie's heart pounded as she remembered how long it had taken her to comprehend and believe the things Ray said that night. "I still don't know why he found such pleasure in making everyone think we had been working together all along," she said softly to Jim. "It didn't make his sentence any lighter. In fact, he all but confessed to the crime right there in the road. And he never stopped telling elaborate stories about how I had ridden out at night to pull jobs with him. There were even witnesses who said he'd been seen with a woman."

Sadie fell silent. Suddenly she was exhausted. "I truly

think," she said after a long pause, "that what convicted me was not the valise full of stolen money and valuables, and not the things found hidden in my room, which I knew nothing about, but the fact that when the sheriff and his men arrested me there on the road, Ray was . . . was trying to . . ."

She couldn't forget the picture she had presented to those men that night, her breasts half exposed and her legs partially showing.

"They decided I was a hussy, and treated me accordingly. They took us back to North Rushing and put us both in jail, in cells side by side. A man came by and took pictures of me. Just me. I heard the wagon with the extra editions of Connerston's *Daily Reporter* arrive just after dawn. They hawked them for sale right outside the jailhouse door. That's what my mother heard after she was awakened by the sheriff's deputy banging on her door. I'll never forget her face as she came into the jail that morning. I told her . . . I told her I was completely innocent, that Ray was telling gross lies about me . . . but the sheriff took her aside. He told her bluntly and crudely what he and his men had seen. I could hear her crying. She left without speaking to me."

"Why didn't she believe you?" Jim asked, his voice thick and soft, as if he was sharing her pain.

Sadie shook her head. "When people came to ask questions, I only shook my head. I was utterly crushed with humiliation. The man I thought I had loved was sitting in the very next cell having a marvelous laugh at my confusion. He told any and all who cared to listen that I had been intimate with him almost from the first day he took up residence in my mother's boarding house. He said I wouldn't stop pestering him for the . . . the sexual satisfaction he could give me. He said I was . . ."

She began to laugh hysterically. If Rayford Stark had been there at that moment she almost thought she could have killed him and delighted in it.

"He said I was insatiable! That I . . . begged him for acts that in fact I had no idea existed in a sane world. At night, alone in those cells, he described those acts for me. That's where I learned the facts of life, Jim. I think for a time he rendered me insane."

Jim took her into his arms suddenly and crooned softly to her. "Sh-h-h, I've heard enough."

"But there's more!" she cried. "There was the trial. And the faces staring at me. I testified, and people snickered. I never knew ordinary people could be so vicious. It was as if they were delighting in my degradation. It was an orgy of insinuation and imagination. When I was sentenced, mother lost her senses and behaved like a madwoman! I was taken away from North Rushing in a wagon fitted with iron bars. They didn't allow me to see my mother so I could try to comfort her. They told me I'd done enough."

Jim hugged her.

"It doesn't matter now. I cried out my heart on the way to the workhouse. Then I learned soon enough that crying was a sign of weakness. If I was to survive, I had to be strong. And I became strong. I remember seeing the high gray walls as we drove nearer the prison. The driver was making some kind of offer to me, something about letting me escape if I would let him enjoy some of what Ray had told everyone about. It was useless to reply to the man. He had a whip and would have used it on me."

"He should have been fired," Jim hissed.

"He could have stopped and had his way anyway. I was lucky he didn't. That I came out of that prison still a virgin was miraculous. Certain women took gratification wherever they found it. And others paid guards to smuggle men in. I came under the protection of Adelaide, a good strong woman. She kept me apart from the rest. I spent my time studying the books she brought me. In all respects she was a good and decent friend to me, though I was aware her feelings for me were . . . not just those of a mere friend."

Sadie went on to explain the letter she had received saying Adelaide had died in an accident, and Jim told her of the two letters he had received. "I can only hope that Otis hasn't written other letters. If I can convince the postmistress to keep quiet about the ones she gave me . . ."

So, Sadie thought. Otis Wheeler suspected her. "Will the postmistress mention the letter?" Sadie whispered. The wind whipped her hair across her face.

"I'll think of something to tell her."

Sadie was silent for a long time, basking in the warm, strong arm around her. It was the kind of comfort she had longed for. "I can almost believe you think I'm telling the truth," she whispered at last.

He hugged her. Then he chuckled just a little. "I do believe you!"

"You sound as if you were afraid you weren't going to," Sadie said.

"If I'm to be honest, you're right. I wanted to believe you and was determined to force myself to believe you. The fact is, I do. Now the question is how do we forget? How do we go on as before?"

"You don't think I should leave town?"

"No one need ever find out!"

"I think we should see less of each other," Sadie said, unable to convince herself there might still be some hope. "At least for a while."

"There's no sense in that. You have nothing to hide!"

She kissed him lightly. "I can't claim innocence any more, Jim. You and I have been lovers."

"That's no crime," Jim said, knowing that in the eyes of some of Warren Bluffs' upstanding citizens it very well might be.

"You have no idea what it's like to be called — and treated like — a hussy," Sadie whispered, shuddering.

"Sh-h-h. I want to kiss you and reassure myself that you haven't changed."

"Prison changed me, Jim. In those first awful days I learned to fight. The scars on the outside have healed, but I'll never again be the girl I was."

"Would you want to be that gullible person again?" Jim asked.

She had to smile then. "I suppose not. Jim, you're so good for me."

His kiss quickly flared into passion. They were no longer strangers. No more doors lay locked between them. Jim's hands went to her breasts, aware that she might be reminded of that other man, now behind bars for twelve more years. For a brief moment Jim wondered what he would do when that man was freed, but the question melted away, leaving him with only one thought. He had Sadie back! This time for good!

She stiffened. "I heard something!"

"Maybe a coyote," Jim mumbled, beginning to undo her buttons.

"Jim, listen! I heard someone snicker. There's someone out there, watching us! I can't stand for it to begin all over again!" She jerked away and righted her clothes.

Convinced she would not relax until he had investigated, Jim climbed down and lighted the lantern. Soft footsteps thudded into the distance.

Jim started after the sound.

"Don't leave me! Let's go away from here!" Sadie called, terrified. "Someone might have heard what I said! Sometimes I wish I had died in that prison!"

Jim climbed back into the buggy and took her trembling hand. "We have to believe that no one heard you." His eyes were quick in the darkness. "I'm wondering what someone is doing up here at this time of night. This is my land." He took the lines and shook them.

"I'm afraid!" Sadie whispered, huddling against his arm. "And I'm so tired of being afraid!"

He guided the buggy down the steep track toward the house. "At the very worst, Sadie, I can sell my land and we can go away."

Her heart twisted. "You wouldn't do that!"

"I would if the people of Warren Bluffs turn out to be like that passel of no-accounts you had in North Rushing."

She laid her head against his shoulder. "Oh, Jim . . . I love you!"

Chapter Fifteen

Marty ran until he couldn't breathe. It was four miles back to town by way of the road west. When he was sure the deputy wasn't trailing him, he slowed, bending over to gasp in lungfuls of cold night air.

Then he chuckled softly and went on at a trot. When he slipped in through the loose board in the fence behind their ramshackle house on First Street he heard his pa just coming in from rounds. He met him at the shed, startling the tall, wiry man as he fished a jug of homemade whiskey from deep within the hay.

"What you doing hanging around out here, boy?" Otis grumbled. "Ain't I got enough to plague me tonight, what with that worthless deputy of mine running off without a word?"

"I been up to the still, Pa."

"Shut your mouth before somebody hears you! What was you doing up there? I told you to stay clear of it." Otis seized his boy's collar. "I got no time for trouble from you, boy! I got bad enough news about your big brother last night."

Trembling with ingrained fear of his father, Marty squirmed like an ingratiating mutt. "What news was that, Pa?"

Otis flung Marty away and took a long pull on the jug, burping deeply afterwards. "That blame fool got himself shot up in Kirkston couple days back in a stand-up gunfight."

"Is he dead, Pa?"

"Yes, you damn fool! He's dead. Everett never was good for nothing but trouble. He didn't know how to stay out of it, just like you. I'm warning you, boy, I don't need no more trouble out of you. And don't tell your ma. I got things going just the way I want them now, and I don't intend for the likes of you to foul everything up."

"But don't you want to hear who else was up on the bluffs, Pa? Alone?" Marty slunk a bit closer to his father in the musty darkness of the shed. He lowered his voice to a hiss. "That deputy and her majesty, the schoolmarm. They was about to have at it, but I was busting a gut to keep from laughing and they heard me."

Otis seized Marty's collar again. "Did they see you?"

"No, Pa! I'm sure they didn't. I ran like hell to tell you what they was saying before they got down to business. You was right about her, Pa! She just got outta some prison back east for train robbery. She stole twenty-five thousand dollars! Can you beat it?" Marty rasped a delighted laugh. "I'm going to take that damn thinking stool of hers and —"

"Shut up a minute! You heard her say she done that? How come I ain't got a reply to all them letters I wrote?"

"Deputy's been getting 'em, Pa. And she's using some other name. What you going to do to her? Let me help, Pa! I'll do anything you say real good!"

Otis took two more long pulls on the jug. "First off, we got to rid ourselves of anybody else likely to find my still. And I think I know just how we're going to do it. You round up your little weasels and do just as I say. I'm going to have complete control of this town again, and that little schoolmarm is going to be standing right behind me, supporting me all the way. Where'd she say she served time?"

The two bent together, whispering for some time. At length, Otis sent his boy off into the darkness with a stinging slap to his backside. Then he adjusted his gunbelt and went in search of the old man who had known too much for too damn long now. Otis had failed to rid himself of the old coot once, but this time he'd leave no room for interference of any kind. And in the bargain he was going to rid himself of another man who had learned too much and thought because of his name he was immune to Otis Wheeler's power.

"You've worked everything out with Jim, then?" Trudy whispered as Sadie slipped in the front door and turned to wave at Jim driving away.

"Yes, it was foolish of us to quarrel," Sadie said, hoping to escape upstairs to gather her thoughts.

"I can't imagine what the two of you would find to —"

"It was nothing, really." Sadie took Trudy's hands. "Everything's fine now."

"Have you eaten?"

Sadie shook her head. "I just want to rest. Forgive me if I go on up." She started up the stairs, but Trudy followed.

"I hope you'll understand," Trudy began in a very low whisper, "but when you left so abruptly I found your door standing open. And I noticed your things thrown into the trunk. You weren't thinking of leaving us?"

Sighing, Sadie knew she could not escape giving the woman some kind of explanation. "I was upset, and yes, for the briefest moment I did think that I must go away, but truly I have been happier here than anywhere in my life. Can I hope that you'll say nothing about this evening?"

Trudy looked as if she was struggling to understand. "The others heard so much, dear. I don't know if they'll discuss it with anyone or not. I'll say nothing, of course. Are you sure you're well?"

"Yes, I . . . I was trying to cover up my . . . . Oh, Trudy, if I could just sleep. I promise to explain as best I can in the morning." Sadie was certain she would say the wrong thing if she went on in her confused state.

"Dear Sadie, you needn't explain a thing to me! I'm your

friend, and whatever you do is your business. You're a good young woman, and we all value you as much as we like you. I won't pry any more. I'm ashamed I had to ask as much as I did. When I saw your clothes in the trunk, though, I just got so worried about you." She gave Sadie a little hug. "Rest well, dear. We're your family now, and if you need anything from us you only have to ask."

Fighting sudden stinging tears, Sadie watched Trudy slip down the stairs. Quickly she shut herself in her room but didn't turn the key in the lock. Was there any hope they would understand? she wondered.

Stripping off her clothes, she crawled into bed but sleep would not come. Memories still crowded her mind — of home, of Rayford Storm's darkly handsome face, of her mother shrieking at the sound of the judge's gavel, and finally of the cold finality of the high iron doors of the prison that closed behind her the winter she was twenty-one and utterly, unbearably alone.

She had put on the gray cotton prison gown and joined the inmates idling in the common room lined by barred cells as dirty, dismal and rank as anything Sadie had dared imagine.

All kinds of prisoners were thrown together, first offenders like herself alongside murderesses, prostitutes of incredible ugliness and age, thieves, swindlers and gamblers, all of a hardened nature shocking at first to a sheltered small-town girl.

In with the criminals, and without any sort of medical assistance, were the drug addicts — many of them the overflow from eastern prisons — and the mentally ill, women too troubled to survive on the outside for long but not sick enough to be confined to an asylum. Women of every stripe were mixed together to fend for themselves, to fight for favor among the guards, to smuggle in drink and tobacco.

The food was atrocious, the accommodations lacking any grace or comfort. The women forgot they were women and behaved like caged animals, quarreling, thieving, forming cliques for protection and companionship. It was a madhouse of torment relieved only by one woman, the matron, who fought for reforms, the simplest of which was for tableclothes and linens for the cots.

Adelaide McAllister had been fighting to overhaul the prison for years before Sadie arrived. Quickly spotting Sadie as a helpless innocent among she-wolves, she decided to make use of her ability to read and write, and kept her apart as her clerk and secretary.

When Sadie wasn't writing letters to state officials, she was reading, studying in preparation for the day she would be free. "That day will come sooner than you think, honey," Adelaide had said so often. "You'll have to be prepared to start your life all over again. And I'll help you. We'll start right now. You've got the training to be a teacher. I know the people who can give you a teaching certificate and renew it as many times as necessary until you find the right man to marry."

"I'll never marry," Sadie had said bitterly.

"Sure you will . . . unless you don't like men, honey."

"I hate them," Sadie had said, only later realizing that what she meant by that and what Adelaide meant were very different things.

In the twenty months Sadie lived among the inmates of the Lincoln Women's Workhouse, Adelaide kept her distance, becoming nothing less — and nothing more — than Sadie's most valued friend.

Adelaide couldn't protect Sadie from the brutalizing effects of prison life, from the screams at night and the fights by day, for Sadie had to learn to do battle for herself; but on the whole Sadie's stay in prison was far less horrible than it was for most.

She lived apart in a cell off Adelaide's office, surrounded by books instead of bars, filling her mind with knowledge and hopes for her future instead of learning the many tricks the thieves and prostitutes could have taught her.

The day Sadie left the workhouse she was mentally and emotionally older by much more than the two years she had been in prison. Her mother had died. Her former life was over just as if she, too, had died. In her hand she clutched false papers that said she was a graduate of a fine women's teaching college, all carefully researched so that she would not go to a new town in the west only to be confronted by some woman who had really attended college there.

She had a trunk of clothes that Adelaide had gathered for her from among her friends in the women's clubs outside the prison. And in another trunk were items that had belonged to her mother, assembled by a few exceptional ladies from North Rushing who pitied Elinor's wayward daughter. In that trunk had been the picture of her mother, the gray serge traveling suit and the double-wedding-ring quilt.

Sadie had not returned to her home town. She had gone directly to a tiny town in Missouri where, after only three weeks, she had left, knowing she could not maintain the pretense of being Sadie Evans, schoolteacher.

Adelaide had understood and had arranged a teaching job in Illinois, but that, too, proved too difficult.

"You have to make a go of this one," Adelaide had said when she sent Sadie the information on Warren Bluffs, Kansas, where a schoolteacher was desperately needed. "Word will get around about you if you give up too many jobs. You'll have to change your name again. If you keep running, you'll find yourself starving to death or working yourself to death in some factory. Or it'll be a saloon or bawdy house for you. Pull yourself together, my friend! Warren Bluffs is your last chance."

Adelaide had been right about so much. She had carefully schooled Sadie on how to behave once free of prison. And yet Sadie had made mistakes from the first, the worst of which was spotting Marty Wheeler and his little band of flunkies picking the pockets of those unwary farmers.

Adelaide had cautioned her to close her eyes to anything that might bring her trouble, and instead she had self-righteously kept her eyes — and mouth — open. She had stuck her nose where it didn't belong and generally acted as if she was a saint. How much better it would have been to behave like a blind, mousy little schoolmarm who was interested only in dusty subjects like history and in teaching by mindless rote. She had dared to become involved with her students as young persons. She had dared to antagonize the sheriff. And now she was paying the price. Worst of all, she had fallen in love with Jim Warren, binding herself to the very place she now most longed to escape!

Writhing on her bed all night, Sadie wearily dragged herself to her feet the next morning. The grasses in the back lot were thick and white with hoarfrost. The sky was gray, the horizon murky.

She could think of nothing to do but go on pretending. This was how it would always be, she thought, no matter where she went. This was her future, the only future she would accept for herself! No factories. No saloons. No bawdy houses.

True to her word, Trudy asked no questions as Sadie forced down a bit of breakfast. Dressing warmly, Sadie set out for the schoolhouse a short time later. She had the eerie feeling of being in a place set apart from time. She smelled the bite of snow in the air and savored the sound of her own footsteps thudding on the cold-hardened streets.

Once in town Sadie was startled by all the activity, especially in the distance where a number of wagons appeared to be unloading near one of the boarded-up old saloons. Sadie was so engrossed, she walked headlong into MargieBelle Cadwallader. For several startled seconds, the two stared at each other.

"Pardon me, MargieBelle," Sadie murmured, thinking that of all the people she must see when she was least prepared, it should be MargieBelle.

Strangely, MargieBelle's expression didn't grow hard. "Good morning, Sadie. How are you?"

"I suppose I'm well," Sadie said, unable to think how she should respond to MargieBelle's cordial tone. Was this a trick of some sort? Did anyone know what Jim had learned the day before? Was she about to be exposed?

Sadie found her mind immediately whirling in confusion as she tried to read MargieBelle's eyes.

"Let me walk with you a ways," MargieBelle said, linking elbows with Sadie and drawing her along to cross Cowtrail Street at the corner. Sadie was so startled she said nothing and allowed herself to be led.

"Forgive me for not seeking you out long before now," MargieBelle said, lifting her face as a gust of chilling wind swept around the corner of the barbershop. "I don't see Jim in there, how odd. I just wanted to say . . . to thank you for letting me take over the school that day. For a time I was furious with you over that business with the mice, of course, and I went around saying a lot of unkind things. I'm like that when backed into a corner; but, you know, after that I was better able to stand up to my mother. I could say I'd proven I wasn't suited to teaching — and not much attracted to it, either. I was finally able to tell her a great many things. If you'll take a look at me I think you'll notice that I'm no longer dressed like a child."

Struck dumb by the change in MargieBelle, Sadie did turn and see that the girl was wearing a becoming cape and bonnet over a fine woolen skirt of soft brown. Her hair was drawn back in a stylish, complicated knot. "You look very nice!"

MargieBelle laughed a little. It was the first sincere smile on her face that Sadie had ever seen. "I think at last I'm beginning to make a little headway with my ma. She has such plans for me, and I'm so disappointing to her. I'm like my pa. I'm sure someone has told you he was no gentleman when he agreed to marry my mother. She had despaired of finding a husband, and she was well-to-do and suspicious of men's intentions. It was never an ideal match.

"Now my brother George has his plain little wife, who is little more than a child herself — and expecting, of course. My sister married a most disappointing man. My nieces and nephews are, as you know, a real trial. Mike finally confessed about the mice. But enough about me. Is there any hope that we might be friends some day, Sadie? I admire you so. You're an independent woman, free to do whatever you choose. You're so competent and fair. I'd like to be more like you."

Sadie was overwhelmed! She had to pause, to look at MargieBelle in amazed disbelief and then smile a bit helplessly at the irony of the young woman's words. "I would be honored to be your friend!" she said, astounded that a person could be so wholly sincere about a change of face. "You're . . . like a different person!"

MargieBelle laughed. "Yes, and it feels good! I was so sick of pretending to be young when every person in town was perfectly aware of my age. And I had to act as ma thought I should, wearing those ruffles and corkscrew curls and . . . trying to act chaste and yet flirtatious enough to snare a husband. Honestly, I thought I'd go mad. And not a man in town wanted me. Least of all the one I admired the most."

"Jim?" Sadie offered, thinking that with MargieBelle suddenly so different she might now prove a real threat to her relationship with Jim.

"Well, yes, if I'm to be honest. He always was my favorite, but it's clear to everyone that he's chosen you. You won't begrudge me an invitation to the wedding, will you?"

Sadie nervously pushed back loose tendrils of hair. "I don't know that it'll come to that."

"Nonsense. Oh, would you look at that! I thought the saloons were on their way out. We had hoped Otis was going to keep all the saloons out of town. You'll have to excuse me. I'd better go wake ma and tell her there's a new saloon opening up. I won't tell pa. He'd be the first man inside!"

MargieBelle released Sadie's arm and started away. Then she stopped and turned. "I don't know why I was afraid to face you, Sadie, after our . . . tussle in the schoolyard, and the things I said about you. It was an awful time for me, but I'm glad it happened. I'm so glad to be free of the burdens my mother placed on me for so long. I should have known you'd be generous." MargieBelle looked strangely sad, as if she regretted the trouble she had previously caused Sadie. "Is everything all right, Sadie? You look rather odd."

Sadie found herself longing to take someone into her confidence. Seeing the sincere concern on MargieBelle's face,

Sadie almost asked to call on her. But in prison she had learned to be wary of unexpected offers of friendship. Though revealing no trace of suspicion, Sadie sadly smiled. "I'm perfectly all right, MargieBelle. I'm glad we're friends now."

MargieBelle rushed away. Whiskey crates and beer barrels were being unloaded from the wagons at the far end of town. Three strange workmen trooped by wearing derbys and long, foul-weather slickers. Jangling tool belts were strapped to their hips, and coils of cable were slung about their shoulders.

Another man in an ugly plaid suit came out of the emporium and went by her. He paused to tip his hat and then went into Roberts' store carrying a large heavy valise of wares.

Sadie felt disoriented, as if too much was going on for her to comprehend. She felt as if she'd been gone for a long time and was just now back. Nowhere did she see Jim, or the sheriff, who would surely be calling on her at any time with the revelation that he, too, knew her secret.

Feeling panic, Sadie rushed on to the school.

She was just untying her cape and noticing how empty the schoolroom looked when a tremendous explosion came from the direction of town. Immediately, the few children in attendance pressed toward the windows and then spilled out the side door to watch a plume of smoke rise into the air.

"That's coming from Cowtrail Street," Cornell said, frowning.

Thinking of her pa's saloon, Winnie let out a squeal of alarm and began running across the field, angling toward School Road.

More smoke began rising in the distance. Then the fire bell started clanging.

"We'll have to go," Johnny Whithers said, running for his hat and coat.

"I'll drive us in the buggy," Walter shouted, dashing out to hitch the horse back into the traces.

Seeing that she would quickly have an empty schoolhouse, Sadie retied her cape. "You may go, but stay clear of —" No one was left to heed her caution.

The eldest boys were already lashing the buggy horse away toward town, with a scraggling of children pounding after them. The girls hurried along at a more decorous pace. Sadie followed quickly behind, thinking she would be needed, if only to keep the children out of harm's way.

Cowtrail Street was a riot of confusion. The town's single steam pumper was gushing a flaccid stream of water from a tank mounted on the old farm wagon pulled up beside it. Two bucket lines had already formed from a trough with a pump. The merchants and their patrons were hastily helping put out a small fire that had blazed for a short time in the midst of some rubble that had been an abandoned saloon moments before.

Amid the smoke and confusion in the street, the ladies of the town were gathering in knots. Some of them wore their kitchen aprons and clutched shawls thrown crookedly around their shoulders.

Olive spied Sadie attempting to herd the youngest of her charges out of the way of a second water wagon that was trying to jockey up the street. She was just crossing from one foot-high boardwalk to the next, where Sadie stood holding Douglas Newcomb's collar and Jerome Crowley's sleeve. Olive started to call out when a gasp of alarm rose from among the men manning the buckets in the first line.

Jim Warren emerged from the smoke billowing up from the destroyed saloon. He had Mike and Danny Shockley by their coats, and the boys looked speechless with terror. A flurry of questions drowned Jim's words, but by his expression Sadie gathered he was terribly angry about something.

Ethel Cadwallader shouted to be allowed to drive her buggy in closer. Beside her on the seat was a white-faced Margie-Belle. MargieBelle scrambled down, saw her nephews and forced her way to the line.

"They's still inside!" Sadie heard one of the boys begin screaming.

Olive clutched Sadie's shoulder. "You don't suppose those boys caused this? My lord . . ."

Sadie transferred her straining young charges into Olive's firm custody, and stepped down to the street. "Mrs. Cadwallader!" she shouted. "Perhaps you should fetch the doctor. Someone here might be hurt!" Sadie seized the horse's harness and helped clear a path so that the bewildered woman could drive away.

Sadie pressed through the crowd that was closing around the two sobbing Shockleys. MargieBelle was shrieking at them. When she saw Sadie, she stopped momentarily, looking as if she had somehow betrayed her good intentions.

"Where's Freddy?" Sadie asked, her tone urgent. "These three work together," she said to no one in particular. "Tell the men to look for Freddy!" She grabbed the two trembling boys whose faces were blackened with smoke and blasting powder. Crouching between them as MargieBelle ran toward the smoldering ruins, Sadie shook the boys' shoulders gently. "Was Freddy with you?"

They nodded, round-eyed with terror.

"What about Marty?"

They nodded even harder. "He told us what to do, but it went off before —"

"Clear the way!" a man shouted, knocking Sadie and the boys aside.

She found her footing and edged the boys away, as several men carried Marty Wheeler from the building. Mrs. Cadwallader was just returning with the doctor, who leaped down and came running toward the boy. MargieBelle pushed in next to him and seized his arm.

"Is he dead? Is he?"

Marty was unconscious and burned along one side of his face. One arm looked bloody and mangled. The doctor laid his head to the boy's chest and then straightened. "Someone help me get him over to the office!"

"Where's the sheriff?" someone nearby shouted.

Almost at once the tall wiry man came loping from the direction of his house. He paused as his son was carried by, his face reflecting shock. Looking around, he started again toward the knot of confusion in front of the destroyed saloon. Next to it was the overturned wagon that had been unloading into the building next door less than an hour before. The new saloon keeper stepped in front of Sheriff Wheeler.

"What's the meaning of this? They're saying these whelps blew up the building next to mine! I could have been burned out! What are you going to do about it, Sheriff? I lost me a good draft horse and two kegs to that blast!"

Those on the bucket lines had managed to put out the last of the fire. Jim emerged from the splintered timbers that lay scattered about like jackstraws carrying a hiccuping boy blackened by powder burns. Jim was covered with soot, too, and his face wore an angry scowl. He marched up to Otis and stared him straight in the eye. Then he thrust the hysterical Freddy Shockley into the sheriff's arms.

Ethel Cadwallader climbed down from her buggy and forced her way toward the sheriff and her grandson. "What were these boys doing here instead of at school?" she demanded.

Sheriff Wheeler turned briefly to the woman. He was about to thrust the boy into her arms.

"Pardon me for having to tell you this at such a time, ma'am," Jim said through his teeth. "But your grandsons and Marty Wheeler just blew up this building."

"You're crazy, Warren," Otis hissed. "Why would they do that?"

"Want me to bring Herman Biggins out, Sheriff? How was it supposed to look? Was he supposed to be burned beyond recognition in the resulting fire? Or just blown to bits. He's dead in any case. Beaten, by the looks of him."

"I don't believe it!" Ethel Cadwallader snapped, taking her grandson. "My grandsons weren't involved in any way! Tell him, Sheriff Wheeler. Arrest him for slandering our family name!"

"I don't know how my boy happened to be in there, but he didn't have nothing to do with blowing up this building," Otis said, ignoring Ethel. "Where would he get the dynamite anyhow? I think you set this up, Warren. You ain't the only one who noticed that Bat Masterson wasn't re-elected sheriff in Dodge City a couple weeks back. It's a fair guess you ain't going to be elected here either. Making me look bad ain't no way to get votes, I can tell you that right now!"

Jim's face went livid.

"I demand that you take back what you said about my grandsons! They had nothing to do with this!"

"Mrs. Cadwallader, your grandsons have seen more mischief in this town than I can recall at the moment. And Marty has been their leader from the first . . . acting on direct orders from the sheriff himself, I'll wager!" Jim looked down on her with contempt.

"Hand over your badge, Warren," the sheriff said softly, with venom in his voice. "You got no proof for them accusations. And you just lost yourself an election for making up such lies. I heard you tell these boys to come over here and help out with the unloading of these whiskey barrels, and everybody knows you allow Herman Biggins to make himself a bed any place he likes. Maybe you beat up the ol' coot yourself and laid the dynamite to cover it up. Everybody in town knows you ain't got Cadwallader's vote in the election next week."

Though no one confirmed the sheriff's words, no one rose to Jim's defense. His brows worked in disbelief as he surveyed the crowd of townspeople gathered around. What were they willing to believe about him? his expression said. And what were they willing to believe about Otis?

Gradually his eyes narrowed. He looked back at the sheriff as Otis ripped the tin star from Jim's vest, leaving a corner-shaped rent in the worn leather. "I do believe you have larger pockets than I ever thought, Otis. You got a whole town in them, and I never realized it." He let the star drop to the muddied street. "Folks, you're welcome to him."

Just as he was about to stride away, he saw Sadie watching him. She had both arms around the trembling Shockleys, and in her eyes was pain, for unlike anyone else in the town, she knu exactly how he felt at that moment. Foolish and betrayed.

He shouldered his way through the crowd and disappeared down Prairie Street to clear his things out of the jail's back room.

Chapter Sixteen

School remained recessed for the rest of the day. Sadie returned to the boarding house to help Trudy with chores while the gossip about the Shockley boys' involvement in the explosion spread to every household in town.

Sadie said little, afraid to express an opinion about the explosion lest it harm Jim's reputation any further. She found instead that listening to the talk run back and forth from sensible to absurd afforded her valuable insight into the citizens of Warren Bluffs.

For the most part, they were practical people, who were willing to look at all sides in an effort to find answers. She had to believe that they were good people at heart, and that though they might for a while consider the possibility that Jim Warren would risk the lives of three children and a troublesome youth just to discredit his adversaries, in the final analysis they were unlikely to believe it.

Otis Wheeler, on the other hand, was not the most easily liked man. He hadn't Jim's social graces or solidly respectable background. Yet he had long ago proven his courage. Why would he need to work through clumsy boys now?

Wasn't it more likely that a series of coincidences had placed the Shockley boys, Marty and Herman Biggins in the same dilapidated abandoned saloon when some old whiskey barrel blew up?

Mike Shockley swore on his grandmother's Bible that he and his brothers were only sneaking a smoke in the place when it went up with no warning. They were spared a whipping only because they were burned, though mildly. Buttered and contrite, they eagerly supported their grandmother's efforts to explain away their presence in the abandoned saloon that morning.

Sheriff Wheeler made a cursory investigation, but said finally that he couldn't determine why the building had exploded. In the year it had been boarded up, just about anything might have been secretly stored there, he said. The boys "sneaking a smoke" might have touched off any number of flammables.

Jim was seen no more that day, and Herman Biggins's body was carted off wrapped in a tarp from the rear of the building by the smithy and livery man long before Sheriff Wheeler began poking the toe of his boot through the rubble.

After dinner, Sadie pleaded exhaustion and was sitting chewing her nails in her room when she heard footsteps on the veranda and a tap at the front door. Thinking it was Jim, she rushed to her door.

Trudy was ushering a guest into her parlor. "Sit down right there and I'll see if she's able to come down. So nice of you to call." Trudy's voice sounded awkward with surprise.

As Sadie rushed down the stairs, she wondered if Trudy was still confused about Jim's part in the day's excitement. She reached the doorway before Trudy could speak, and stared with dumb confusion at Dr. Gary Hamlin sitting on the sofa couch, his hair slicked back and a box of chocolates in his hands.

"Oh, Dr. Hamlin . . ." Sadie paused and pressed back her untidy hair.

He stood and smiled stiffly at her. "You did give me permission to call."

"Well, of course. I . . . . How is Marty? Was he seriously hurt in the explosion?"

She went into the parlor, accepted Dr. Hamlin's offering and took a seat on a horsehair chair across the room from him.

The doctor sat when she did. Trudy had made herself scarce. "He's going to be just fine. His arm'll take a while to heal, but otherwise he got off lucky. That blast knocked him unconscious at first. I'd say his wings will be clipped a spell. I left Miss MargieBelle to tend him."

"I had no idea she was a trained nurse," Sadie said, still trying to understand why the man was there to call on her when it would seem more appropriate for him to be looking after his patient.

"She isn't, but she has a gentle touch. I'd say she's going to be a great help to me in the future." His tone had dropped to a near whisper.

"I'm so glad to hear that."

He leaned closer. "Miss Sadie," he whispered very softly. "I've come on behalf of a friend." Then he returned his voice to normal. "Who do you think will be elected sheriff on Monday, Miss Sadie?"

"I hadn't given it much thought, actually," she said, bewildered by his behavior.

He craned to see if anyone was within sight of the open parlor door and then half rose to thrust a folded note toward her. She took it and was about to read it when he cautioned her to wait. "I just hope folks keep in mind which man had the interests of this town at heart."

She gave the doctor a questioning smile, wishing she could speak freely, but knowing somehow she could not. "Is there any hope that Jim Warren will be elected now that the sheriff fired him as deputy?"

The doctor looked pointedly at the note she held clutched in her hand. They talked on for several minutes more. The doctor strained to keep their conversation alive, looking as if he knew Sadie's mind was on something and someone else. Finally he rose. "I suppose I should be getting back now."

Sadie got to her feet and shook his hand. "Thank you for calling. If there's anything I can do, please let me know."

He just smiled. She showed him to the door and watched as he strode quickly away, back toward his office.

Trudy slipped up behind Sadie. "I was never so surprised to see anyone. I just wasn't expecting him. I thought perhaps Jim would stop by. It's so unlike him to just take off. I don't think for a moment that he tried to discredit Otis Wheeler, but I don't like it that he hasn't been around to —" She broke off with a shrug. "I guess I'd like for him to set my mind to rest. Mr. Charles says he'll vote for Jimmy, but Mr. Bennett is the first to believe anything bad about a person. They've had Alvinia and me tied in knots all evening. Will you be going back to bed?"

Sadie kept the note concealed in the folds of her skirt. "I think so, Trudy. Dr. Hamlin seems like a nice enough man."

"Oh, he is, surely! I knew his wife years ago. He has two grown sons going to college at Harvard Medical School, you know."

"No, I didn't. Good night, Trudy. Thanks again for a lovely dinner."

"Why, you're always just as welcome as you can be."

Sadie closed her bedroom door moments later and leaned against it as she unfolded the hastily written note.

Take extra lunch Monday. Look in hay barn. Stay after school. I will meet you.

The note was signed with a sprawling, crooked "J." Sadie's heart leaped. What was he up to?

Asking Trudy to pack extra in her lunch box Monday morning on the excuse that some of the children hadn't been bringing enough lately, Sadie set out early for school.

The morning was crisp, the sky clear and pale. The cottonwoods along the riverbank were bare and looked faintly hazy in the early morning mists.

Inside the schoolhouse everything was blessedly in order. With Marty lying in bed at the doctor's office, and the Shockley boys recovering at their grandmother's house in town, Sadie knew she would have no pranks to trouble her for some time.

Setting down her generous lunch — Trudy had welcomed the opportunity to send along some of the leftovers from her laden pantry — Sadie rushed out to the hay barn. She half expected to find Jim hiding there, though why he would hide she couldn't imagine.

Saying nothing, she crept under the wide low roof. A load of hay had been delivered over the weekend, she observed, glancing at the fresh wagon tracks in the dust. One side of the sweet-smelling three-sided building was heaped so high she couldn't see the corners. "What am I supposed to find here?" she wondered aloud.

The hay heaped in the farthest corner shifted suddenly. She heard a faint, muffled snore followed by a snort and a sneeze!

"Who's in there?" Sadie yelped.

Then she heard a long moan and groan. At once she was burrowing into the hay. She found a battered boot. The man jerked his foot away the moment she touched him. In seconds she had uncovered a woolen blanket and the bewildered, battered face of the handyman, Herman Biggins.

Gasping in shock, Sadie sat back on her haunches. "I thought Jim said you were dead! Oh, Mr. Biggins, your eye. Have you been to the doctor?"

"Yes'm," he said through swollen lips. "Don't ask me to explain what deputy's up to. I can't remember the half of it. You got anything to eat on you? Got a dollop of whiskey for an aching old man?"

"I've got plenty of food, but no whiskey," Sadie said. "Don't move. I'll bring you something." Moments later she was back with the lunch Trudy had packed. "How long do you expect to hide here? Why are you hiding here? Why did Jim say you were dead? Who beat you like that? What were you doing in the saloon when it blew up?"

Herman waved off her questions with a grimace and plundered her lunch, taking the dainty sandwiches Trudy had made and stuffing them unceremoniously into his mouth. Over the mouthful, he said, "Jim'll be by later to tell you all that. All I know is that I'm to stay under this hay till he pulls me out hisself. Now git, schoolteacher, 'fore some young squirt comes along and sees me. See about some whiskey, will you, dear lady?"

He drew her lunch box under cover of the hay and pulled his tattered blanket around himself and over his head. Seeing that her questions would have to wait, she pushed back all the hay she'd moved aside and thought with amazement that no one would ever guess that the old man was hidden in the heap.

With Herman's safety to consider, Sadie had no time to dwell on her own problems. To her amazement, the Shockley boys had come to school. She informed everyone that they would skip the rehearsal for the tableau that afternoon. After an hour of quiet study Sadie decided she was too nervous to endure the silence. She changed to a lively lesson that everyone enjoyed.

Susanna Wheeler behaved as she had since her brother quit the school. She was sullen and uncooperative. Today she was particularly unpleasant, and the small pocket of tension she generated was made worse by Dawn Shockley, hunched motionless at her desk. Dawn refused to participate in any of the lessons.

Thinking the girls were merely being obstinate, Sadie ignored them. At lunch she expected to take Herman a cup of water, but Dawn refused to go over to her grandmother's for lunch with her contrite brothers.

"Then I won't go either," Susanna declared, looking faintly worried by her best friend's oddly pinched expression.

Sadie had nothing to eat, but resigned herself to the minor discomfort, and took her customary place on the bench outside the side door where she could hear the two girls whispering heatedly in the schoolhouse. Whatever was troubling them, they were not in agreement about what to do.

During the afternoon session, Dawn looked considerably

better. By the time the long day was done, Sadie had had ample opportunity to observe Dawn, and the girl looked furtive and nervous. On guard for a prank, Sadie dismissed for the afternoon.

Everyone left as usual except Dawn and Susanna. The two girls lingered at the iron gate, until finally Dawn flew into a rage. "If you don't go on without me, I'll never speak to you again! I got a question for Miss Evans. A private question! Git, you slow-minded Wheeler! You're as snoopy as your pa!"

Sadie shuddered to think what revenge Susanna might be capable of in the face of such insults from her only friend. Instead of setting everything in order as she would have on any ordinary school day, Sadie waited breathlessly at her desk. In a moment, Dawn slipped back into the school and closed the door.

"Can I help you clean up or something, Miss Evans?"

"I'd be glad for the help. Are you feeling better?" Sadie said gently, seeing that the girl was pale with agitation.

"A little." Dawn's young face twisted with anguish. "Where shall I start? I can —" She looked ready to burst into tears.

"I need a sip of water. Would you like some?" Sadie said, thinking the girl needed a moment alone to compose her thoughts. Her mind was racing back to the afternoon she had seen the girl and Marty making love on the river bank. At Dawn's slight nod, Sadie slipped outside.

She saw no movement in the hay barn and thought that by now Herman must have a terrible thirst. Yet she pumped a fresh cup full of water for Dawn and took it back inside. She must finish with Dawn and get the child on her way.

Dawn took the cup and looked at it, clutching it with trembling little hands. Her voice came out a rasping whisper. "Susanna says her ma claims that if a boy touches a girl in just the right spot she'll get a baby. Is that true, Miss Evans?"

Sadie felt an icy wash go over her. "In a manner of speaking, I suppose it is, although there's more to it than that."

"Where's the spot, Miss Evans? Is it the belly button, or what?"

"Not the navel, no, Dawn. Would you like me to explain the entire process?"

The girl hastily shook her head. "No'm, just the part about knowing . . . knowing there is a baby coming."

"You mean signs of pregnancy."

"That and . . . something to do about it."

"I know nothing about that, Dawn. You'd have to see a doctor, and few doctors on the right side of the law perform such . . . operations." Sadie's voice was trembling now, for she had heard any number of methods for abortion discussed in hideous detail while in the workhouse.

When the girl said nothing more but waited, staring at the cup of water in her hands, Sadie went on to describe the signs of pregnancy in the same clinical language that she had read them herself seemingly ages ago in Adelaide's office. She herself had feared that Rayford might have made her pregnant by "touching" her. For months her monthlies had been irregular, but later she realized that it was her anxiety that had upset her system so drastically. What terror this poor girl must be feeling now, Sadie thought.

Tears started dripping into the cup. Hastily, Sadie took it from her, set it down and gathered the quivering young girl into her arms. Suddenly Dawn was sobbing in complete despair. After a minute her voice came out thick with agony. "I don't know what to do, Miss Evans! I got to stop it somehow. I once heard ma say that falling out of a hay loft is one way . . ."

"Hush! Don't think such a thing! Lift up your face now, and show me the smile of a strong young woman, for that's what you've become, Dawn. Dr. Hamlin is an understanding, kind man. He'll tell you if what you fear is certain, and I'm sure he'll be willing to break the news to your parents."

"No! They can't know! I'll run away first! You don't know, Miss Evans! They'll throw me right out the door! You should have heard the things my folks were saying to each other last night. Grandma won't turn over my brothers to them. She says ma's no kind of mother, and pa's a no-account bastard!

Grandma is a hard, hard woman, Miss Evans! She'd send me away forever! I thought you might help me, somehow. I hoped you'd tell me I was wrong to think that I could be . . . . Miss Evans, I don't want to marry Marty! He said he wasn't touching me in the right spot! And besides, I'm scarcely thirteen!"

Sadie had just pulled the girl back into her embrace, when the sound of footsteps brought the girl's head up. Her skull knocked hurtfully against Sadie's jaw.

"Who's that?"

"Just the deputy," Sadie said softly.

"No, it's not. He's come to get me!" Dawn bolted out the side door, holding her skirts high and pounding away.

Sadie whirled and stood. Otis Wheeler stepped into the schoolroom and took off his hat. "Afternoon, honeypot. Nice of you to stick around so's we can have us a private little talk."

Sadie's heart had leaped into her throat at the sight of the man. It dropped into her feet as she read by his expression that he knew about her. He was wearing his pistol and a smile. She wondered if he had come to run her out of town. "Afternoon, Sheriff," she said, praying she was wrong.

"What ails the girl?"

Sadie swallowed over a dry tongue. "Things are very hard for her at home now that her brothers have been exposed."

"Damn little fools. What do you think made them boys blow up that saloon anyhow?"

"You and everyone else in town knows they didn't do it without help from Marty. It's a shame, nevertheless, that Marty was injured. He might have lost his arm."

The sheriff ambled across the room to lean against her desk. She wouldn't be able to dart out either door without passing close to him first. "I always did wonder where you got your gall, Miss Whiting, but now o' course, I know."

Sadie straightened, her heart bounding now to hear her old name. She had never fought a man with the intention of doing him real harm, but she felt the power necessary suddenly spurting in her veins. Let him try to touch her.

"I really admire that look you got in your eye right now, honeypot. I knew from the first that you and me would have us some fine times. I imagine you think I'm about to run you out of town. Chances are the school board will when they find out, but I ain't about to say a word about you being in a prison two years for stealing twenty-five thousand dollars, and who knows what-all else. If anybody finds out, it'll be because the deputy lets the news out, and if my calculations are right, he's long-gone from here. He ain't got a chance in this town now. All day long the men of this county have been putting their vote in for me because they know I can handle the job."

"What are you doing here then?" she whispered.

"Why, I'll bet you know perfectly well. I got a proposition to make. I won't tell nobody about your past if you prove yourself to be my good and loyal friend. A woman of your sort can understand a relationship like that. I take it you want to stay in this town? Why, I ain't too sure, but it suits me to know that you do. It's mighty hard to keep starting over again and again. You got a few friends now, like you said before. You can stay as long as you like. I'll keep your secret close to my heart." He grinned and his overlapping teeth showed plainly in the waning afternoon sunlight that slanted through the windows.

"In return for . . . friendship, Sheriff Wheeler?"

"And a good word to your friends, and your support whenever I do something that's likely to cause a stir, and other . . . considerations." He started slowly down the center aisle. He had left his hat on her desk. One hand played at his gun belt. "I got a need for a good woman like you," he said softly. "I had my eye on you from the first. Said to myself I could see the need burning in them green eyes of yours." His eyes played lingeringly over the swell of her bodice. "I can't think of nothing that would keep me quieter than having you undo them buttons right now."

He kept advancing inch by inch, his hand on the pistol. She couldn't let him shoot her, she thought.

"I don't think the schoolhouse is any place for that sort of thing," she murmured, keeping her eyes lowered so that she could just barely see his expression through her lashes.

"I don't suppose not. But you agree, then? I won't run you out of town, and you'll be my friend . . . my very special, very private friend? Like, at least once a week?"

"And if the truth about me gets out anyway?" she whispered, trembling.

"Then I stand behind you, and I get . . . proof that you ain't that Sadie Whiting who helped rob the train with that outlaw. I can get any papers I want. For instance, I could have papers proving you'd spent a lot more time in prison than you did . . . just as an example of how much harm I could do you. 'Course, I won't do that to my special lady friend."

With her heart thundering, she turned away as Otis reached her. His hands slid around her shoulders. If she could just get away one last time, she thought, looking up as he drew her close.

In the window was the round, aghast face of Susanna Wheeler. "Oh, no —" Sadie gasped softly.

Instantly the face disappeared.

"What did you see?" Otis said, noticing the direction of Sadie's wide-eyed stare. He let her go.

"Nothing! Oh, God, I don't know what to do! If . . . if anyone finds out about . . . this, I'll be thrown out of town in any case! You've got to leave. Maybe I can meet you somewhere later," she said just to get him out of the schoolhouse.

He fought his way through the rows of desks to thrust his head out the door. His daughter had long since dashed away, and Jim Warren was approaching on horseback from the direction of the river bank.

Otis slammed the door. His mouth worked in a nervous grimace. "I'm going to have to shoot that bastard! Always showing up at the wrong times . . ."

In the growing dusk, Sadie saw Jim dismounting out by the gate. As he looped his reins around a sagging post, she made a mad dash for the schoolhouse door. Otis easily caught her. She felt the iron bite of his pistol barrel nudge into her side as he jerked her against his chest.

"Tell him to be on his way, honeypot. I'll even see that you get a raise in pay. And I'll set you up in your own little place way far out of town where we can be together without having to worry about all the snoops —"

Jim threw the door open. He was wearing a pistol, too, and a long traveling slicker. The cold evening air rushed into the room as he paused to look at Sadie held so tightly against Otis.

"Just turn yourself around, Warren," Otis said, with a chuckle in his voice. "I've staked my claim here. You lost out on both counts. Returns from the polls are probably being counted right now. In a few days we'll know who the sheriff for Warren County is, and his name ain't going to be Warren. If I was you, boy, I'd put that land o' your grandpappy's up for sale and head further west. You might even get a sheriffing job someplace. Plenty o' lawless towns for a young buck like yourself to tame. Tell him, honey. Tell him which of us you prefer." He jammed the pistol barrel deeper into her side.

She watched Jim's eyes go over her. She was sure he couldn't miss the fact that Otis had a gun on her.

Jim stood for the longest moment gazing steadily into her eyes. Then he tipped his imaginary hat. "S'cuse me, Sadie. I didn't mean to barge in where I'm not wanted."

Her heart dropped as he disappeared out the door. Through the windows she could see him mount and ride away. Otis slid his pistol into his holster and started to nuzzle her neck. "You done real fine, honeypot," he said, chuckling. "You and me is going to have some fine times together, now that I know the kind of woman you really are. I bet you'll teach me a few things."

"We should leave now," Sadie whispered, gritting her teeth. She wondered if there was any hope at all of escaping him.

They both heard a noise off to the side of the school. Otis flung her aside and slunk low to the side door. Throwing it wide, he lunged out, pistol drawn. At the same moment, the other door opened, and Jim vaulted across the room and leaped onto Otis's back.

Sadie heard both men land in the dirt and scrabble about, landing punches and grunting. She went to the door and watched helplessly as the men found their feet and battled into the field, each giving and receiving punches that made her want to scream in horror.

Jim took several brutal blows to his mid-section and one savage jab to his kidneys that sent him to his knees. But the moment Otis tried to take the advantage, Jim caught him in one blinding slug to his jaw that sent him sailing backwards.

Otis landed on his back and tried in vain to climb to his feet. Jim was immediately on him, pummeling his face harder and harder until Sadie was dashing at them.

"Stop! Jim, you've got to stop! You're killing him!" She grabbed his coat and jerked furiously. "You've got to stop. He knows about me now, too. Jim! Jim! Stop and tell me what I must do! Should I leave town now?"

That question seemed to rouse Jim from his blood-rage. He dropped Otis's bloody head into the dust and stood, heaving breaths that made white gusts in front of his face.

"I hate that man!" he hissed, turning away to rub his jaw. "Are you hurt, Sadie?"

"I'm all right. Let's get out of here before he comes to."

"No, I'm driving him out of town. You . . . you get on back to town before he thinks up anything more to do to you. He won't say anything about you, Sadie, I'll see to that. I just found his liquor still hidden up on my grandfather's land, and I smashed it. If folks hear he's been selling homemade whiskey to the men hereabouts and was planning to make a regular business of it after the prohibition, they'll tar and feather him. Go on, I'll be all right."

"Take his pistol first," she said, loath to leave Jim.

Jim paused to look down at her and smile. "You'll make a handy sheriff's wife," he said.

She wanted to shake him. "What about Herman?"

"Is he all right? Then he'll stay where he is until I know what to do about him. I know Otis got Marty to blow up the saloon. And Herman's mixed up in it somehow. He said something about knowing all about Otis's operation. As soon as the doc gets Marty to admit what he knows, we'll be rid of Otis. I'm going to lock him up and ride to Topeka for help. If you can just hold out for a few more days . . ."

"If you lock him up, he'll be sure to tell every secret he knows in order to get out. Come on, Jim. Go now before he wakes. I'll stay as long as I dare. It's not that I'm so afraid for myself any longer," she finally said, thinking that to be exposed might be a welcome relief from the strain of trying to keep her secret concealed. "It's just that so many people need my help. Dawn Shockley is pregnant. She needs someone on her side. Jim, go! And be careful. Hurry back."

He slipped his warm, slightly trembling hand to her cheek. "I hate to leave you with him still on the loose."

"How long will you be gone?"

"Two days. Maybe less if I ride hard." He bent and kissed her. He seemed to want to linger.

Otis stirred, moaning.

"Go! Leave me the pistol, Jim, just in case. I'll check on Herman."

The heavy pistol sagged in her trembling hands. She listened to Jim pound away into the deep blue shadows. At once she ran back to the hay barn.

"Herman, I need my lunch box. Hurry! I'm sorry, but I won't be able to bring you anything more until morning. The sheriff's not far off. You'll have to be very quiet."

When the old man didn't answer, she burrowed into the hay and woke him, repeating her warning. With the pistol hidden inside the lunch box, she locked the schoolhouse and dashed away, praying she would reach the boarding house safely. She took the back way, through the park and the grassy lot behind Trudy's.

She was just climbing wearily up the front steps, racking her brains for a clever excuse to cover her tardy arrival for dinner, when she saw through the parlor window that Trudy had a passel of company.

Trudy was opening the door the moment Sadie set foot on the veranda. "Dear me, you're late." Her expression was tight with worry. "Oh, Sadie, they're all here, and they seem so . . . unfriendly. What has happened?"

Clutching the lunch box to her stomach, Sadie felt herself go stiff with dread. It was as if she was stepping into the courtroom again as she entered the boarding house and turned to see Ethel Cadwallader, MargieBelle, Mrs. Shockley, the Davidson twins' mother and her friend Lindie Purcell, the barber's wife, all sitting stiffly across from Olive Crowley and the preacher's wife. Seated a bit to the side and by herself was Mrs. Wheeler in a dress far plainer than the others were wearing. She stared straight at Sadie without flinching, her expression icy.

"Good evening, ladies," Sadie said like a frightened child. She was growing disoriented again. Her head started to spin as she imagined what the ladies were going to say to her. Somehow they had found out her secret, she thought, feeling ill at having so many people against her.

MargieBelle looked away, her face faintly red. Ethel's eyes bored into Sadie as she stood trembling in the doorway. The other ladies held themselves in self-righteous postures, their faces pinched, their gloved hands rigidly folded. Only Olive looked upset to be there, as is she was being forced. And Mrs. Whithers looked as if she was trying to recede into the background.

"Can I take the lunch box for you?" Trudy said, her voice strangely small, as if to have Sadie a grave concern of the ladies' society somehow reflected badly on her.

Sadie scarcely heard her request and held all the more tightly to the box containing the pistol. "Can I help you ladies?"

Olive looked about to speak, and then balled her fists at Ethel Cadwallader's frigid look that silenced her.

"Miss Evans," Ethel began, rising with dignity to her feet. "Something has come to our attention that can no longer be swept under the carpet. I'm afraid we've come to ask for your resignation."

The words cut through Sadie, leaving her stunned. "Might I ask exactly what has come to your attention that warrants such a request? Might I ask that you grant me the right to speak in my own defense?"

"That's hardly necessary, since we have witnesses to your transgression," Ethel said.

"Witnesses?" Sadie breathed, realizing they might not know the worst of her secrets at all! She was almost tempted to laugh. Such foolish women they were! Such innocents!

Mrs. Wheeler sprang to her feet. She was a homely, rangy woman with a careworn face and big, ungainly hands. "We've stood by while you chased after every eligible man in town, but when you start in on the married ones, that's where we must draw the line! And if you thought such a tawdry effort would cost my husband the election, you're very wrong. My husband is clearly the better man to keep law and order in this county. You can stop chasing after my husband and get out of town!"

Chapter Seventeen

"I can assure you, Mrs. Wheeler, I have never chased after your husband! On the contrary —"

MargieBelle turned toward Sadie sharply, her expression filled with warning. "Careful what you say."

With her mouth hanging open, Sadie struggled to control her urge to throw the facts about Otis in his wife's face, humiliating her in front of everyone.

Suddenly she knew she could say nothing about Otis. His wife was a blind fool if she didn't already know the sort of man he was; and if she did know, she was merely trying to hold onto her dignity. In any case, Sadie had nothing against Mrs. Wheeler and couldn't deliberately hurt her.

"You can all force me to resign if you like," Sadie said, her voice quivering with anguish. "But I'd like the opportunity to explain to my pupils why I'm leaving and ask their assurance that the next teacher won't be treated to the pranks I've had to endure. I would also like to stay long enough to hold the pageant. The students have worked marvelously hard. It would be such a shame to cheat them of the honor to perform for their parents."

Mrs. Cadwallader huffed as if Sadie had submitted too easily. "MargieBelle will have no trouble controlling the students —"

"I told you before, Ma. I'm not taking that job! It's Justine Wheeler, or someone else — or no one. I'm going to be working for Dr. Hamlin from now on. He agreed to take me on today." She got up, looking glad she'd found an excuse to leave. "I'd better get back now. Marty's feeling a lot of pain on account of his arm. Mrs. Wheeler, why don't you come along with me and visit him? I could do with a word from you to help keep him abed."

"He wouldn't listen to me," Mrs. Wheeler muttered, her face red and her eyes growing uneasy as she thought of what would be said about her if she left now. "No, I think I'll stay on and stop by after we've done with Miss. Evans." She nodded her head, confident of her decision.

Olive rose, tugging on her gloves. "I'm sure we've said plenty. I want everyone to know I still think Sadie did nothing to warrant our shameful treatment of her. I vote she be allowed to stay as long as she's got the stomach for us."

Sadie forced herself not to dwell on Olive's words for fear she would burst into tears.

Mrs. Whithers stood, too. "My husband has been more than satisfied with her ability to prepare our son for college. I vote with Olive that Miss Evans be allowed to remain in the schoolhouse as long as she likes. It's my hope that she's still here when Cory is preparing for college."

Sadie could no longer meet the eyes of the women. Her heart was twisting with the desire to flee and the faintly glimmering hope that she might have enough friends to stay.

"I vote that she resign," Lindie Purcell snapped. "I'm not wishy-washy in the face of her kind. I don't want a hussy teaching my little ones."

The word brought Sadie's head up sharply.

"I, of course, vote for resignation," Ethel Cadwallader said coolly, nudging MargieBelle. MargieBelle didn't speak.

Mrs. Davidson looked confused. "My boys told me about

the day she was lollygagging in the cloakroom with the deputy. She's not the kind of woman I want as an example of a lady for my boys. I vote . . . she resign." She looked to Lindie and Ethel for approval.

"I agree. She should go," Mrs. Wheeler said, gratified to see the amount of support in her favor.

"Well, I vote she should stay!" MargieBelle snapped. "None of you knows what she's put up with."

"Nevertheless, the vote is against her, four to three," Ethel said, leading the way out of the parlor. "But we'll allow you to remain until after the foolishness with the tableau, Miss Evans."

Trudy stood agape in the entry. "You ladies make me ashamed! I vote that she stay! If Jimmy Warren was here, not a one of you would treat Sadie this way!"

Ethel gave Trudy a scathing look. "Jim Warren hasn't the grit to defend this town. Aside from toying with the affections of my daughter, he has openly soiled the reputation of this . . . woman. I should think you'd be ashamed to have such a creature under your roof."

Trudy brought herself up. "Ethel Cadwallader, you take on airs that are mighty tiresome! I'll thank you to go on home now. You've quite upset my boarders."

Alvinia crept from the drawing room in the rear. Her cheeks were bright with the excitement of eavesdropping. "What about me?" she asked, timidly coming forward. "I'm a voting member of the ladies society."

Everyone turned to the shrinking little woman with the powdery face. "Vote then," Ethel snapped. "We have better things to do than dawdle here over your opinion on a matter that has nothing to do with you. I thought we had clearly discussed this issue and made up our minds before we came that Sadie Evans' morals were too loose for her to make a suitable teacher."

"We'll have a good deal more to discuss if you keep carrying on in this way!" Olive said, her face flushed with anger. "Tell us your opinion, Alvinia dear."

"I've always said you can tell a good woman by her table manners and her daily habits," Alvinia said in her sweet, childish tone. "She's always been very kind to me, unlike some I could name." She looked at Ethel with a sniff. "I think Miss Evans should stay."

"Thank you," Sadie murmured, letting out her breath.

"No matter," Ethel huffed as she started out. "I need only ask for Nancy Newcomb's vote. Her boy was constantly in peril in that so-called classroom. And Mrs. Runyon will certainly have something to say now that she realizes the gravity of this rift in a social club that was never before disturbed by such foolishness. She didn't think a woman teacher was right for this town, either! If that isn't enough to pass a vote of resignation, there's still the mayor's daughter-in-law and Mrs. Roberts, whose husband could tell us a good deal about a certain incident that took place in his store . . ."

"Don't count my daughters-in-law," Olive put in. "They know Sadie, and they like her. And I think you'd be surprised by the way the Runyons would vote."

Sadie wanted to scream. "Ladies, please! I won't have this!"

"Then leave with dignity and let us settle our own affairs," Ethel said, with a toss of her head.

Olive pushed passed the small hard woman and started down the front steps. "I move we call a special election. It's time we had a new president. We'll continue this meeting at my house!"

"I second!" someone called out.

One by one the startled ladies trailed out after Olive, leaving Ethel to follow protestingly until the argument finally drifted out of earshot.

Sadie started to drag herself up the stairs.

"You haven't eaten! You can't go on like this, Sadie! And let me take the lunch box. Will you need extra lunch tomorrow, as well?" Trudy was alarmed by Sadie's dazed expression.

"Y-yes, extra lunch. I can't eat now . . ." Halfway up the stairs Sadie took out the pistol and handed down the box. She didn't see Trudy and Alvinia gawk at the pistol as she pulled herself up the last step and into her room.

The night seemed eerie with ringing silence. Sadie finally ate a little from a tray that Trudy brought up. Wisely, Trudy chose to talk of inconsequential things, which helped Sadie relax somewhat.

Finally Sadie just sat on the edge of her bed, sorting through the last bewilderingly long days. She felt the pressure of them building in her head. She longed for peace and thought again of simply throwing on her cape and escaping.

Then she remembered Jim riding hard for help to expose Otis's part in the destruction of the saloon, and Herman Biggins waiting trustingly in the hay barn. And there was little Dawn Shockley, who had good reason to fear her grandmother's wrath if her condition was revealed.

Sadie was trapped by obligations beyond her control.

After she blew out her lamp, she stood at her window, looking out over the prairie. The air outside her window was sharp with frost, the darkness soothing and still.

Late that night, she heard a commotion downstairs and went to investigate. Trudy was just slipping into the dining room, wearing her wrapper and nightcap. In her arms was a long rifle that had once belonged to her husband.

Sadie rushed down to her. "What is it?"

"Oh, nothing dear. I thought I heard someone out back. Without Jimmy in town I don't feel quite safe. And you have me a bit jumpy with that pistol in the house."

"Jim gave it to me," Sadie whispered.

"Then you have seen him since the explosion." Trudy peered out the side window.

"Yes, let me take the rifle. It looks heavy."

"No need to worry, dear. I'm no stranger to this old thing. Besides, I have Mr. Charles on alert, and Mr. Bennett, if necessary. We'll protect you."

"Protect me? From what?" Sadie whispered in alarm,

thinking that the two old gentlemen would be quite useless when it came to firing heavy old rifles.

"Why, that Ethel woman. I wouldn't put it past her to try to scare you out of town. The things she said about you . . . . If you hadn't come in when you did I would have slapped her face! She said you'd gone after her George at her party, and that you'd gotten mighty friendly with Preacher Whithers, too! I swear, the woman's got the mind of an alley cat! I can just imagine what's going on at her house tonight with MargieBelle taking a stand against her in front of everyone."

"Get back from the window! I see someone out there," Sadie said, thinking it might be Otis. "Check the doors. Don't forget the one to the cellar. Can it be bolted from the inside?"

Trudy was quiet a moment. "Are you in any sort of trouble, Sadie?"

"I would explain, but it's too complicated, and I would like to rest easy tonight. Forgive me for bringing you such . . . trouble."

"I'm no stranger to trouble, either," Trudy said as she slipped away to attend to the doors and windows.

The remainder of the night passed without incident. As if she had not been up all night prowling in the darkness with the rifle, Trudy served breakfast as usual the next morning. Sadie left for school with a lunch box laden with enough for three people, and the pistol.

She found Herman down by the river bank looking battered but chipper. He described hearing Otis prowling in the hay barn the night before and then proudly showed her his discovery.

"Just looky here, missy," he said, dragging her to the hay barn as he gobbled sandwiches from the lunch box. He showed her a spot opposite his hiding place. With his boot he cleared away some of the old hay and reached for a loose board in the rear wall. Prying it back, he exposed a dugout in the foundation where several dozen bottles of whiskey were hidden. "I already knowed about the sheriff's cache in the hills, and he's got one in a warehouse back of my shack.

Chances are he's got some at his place, and maybe the jail-house, too. But I never knew about this here place. It's sure he had something hidden in town, maybe that place where he left me after he tried to stove in my head."

"The sheriff beat you and left you in that abandoned saloon?" Sadie gasped.

"Sh-h-h, I hear them youngun's o' yours coming. You'd best get on about your schoolteaching. I'll be fine here. I just naturally sleep all day anyways."

As usual all her students were present but Marty. Dawn looked as green as she had the morning before. Sadie left her out of the lessons. Susanna was troublesome, answering back and generally disrupting the lessons whenever she could. Sadie wondered if she dared assign her to the thinking stool, but decided against it. The best thing she could do would be to explain what Susanna had seen through the window the evening before. She would undertake that during lunch, she decided.

At eleven-thirty that morning, the middle grade was just finishing reciting the multiplication table when a series of shots rang out from the direction of town.

Instantly the room was silent. "Stay in your seats," Sadie said, going to the side door to see if she could determine if anything was wrong in town.

Another volley rang out, and then several scattered shots popped at irregular intervals. Strangely, Sadie saw no movement on Prairie Street, where traffic was usually light but steady.

"I want you all to remain in your seats. I have no idea what would account for so many gunshots in town, but I'm sure if there's any real trouble we will hear the fire bell as a warning."

The children erupted with questions she couldn't answer. Sadie attempted to go on with the lesson, but was interrupted by more shots, singles, then a series of exchanges that sounded like some kind of battle.

With her heart in her throat, Sadie commanded the children to remain seated.

"But we should go, Miss Evans! There could be serious trouble!" Walter said impatiently.

"That's exactly why you must stay here and obey me," Sadie said, her voice ringing with authority. "You are all in my charge. I know of a way we can learn if there's any trouble. I must ask you all to remain in your seats and not come to the door. Word of honor," she said, eyeing the eyebrowless Shockley boys until she had received their nod of agreement.

Slipping outside, she scanned the portion of town that she could see, and saw a number of riders moving along at an easy pace. Nothing seemed out of the ordinary in that. "Herman!" she called, yelping with alarm when the man appeared from a shadow across from where she expected to find him. "Oh, you heard them, too! Here, take this pistol." She lifted it from the lunch box. "See if you can slip into town unseen. I think a bank robbery may be in progress. I can't send the children home for lunch until I know the way is safe."

Herman's eyes rounded at the request. Charged with such responsibility, the old man stiffened his spine and nodded to her like a brave soldier. He took the heavy pistol in his gnarled fingers.

"Hurry right back as soon as you know everything is all right. I know you can keep from being seen, can't you?"

"Sure can!" he said, hefting the pistol with appreciation and then scuttling away up the road. He was quickly lost to view in a series of hillocks and hollows thick with dried grasses. Sadie watched him slip in behind the store.

Sadie returned to the schoolhouse gratified to find every student still in place. "We'll remain here until we know that it's safe to go home for lunch. I'll read to you from Ellsworth's Primer."

By half-past twelve the room bristled with tension. The younger children were restless with hunger. Sadie was worried and annoyed because Herman hadn't returned. She'd heard several more distant shots, and was certain she heard the church bell peal once.

Finally she looked at Johnny, Walter and Cornell, her

eldest students, and motioned for them to join her outside. After closing the door, she looked up at the young men with a serious frown. "Listen to me very carefully. It's possible the bank was robbed, and just possible that outlaws are still hiding in the area. With Deputy Warren out of town —"

"How do you know he is?" Cornell asked.

"Never mind! I know. And it's possible the sheriff is chasing the ones doing the shooting . . . or doing just about anything, actually. All I want you boys to do is slip into town from the direction of the park. Go together so that you'll be safe. You might stop at the Crowleys and relay the message that I'm keeping the rest of the children at school until —"

Another shot rang out. Then a steady series of them followed. They were moving closer.

"I will not release the children until one of you returns. Don't try to handle anything yourselves. I'm serious about this, boys! There are plenty of grown men in town who can handle anything that comes up."

Eagerly they dashed away, jackets flying as they clapped on their hats and darted across the field in the direction of the park. She felt a knot of dread settle in her stomach. Almost as quickly she shook off the feeling, thinking to herself that she was being needlessly dramatic. She was probably just trying to convince everyone how concerned she was about the students. Her efforts were certainly hopeless, for as soon as Jim returned she was determined to leave town and head west. Maybe he would go with her.

Though Sadie couldn't hope that the boys would return after only half an hour, she was having an increasingly hard time keeping the children from complaining of her foolishness and their own hunger. The Davidson boys were furious that she hadn't let them go with the older boys, but they were only thirteen. "I need you boys here to help me," she told them, hoping they would realize how sincere her words were.

Christa's mind was working in leaps as she, too, imagined that outlaws had come to rob the Crowley bank. And she was thinking of her father's store, another possible target for thieves. Betty Runyon had good reason to fret for her father, whose law office was not far from the bank, and for her grandfather the mayor. Mary and Sara Whithers and Cory managed to keep fairly calm, sustained by their father's teachings.

Annabelle, Cornell's sister, was naturally concerned that he hadn't yet returned. Winnie occupied herself by distracting Annabelle with a game of cat's cradle. Susanna and Dawn whispered and fretted together. Now and then Dawn cast Sadie a worried look, and then resumed gnawing on her fingernails until Sadie was certain they were worn right down to the quick.

Just as the Shockley boys were beginning to go too far in their teasing of Jerome Crowley and Douglas Newcomb, Sadie heard hoofbeats pounding up the road. The horses and riders passed by too quickly for her to see if it was just the boys returning. A roil of dust rose at the windows on that side, and then the door fell open.

Two men in long, buff-colored riding slickers burst into the room. The girls and younger children screamed. Sadie saw nothing but the ugly muzzles of long rifles tucked carelessly beneath each man's arm. They held drawn pistols in their free hands.

Sadie held her hand flat at her side as a signal for the children to remain motionless. She heard behind her the quivering silence as the children froze in postures of flight. "Sit down, children," she said, her voice strangely thick. "These gentlemen have no reason to harm us. We have nothing here," she said to the two men as they stared, grinning, at her.

One man of about thirty had longish auburn hair and a thick curling mustache of brown over a pouting lower lip. He swept off his dusty, weather-worn derby and scowled at her suddenly. He had the passionless, stolid eyes of a cutthroat. Half the cartridges in his gunbelt had been used, Sadie observed.

The other man was younger, perhaps only twenty. He wore

a strange narrow-brimmed hat slightly too large for his head. He had no mustaches, only ragged chin whiskers, and his greasy gold hair hung in sweaty ringlets along the back of his collar. His smile faded, too, to be replaced by a petulant, worried frown.

"No trouble from you," the older man said softly. "All valuables on the desks, if you please."

Winnie burst into tears.

"We have nothing of value, gentlemen," Sadie said. "You're welcome to search my desk, but then I must ask you to leave us. These are only children. You can't harm them."

"Jasper," the older man said, jerking his head to the side, his eyes showing no concern for the terrified children shrinking in their seats. "See to the cloakroom."

The younger outlaw sidled into the cloakroom and went through all the jackets and belongings hanging on the hooks. The older man jerked Sadie's desk drawer out, dumping the contents on the floor. "Got a bar for that side door?"

Reluctantly, Sadie nodded.

"Jasper, get the door."

The one called Jasper came out examining a brooch he'd found pinned to one of the coats. His eyes flickered across the children's faces as one of the girls gasped.

"Miss Evans, I'm feeling poorly," Dawn whispered.

Sadie turned, about to go to the girl.

"Don't you move, schoolteacher. Set yourself down right there. That's it. Don't none of you children move a muscle. We're here to wait a bit."

Jasper slipped the wooden plank into the brackets so that the side door was held closed.

"Keep an eye out at that window," the older man said, motioning with his pistol.

Jasper smashed the barrel of his rifle through the lower three panes of the window, making the Shockley boys scatter backwards in terror. Ignoring them, he thrust the barrel outside, resting it on the glass-littered sill. "Got the road covered, Daryl," he said.

"Yeah, now shut your face. Damned idiot." Daryl swept the top of Sadie's desk clean with his pistol and then perched on the corner. "You Sadie Evans?" he asked casually, glancing up when he didn't hear her answer. "Well, are you?"

"Why . . . yes," she whispered, astonished.

He barked a humorless laugh. Scratching his chest thoughtfully, he then laid his rifle down and fiddled with his pistol, filling the three empty chambers with bullets from his gunbelt. He took aim at the rafters, squinting along the sights. Then he leveled the weapon at Sadie's breast. "Am I going to have any trouble out of you, Sadie Evans?"

"Not unless you harm one of these children," she said softly, her eyes narrowed, her jaw clenched. "It will get cold in here soon, with that window broken. Can the children put on their coats?"

"You hear that, you damn fool?" Daryl said, kicking the nearest desk to get the younger man's attention. "Git the coats and things. Got enough firewood to last the afternoon?" he asked Sadie then.

"Only enough until the end of the class day. If you keep us here after three, the children's parents will come for them."

He shook his head, picking at one of his back teeth. "T'ain't likely. Most folks in town are otherwise occupied, you might say."

Jasper brought out an armload of jackets and caps he'd scooped up from the floor where he'd thrown them after going through them.

"May I?" Sadie asked, indicating she wanted to pass the things among the shivering children.

"Just you remember who I'm pointing this gun at," Daryl said softly. Then he rolled his eyes around the room, stopping to take in the features of each of the eldest girls. His gaze lingered longest on Christa.

Sadie's blood ran cold.

Trying to act as if she dealt with gun-toting outlaws every day, Sadie calmly took the jackets and capes around to the children, loudly urging them all to the farthest corner where "the cold wouldn't reach."

Outside, the sun was pouring from a cloudless sky. In the distance several more shots rang out in rapid succession. Annabelle began weeping with Winnie.

"Girls, everything's going to be just fine. Try not to cry. Help is on the way," Sadie said.

"Ain't so," Daryl snapped. "We got this town sewed up. We're staying just as long as we care to. We got every last coin from the bank, and we're helping ourselves at the stores along the way. Ain't a man in town with the gumption to stop us. You know, you got a lawman in this town about as lily-livered as a puny little woman."

"That ain't so!" Susanna yelped, leaping to her feet.

Sadie grabbed the girl's shoulders. "Don't say another word," she hissed into the girl's ear. "If he finds out you're the sheriff's daughter, he might —"

"What's that you're whispering to the little brat?" Daryl said, smirking at Susanna's smoldering look of terror and fury.

Jasper interrupted. "The others are coming now," he said. "I'm going. You want to?"

"Will you just shut your face, you stupid jackass? You want her knowing everything we're about?"

Jasper glanced at Sadie. "She ain't nothing." He started for the door.

"You got the brains of a peahen," Daryl said, joining the young outlaw at the door.

Jasper went out as riders thundered into the schoolyard. He and one other rode off again. Sadie couldn't determine if more than four or five horses had arrived. Trying desperately to calm Winnie and Annabelle, she watched the door.

A stiff breeze stirred the dry grasses outside, sending a whisper of warning through the quiet. Dust and cold air swirled into the room. Sadie saw three men beyond the door, one tall, wearing a long dark coat. He was clean-shaven except for a day's growth of stubble. His brows were knit as he looked back up the road and fondled his rifle nervously.

Another man had long sleek hair and a full beard. He was tall, too. He wore the long black riding coat of a traveling preacher, but he was loaded down with so many pistols and rifles that he looked more like a bandito.

Sadie's attention was drawn to the man coming in ahead of them, a man of average height but stocky, a man with wavy brown hair and a handsomely formed face. His expression was calculating and slightly suspicious as he entered the schoolroom. Pushing back the brim of his stetson with the muzzle of his pistol, he squinted at Sadie. A slow smile spread across his full, provocative lips.

The room began to spin, and Sadie's breath came in shallow, constricted gasps. A dull thudding filled her ears, deadening the muffled whimpers of the younger children as they pressed in around her.

Fighting to keep from fainting, Sadie stared at the man, who was wearing a brand new frock coat with a long coat over it. His stetson was new, too. He brandished his pistol, still gleaming with oil from the gunsmith's display case. He had on shiny new boots, and slung over his left shoulder was a weighty saddle bag. He swung it to the desk with a chinking thud, waving Daryl away as he made a move for it. "Later," he hissed. "I got business with the schoolmarm first."

Sadie dropped into the nearest seat. She couldn't think.

The stocky, curly haired man grinned at her. "And how are you on this beautiful November afternoon, Sadie? You're looking mighty good. Better, in fact, than the last time I seen you. Been keeping yourself busy, I see. All upright and respectable again. Well" — he chuckled to himself — "we'll see about that before we're through."

Sadie felt someone tugging on her sleeve. "Do you know him, Miss Evans?" one of the children whispered in amazement.

Sadie's head was whirling with thoughts and memories. Her first instinct was to run, to make him fire and kill her so that the pain of seeing him again would cease.

But the pain remained. She was rooted to the desk, staring at eyes she had once thought handsome, a smile that had once been dear.

"Evans, is it now?" he said, motioning the two tall men to enter.

Sadie couldn't respond.

One man had the dark, disappointed look of a man capable of great evil or surprising gentleness. The other had the removed, self-righteous, relaxed expression of one completely without moral scruples or sane reasoning.

"Boys, I want you to meet Sadie. My dear," he said, removing his outer coat. "I would like to introduce my friends. Over here is Daryl Craig, whom you've already met." He took on the expression of an extremely proper gentleman with affected mannerisms.

One of the girls giggled in terror.

Sadie reached out and seized the girl's icy, trembling hand. It was Susanna, no longer a troublesome brat but a shivering child. "Don't be taken in," Sadie whispered, trying not to move her lips.

"Over here we have Verle Potts." The stocky man waved toward the man with the beard. "And Glen Preston." He pointed to the frowning one with stubble. "You met Jasper Potts already — Verle's baby brother who rode off. We've come to this fine little town at the recommendation of a mutual acquaintance, Miss — what was it again? — Evans? Yes, she didn't want to tell me where you were at first, or your new name, Sadie, but I persuaded her. Warren Bluffs, Kansas? I asked. Where the hell is that? And eventually she told me."

Sadie stiffened. "I doubt you received parole so soon," she hissed, shocked that she could still speak.

"No. Just took a little time off to look up my best girl."

"Adelaide's dead, you know," Sadie hissed more loudly, growing reckless. "Did you kill her?"

He looked distressed. "Not that I remember. Let's have a look at your charges. Ain't they a fine-looking bunch? Want to introduce them to me? You know me as Rayford Storm, of course, but most folks just call me Stark."

Chapter Eighteen

"Regardless of the election results, Jim, this temporary writ will remove Otis Wheeler from the duties of sheriff long enough for my investigators to look into your allegations. In the meantime, I assign you as a state marshal under my authority charged with arresting and holding over for trial this sheriff who is accused of misusing his power."

Jim shook the governor's hand. "Thank you, sir. If you'll excuse me, I'm heading back for Warren Bluffs right away."

"You look ready to drop, son." The governor handed over the papers Jim needed to remove Otis from office. "You can afford to join me in a drink, can't you? I'll have something brought in for you to eat. Send a dispatch to your mayor so he'll know what we've decided."

Gratefully, Jim accepted a shot of the governor's best bourbon and dropped onto a comfortable sofa in the governor's private office to discuss in more detail the events that had led him to make the hard hundred-mile ride to the state capitol.

He was just finishing a plate of delicacies brought over from the formal luncheon the governor had been attending before Jim insisted he come away to hear his news, when the governor's secretary came in.

"Excuse me, sir, but I can't seem to get a telegraph dispatch through to Warren Bluffs. The lines must be down."

Jim's head came up. "I don't like the sound of that. Try Abilene or Hays City. Governor, you'll have to forgive me, but I probably should get back right away. Otis may be trying to delay the returns for the election. Who knows" — he smiled, with an effort — "I might be winning after all."

By the time Jim had retrieved his hat and coat, the secretary had returned saying he had sent dispatches to both towns on either side of Warren Bluffs, but both towns had reported that they could not get messages through to Jim's home town either.

"I could spare a few well-trained and reliable deputies," the governor said as Jim started out the door.

"Thank you again, sir. You've been a tremendous help."

Within the hour, Jim and three deputy marshals were headed back to Warren Bluffs. Jim's mind raced with the possibilities awaiting him there, and with every mile he grew more anxious.

By dusk that day he was within sight of the town, and he and his companions stopped to rest and consider their options. After careful thought Jim sent the deputies around to scout the town from the other three directions. For himself, he decided his best tactic would be simply to ride into town as though he suspected nothing. He would be most likely to catch Otis unawares if he did nothing to alarm the man.

A mile from town, however, a gunshot rang out, and a bullet whizzed by Jim's head. He tumbled to the roadside, and lay still as his horse galloped on. At the sound of footsteps approaching from a cover of bush not far off, Jim rolled, drew and fired, felling a young stranger.

Rising, Jim stood over the stranger, a youth with chin whiskers, and wondered why the man fired on him. Jim hadn't been forced to kill a man since the earliest days of his job as deputy, when the town was wild and nearly lawless. The deed left him tense with regret.

Approaching the town on foot, he decided to leave the road to seek the cover of the cottonwoods that shaded the homes of the poorer east-side residents along the river. It was there, creeping between sheds, barns and harvested truck gardens that he first saw the strangers on horseback who stood sentry along Cowtrail Street. He made his way undetected as far as the rear of the livery barn and finally into the loft.

From there Jim could see broken windows in Cadwallader's store. The town was strangely silent. He eased back into the shadow of the livery's loft to await something that would tell him what was happening in Warren Bluffs.

"Let me tell you about your brave little schoolmarm," Stark said, settling himself comfortably on Sadie's desktop. "When I met her she was the sweetest little lady I'd ever run across. Why, she was just as proper as a saint."

The children around Sadie listened with their eyes wide and disbelieving. Sadie felt them shifting uneasily as Stark went on to describe the boarding house where he had found Sadie and her mother. With every word Sadie longed to flee, but instead she silently endured with increasingly fatalistic calm. This was the end of her stay in Warren Bluffs. She felt sad and a bit resentful that it should be Stark who exposed her, but it was a relief to know beyond any doubt that she had nothing more to hide.

Stark was laughing to himself and shaking his head a little. Then he lifted his eyes and gazed at Sadie. "Yessiree, she was the most innocent thing. I must've pulled a score of jobs while living at that run-down little boarding house. And can you believe it? I hid most of the loot in her bedroom closet, right under her nose!" He leaned forward, having fun with his story. "I told her I was hunting for mice."

Mike Shockley snickered, but at his sister's sharp look he grew quiet again.

"She never suspected a thing," Stark said, drawing in a self-satisfied breath. "The best part was when I asked her to marry me."

Sadie felt the children stiffen with surprise. She glanced at Dawn and saw that the girl looked amazed and somewhat taken aback. As if to probe the depth of her ruin, Sadie forced herself to meet the eyes of Susanna and then Winnie, both bitterly scandalized, and finally Mary and Sara Whithers, rigid with shock that would have warmed Ethel Cadwallader's heart to see.

"I told her to meet me and we'd run away together," Stark went on. "And she did, the little sweetheart. I robbed the train with a friend wearing a dress. It wasn't even the same style or color as the one Sadie was wearing that night, but folks swore she was the one with me. Ain't it something how they was taken in, Sadie?" he asked.

"Must you go on in front of my students?" Sadie whispered.

"They like a good story same as the next person, don't you, younguns?" Ain't you dying to hear what happened to your prim and proper Miss Sadie then? Why, we was arrested. Crime don't pay, so they tell me. She got sent to jail, same as me. How long was it, Sadie? A year? Two? I don't begrudge you the time I spent behind bars, mainly because we're going to make it up. Ain't that so?"

The girls turned to Sadie, confused now. "Miss Evans, is anything he's saying true?" Winnie whispered.

Sadie tried to swallow. Her throat was thick. "Yes, it's all true. Stolen items were found hidden in my bedroom closet. I was arrested and convicted, sentenced to two years in the women's workhouse."

"Oh, Miss Evans, but if you were innocent . . ."

"In the eyes of the law I was not. If nothing else, I was guilty by association. One should be careful choosing one's friends," she said for the benefit of the Shockley boys. But they appeared to be too absorbed in snickering and side-of-the-mouth whispers to heed her warning about associating with Marty.

"My story, younguns, is true, which just goes to show you that law and order ain't all it's cracked up to be. She didn't do a thing and got sent to prison just the same." Stark grinned, then slid off the desktop and stretched. "I figure that pretty well makes you belong to me now, don't you agree, Sadie? Ain't nothing else for you, now that everybody knows you're a jailbird. At least they will know as soon as these lads and lassies toddle on home and spill the beans.

"Now tell me," he said, wiping his mouth with the back of his hand. "Who knows where I might find a sip of Sir John Barleycorn around here?"

Sadie shook her head. "You'll find no liquor near a school-house," she said, feeling her cheeks warm as she remembered the cache of whiskey Herman had showed her only that morning.

Herbie Shockley sprang to his feet. "I know where there's some, mister!" He grinned proudly at his brothers as if expecting their admiration for his boldness in the face of an armed outlaw.

"He doesn't know what he's talking about," Sadie said quickly, jerking the boy back.

Stark silenced her with a single sharp warning look. "Come here, sonny. Tell ol' Stark what you know. If I find out you're telling the truth I'm going to give you a shiny new twenty-dollar gold eagle fresh from the Warren Bluffs bank." He dug a big heavy coin from the bottom of the saddlebag that lay on the desk beside him. "Ain't this a pretty sight, sonny? A gold coin that ain't never seen the inside of another man's pocket. 'Course, if I find you're telling me a lie . . ."

Herbie's eyes glowed with wonder as he gazed at the huge gold coin. At Stark's warning, he faltered.

"Come on, son," Stark said, spinning the coin on the desk. It sang and glittered tantalizingly.

Mike tried to stop his littlest brother. "Wait till I tell pa!" Mike hissed when Herbie didn't stop.

"I ain't going to hurt the boy, son. Now come here, Herbie, my boy, and sit on ol' Uncle Stark's knees. That's a good kid. Where's that liquor you mentioned? Whisper it in your ol' unk's ear."

Stark sat again and helped Herbie onto his knee. Sadie hated to see Herbie whispering to Stark, but felt that so long as the man was behaving amiably she dared not antagonize him.

"Well, you run out and get me a bottle like a good lad," Stark said, grinning across the room at Sadie. "Mighty helpful youngun you got there, Sadie."

In moments Herbie returned, bursting in the door holding up a whiskey bottle in each hand. Daryl turned from his watch by the back window. The other two men straightened. Stark took the bottles, examined the labels and then tossed one to Verle. They uncorked them together and took long pulls. Verle swallowed with hesitation. Stark grimaced as if he'd taken a mouthful of kerosene and gulped it down with a gasping cough. "Suffering snakes! What the hell is this witches' milk?"

Herbie went white and scrambled back, away from Stark.

"Never mind, sonny. Here's your gold eagle. And since you were good enough to bring us two bottles, here's another. That's probably more cash money than the sheriff makes in a month! Don't spend it all in one place!"

Herbie accepted the coins and slunk back, near Sadie but far enough from his brothers so they couldn't take his coins. For a moment he gazed in the wonderment at the money, dazzled more by its unmarked beauty than its inconceivable worth.

Stark passed the bottle to Daryl and then grabbed it back after the man took several eye-watering gulps. "This isn't no real whiskey, let me tell you, Sadie. This is some homemade brand of skull varnish if I ever tasted any. Whoever's making it hereabouts is probably making a lot of money. He's a man after my own heart."

"Miss Evans, I feel real puny," Dawn whispered, holding her stomach with both hands.

Sadie moved to take the girl's shoulders, but the room exploded with two gunshots that splintered the floorboards two feet in front of Sadie. Sadie jerked back as the children shrieked. Herbie looked up at the outlaw who had smiled at him only moments before and who was now holding out his smoking pistol. Herbie swallowed and laid his two gold eagles gingerly on the desk before him. Rising cautiously, he backed away as if wanting nothing more to do with the unpredictable outlaw's loot. He took refuge behind Sadie's skirts.

"Dawn needs a little fresh air," Sadie said, her voice trembling from the shock that Stark would actually fire at the children.

Stark was chuckling. "Thought I'd just let you know I ain't here for a picnic. I'm a personable man, as you well know, Sadie, but you make another sudden move like that and I just might have to prove what we're about in this town. It's nothing to be snickering at, younguns," he said, eyeing the Shockley boys, who had been growing irritatingly free with their whispers. "That reminds me, Glen, why don't you ride over to that restaurant and bring us back something. Sadie and me still have plenty to talk over while the boys finish up in town."

The man gulped from Verle's bottle and then shuffled out, looking annoyed.

"Stark, let me take her outside. She really is ill!" Sadie said, holding Dawn's quivering shoulders in her own shaking hands.

Seeing the pale girl bent over, Stark made a sharp motion. "Get her out then before she pukes all over the place. Damn silly brats."

Casting the children a warning look, Sadie rushed Dawn outside. The fresh air did wonders for her own swimming head as she steered Dawn toward the fence, thinking perhaps the girl might escape.

"Hold it right there, Sadie. If she's going to chuck her guts, she can do it right there," Stark said from the doorway.

"I'm all right now, Miss Evans," Dawn whispered, breathing deeply and straightening. "I guess you don't need me going to pieces on you. Is he going to kill us?"

"He's just tormenting us. He wants to take me away with him. But you mustn't worry," Sadie hissed very softly. "I won't leave you children. Go back inside when you're ready. If you can, get the older ones to pair up with the younger ones. A chance to get away might come, and I want to be certain each of you is safe and looking after the little ones. Can you do that for me?"

Stark ambled toward them. "Want to stop that whispering, ladies? Missy, how about you going back inside now? You look fine to me."

Dawn stuck out her chin. "I ain't scared of you! You lay a hand on any one of us and my pa'll blow a hole in you big enough to drive a team of horses through."

Stark chuckled.

"And even if Miss Evans did go to jail, she's the best teacher we ever had. You're just a no-account outlaw, and in these parts we hang outlaws!" Dawn said, flouncing back toward the school. "We hang 'em high and watch 'em dance."

"Dawn, hush!" Sadie gasped, reeling at the girl's astonishing, foolhardy courage.

"Is she crazy or does she think I'm still playing?" Stark said with less humor.

Sadie shivered in the wind. She had come outside with no wrap. Frantically searching her mind for a plan, any sort of plan that would save the children from further trauma, she remained motionless as Stark's hands closed over her trembling shoulders. "Why did you come here?" she whispered, feeling his body shield her from the cutting wind.

"Ain't that obvious, Sadie? I spent a good deal of time in prison, and you know that's no place for a man like me to be. I belong on the outside with a good, willing woman in my bed every night. I sure did have plenty of time to think about you, though. About all I ever thought about was how you felt in my arms that night we got caught together. Have you missed me a little bit? Maybe a lot?"

"I hate you," she whispered softly, letting the venom of her hate fill her throat. "You know that I hate you with all my heart and soul and mind! You all but killed my mother!"

He gave a throaty laugh of dismissal. "She was no saint.

Don't you know that I went to a lot of trouble to find you? You're my best girl, Sadie, and I ain't even had you yet. We're going to take care of that later on tonight, but for now you got to know we belong together from now on. There's nothing left for you but to join up with me now. Towns like this ain't no place for a smart woman like yourself. Why, you and me, we could make so damn much money together it'd be downright sinful!"

"I'd sooner be dead," Sadie whispered.

"Well, that can be arranged, but it doesn't have to come to that. I think when you've had a few hours to consider you'll see my way of reasoning. You ain't going to get rid of me except if you kill me. I don't see how a sweet little slip of a thing like you is going to do that. And I ain't leaving here until you're on the horse with me." He caressed her shoulders, finally sliding his arms around her. With a hand clamped over one of her breasts, he hugged her with his other arm. "Umm-m-m, you're warm, Sadie. I'll bet you been dreaming on me all these months we been apart. You were so eager for me. You were all set to marry me. Remember?"

"How could you possibly think I would remember anything good about you?" Sadie said, twisting away to be free of his fondling hands. "After the way you treated me that night? After the things you said to the sheriff, and after the things you said to me when we were in jail?"

He let her stumble several feet away.

She turned, raking him with a burning look of loathing. "I hated you then, and I still hate you!"

He shrugged and stroked his pistol. "That doesn't change what you wanted with me. I'd say we could work real good together without something as foolish as love between us. You got to make a living, and so do I. You could start work in a town something like this, and get to know the folks with the most money and where they keep it. I could come in and clean the place out.

"I don't expect to keep on with this bone-headed bunch of rowdies I took up with. I'm only doing it this once to get a start. I been planning to come get you a good long time now, and this was the best way I figured I could get you and a stake, too.

"You think on my offer, Sadie. Now, either you soften up and come over to the side of the building with me where we can have a little privacy, or you go back inside for a while. I'll give you another chance. I'm not a hard man. I got all day and all night to wait. As long as all the men in town are crowded into that jail, and anybody else worth bothering with is at that big store under the guns of several mighty trigger-happy yokels — and here I am with a schoolhouse full of sniveling little brats willing to bring me whatever I need and tell me whatever I want to know — I figure I got this town by the short hairs. You can come along afterwards if you like. Or you can go back to prison afterwards. It's up to you. I can't see that you'll be too welcome among your new high and mighty friends after those darlings in there tell how it was you I come looking for. All this business is on your head, my dearest Sadie. If I was in your little shoes, I wouldn't want to be around when those folks were turned loose. My boys and me, we shot up a few stores, and cleaned the cash boxes down to the last pennies." He jingled his pockets. "Those folks are eventually going to take it out on somebody."

Sadie was terrified that he might be right. She forced herself to mask at least part of her hate for him. "I have to think," she finally said.

"That's my best girl. Now, come here and give ol' Stark one of your sweet kisses. That's right, right here in front of God and the kiddies in the schoolhouse."

"Ray, please!"

He grabbed her wrists and pulled her close. "Just Stark, Sadie," he whispered, looking down into her face. "Just call me Stark. No pretending. You know what I really am, and I know what you really are. It'll be good between us. You know it will be." His eyes were so dark and moody, his lips soft and sensuous. Then his lips were on Sadie's mouth, slighty hard and faintly cool. He jerked her close, crushing her breasts against his chest as he forced his tongue between her teeth, thrusting it deep to show her how it would be for them . . . later.

She moaned and beat her fists on his shoulders until he released her. "Let me go . . . back inside," she gasped, shuddering with revulsion.

He seized her arm and forced her back to the door, kicking it open and shoving her inside so that the children could see her reddened cheeks and moist lips.

She wiped her mouth with the back of her hand. Composing her face, she finally looked at her students. She could see that they had paired off just as she asked. All she needed to do now was think of a way to distract all three men long enough for the children to slip out the door and run.

"Webb's dead!" the one called Glen said, galloping into the schoolyard an hour later and thundering in the door. He dropped a tablecloth filled with all manner of foods, now mixed together in an unappetizing mess, onto the desktop. "Some crazy little woman with a fifty-fifty buffalo rifle walked into that one big store on the main street and blew his chest in."

Stark looked up from his perusal of his saddlebags. "Do I need to ask what Sutherland did about that?"

"Well, he got the rifle away from her, luckily. And I guess she was satisfied because after that she didn't cause no more trouble. Seems she was upset about her husband getting wounded in the arm or something. I say we clear out of here before morning."

"I'll decide when we clear out of here," Stark muttered. "What is this mess you brought us?" He started picking through the berry pies mixed with meat pasties and several loaves of bread.

"I didn't think I should hang about when there might be more crazy females about with big fifties," Glen said.

Stark gave Sadie a look of rolling-eyed disbelief.

"The children have had nothing to eat all day," Sadie said. "Can I give them some of that?"

He shrugged and allowed her to take one of the loaves and break it into several large pieces, which she gave out to the children. While the children ate, the men talked quietly together and finished both bottles of whiskey.

"Any more where this came from?" Daryl asked, pinning Herbie with his passionless eyes.

The boy seized up with terror.

Daryl made a sniff of contempt and started out the door.

"Where do you think you're going?" Stark asked.

"I seen the kid get these bottles from the hay barn. Thought I'd go see if there's more."

"You've had enough," Stark said.

Daryl screwed up his lip beneath his drooping mustache. "I don't think so, Unkie Starkie," he said with a note of contempt as he swung out.

Stark was waiting for the man when he returned with an armload of bottles. He cuffed the man on the side of the head, causing two of the bottles to slip from his hold and shatter on the floor. The stinging odor of raw alcohol began to fill the room.

Daryl controlled his urge to return the blows and instead took a bottle and resumed his place at the back window. The afternoon light was waning. Verle drank from another bottle. Before long Sadie realized he was watching the girls.

"Why don't you get one of them boys to stoke up the stove there, Sadie?" Stark said after a while. "It's colder than a witch's tit in here."

Mike Shockley snickered. Stark seemed to enjoy provoking the children.

Burt Davidson fed more kindling into the stove and then returned to his seat next to his twin. "How long are we going to have to sit here like this?" he muttered under his breath.

"Till I'm good and ready to be on my way," Stark answered

softly, surprising everyone that he'd heard. "And I ain't going until I know what my best girl intends to do."

"Might we have more of that bread and some of the pie, if you're done?" Sadie said, surprised at how calm she sounded. But she couldn't seem to stop the heavy breathing that caused her bosom to rise and fall so noticeably.

When Stark motioned for her to take the rest of the food, he caught her hand and detained her long enough to make her cheeks flame with embarrassment and alarm. She couldn't go on much longer, she thought. He might get bold . . . or drunk, and do something that the children should not see.

Sadie took everything left in the tablecloth and brought it back. The children gathered around her, picking through the mess, eating and licking their fingers.

"Listen," Sadie hissed just loud enough for them to hear her. "No matter what happens, no matter what I do" — she paused to see if Stark was able to hear her — "I'm doing this only so you all can get away. Understand? As soon as all the men are outside you slip out the side door two by two."

Winnie touched her arm. Her fingers were icy and trembling. "Ain't the deputy your beau, Miss Evans?"

"Yes, but he's not in town to help us. We must help ourselves. Pay no mind to what I say or do! Promise me!"

"You're whispering again, Sadie," Stark said.

"I'm afraid we're going to have to ask a favor of you," Sadie said, seeing the strained look on several of the children's faces. "The children have long since missed their afternoon line-up at the privy. And they need a drink at the trough out back if you're going to keep us here much longer."

Stark began to smirk. "Daryl, ride into town and see if the boys are done. Get back right away, and see that they relieve the boys stationed out on the roads. They might be hungry by now. And take 'em a drop of this fine rot-gut while you're at it."

"I thought Jasper was your errand boy," Daryl muttered, shuffling out.

"He ain't here, is he? That seems to leave you."

Daryl took up several of the bottles and was soon pounding away, his expression dangerous.

As Sadie guided the children out to use the privies, the Shockley boys paused to gawk at Verle's arsenal — the weapons that hung all over his chest and hips.

"Like shooting irons, do you, boys?" the man said, the first words Sadie had heard him speak. His voice was low and resonant, just the sort of voice to preach a hellfire and brimstone sermon. "Let me show you what a few of these pieces will do," he said, going out with them.

Stark motioned Glen to follow. "Keep an eye on that varmint."

While Verle entertained the smaller boys with feats of truly amazing marksmanship, the rest of the children rushed to the privies. Winnie and Annabelle were able to slip away to the shelter of some bushes and make their way to the park.

While the others filed back into the school, nervous now because the men were outside and this might be their chance to escape, Verle's explosive shots echoed one after another in the twilight.

As if answering, several shots destroyed the long silence from town. Stark looked up in irritation. "Damned fools," he muttered.

"Hey," Glen said, the first to notice that two of the students were gone. "We're missing a few kids." He nudged Stark. "I only count fifteen."

"Didn't know you could count, Glen," Stark muttered. Looking up, he surveyed the room and then took Sadie's arm as she started in after the students. "I warned you about that whispering. I think it's time you made up your mind about me."

"I've been trying to, but as long as I have charge of these children . . . Would you let them go on home? I'm free to go with you after that," Sadie said softly.

"I'll consider it, Sadie," Stark replied, guiding her inside.

Verle continued to take practice shots at the trees along the river bank. Glen was draining yet another bottle; he was clearly growing quite drunk. He eyed the saddlebags lying across the desk and then turned his attention to Betty Runyon and Christa Roberts, who were huddled together nearby.

"Hey, you two, didn't Stark warn you about whispering? Come here, both of you."

Sadie stepped between the bitter-looking man and the two cringing girls. "You're not to lay a hand on them or any of the others. Stark, I want your word that you'll keep your men away from my students," she said, never taking her eyes from Glen's face.

"I got no hold over these boys," Stark said with a hint of amusement in his voice. "All I got is this money we're going to divide up, and since the take's not all in yet, we can't leave. 'Course, me and you can ride into town and pick up what the rest of the boys have gathered."

"What makes you think they're still there?" Sadie said softly. "They might have gone on with all they got from the stores. If I remember correctly, the merchants in this town have a habit of keeping large amounts in their private safes."

Christa gasped. Someone shushed her.

Stark considered that. Gradually he saw through her effort to make him suspect the men he'd left in charge of the town. "Try again."

Sadie heaved a sigh. "Well, hell, what's the use of keeping on with this nonsense?" she said, hating the stunned looks of the children as they listened to the abrupt change in her tone.

She straightened, jutting out her chin and taking a breath deep enough to accentuate the curve of her bosom. "I don't know why I'm worrying myself over these kids. They've been nothing but trouble since the first day I walked in the school. Every time I turned around some woman was telling me I wasn't a good teacher, and . . . and . . ." She found she couldn't go on. That subject was too dangerous to expose to the children. "Let's just get out of here. I'm sick of this dusty little hole in the wall. I'm sick to death of putting on airs and trying to fool everyone into thinking I'm a lady. I never should have tried to work here. Come on, Stark. I've made up my mind. I'm going with you."

A grin spread across his face. He settled back and folded his arms. "You sound better already. You've got the kiddies convinced that you've been play-acting with them all this time. Now all you have to do is convince me that you really mean what you're saying."

Sadie's blood surged in her veins. If she delayed even another hour she might lose control of the situation and be a witness to the degradation of her most innocent students. Giving Stark a look she'd seen on the most practiced women at the workhouse, a low, smoldering look of knowledge and desire, she softly smiled. "I think if we go outside I can convince you."

Stark was on his feet at once. Taking the saddlebags and giving Glen a wink, he opened the door to the deepening darkness outside and showed Sadie the way. "I don't think you'll need your wrap this time, either," he said, grinning.

Without a backward look, Sadie stepped outside. "Send your men on their way."

"I'm not doing a damn thing until you've convinced me that you aren't just playing cat-and-mouse with me," he whispered behind her.

"Over this way," she said, leading him behind the schoolhouse where they wouldn't be seen from the windows.

Verle was squeezing off shots into the dark of the river bank now. Every shot made Sadie's heart leap with alarm. As soon as she and Stark were in the shadows, Stark had his hands on her and was drawing her close. His mouth was all over hers, and she had to return his kisses as if she desired them.

With one of his hands groping at her backside, his knee probing between her thighs and her heart pounding so hard she was sure she'd faint, she let Stark handle her. Quickly she knew he was aroused. She twisted away. "Convinced?" she whispered huskily, panting. "I'll go away with you, but not with your men. I don't trust them."

A chorus of squeals rose from inside the schoolhouse. Stark wanted another kiss, but Sadie held him off. "I warned you! Send the men away!"

With a muttered curse, Stark stormed back into the school. "All right, you bastard. Let her go! Go on out to the roads and tell the boys to meet back at the cabin. We'll divide everything there."

Glen released Christa when Stark cuffed the back of his head. "I want my share now!" Glen yelled, drawing his pistol.

"I think you've made a serious mistake, my friend," Stark said coolly, staring down Glen and the drawn, cocked pistol.

"Not in here! Not in front of the children!" Sadie gasped, pushing Stark back into the darkness. "Outside!" she screeched at Glen.

Christa fell sobbing into Sadie's arms. "He kissed me! Papa will kill me!"

"Hush!" Sadie hissed, watching Stark and the other man advance into the darkness. Finally she was able to fling the door closed.

"Down!" she shouted just as a rifle shot rang out. Something heavy hit the door, knocking Sadie to her knees. Glen sprawled backwards partially into the schoolroom, his arm flung back.

The children were screaming.

"Go!" Sadie said, pushing the man's body and trying to close the door with her foot. She thrust Christa toward the side door and heard the Davidson twins lifting the bar from the brackets.

Just as the last child slipped into the darkness, Stark managed to shove the door wide. Momentarily he looked down at Sadie, thinking she had been shot. Seeing that she was unharmed, he looked up and scanned the empty room. "Verle!" he shouted back over his shoulder. "Round up the boys! Meet me at the cabin." He slipped inside the shadowed schoolroom. He still had the saddlebags.

His face was lit with stripes of flickering yellow light from the grate in the stove door. "I don't think for a minute that you're going with me willingly, but that doesn't bother me, because we can still work together."

Sadie struggled to her feet. Her legs felt like jelly. "I said I'd go with you, and I will," she said, knowing she had to continue to deceive him long enough to rid the town of the thieves. She couldn't risk having him chase after the children.

He seized her and jerked her close, gazing balefully into her eyes. Then he kissed her and there was no restraint now that the children were gone.

Her body quaked in alarm as she felt involuntary shivers of fire race through her blood. "Not here!" she gasped, tearing her mouth free of his devouring kiss. "Let's go. Let's just go!"

Looking drugged, he dragged himself through the doorway into the darkness. He tied the heavy saddlebags to his saddle and then mounted. He extended his hand to Sadie and turned the horse slowly until he was in a position for her to mount behind him.

After what seemed like an eternity of hesitation, she took Stark's hand and squirmed up behind him, circling his waist with her cold, aching arms.

"Hold me like you want me," Stark whispered, touching his spurs to the horse's flanks.

She thought of Jim then, the first thoughts of him she'd dared allow into her mind in hours. Where was he? What would he find when he returned? A devastated town and her gone away with an outlaw? She laid her head against Stark's back and spread her hands across his chest. He wasn't as muscular and broad as Jim. She felt the first stinging tears gather in her eyes. His coat didn't smell the same. It had the impersonal smell of the store where he'd stolen it that afternoon.

Stark guided the horse west across the field into the park. Not a soul stirred near the courthouse on Park Circle, and all the houses were dark. Sadie closed her eyes. "Was anyone hurt today when you rode into town?" she whispered.

"I didn't take notes," Stark muttered, turning onto the road that led toward Jim's grandparents' home.

Her thoughts raced back to the times she had traveled this road with Jim, to wonder of the love they had shared in the bluffs. What a fool she had been to think that she could ever have what decent women are entitled to after what she'd experienced thanks to Rayford Storm — Stark.

"I like the way your hands hold tight to me," Stark whispered, urging the horses to hurry.

She wanted to crush him to death, she thought, grinding her teeth. Instead, she forced her voice to come out softly. "Where's this cabin you're meeting your men at?"

Stark laughed out loud. "You don't think I'm going back there, do you? Hell, I've got the cash money. What do I need with a bunch of brooches and earbobs from dusty ol' sodbusters' wives? There wasn't enough gold to fill a tooth in most of the cash boxes of this town. I know, because I went through most of them myself. Hell, Sadie! I ain't stupid, except when it comes to picking up little small-town virgins to help me hold up trains. You and me are taking off for parts unknown! We'll change our names, buy us some real nice clothes, hole up in some fancy hotel for a while until we figure out a way to clean out the cash boxes of other towns along the way. Those boneheads can keep their homemade whiskey and their trinkets."

Sadie's heart slowed to a dreadful thud. "Won't they come after you when they realize you've taken off with the . . . the saddlebag?"

"Let them try to find us, Sadie my darling! You and me will find us a safe spot to hide in the bluffs all night. Come morning we'll figure out where to go. I hear Dodge City is one fine place. None of this prohibition business going on there."

Nothing more lay between Sadie and the promise Stark had made earlier, that they would soon make up for lost time. Together.

Chapter Nineteen

"I have an extra key," Jim called to the mayor, who was grasping the bars in the crowded jailhouse cell. As Jim herded four of the outlaws inside the jail, he tossed over his ring of keys and waited while Lex Runyon let himself and the others out. "In you go, boys," Jim said, nudging the prisoners into the cell.

The townsmen spilled into the street, bristling with indignation and wounded pride. They had been confined in the cells since early afternoon. Hungry, thirsty and weary, they grumbled among themselves as they began to disperse. If they had not been so concerned for the safety of their families and businesses, they might have turned on the outlaws. Jim had been prepared for that, but breathed a tense sigh of relief when he saw the men wanted only to relieve themselves and get home.

The women who had been held at gunpoint all afternoon, were pouring from Cadwallader's store, crying for joy as they found their men and embraced in the street. Jim had freed them all a short time before, killing an outlaw named Sutherland and felling another with a bullet to the chest as the outlaw galloped through town trying to flee with an armload of whiskey bottles.

Over the joyous commotion, Jim shouted directions for the wounded outlaw to be tended by the doctor. Dr. Hamlin was already tending minor wounds and abrasions caused by the outlaws' abuse. One of his patients was George Cadwallader, who had been shot in the shoulder moments after the outlaws swarmed into his store.

"A couple of you men take that second man over to the Doc's, please. And Henry?" he shouted to the rancher. Henry Shockley was still astride his horse alongside the mounted deputy marshals and several other ranchers who had made up Jim's army. "I left a man shot out on the east road. See that he gets to the undertaker, will you?"

The man nodded and rode off.

"Akins? Johnson?" Jim called, spying the men who had helped carry Biggins secretly from the demolished saloon, when Jim had decided to trick Otis into thinking Biggins was dead. Moments after the explosion, Otis had proved to Jim's satisfaction that he, Otis, had known Biggins was inside the building. "I want you to ride north to see if you can spot that other man they claim was with them. Verle Potts is his name. Just trail him if you can. He's an escapee from the asylum in Topeka. His wanted circular came through here just a few months back. I'll try to join you in a few hours."

"Where are you going, Jim?" Herman Biggins said, hobbling from the shadows between the jail and the railyard.

A murmur of shock spread among the people scattered in the street. "Thought you was dead, Herman!" someone called out.

Herman removed his hat and did a theatrical bow. "Miss me, did you?"

Jim was about to explain what was going on as the first of Sadie's students appeared from the tall grasses along School Road. In the resulting chaos, Jim steered Herman to the side. "I want you to tell everyone just exactly what happened to you the other night when Otis took you from your shack and beat you. Can you remember?"

"And about the big bang and the fire and me hiding in the hay barn?"

Jim nodded. "I was going over to the school, but Sadie should be along any minute now." He glanced up, expecting to see her hurrying after the pairs of children emerging from the darkness.

The angered voices of the townsmen rose as the children shouted out the details of their afternoon ordeal. Christa Roberts' voice was loudest. ". . . shot him! And he fell dead in the doorway right in front of us. And I think the fancy-talking one has taken her! He told us the most awful story about her, Papa, but she . . ."

Jim didn't stop to listen to the rest. Sadie wasn't coming up the road. She'd been taken! He was swinging onto the nearest horse. "Can you keep this from turning into a lynch mob?" he shouted to the deputy marshals.

The three nodded and dismounted, taking charge.

At the schoolhouse, Jim didn't bother to dismount. He rode past the windows, leaning to peer into the shadows that encroached as the glow from the potbellied stove dwindled. He found the body of Glen Preston sprawled on the doorstep.

Pausing, he couldn't fathom why one of the outlaws should take Sadie along as a hostage. The siege had been broken, and nearly all of the outlaws were captured or killed. He wheeled his horse, trotted to the riverbank, then followed the river around to the park. Seeing a movement at the pavilion, he climbed down, drew his pistol and crept forward in the dark.

"Want to come out of there?" he said softly when he drew near enough to hear sniffling. "Annabelle! Winnie Akins! What are you doing out here?" He eased his pistol back into his holster. "It's safe now. You can go —"

"We saw him taking her away!" Winnie shrieked when she raised her head above the rail and saw Jim staring down at her. "They were headed that way, out of town, and he had her, just like he said he would. He's taking Miss Evans away!"

Jim hauled both girls from the pavilion, starting them toward Park Circle and the safety of the houses there. Lights were on at the Cadwalladers' and the Crowleys' now. "Go on home now, girls. Who had Sadie? Why?"

"Oh, it was just awful the way he talked to her!" Winnie gasped in a scandalized whisper. "He was no gentleman! He told us how she went to jail for something she didn't do! It was just awful to see her face, Deputy Warren! Just awful. She was so ashamed."

"And so brave," Annabelle said, her voice quivering. "She went off with him to save us!"

"How did he — what was his name? Did he say his name?" Jim demanded.

"Y-yessir, he did! It was Stark," Winnie whispered in hushed terror. "He called her his . . . his best girl. Oh, hurry, Deputy Warren! Save her from him!"

Stark's horse struggled up a steep ravine to the top of the bluff. Reining, he paused to look back at Warren Bluffs. Sadie lifted her tear-stained face from where it rested against Stark's back and looked, too, thinking that she was leaving behind all she had fought so hard for.

Lights were winking on all across town. Though the night was growing bitter, with the bite of frost already in the air, Sadie scarcely felt the cold. She stared down on the little town wondering if Jim had returned safely from Topeka yet. Then, too, he might be lying shot to death on one of the streets below, the light from his penetrating pale blue eyes forever dark.

She shuddered.

"Ugly little town," Stark muttered, as if he understood the reason for her shudder.

"I had almost been accepted there," Sadie said flatly, remembering how MargieBelle, Trudy, and Alvinia had sprung to her defense the evening before.

"And what would that have gotten you? A paltry school-marm's pay and a lifetime of living up to impossible expectations," Stark said, jerking the horse around and galloping off. "You're better off with me to look after you."

Sadie clung to him to keep from being thrown off into the rocks.

"I come from just such a town," Stark shouted over the thunder of the hoofbeats. "Bunch of stupid boneheads live in them. Nothing but gossip and church socials. Stupid people. I got out as soon as I was old enough to steal a horse and a gun. I'm telling you, Sadie, my darling, I owe myself a better life than that."

Jostling behind Stark, Sadie gritted her teeth. She owed herself a better life than the one Stark offered. She had come close to being accepted by a town dominated by one bitter little dragon of a woman. No other small town would ever have a woman more difficult to please than Ethel Cadwallader.

Sadie suspected Ethel was the one with the fifty-fifty buffalo gun. For all the woman's airs and mean-minded ways, Sadie had to admire her. She could just picture the little woman marching into her husband's store in her rustling Kansas City foulard silk to blast an outlaw.

Yes, there would be gossip and church socials, and snooping and children thinking up pranks. Strangers would always have to prove themselves to suspicious people who had good reasons to view outsiders with a skeptical eye.

It was the world she had been born to, the world where she had been happy. It was the world of ginger beer and double-wedding-ring quilts. It was box suppers and school pageants, dusty streets and merchants who all knew her name.

There were other towns like that, she thought, though there would never be another Jim Warren. She had come so very close to success in this one foolish, unimportant little place that she would be crazy to throw away her hopes of a decent life yet, in spite of the double injustice done her by this man she was with.

The horse thundered ahead, carrying her farther and farther from all she'd fought to regain. Once before, Stark had torn her from a world she had loved. He wouldn't again, she thought, relaxing her hold on his chest. It was better to be dead than dishonored.

Squeezing her eyes closed, summoning the image of Jim's easy smile to her mind, Sadie released her hold on Stark. With the next racing step she was flung from the horse's back.

She landed hurtfully on her left shoulder and arm. Stunned by the pain, she lay still, straining to hear. Yes, Stark was reining in, calling back to her, turning. If she could only move. If she could only hide.

The breath had been knocked from her, but she struggled, moaning when she was able to drag herself only a few inches through the grass.

Then Stark was there, grabbing her up. "What are you doing? Are you trying to get yourself killed?" She could just make out his face by the wan light of the quarter moon.

"You can't understand what it means to be decent, can you?" she whispered, gasping in pain as he wrenched her up. "My shoulder!"

He examined her, making a disgusted, impatient noise. "It's dislocated. Let me see if I can —" He attempted to twist her arm back into place.

She let out a shriek of pain. "Don't! Just leave me."

He crouched over her. "I told you I was taking you along. Now you're coming, dislocated shoulder or no. On your feet!"

"I can't," she panted, blinded by pain as he jerked her to her feet and held her against him. The vicious effort had moved her shoulder joint back into place. The pain was dull and throbbing now.

"I'm taking you," Stark hissed against her face. "I decided a long time ago that I wanted you, and I still do. If we hadn't been caught, I would have married you. I had that bridal suite waiting for us. I even had the clothes waiting not far from where we stopped."

"Why did you stop then?" she whispered, trying to stand on her own. She reached suddenly for his pistol. Her left arm and hand were clumsy with pain, nearly useless.

He struck her down, away from the pistol. She fell in a heap, panting, thinking now that if he wouldn't leave her she would have to kill him, or be killed. She curled her fingers around a rock at her side, trying to take it in her right hand before he realized what she was doing.

He saw her and dropped to his knees astride her chest, wrenching both her arms back and pinning her wrists to the ground. She wailed in pain. Her shoulder felt on fire.

"I hate you! You killed my mother!" she gasped, overwhelmed by the agony in her injured shoulder. She realized he was trying to kiss her. She twisted her head to the side, wanting to spit on him.

"I told you she was nothing. I knew all about her, practically from the first. I found out not long after I started walking with you. Someone from your high and mighty little home town took me aside . . . to tell me all about your ma."

"Don't," Sadie whimpered, fearing that if Stark reminded her of the awful night she had been allowed to return to North Rushing to witness her mother's passing she would go mad because of it. "Don't. I won't fight you any longer. Ease up on my arm. It's killing me."

"No more tricks?" Stark hissed, his lips only a fraction of an inch from hers.

"No. My word."

"That should be worth something, coming from you," Stark said, his tone derisive. "Prove to me that you won't try falling off my horse again or shooting me in my sleep some night. Prove it!"

"What do you want me to say?" Sadie said, groggily, barely half-conscious from pain and despair.

"You know what I want, what I've always wanted from you. Prove yourself to me, Sadie Whiting. Show me what you're made of."

He released her arm. The sudden lessening of pain made her weak with relief. Then she realized he was tearing open her shirtwaist. She could feel the night's cold on her throat, and then the hot moistness of Stark's kisses.

Give up! Give up! she thought, still wanting to fight as she felt the coldness of the night air touch her breasts when Stark exposed them.

Then he was heavy on her, his mouth on her breasts and his hands stealing up beneath her skirts again just as they had that night the posse caught them and dragged them off to jail. It was all happening again for her, the shock, the degradation, the whispered promises of sexual fulfilment coming from the cell next to hers while her mother wept in despair out in the next room.

Confused, terrified, Sadie felt hands on her thighs, heard her mother's wailing scream fading away. "Guilty! Guilty! Guilty!"

And then it was the dark night only a few months after her imprisonment when the urgent message had come. Her mother lay dying. Sadie would be granted a few hours' visit. Adelaide had taken her home, handcuffed and in disgrace. The town had been closed up tight, and quiet. Almost everyone had been asleep. She had gone into the boarding house, now dusty and cluttered. Her mother had been packing when she suffered the attack.

Sadie was taken back to the bedroom that she and her mother had shared, and she stared down into the sunken, now almost unrecognizable face of the woman she had so admired and adored.

"Mother?" she had whispered, terrified that her mother would not want her there in her last moments.

"Sadie?" her mother had said thickly. "Where's my Sadie?"

"I'm here," Sadie had wept, dropping to her knees at her mother's bedside. "I'm sorry."

Adelaide had removed the handcuffs so that Sadie's mother wouldn't be reminded of Sadie's circumstances.

"Your father won't be coming," her mother whispered. Then she was crying softly. "I did all I could to forget him and what he did, but it was no use. He had bad blood and he passed it on to my Sadie. My dear, innocent little Sadie. Fornicating with that thief, taking all that money . . ."

"Mama! What are you saying? I never let him touch me! Please, Mama, listen to me! I didn't do any of those things. Why won't you believe me?"

Adelaide had started to tug on Sadie's arm then.

Pain shot through Sadie's body. The memory began to dim as Sadie relived a moment out of time that she had tried to bury, that she had almost succeeded in forgetting. At the same time a man named Stark was kissing her, caressing her and struggling to free her legs to claim her.

"No! Don't say that! Don't!" Sadie wailed, erupting in fists. She bit down on something and tasted blood. A yelp of pain deafened her. She grasped a rock. "Don't say that! He didn't! He didn't!"

But the words were rushing from her mother's lips, those slurred dying words that so crushed Sadie she had feared afterwards that she would never recover. "He was working in the store, and they said he had been embezzling funds for three years, ever since the very first day we were married! They took him away just as they took my Sadie away!" Her mother sobbed uncontrollably, remembering, sinking deeper and deeper into the pillow of her death bed.

"Mama!" Sadie had said, shaking her mother, seizing her and shaking her. "Listen to me! I didn't do anything. I'm innocent! *I am innocent!*" Sadie's throat was raw from screaming.

A sudden blow to the side of the head left her dazed. She was lost to remembering the last moments of her mother's life, to seeing the blessed recognition in her mother's faint, moist eyes.

"Mama," she had whispered, laying her cheek against the cool one of her mother. "I'm innocent."

"Truly?" her mother had whispered, beginning to believe.

Sadie had nodded, and then the light had gently lifted from her mother's face. The flesh became pale and flat. The tears on the old cheeks began to dry.

Sadie had collapsed, relieved to have been forgiven, only to take up moments later the burden her mother had left her, the truth about her father. He had been sentenced to prison, too, for embezzling, and had died there when Sadie was seven years old. Everyone in her home town had known. They had pitied her all those years . . . and they had been watching her, waiting for the bad blood to surface.

Sadie lay still on the cold hard ground in the dry autumn grasses, the tears drying on her own face as she remembered. Stark rolled away from her, blood streaming from a gash in the top of his head. She had struck him with a rock while she raved something about her mother, and now he couldn't think, and he had lost his desire to take her. Looking at her with a wary frown, he fingered his tongue where she'd bitten him. Damned crazy wildcat!

Once before, his weakness and his downfall had been his desire for Sadie's innocence. He couldn't risk getting caught again on her account.

"Come on. I can wait until we find a safe place for the night. Get up," he said, struggling to his feet.

She lay motionless on the ground, her arms limp where they'd fallen when he pried them from his throat and struck her. Her breasts were so beautiful, so perfectly, tantalizingly ripe, exposed there in the pale moonlight like that.

Stooping, he almost lost consciousness as pain radiated through his head. He grabbed her good hand and tried to shoulder her up so he could carry her back to his waiting horse and the future he saw for them both.

"Might as well lay her back down," came a soft, hair-raising voice from the shadows behind.

Stark released Sadie's limp hand and let her drop back down. Motionless, still bent, he listened to the crunch of footsteps behind him, and the snort of a horse. By all his best reckoning, there was only one man behind him. In one fluid motion, Stark straightened and twisted around, drawing and firing his pistol in the direction of the footsteps.

The flash from the shot illuminated one bare-headed man leading a horse, pistol drawn. An answering shot whizzed by Stark's shoulder. Then the man facing Stark was falling to his knees with a grunt. Stark's shot had found its mark.

Stark tripped over Sadie and fell headlong into some rocks that smashed into his ribs. Scrabbling to his feet, he lunged with a groan behind them for cover, and shot again into the darkness.

He waited, listening. Had he killed the man or just wounded him?

"Sadie," the man whispered.

Stark squinted into the darkness, trying to make out the form crawling toward Sadie. If he shot now he might strike Sadie, and, if at all possible, he wanted her alive and in one piece for the time ahead when they would work together as a team.

She moaned. "Oh, Jim. Oh, God! You're bleeding all over!"

Stark heard the tender way Sadie said the man's name. Without thinking, he reared up, taking aim and thinking to shoot her first. She was his!

Stark saw the man's pistol flame, but strangely he didn't hear it. Then he was staring up at the starry sky wondering why he wasn't standing any longer, wondering why he couldn't move. He could hear faint sounds of weeping coming from a great distance, but he knew the weeping wasn't for him.

"Sadie! I'm okay. I think I got him. Are you all right?" Jim asked. "Did he hurt you?" Jim could just make her out in the weak moonlight. Blood was streaming down his face from the crease the bullet had made in his temple. He pulled out his kerchief and cleared his eyes, finally tying the kerchief around his head. The wound was making him fuddle-headed.

Suddenly her arms were around his neck. She was quivering, but her tears had stopped. Then her hands were gingerly patting his face. "I didn't know what might have happened to you." She grunted in pain as she sat up.

He helped her to her feet. Her shirtwaist was torn from shoulder to waist. He pushed up the fabric, helping her cover herself.

"I'm all right. He didn't hurt me," she whispered. "What about the town? The children?"

"It's over. The outlaws are in jail, all but one, I think. I may have miscounted. The children are fine. George Cadwallader took a shot in the shoulder, and one of the tellers at the bank was pistol-whipped, but we survived. Come on. I have to get back to town."

She explained about her arm, and then found her footing. Clutching her shirtwaist closed, she looked back at the motionless body in the shadows beyond. "Is he dead?"

Jim steadied her and then went to Stark, crouching over him. "Yes. Let's go now. Can you ride?" He rejoined her, putting his arm protectively around her. "You're free now."

She hesitated. "Seeing him again . . . made me remember so much. He made me remember all I'd lost and all I tried to get back in Warren Bluffs."

"Is small-town life still what you want, Sadie?"

"Yes, but — Jim, I never told you, my father went to prison, too." Softly she explained what she had learned the night her mother died. "I felt you should know."

Her heart was so heavy, as she waited in the darkness for Jim's reaction. The cold had numbed her, but pain was still throbbing through her body, and she was so tired, so very weary of the long, seemingly impossible struggle.

Jim encircled her with his strong arms. He brushed the warm tears from her cheeks. "I can't believe that after all this you still think there is something that will turn me from you."

She sagged against him, stunned by the sweet tenderness of his words. She could almost see his smile. Lifting her face, she felt his warm, possessive lips close over hers. There was fire in his kiss, fire that warmed the fearful chill in her heart and brought it back to life. The fire erased the pain and anguish of the last long hours, and the apprehension that still remained for the long hours ahead.

For that wondrous moment she knew only the feel of him surrounding her, the strong arms tight across her back, beneath her cheek the wall of his broad chest where she would always be able to lay her problems and know that he would care and would help.

She could hear his heart beating strongly, quickening when she tightened her own arms around him. It was too good to be true, too impossible. After everything she had done, after all the lies she had been forced to tell and all the scandals in her past, he still wanted her unhesitatingly.

"Nothing will ever change how I feel about you, Sadie," he whispered. "I love you. I told you, my love is fierce and furious. I'll never let you go! Whatever is ahead, we'll face it together. I'll always be there for you, Sadie. No matter what. We've been tried by fire!"

She could taste blood on his lips as he kissed her. His love had saved her. She ached to think of the torment her mother had known all those years. To live with shame was the greatest heartache, and for her Jim had erased it all. Her shame had been exposed and overcome. There was nothing more for her to hide from! She was, indeed, free!

Chapter Twenty

November 26, 1879

An hour before dawn the wide sweep of the sky lightened in the east, turning a dark lavender. All across the prairie the dry grasses of autumn were crisp and white with frost. The air was still and cold, the silence broken only by the soft, padding hoofbeats of two horses.

Jim and Sadie rode slowly together, in no hurry to break the delicious spell their love had cast over the night. Sadie rode in front of Jim with his coat sides pulled around her arms. She was enveloped in his warmth and scent, feeling the steady heat of his breathing just behind her right ear.

Moving together so closely, they were wondrously aroused, yearning for time alone, but Sadie's arm and Jim's grazed temple needed tending. Banking the heat of their desire for one another, they rode on into the murky morning mists of Warren Bluffs.

Behind them on the second horse was Stark's body across the saddle, and the saddlebags containing the bulk of the cash stolen from the Warren Bluffs bank the afternoon before.

Sadie tugged on the reins for Jim. "Stop here a moment. I want to look at everything," she whispered as the horse came to a halt at the southern edge of Park Circle.

Several lights were still burning in the courthouse windows, but the rest of the town quivered with silence. A cock crowed from the west, and the light in the eastern sky changed to pink and yellow.

"It's a nice little town, Jim," she murmured with a tug at her heart that told her this had become home for her. "Could you take me across the field again? I want to clean up a bit and change my clothes before anyone sees me."

"Everything will be fine," he said, guiding the horse around to the field behind Trudy's boarding house.

"I know, but I might as well not shock everyone by letting them see me all bloody and torn like this."

Leaving the horses, Jim helped Sadie down and then picked her up in his arms again just as he had the night of the Cadwalladers' party. As he carried her through the frost-brittle grasses, she lifted her face for a kiss.

"You look like a battle-scarred soldier," Sadie said teasingly, her heart fluttering with nervous anticipation.

He smiled disarmingly. "I'll leave you here and fetch the doctor. There will be a lot for me to take care of today, but will you save me a seat in the parlor?"

"I hope I can just sleep for a week or two," Sadie sighed as he placed her on her feet at Trudy's back porch.

"My sweet Sadie, I think you will be swamped with callers today. If a schoolmarm had risked her own life and virtue to save a child of yours, wouldn't you want to call and heap your thanks at her feet?"

"Don't be silly, Jim. I did what any woman would have done."

He kissed her cheek playfully. "Your modesty becomes you, my dear."

Chuckling, she watched him trot back to the horses. Gathering the last shreds of her strength, she lifted her skirts with her good arm and struggled up the rear steps. Trudy appeared, holding up a lantern and gaping down into Sadie's haggard face.

"Lord preserve us! Sadie, we feared something awful had happened to you! Where's Jimmy?"

"A bullet grazed his temple and he needs to see the doctor." Sadie felt oddly fearful of meeting Trudy's eyes. She stepped into the porch and paused, listening to the waiting silence in the house. "I've wrenched my arm and shoulder pretty badly, so he's likely to bring the doctor over in a short while. Is there any hope of slipping up to my room unseen?"

Trudy was staring at the painfully awkward manner in which Sadie clutched her shirtwaist closed with her stiffened left arm. At last Sadie lifted her eyes. She would have to face every person in Warren Bluffs today. She might as well start now.

Trudy's eyes glistened. Then she blinked and lifted her brows, turning matter-of-factly toward an old shawl she kept draped on a peg by the back door. "You look chilled through, dear. I'm going to bring you up a cup of hot chamomile tea. You'll feel a world better." She covered Sadie's shivering shoulders, effectively concealing Sadie's ravished appearance. "Just as soon as the breakfast dishes are cleared I'll bring in the tub and you can wash off all that dirt. You look like you've been fighting a pack of wild Indians!"

"Are you all right after . . . yesterday, Trudy?" Sadie whispered, seeing the boarders in the hall beyond the kitchen craning to catch a glimpse of her.

"Spent the day clutching that old rifle in the cellar. I half wished the outlaws would've showed their faces at this end of town. Alvinia and Mr. Charles were a trial to be cooped up with, I can tell you!" Then quickly Trudy turned and clutched Sadie's good hand for just a moment, giving her a heart-felt, reassuring squeeze. "Let me shoo them into the dining room."

As soon as Trudy had closed the dining-room door on the boarders, Sadie dragged herself to her room. She dared not lie down, she thought, or she would be dead to the world for the remainder of the day.

Going to the mirror over her dresser, she let Trudy's shawl fall to the floor. She took her hand away and let her shirtwaist fall open. How often she had been forced to examine herself like this, she thought, noting the bruise along her jaw and the scratches. Her hands were battered and dirty, her clothes beyond repair.

But she was free now! Stark was dead.

Stripping quickly, she heaped her things in a corner and awkwardly drew on her wrapper. She had just begun to pull the stray pins from her hair when she heard Trudy's heavy tread on the stairs.

"Dr. Hamlin's here," Trudy whispered.

Admitting the doctor, Sadie forced herself to meet his eyes immediately. With relief she saw he no longer devoured her with his hungry gaze.

"Jim tells me your shoulder was dislocated," he said, guiding her to the bed for the examination.

After Sadie described her fall from the horse, he pronounced her healing already, and advised Trudy to help comb out Sadie's tangled tresses. When he was gone, Trudy helped Sadie bathe and dress in a morning gown that had once belonged to Adelaide. Lost in thought, Sadie grew drowsy as Trudy brushed out her long hair and knotted it carefully.

"Oh, thank you, but that's not necessary. I'm going to lie down for a while now."

"I'm afraid not yet. There's someone waiting for you downstairs in the parlor. You have enough strength left to see Jimmy for a moment, don't you? And there are others eager to speak to you. Alvinia, Mr. Bennett and some others I've asked to wait out front on the veranda, since there's not room enough in the house for them all."

In alarm, Sadie's eyes shot to Trudy's.

Trudy kept hold of Sadie's good hand, rubbing it and patting it. "Dear Sadie, what you must have gone through all these months, trying your best and fearing what we would think of you when we found out." Her eyes grew moist again. "I'm full of questions about things that are none of my business, but I just want to say that you are welcome in my home as long as you care to stay." Then she smiled as if she had a secret. "Come along now. We've kept everyone waiting quite long enough. Oh, let me fix up a sling for that arm."

Sadie forced herself to think of nothing. Following Trudy down the stairs, she allowed herself to be steered into the parlor.

Jim rose as she entered. He'd thrown on clean clothes and had washed the night's blood and dirt from his hands and face. The doctor had dressed his wound with a band of gauze around his head.

"You still look like a war hero," she smiled.

"Would you sit here, please?" he said, grinning as he led her to the divan.

Trudy had drawn the drapes against curious eyes. Sadie could hear the gentle thunder of restless feet shuffling on the veranda.

"I'll make this short and to the point, Sadie," Jim said, taking up a bunch of silk daisies he'd brought from the ladies' dress shop. "Otherwise Trudy's front porch may collapse from the weight of your callers."

Sadie chuckled. "You and Trudy make it sound as if the whole town is out there," she said, shaking her head. She accepted the flowers and laid them in her lap.

"If I had a hat, my darling Sadie, I would sweep it off," he said, smiling down at her. "My God, you're beautiful. I didn't think it was possible, but you are more beautiful right now than even that first day I saw you in the park."

"You flatter me, sir," she said in the old teasing manner that they had enjoyed together in those early weeks.

He looked thoughtfully at the carpet. "Now, how should I do this? Is it on bended left knee, or bended right knee?" He went down first on one knee and then the other, looking delightfully confused.

"Oh, do stop! Don't be so silly, Jim —"

He settled on his left knee, plucked up her trembling hand from her lap and drew it to his lips for a kiss. "My darling Miss Whiting-Evans, I am smitten by your beauty. Long have I waited for the perfect woman to take as my wife, and here you are before me. Would you, could you . . . consider . . . ? He looked imploringly up into her face. His blue eyes danced with delight, and a grin twitched on the corners of his lips.

"Oh, Jim," she whispered.

"I know you're overwhelmed by the suddenness of it all, but I beg you, dear lady, consent to be my wife forevermore." He laughed out loud then at the way he was saying words that were bringing tears of joy to her eyes.

Slowly he took a kerchief from his breast pocket and unfolded it before her. Then he shifted to his other knee. "This floor is hard on a man."

Sadie bent forward, laughing, and kissed him. "Jim, you're such a darling."

"In all seriousness, Sadie, I asked you once before to reach into my breast pocket for this. Now I'm offering it to you as my token of our betrothal. I love you. Say you'll marry me." He lowered his voice. "As soon as possible, please. I'm wild for you!"

She laughed. Tears flooded her eyes. Struggling to maintain control of her emotions, she smiled down at his open, eager face. "I love you, Jim Warren. I would be pleased and proud to marry you." She was just reaching to take the slim gold ring from the folds of his kerchief when she heard an excited squeal from the hall.

"She said yes!" Trudy whispered out the front door.

A murmur of approval filled the morning quiet.

Sadie frowned. "How many people are out there?" She heard the floor boards creaking.

"I guess I've had you to myself as long as I'm going to get today. I have a lot to do over at the jail. My deputies are busy on the paperwork, and we're planning to transport the outlaws to Topeka, since there are outstanding warrants for them all over the state. As for Otis, his whole operation has been exposed. He was making homemade whiskey in a still on my land, mixing it with shipments smuggled in and selling it as the real thing.

"Marty's been talking a blue streak since he woke up in the doc's office. It turns out Otis is also a horse thief and has a few men up north buying and selling the stolen horses from all over Kansas and Nebraska. Yesterday, when the outlaws took over the town, Otis didn't even try to deal with them. He rode off, headed someplace west, not even caring what became of friends and neighbors he'd known for years. Or his family. I can't figure it, either. He was once a good sheriff. I guess Warren Bluffs got too tame for him.

"I don't know what else broke loose yesterday, but it's for sure that it'll go down in the history of Warren Bluffs as a mighty peculiar way to welcome in the new sheriff." Jim grinned.

"You won?" Sadie gasped, as they both got to their feet.

"The doc told me when I got to his office this morning."

With her good hand, Sadie drew Jim's face down to hers and kissed him. "I knew you were the man for the job," she whispered.

At last Trudy opened the parlor door a crack. "Oh, do hurry, you two. The porch is beginning to sag!"

Jim's arm encircled Sadie's shoulders. Sadie took a deep breath and lifted her face. There was no time to wonder what everyone wanted with her, for she was quickly at the front door, being guided onto the crowded veranda.

Blinking in disbelief, Sadie found herself facing a crowd as large as the night of the town meeting. In front were the gentlemen from the school board, and next to them stood MargieBelle and Ethel Cadwallader. Beyond were the mayor, and Olive Crowley clutching her grandson by his shoulders.

In the yard and poised on the steps were her students and their parents, and the younger children not yet of school age, all standing silently, patiently. They noted her sling and the bruise on her jaw. And beside her was the newly elected sheriff.

Sadie felt she should speak, but no words came. What did

they all want? Bewildered and somewhat frightened, she edged back into the protective circle of Jim's arm. She remembered what Stark had said about her being the reason the outlaws came to town in the first place. She began to tremble.

Olive began clapping. Suddenly they were all clapping. The older boys down in the yard whooped and tossed up their hats. The smaller children cheered. The tumult went on for a full minute, and all the while Sadie stared in complete confusion.

At last the applause dwindled away. Olive was the first to step forward. "We all want you to know what a debt of gratitude we owe you for protecting our children while they were held hostage in school. If we had a medal to offer you, it would be a gold one and engraved with the names of the children dear to us who will never forget your strength and courage."

Sadie was trying to shush Olive, and shook her head. "It was nothing . . ."

"In place of the medal we all wish for you, Sadie Whiting, will you accept our hug of thanks for being such a dear friend to us all?" Olive's lips quivered as she spoke. She put her arms around Sadie and hugged her gently.

As Sadie broke down in tears, Olive supported her. Whispering, Olive said, "We know the whole story, dear, and, as of today, all the unpleasantness in your past must be forgotten. This is your new home. I hope in some small way that we can make up for the mother you lost and the life you were forced to leave behind."

Sadie buried her face in Olive's neck, and then Olive turned her to Jim, who held her.

"Thank you for coming, all of you," Jim said, his voice husky. "Your vote for me as your new sheriff and your presence here today mean more to Sadie and me than we will every be able to say." He paused to rouse Sadie.

With tears still shining on her face, Sadie straightened suddenly and faced everyone. "Perhaps some day I will know how to thank you," she said, beaming.

Ethel came forward to shake Sadie's hand. She looked up into Sadie's eyes as if seeing her for the first time. "You made a woman of my daughter, Sadie. Thank you. I think you showed me a thing or two, too. I hope you and Jim will be very happy. I expect an invitation to your wedding, mind."

Laughing suddenly, Sadie nodded. "You'll be very welcome."

Then one after another Sadie's new friends filed by to shake her hand and say a private word of thanks.

"I feel as if we're already married," Jim whispered as those who had waited on the veranda went on their way and those from the yard came up.

Dawn Shockley and her mother were suddenly there, and the boys, and Henry, who had helped Jim round up the outlaws. Dawn's face was streaked with happy tears. "I'm going on a trip, Miss Evans. . . . Is that what we're to call you still?"

Jim broke in. "It'll soon be Mrs. Warren. Don't go before we're married."

"I wouldn't dream of it!" Dawn said, giving Sadie a gentle hug. "I'm going to visit my aunt back east and go to school there a while. It's a chance I can't pass up."

"Will you be back?" Sadie asked, reading the knowledge of Dawn's condition in her mother's eyes.

"Oh . . . in a year or so. Thank you, Miss Evans. We all love you dearly!"

In time everyone had gone, leaving Jim and Sadie alone on the veranda.

"It's cold out here now. You belong in bed, resting," Jim said. "And I have my chores."

Sadie pulled him close suddenly, hating to let him out of her sight even for a few hours. She felt his arms go around her again. "I didn't know it was possible to feel this happy," she whispered.

"You're a good woman, Sadie. You deserve all the happiness we can give you."

"Life will never again be as perfect as it is now at this very moment," she said.

"Oh" — he began kissing her — "I don't know about that. I think we have a lot of perfection ahead of us. Will you marry me Sunday morning at ten o'clock. What do you think of a honeymoon out at my place? Do you relish cleaning out a house that hasn't been lived in for three years as your wedding trip?"

"Sheriff Warren, nothing would suit me better!"

They were kissing then, oblivious to the sweet powdery face watching wistfully from the parlor windows. They were still kissing as Alvinia began playing, "Oh, Promise Me."

Across town at the doctor's, Marty Wheeler sat up for the first time since the explosion. MargieBelle started spooning broth into his mouth. When Dr. Hamlin looked in, MargieBelle smiled up at him. Hungrily, he thought of the startlingly exciting creature Miss Cadwallader had turned out to be two evenings before.

On Cowtrail Street they were marking down orders for window glass to replace panes filled with bullet holes. Herman Biggins was telling for the hundredth time how Jim had found him in the demolished saloon and said he must play dead. "Getting carried out with a tarp over my face has cured me!" he said, swearing off Demon Rum forever . . . or at least for a few hours.

One of the deputies was conducting a search of the town for Otis's many caches of rot-gut. Mayor Runyon was organizing a citizen's committee for the town's defense.

School was recessed until further notice. The Shockley boys were doing chores for their pa, and not a one had yet forgotten what a real dead outlaw looked like.

Bea Wheeler and Justine were packing, while Susanna sat glumly on the doorstep contemplating the fact of a father who had deserted not only his town but his family in its hour of need. She still couldn't get out of her mind the picture of her father trying to take Miss Evans into his arms. Putting her head in her hands, she cried silent, bitter tears, wondering if there was time to see Miss Evans again before they loaded everything into the wagon and lit out for parts unknown. She wanted to say she was sorry about the poison ivy in the flowers. And perhaps Miss Evans would have a word of advice for her.

Preacher Whithers was preparing for a wedding on Sunday. At the jail the new sheriff paused in his crush of duties to think of the woman he loved and had won. A smile spread across his face, and his friends began ribbing him again.

Sadie was curled beneath the double-wedding-ring quilt, unable to sleep, trying to decide which of her many new friends should be in her wedding party.

Then finally she closed her eyes, saying a prayer of thanks for the miracle of love. Jim's smiling face filled her mind. She hugged her pillow, free from all cares. For her, the future promised long tender nights with the man who had set her free from the sorrows of the past. Without them she would never have come so far nor found so much to once again call her own.

FREE!!
BOOKS BY MAIL
CATALOGUE

BOOKS BY MAIL will share with you our current bestselling books as well as hard to find specialty titles in areas that will match your interests. You will be updated on what's new in books at no cost to you. Just fill in the coupon below and discover the convenience of having books delivered to your home.

PLEASE ADD $1.00 TO COVER THE COST OF POSTAGE & HANDLING.

BOOKS BY MAIL

320 Steelcase Road E.,
Markham, Ontario L3R 2M1

In the U.S. –
210 5th Ave., 7th Floor
New York, N.Y., 10010

Please send Books By Mail catalogue to:

Name_____
(please print)

Address_____

City_____

Prov._____ Postal Code _____

(BBM1)